W—

Felicia tested the narrow bed with one hand, and heard the rustling of the cornhusk mattress beneath the buckskin padding. She started to sit, then became aware of her damp skirt and petticoat. She knew sleeping in them would be miserable. She glanced at the closed door, and decided that she had enough privacy to sleep in her chemise.

She removed her kerchief, dress, and petticoat, and wrapped her blanket around herself as she looked for the saddlebag that contained her chemise. Suddenly the door opened, and Hawk walked in, carrying an armful of firewood.

His unexpected entrance startled her, and Felicia lost her hold on the blanket. As it fell, she quickly regained her senses and grabbed it, stretching it tightly across her breasts, but not before Hawk caught a tantalizing glimpse of her nakedness. Felicia knew he had seen her, when his dark eyes blazed with unconcealed desire. She watched, pinned to the spot by that hot gaze, as he kicked the door to with the heel of one moccasined foot, then walked towards her. Even when he bent and dropped the logs into the wood bin, she couldn't move, for he still kept eye contact. Hawk stepped up to her, so close she could feel his heat and smell his heady essence. His breath fanned her face as he said, "I brought you firewood, in case you got cold during the night, but you're not going to need it."

Felicia was shocked at how breathless she felt. Her words were a mere whisper. "Why not?"

Hawk's smoldering gaze moved slowly down her body and then back up, stripping her with his eyes and bringing a warm flush to her skin. Then, as his eyes once more met hers, he answered in a husky voice, "Because tonight I'm going to keep you warm."

LAUREN WILDE
SWEET SAVAGE SPLENDOR

ZEBRA BOOKS
KENSINGTON PUBLISHING CORP.

ZEBRA BOOKS

are published by

Kensington Publishing Corp.
475 Park Avenue South
New York, NY 10016

First Printing: February, 1993

Printed in the United States of America

*To Laura, with her black eyes and her
valiant Cherokee spirit, with love—*

Chapter One

The sharp crack of a whip was heard, and then seemed to hang in the hot, humid air as if suspended in time.

Felicia Edwards noted the noise, as the open carriage she was riding in passed the town prison. It was a sound she was long familiar with. Almost every time she had come to Camden since her birth nineteen years before, there had been some poor soul tied to the whipping post outside of the jail, being publicly beaten. Ordinarily she ignored the spectacle, finding it both distasteful and disturbing, but there was something strange about this crack of the whip, something missing, that aroused her curiosity. She turned her head to the platform where the sound had come from.

Felicia briefly glanced at the man manacled to the whipping post, his dark head hanging limply to one side of the heavy wooden beam as he knelt where he had collapsed on the floor of the platform, then glanced at the burly jailer towering over him and wielding the wicket whip, be-

7

fore her full attention was captured by the sight of the British officer who stood beside the pair. She knew that man, she realized with a jolt of surprise, for the last place she would have expected to find Col. Banastre Tarleton was supervising the punishment of a common criminal.

At the same moment, Felicia's father, Thomas, also spied the officer, who was considered the hero of the hour by every loyalist in the Carolinas. Quickly ordering his driver to bring the horses to a stop, Tom rose in the carriage and called out, "Colonel! Colonel Tarleton!"

At the sound of his name, Tarleton looked up, saw Tom, Felicia, and her mother in the carriage, and waved congenially. But he made no move to leave his business at hand.

"May I have a word with you?" Tom called.

Just a hint of irritation passed over the young officer's handsome face, before he crisply ordered the guard to continue the beating, then walked down the stairs of the platform. As he crossed the green to the dusty street where the carriage sat, the townspeople who had crowded around to avidly view the whipping cleared a path for him, and bowed in awed respect at the man who had been responsible for the daring calvary charge that had broken the Americans' line and won the Battle of Camden for the Crown, sending General Gates and his half-starved, ragtag patriot army fleeing for their lives. Watching him as he approached their carriage, Felicia had to admit that despite the fact that the slender Englishman was a bit of a dandy, he did present an impressive sight in his immaculate green coat, gleaming white ruffled shirt, high black boots, and skin-tight buff pants that showed off his muscular horseman's thighs, a uniform he wore in deference to the elite loyalist ranger unit he commanded, rather than the usual scarlet and white British uniform. The only Englishman in the legion formed from New York, Pennsylvania, and southern Americans loyal to the Crown, the colonel had named his dragoons Tarleton's Loyal Legion, and the unit had gained such a splendid fighting reputation that every young loyalist in the colonies would give his right arm to become one of the group and share in the glory. That was why Felicia's brother, Robert, had joined the legion shortly after the surrender of Charleston, and how Felicia's family had come to be on personal terms with the colonel.

Tarleton came to a stop beside the carriage and swept off his bearskin hat, a hat he had a particular fondness for, which would have looked ridiculous with his otherwise resplendent uniform, had he not worn it with such utter self-confidence. "Good day, Mr. Edwards," he said to the graying, slender planter who had climbed from his carriage to meet him. Then turning to Felicia and her rather rotund mother, the officer bowed slightly and said, "Good day, ladies."

While the two women returned his greeting,

Tarleton's eyes rested just long enough on Felicia's beautiful face to tell everyone watching that he was attracted to the young woman with her startlingly golden green eyes and thick chestnut hair. The appreciative look made Felicia's mother, Mary, titter nervously, while Felicia blushed, more in embarrassment at her mother's silly behavior than the officer's blatant admiration. The flush only increased the Englishman's appreciation, for it gave the girl's flawless creamy complexion a rosy tint that was most becoming. Christ, Tarleton thought, with her unusual coloring, beautiful classic features, and curvaceous body, she was a woman to tempt the gods. His eyes dropped ever so slightly to view the creamy rise of Felicia's proud young breasts, for the sheer fichu she modestly wore over her shoulders and bosom did nothing to hide her lovely curves.

"What are you doing here, Colonel?" Tom asked, drawing the Englishman's attention from his daughter's tempting body. "I should think you would have more pressing things to do than watch a thief being punished."

Tarleton's eyes darted to the platform. An angry look came over his face. "That's no thief," he answered in a tight voice, "at least not in the strictest sense. Nor is he any common criminal. That man is a spy!"

"A spy?" Tom repeated in surprise.

"Yes! We caught him skulking around my quarters the other night."

"I thought you hung spies," Tom remarked, turning his full attention to the man on the platform.

"We do! After we've gotten the information we want from them, that is. That's why I'm having him beaten, in hopes he'll confess. I want to know who sent him. That damn Marion or Sumter? And then I want to know where that bastard's headquarters are!"

Tom glanced over his shoulder, wishing the officer would be a little more careful of his language in front of the ladies. But Tarleton had momentarily forgotten their presence, as he continued in exasperation, "For the life of me, I can't understand these rebels. You'd think that after our decisive victory here at Camden, they'd realize they're beaten and lay down their arms. Christ, General Gates has completely flown the colony! He's in North Carolina now, but we can't pursue him, because Marion's swamp rats and Sumter's backwoods militiamen keep raising hell, and we can't leave South Carolina until it's totally secured. General Clinton's orders were very explicit on that matter. Yet we can't fight the blasted rebels, because they refuse to stand in the open and fight like men. No, they ambush us, hit and run, then hide. The cowards!"

"Perhaps you need to increase your punitive raids on the rebels' plantations," Tom suggested. "That's where they're getting their food and supplies from, you know."

"I've been doing that!" Tarleton answered testily, highly resenting the planter's audacity in trying to tell *him* how to wage war! Why, he was an authority on the effects of spreading terror among the enemy. He and his men had raided countless Whig plantations and burned them to the ground, after confiscating their slaves and movable property. The loot he and his men had taken during this war would make them very wealthy men, but the knowledge brought him no satisfaction. It angered him that no matter how brutally he dealt with the Whigs, how much destruction and death he wrought on them, the stubborn southern rebels kept resisting. It was almost as if his scorched earth techniques were spurring them on, instead of terrifying them.

Tom had heard the resentment in the young officer's voice and wisely held his tongue. Seeing the dark glower on Tarleton's face, he also read the Englishman's thoughts and could sympathize with his utter frustration. Long before the British army had arrived on the scene, the deep South had been waging a bloody civil war, despite the fact that a larger portion of the population there were loyalists, which was exactly why General Clinton had decided to move the war to the area where he thought his chances of winning would be better. Unlike the middle and northern colonies, or even Virginia, where at least a third of the population were fence sitters, in the lower colonies they were more evenly divided and clearly defined, and had gone at each other's throats with a ferocity that far surpassed the conflict between the two in the other colonies. It had been open warfare, with neighbor against neighbor, brother against brother, father against son. Both sides raided, plundering and burning plantations, and tarring and feathering were common occurrences in towns. There had even been a few hangings. Yes, here in the South, feelings ran very high, and Tom had been vastly relieved to see the British Army appear on the scene, not knowing how much longer it might be before he felt the wrath of the rebels. But now, learning that Tarleton wasn't coping well with the patriot's guerrilla tactics, he wasn't too sure the King's army was going to be his salvation, after all; and that knowledge made him feel very uneasy.

Tom peered at the man being beaten on the platform. The jailer was going at him hot and heavy, laying lash after vicious lash on his back. "What makes you think the spy is with Marion or Sumter?"

"Because he was wearing buckskin pants and knee-high moccasins, like their men do. At least Gates' army wore uniforms like real soldiers, even if they were nothing but rags," Tarleton answered.

"Has he divulged any information at all?"

"Not a word!" Tarleton answered angrily, his eyes flashing.

Felicia had been listening to the conversation from where she sat, and it was then that she realized what had been so unusual about the beating that it had caught her attention. It was the absence of sound *after* the crack of the whip that she had noticed missing, for there had been no cry of pain or even a moan.

"The only time he's opened his mouth," Tarleton continued, "has been to taunt the man beating him." A look of disbelief came over the officer's face, as he said, "Can you believe that? He actually taunted the jailer into beating him harder and faster. I've never known a man to do that before! I had to stop the jailer at sixty lashes the other day, for fear he'd kill the spy before I could get the information I wanted. And then I had to give the rebel two days to recuperate before trying again."

Sixty lashes? Tom thought in horror. My God, the man's back must have been cut to ribbons! No wonder he had to be given time to recuperate. "Perhaps that was his motive in taunting the jailer," he suggested. "He hoped to escape in unconsciousness."

"The bastard never lost consciousness!" Tarleton exclaimed, in a voice that was part fury and part incredulous. "He was still standing when I called a halt." He paused and looked at the man on the platform, a man who had become his personal nemesis over the past few days. Damn, he'd break him if it was the last thing he did! he silently swore.

Tom was shocked at Tarleton's revelation. The

spy must have superhuman strength, he thought, then, remembering that his wife and daughter had been listening to the entire conversation and probably found it distasteful, Tom decided to change the subject. "Well, I won't keep you from your business any longer. I just wanted to be sure Robert hadn't forgotten to invite you to the victory ball we're having at our plantation next Thursday."

"No, he didn't forget."

"We would have sent an invitation," Mary quickly interjected from the carriage, not wanting the colonel to think they didn't practice proper etiquette here in the colonies, "but Robert wasn't sure just where you were staying."

"Yes, I have been moving around a bit," Tarleton admitted, "but you can rest assured I will be there."

Turning his attention directly to Felicia, Tarleton reached for one of her hands that had been resting on the edge of the carriage, saying, "Ah, Felicia, you will save the first and the last dance for me, won't you, my dear?"

As he bent his head and kissed her hand—lingering much too long to be proper—Felicia became suddenly aware of every eye on her, including those of several slaves in the crowd. A flush rose on her face. She knew the colonel was only being flirtatious and that his kiss meant absolutely nothing, but she'd be willing to wager that the townspeople would have her engaged to the officer before the sun went down. The residents of Camden were mostly merchants and country bumpkins, who knew nothing of the social manners practiced by her class. Undoubtedly they would read much more into the kiss than there actually was, and they were terrible gossips. But even though she knew the Englishman wasn't serious, Felicia couldn't help but be pleased by his attentions, for she was just as vain as the next young woman. After all, he was the man of the hour, besides being very good-looking and charming, and she knew every girl in the countryside would envy her when they heard about it. And they *would* hear about it. Of that, she was positive. The slave grapevine would see to it. And she wasn't adverse to a little meaningless flirtation. It might help relieve the boredom.

Becoming aware that Tarleton was waiting for an answer, Felicia dropped her eyelids and tilted her head. Peering through her long lashes, she answered, "If you wish."

The smile that followed Felicia's answer was just provocative enough to make the Englishman's breath catch and his heart suddenly race. Yes, he thought, she was a tempting bit of baggage. He wondered if he could seduce her.

Both Tom and Mary were pleased with the Colonel's attentions toward their lovely daughter, Mary because she was very socially conscious, and Tom because of the favors the officer might be able to grant him, and thereby give him the edge over the other planters. Both smiled broadly, then Tom climbed back into the carriage and shut the door behind him, saying to the Englishman, "Well, I won't take up any more of your valuable time. You've a job to do." Seeing the dark look coming over Tarleton's face, Tom glanced once more at the platform and, searching for something to further please the officer, said, "Cheer up. Maybe your fortune will be better today. At least, you've brought the spy to his knees."

Tarleton's eyes darted to the platform, then lit up with anticipation. A smug smile spread across his lips, as he answered confidently, "Yes, that I have. Perhaps the stubborn fool has finally realized the folly of resisting any further. Even death would be preferable to what he must be feeling."

And surely he must know that he will eventually hang, Tom thought, feeling a twinge of compassion for the rebel. Then he motioned for his driver to proceed.

Just as the carriage moved forward, Felicia heard the crowd gasp. She turned and saw that the spy had somehow managed to pull himself to his feet. He stood on the platform, swaying slightly, and she couldn't help but wonder if he had heard her father's comment about being brought to his knees and taken it as a challenge. It would have taken extraordinary hearing, and even if he possessed such, she would have

17

thought he would have been too engrossed in his agony to pay any attention to them.

Her curiosity aroused, she turned full in the carriage and stared at the man. She couldn't see his bloody back, and for that she was thankful, but the spy looked to be exceptionally tall and broad-shouldered, as he brought himself to stand erect, a movement that she knew must have caused him excruciating pain. And strange as it seemed, she could almost feel the raw power radiating from him, a power so strong that it overshadowed everything and everyone else present, so that even Tarleton, with his considerable charisma, seemed as insignificant as an ant.

Fascinated, Felicia's eyes darted upward to the man's face. But she didn't see the rebel's rugged good looks, or even take note that his black, shoulder-length hair was plastered with sweat to his head, a silent but eloquent testimony to his supreme will that forbade him surrendering to his tormentor. Her eyes were locked on his dark ones, as he glared straight at her and held her as if spellbound, until the carriage turned a corner and she lost sight of him.

But even then Felicia couldn't relax. The experience had left her feeling shaken to the core. Never in her life had anyone's look affected her so strangely or so profoundly. It was as if the stranger had stripped her of all pretense, peered deeply into her soul, and somehow found it grossly lacking. She had never seen such utter contempt in anyone's gaze, nor had she ever seen such fierce black eyes. Had she peered into the eyes of the devil? she wondered nervously. Despite the August heat, a shiver ran over her.

Chapter Two

Five days later, Felicia paused in her dressing for the victory ball and walked to the window where she stood and gazed out; something she frequently did when she had time on her hands. From that particular point on the second story, she could see through the boughs of the massive oaks that surrounded the plantation house, to the rice fields in the distance, and watch the slaves as they worked. But there were no workers there that day. Now it was just a matter of waiting, for rice was almost ready for harvesting, the long heads heavy with starchy seeds, and the fields looked golden red in the light of the setting sun. In a few days, the slaves would cut the rice with small reap hooks, lay the stalks on the stubble to dry, then tie the stalks into sheaves for threshing. Then loaded in barrels in flat-bottomed vessels called Santee boats, the rice would be taken from her father's wharf on the Wateree River to Charleston, over rivers and through fifty miles of coastal swamps.

A noise at the door caught Felicia's attention and she turned, seeing her mother coming into the bedroom. The older woman was already dressed in her ball gown and jewels for the evening, the diamonds and rubies around her neck, wrist, dangling from her ears, and entwined in her elaborately coiffured and powdered hair, glittering in the light.

Coming to an abrupt halt, Mary glared at Felicia's hair and said sharply, "Don't tell me you're going to be stubborn again tonight."

"What are you talking about, stubborn?" Felicia asked, pasting an innocent look on her face.

"You know perfectly well what I'm talking about! Your hair! Why do you persist in refusing to wear it powdered?"

"I've told you why. The powder makes my head itch! Besides, I think it's stupid. Only old people have white hair. Why should I make myself look old?"

"Because it's fashionable, that's why!" Mary answered, throwing her hands up in exasperation. "Because everyone does it!"

"Not everyone," Felicia pointed out calmly.

"If you're talking about the common people, of course not! That's how you can tell the gentry from them, by how we dress, how we behave. And for evening wear, we powder our hair. Now, no more arguments, please!"

"Mother, I am not going to powder my hair," Felicia answered firmly. "It's enough that I suffered sitting through three miserable hours while the hairdresser smeared all of that sticky mess on it, so it would stand up in this ridiculous hairstyle," she said, grimacing at the strawlike feel of her hair as she passed one hand over the high coiffure, "but I will not endure having it powdered. I almost choked to death the last time I had that done."

Mary watched in vexation, as Felicia turned her back on her and walked to where her gown was being laid out on the bed by her personal maid. There were times when dealing with her strong-willed daughter was almost too much for her—times that were too frequent—and Mary wondered where Felicia got her irritating stubbornness from. Deciding to try a different approach, Mary's voice took on a coaxing tone, as she said, "Please reconsider, my dear. I'm only thinking of your good. Have you forgotten Colonel Tarleton will be at this ball? The rest of the countryside is used to your . . ." Mary hesitated, not wanting to further anger her daughter by calling her stubborn again. That only made her more determined. ". . . your unusual behavior, but he isn't. Surely you don't want to give him a bad impression?"

Felicia whirled around, making the whalebone pannier that was sewn into her stiff petticoat rock wildly. "A bad impression?" Felicia demanded, her golden green eyes flashing. "What is he going to think? That I'm a loose tavern wench, simply because I didn't powder my hair?"

Mary winced, more at the cutting tone of her daughter's voice than her words. "Well, I don't think he would go that far," she admitted, "but still, he is a gentleman of the highest rank. You wouldn't want him to get the wrong impression. Why, he's a personal friend of General Cornwallis, who's an earl, no less, a man who freely mixes with royalty. You don't want him to think that we colonials are nothing but a bunch of country bumpkins, do you?"

Felicia sighed deeply in disgust. Unlike her mother or, for that matter, most of the loyalists in the colonies, she had never been particularly impressed with royalty. No, she was more in agreement with her father, who supported Great Britain in this conflict for purely practical reasons, rationalizing that a powerful empire both feared and respected the world over could offer him more protection and better business opportunities than a bunch of rabble-rousing rebels who couldn't even scrape up enough money to feed and properly clothe their army, much less enforce any laws they made; and Tom was a business man through and through. To his way of thinking, what good would it do to win his freedom from one country, if it would leave him prey to another European power that would tax him equally as heavy, if not even heavier, and perhaps not allow him his religious freedom either. As the descendent of a French Huguenot who had come to this country because of religious persecution, Felicia had heard her father swear more than once that he'd be damned if he'd give his loyalty to any country with a papist king, and Felicia felt the same way. Her full loyalty was to Great Britain, not its king or its silly royalty.

"I don't give a tinker's damn *who* Colonel Tarleton's friends are!" Felicia threw out. "Nor do I care what he thinks of me. Why should I?"

"Sssh, dear! Don't curse! It's not at all becoming," Mary chided, only making Felicia roll her eyes in her head at her mother's idea of cursing. "And you know full well' why you should care what the Colonel thinks. He's made it very clear he's interested in you, and he'd be quite a catch. Why, every young lady in the colonies would give her eyeteeth to have him for a husband. He's young, handsome, and very successful in his career. Goodness, he's only twenty-six and already a colonel! Why, I'll wager he'll be a general by the time he's thirty."

"That may be true, Mother. He's obviously very ambitious, and I admit he's very attractive. But he's *not* interested in me. Just because he kissed my hand doesn't mean he has any serious intentions. He was only flirting."

"No, my dear. I saw the way he looked at you. He wasn't simply flirting. I think he's very interested. After all, you're a very beautiful girl."

Felicia sensed that her mother meant desirable, for there had been a moment there when Tarleton's look had been a little too warm for just simple admiration. "Just because a man finds a woman desirable, doesn't mean he's interested in courting her, Mother. His interest may lie more towards just tumbling her," Felicia answered saucily, shocking her mother with her candid observation. Then, before her mother could summon an appropriate answer, Felicia continued, "Besides, even if he were interested in courting me, I don't think I'd want to be the wife of a professional soldier, someone who would always be gone, off fighting a war someplace, and I'd hardly ever see him. That wouldn't be any kind of a marriage, at least not the kind I want."

"And what kind of a marriage do you want?"

"The kind where you and he are together, where you share your everyday experiences, your thoughts, your dreams, your disappointments. Where you sit across from him at every meal, and lie beside him every night."

Mary noted the flush on Felicia's face at the last, and wondered just how much she knew about sharing a man's bed, for Mary had yet to tell her daughter the facts of life, but this was not the time or place to inquire. The two had never shared such a serious conversation, and Mary didn't want to risk ruining it. "Perhaps the Colonel will give up the military, and become a politician. Many officers do, you know, and he certainly has the powerful contacts for it. Why, he might even be prime minister some day."

Felicia remembered her brother telling her that Tarleton was a hell-for-leather commander, who was happiest in battle. That kind didn't settle down. No, he'd be chasing one war after the other all over the world. Besides . . . "Oh, Mother, it's pointless for us to be discussing this. I really don't think he's all that interested in me, and I'm not really interested in him."

Felicia turned and motioned to her maid that she was ready to don her gown.

"Then maybe you ought to *get* interested!" Mary answered sharply, as the Negro woman lifted the gown over Felicia's head. "At least a dozen young men have shown a desire to court you, and you've spurned them."

"I'm waiting for the right man," Felicia answered from beneath the yards and yards of light green lawn and frothy lace.

"And what man is that?" Mary asked archly.

"I don't know. But I will when I meet him."

This time it was Mary's turn to roll her eyes in her head, before she said, "My dear, I hope you are not entertaining any foolish romantic fantasies about the man you're going to marry. There is a big difference between the man of your dreams and what actually *exists* in this world, and there's been more than one girl who's set her sights too high and then lost out. You're not getting any younger you know."

By this time the gown had cleared Felicia's head. She laughed and said, "Mother, I'm only nineteen."

"I was married and with child by the time I was your age," Mary pointed out.

As Felicia's maid stepped before her to tie the laces on the front of her bodice, Felicia peeked around her and said with a teasing twinkle in her eyes, "I still think I have plenty of time. Great-grandmère was thirty when she married."

A hot flush rose on Mary's face. She stamped her foot and said firmly, "I have told you time and time again, you are not to mention your father's grandmother!"

"Oh, Mother, for heaven's sake!" Felicia responded in exasperation. "There's no reason to be ashamed of her. We're not the only family to have an indentured servant for a descendent. Why, I'd wager half of the people in the colonies have at least one ancestor that was an indentured slave."

"But not a criminal!"

"She was a pickpocket! That's hardly a hardened criminal! And she only did it because she was starving."

"We will *not* discuss that woman! I rue the day I ever allowed you to talk to her while she was living with your grandmother. An old woman filling your head with all kinds of tales—tales which I'm sure weren't fit for your ears!" Mary whirled around, sending her skirt swaying and saying over her shoulder, "Now, hurry and finish dressing. Our dinner guests will be arriving soon."

Mary stopped at the door with her hand on the knob, then turned and said, "And please try to be gracious to Colonel Tarleton, if not for your sake, then your father's. Remember, he's a very powerful and influential man. He could be very helpful to your father."

As Mary closed the door behind her, Felicia grimaced. To her way of thinking, it was just as dishonest to be nice to someone because of the favors they might be able to do for you, as to pick their pockets.

Seeing the frown on her face, Betsy, her maid, said cheerfully, "Don't you fret, Miss Felicia. You're not gettin' too old. Why, you're the prettiest girl in the Carolinas, and there ain't a young gentleman in this country who wouldn't give his eyeteeth to have you."

Felicia smiled at the black woman fondly. No matter what happened or how much trouble the young girl had gotten into in the past, Betsy had always given Felicia her total support, even when Felicia had been wrong. "Thank you, Betsy. I'm afraid my mother has never understood me."

"No, she ain't," Betsy agreed readily, straightening the line of bows that hid the lacings on her mistress's bodice, then fluffing the lace ruffles on Felicia's three-quarter-length sleeves. She stepped back and looked at Felicia admiringly, then bending to straighten one of the tiers of lace ruffles that cascaded down the center of the gown, said, "And don't you stop hopin' for that special man, either. He'll come. You'll see. Why, you might even meet him tonight!"

"Perhaps," Felicia answered, feeling very little hope of that happening. Maybe what her mother had said was true, she thought gloomily. Maybe she was just dreaming. Maybe the man she was waiting for didn't even exist. But she was reasonably sure of one thing. Col. Banastre Tarleton was *not* that man.

Chapter Three

That evening, during a break in the dancing, Tom crossed the ballroom floor to where Felicia and Colonel Tarleton were standing. As the planter threaded his way around the elegantly dressed guests, Tom smiled, thinking that the Englishman had held Felicia to her word and more. Not only had Tarleton claimed the first dance, but he had almost totally monopolized Felicia, and despite the fact that the other young gentlemen were anxious to dance with his beautiful daughter, none had been brave enough to challenge the daring cavalryman's possessiveness, particularly in view of the fact that Tarleton was the commanding officer of many of the male guests. Tom had no objections. He was as pleased as his wife that Tarleton was so taken with his daughter.

When Tom reached Tarleton and Felicia, he stopped beside them, smiled broadly, and said to the Colonel, "I hope you are enjoying yourself."

"Most emphatically," the young officer answered, then shooting Felicia a warm glance, added, "Felicia is a marvelous dancer."

Felicia smiled graciously at Tarleton's compliment, then looked about her, wishing there was some way she could escape him without risking offending him. Oh, he was charming enough, she admitted silently, and a good dancer, but not an interesting conversationalist. All he could talk about was the battles he had fought, and expound on his ideas on how to beat the rebels, and Felicia was tired of hearing about the war. She would have much preferred hearing about the Englishman's travels to foreign lands, for she had never traveled any farther than Charleston. Even hearing about the northern colonies would have been appealing.

For several moments, Tom and Tarleton discussed the war, much to Felicia's utter disgust and total boredom. Then Tom said to the officer, "Oh, by the way. Did that spy give you the information you wanted the other day?"

A furious expression came over Tarleton's face. "Indeed not! He escaped that night!"

"Escaped?" Tom asked in surprise. "How did that happen?"

"I wish to hell I knew!" Tarleton snapped. "We found both of his guards in his cell with their throats cut, so somehow or another he came into possession of a knife. It must have been slipped to him that night through the window, probably from some blasted Whig in town. Not all of them fled after the battle, you know. There are several men in town that we suspect of having rebel sympathies."

"But surely you had more than two guards on him, a prisoner that valuable?" Tom blurted, then belatedly realized he should have phrased the question differently, for it only served to anger Tarleton more.

"I *did* have more guards on him!" Tarleton answered in a tight voice. "And not civilian guards. Military guards! I only used the town jailer to whip the prisoner, because he was more experienced. There were two guards at the front of the prison, and two at the back door, but the two at the back underestimated the prisoner. They thought him incapable of moving after the beating he had received, much less that he might have the strength to overpower the guards inside and kill them. One was asleep and the other dozing, when the back door opened. The guard that was dozing roused just enough to open his eyes. He said he never dreamed it could be the prisoner. He thought it was one of the inside guards coming out to get a breath of fresh air. By the time he realized who it was, it was too late. He was knocked unconscious."

"And the other guard?" Tom asked.

"He never even woke up!" Tarleton answered angrily. "Needless to say, both men have been punished."

Probably hung, Tom thought, for the British Army was notorious for severe punishment.

"As soon as we discovered the spy's escape, we searched the town," Tarleton continued. "We didn't find him, but we did discover that a horse had been stolen from the blacksmith's stable. He had just reshod it that day, and the owner was supposed to pick it up that morning. We were left to assume that the prisoner had stolen it, although I can't for the life of me imagine how he could ride in his weakened condition."

"Perhaps he didn't," Tom suggested. "Perhaps the person who slipped him the knife hid him until he could recuperate enough to flee."

"No, he rode from Camden that night. We found the horse's hoofprints on the road outside of town the next morning. Being newly shod, they stood out like a sore thumb. And the spy was alone, there were no other tracks with his. But we lost them in the forest. We searched the entire countryside for days, but we never found him, and we tore every rebel plantation and farm in the locality apart. By now he's either escaped and is back with Marion in the swamps or Sumpter in the backwoods, or he's skulked off someplace and died. And I hope to hell the last is true. God, it galls me to think he got away from me!"

Felicia had been listening avidly to the story. She remembered the aura of power that had seemed to surround the prisoner, and how he

33

had frightened her at the time. But strangely, she found herself hoping he hadn't died, that he had somehow managed his escape. There had been something magnificent about his vitality, his sheer determination that placed him above and beyond the pale of an ordinary man. It would be a shame for someone that alive to meet an untimely death, particularly one as shameful as being beaten to death.

At that moment, the music resumed, and the ballroom became a beehive of activity as the men led their partners onto the dance floor, and the couples lined up for a stately minuet. Seeing several young men hurrying towards Felicia in hopes of a dance, Tarleton cut them off by stepping forward and asking, "Would you be so kind as to show me your gardens, Felicia? I couldn't help but notice them when I rode up. They looked to be quite lovely, and I could stand a breath of fresh air."

Felicia would have much more preferred dancing, but she couldn't think of a graceful way to refuse. She strongly suspected the Colonel of ulterior motives in asking to see the gardens. Like every other young man in the Carolinas, he was probably only using it as an excuse to get her alone. She glanced at her father, hoping he would give her an out, but to her dismay, he smiled congenially and said, "Yes, Felicia, why don't you? It is rather close in here tonight."

As her father turned and walked away, Felicia glared at his back. Why, he was all but throwing her at Tarleton, she thought in disgust. Then, aware of the young officer extending his arm to her, she accepted it, smiled wanly, and said, "This way . . ." She hesitated, for twice she had called him Colonel and he had corrected her. "Ban."

As they stepped from the ballroom onto the wide veranda that overlooked the back of the plantation, Tarleton looked about him. At one side of the house, sat the brick hot house, the plantation kitchen that was built apart from the main building to keep the cooking heat from spreading throughout the living quarters during the warm summers. It also served to lessen the danger of fire, a disaster that occurred frequently in the colonies where open fireplaces were used for both heating and cooking. Beyond the kitchen, he could see the dark outline of the smokehouse, the dairy, the stables, the carriage house, the hen coop, and even further in the distance, the long row of cabins that served as the slaves' quarters. Tarleton recalled the first plantation he had seen. With its numerous outbuildings, he had thought it a town, rather than one homestead. And in truth, most of the plantations were towns within themselves, with their own gristmills and kilns for making bricks, as well as their own orchards and kitchen gardens. The majority had their own herd of cattle and pens of hogs, producing their own meat; they even bred their own horses, and grew their own fields of flax for making linsey to clothe their slaves. For that reason, it had been necessary for him to destroy the Whig plantations. They supplied the rebel army with almost everything they needed to sustain them but their guns and gunpowder. Those couldn't be eaten. Tarleton had been taught that a starving army could not continue to fight, and despite the fact that everyone credited him personally for breaking the enemy's lines at Camden, he knew it was more the rebels' weakened condition that beat them than anything else. After weeks of nothing but watered-down molasses, they were so debilitated from diarrhea that they could hardly hold their guns. Nor could they run fast. Damn, Tarleton thought, if it weren't for the blasted guerrilla fighters, they could have caught Gates's militia and wiped it out once and for all. He was in total agreement with General Cornwallis on that matter. That was all it would take to win this war. One great battle and one big victory.

"Is something wrong?" Felicia asked, when Tarleton stood and stared into the distance for so long.

"No," Tarleton answered, dragging his thoughts away from his favorite occupation, the war. "I was just thinking how large these plantations are. Someone told me that almost all are over twenty thousand acres."

"That's true, but only a portion is under cultivation. My father has twenty-three thousand acres here, but only a thousand are being used for his rice crop."

"Why only a thousand acres? Why not cultivate the entire estate?"

"Why, that would take an army of slaves!" Felicia answered, astonished that the Englishman had not realized that. "And it takes time to clear the land. All of this was once heavily wooded. You can't grow rice like the lazy uplanders in the piedmont do their corn, just gird the trees to kill them and plant between them," she informed him with a hint of contempt in her voice. "For rice farming, the stumps have to be removed, and an irrigation system built. That takes time and labor. Besides, my father gets two barrels of rice per acre. That more than supports us."

Tarleton was surprised Felicia knew as much as she did about rice farming. He had gotten the impression that the upper-class women of the south were terribly spoiled, and not very intelligent. Strangely, knowing that she wasn't an empty-headed flirt as he had thought, seemed to make her all the more intriguing and therefore appealing, only increasing his determination to seduce her, for he was a man who loved a challenge. He gave her a smile calculated to dazzle her, then said, "Well, you certainly showed me how little I know about it, but how did we get off on that subject? We came out here for a walk, remember?"

As Tarleton led her from the veranda, Felicia glanced about and saw that there were several other couples in the gardens. That, plus the fact that the servants had lit the pathways with lanterns in anticipation of the guests taking a stroll through them, made her relax, despite the husky tone she had heard in the young officer's voice. And he couldn't get familiar as long as he was just walking beside her. Her wide panniers would see to that. Besides, Felicia thought, silently laughing to herself, even if he *did* try something, he wouldn't be the first, and she'd handled them.

As they walked down the paths, passing couples going in the opposite directions, Felicia couldn't help but notice the envious looks the women gave her, looks that told her they would give anything to be in her shoes. She stole a sideways glance at Tarleton, thinking he was indeed a very handsome man, and cut a dashing figure in his impeccable uniform and his dress sword. She should be attracted to him, not necessarily as marriage material, but at least physically. But she wasn't, and wondered why. Every other woman seemed to be. Was there something wrong with her?

"Ah, the air is so refreshing out here," Tarleton remarked, breaking their long silence.

To Felicia it still felt rather close, which was

unusual. There was usually a slight evening breeze here in the gardens. "Yes, it's pleasant," she answered agreeably.

"That sweet smell," Tarleton muttered, glancing about him. "Is it coming from the roses."

Felicia took a long breath through her nostrils, then answered, "No, I think that's coming from the honeysuckle, in the woods back there."

Tarleton stopped and gazed at the dark outline of the trees that Felicia had indicated in the distance. "What's back there?"

"The river and my father's pier," Felicia answered.

"Is that where your brother keeps his racing boat?"

"Why, yes," Felicia answered in surprise. "But how did you know about his conner?"

"He told me about it, and I'd like very much to see it."

Despite her confidence that she could handle the officer if he tried anything, Felicia glanced nervously at the woods. They looked very dark and deserted. "Oh, it's not all that much. It's just a log canoe with a sail. It wouldn't be worth the walk."

A sudden thought occurred to Tarleton, and being the direct man he was, he voiced it by asking, "Are you afraid of me?"

The question was asked in a challenging tone of voice, and Felicia had never been able to refuse a challenge. It was a weakness that had gotten her into many scrapes during her childhood, yet she had never learned from her mistakes. Her pride wouldn't let her. "Of course not!"

There had been just enough heat in Felicia's voice to tell Tarleton that he had hit upon a weakness. Fast on the heels of that realization came the thought that perhaps he could play even more on that weakness, goad her further and further until he had aroused her passion so much she was beyond reason. He smiled smugly and said, "Then let's go."

As Tarleton dropped her arm and grabbed her hand, pulling her rapidly down the path that led to the woods, Felicia had to run to keep up with him. She glanced over her shoulder, saw several couples watching them, and realized how their going into the woods must look. Running hand-in-hand as they were, the couples would probably think they were lovers sneaking off for a romantic tryst. She should call a halt right now, before her reputation was in shambles.

"We shouldn't be going off like this," Felicia objected as Tarleton hurried her along. "Someone might get the wrong impression."

"I thought you said you weren't afraid of me?" Tarleton tossed back over his shoulder.

"I'm not. I'm worried about gossip," Felicia answered rather breathlessly, for she was not dressed for such physical exertions, with her bodice laced so tightly. "We were seen leaving the gardens, you know."

Tarleton came to a halt, turned to her, and peered into her eyes. "I must have misjudged you. I didn't think you were afraid of anything, much less something as silly as gossip. I credited you for having more intelligence than that."

Felicia strongly suspected she was being manipulated, but couldn't quickly think of an appropriate retort. Seeing her hesitation, Tarleton seized his opportunity and said, "See, I knew you were adventuresome, and not one of those simpering women afraid of their own shadow."

Not giving her a chance to collect her wits, Tarleton turned and once again hurried her down the path, using the same tactics that he used in battle, moving so swiftly that the enemy didn't even have time to formulate a defense. Within minutes, they were in the thick, dark woods, following the twisting shadowy path that led to the river. Not until they had cleared the forest and run halfway up the pier that jutted into the wide waterway, did Tarleton come to a halt.

Looking around him, he saw two boats tied up to the pier, the larger one a good eighty feet long, with a huge rudder oar at its rear, and the other no more than a log canoe. Pointing to the smaller vessel, he asked, "Is that the conner?"

"Yes," Felicia said, still trying to catch her breath after the long run.

"Well, I'll have to admit I'm disappointed."

"I told you it wasn't worth the walk! Or should I say *run?*" Felicia threw out hotly.

Tarleton turned. There was just a sliver of a moon, but it put out enough light for him to see Felicia's flashing eyes and her breasts heaving in her low-cut bodice. She looked both beautiful and very seductive. His desire rose. He stepped closer, asking in a low, husky voice, "Has anyone ever told you how beautiful you are when you're angry?"

Felicia knew what was coming. She could tell by the hot look in the Englishman's eyes. He was going to kiss her. She had suspected all along what he was up to, but she would have expected him to lead up to it more gradually. My God, did he take everything by storm, even seduction, she wondered. And how she was going to spurn him without angering him, for she didn't want to make an enemy of this man. He was too powerful and influential. As he stepped even closer, and she felt the heat of his body, she muttered, "No, Ban, I . . ."

Felicia never got to finish. Tarleton's lips closed over hers and cut off her words, as he swiftly stepped forward and took her into his arms. He kissed her so passionately that Felicia was at first shocked at his intimacy, for no man had ever put his tongue in her mouth. When he boldly took possession of one of her breasts, Felicia finally gained her senses and tried to struggle, but Tarleton was in prime physical condition and strong. He only embraced her tighter, and Felicia feared for her ribs. The kiss seemed to go on and on, making Felicia feel weak and light-headed. Then, faintly, she heard someone calling, "Colonel Tarleton! Colonel Tarleton!"

Tarleton apparently heard the call, too, for he released her so suddenly that Felicia had to reach out for him to keep from falling. Steadying her with one arm, he turned the direction the call had come from just as a dragoon cleared the woods, followed closely by three other soldiers.

The dragoon shot a quick glance at Felicia, then smiled slyly before saying, "Sorry to interrupt you, Colonel, but I've been looking all over for you. A couple back in the gardens told me they saw you come this way."

Tarleton wasn't in the least concerned that his men had caught him in what appeared to be a lover's tryst. He didn't even bother to straighten his clothing, which had become disarrayed when Felicia struggled. "Yes," he replied calmly. "What is it?"

"A messenger just rode in from headquarters. He said there's a farmer from up-country who thinks he's seen the spy you've been looking for."

Tarleton's plans for seduction were completely swept away. His eyes lit up with anticipation, and Felicia couldn't help but notice their almost diabolical gleam and the cruel twist of his lips as he smiled. "Tell the grooms to bring our horses around!" he snapped.

"Shall I gather the rest of the men?" one of the other dragoons asked, as the first ran to do the officer's bidding.

"Yes, but I'm coming." Tarleton answered, then turned to Felicia and said, "Sorry, my dear, but duty calls. We'll continue this another time."

Before Felicia could respond, Tarleton turned and ran down the pier. As he tore down the path, his men whirled around and followed him. For a moment all Felicia could hear was the pounding of their boots on the ground, then the faint drumming as the sound faded, and finally, just the gentle lapping of the water against the piles.

Felicia enjoyed the soothing sound and took a moment to compose herself, silently thanking the spy who had unknowingly saved her from making an enemy of Tarleton or, for all she knew, saved her virtue, for she had never seen anyone as daring or as determined as the Englishman. The more she thought about how Tarleton had tried to overcome her by sheer force, the more outraged she became. And to think he thought he was going to come back and take up where he had left off, she mused, as she turned and walked from the pier. The audacity of the man! No, the only thing he was going to get from her was a piece of her mind. She smiled, planning

44

the scathing dressing-down she'd give him the next time they met.

Then, as she stepped onto the darkened path in the woods, Felicia's thoughts were abruptly ended as she was grabbed from behind and jerked back against someone so hard it knocked the wind from her. Terrified, she opened her mouth to scream, but the sound died in her throat, as a cloth was stuffed into her mouth and the ends were tied at the back of her head with a swiftness that stunned her. She was whirled around to face her attacker, and before she could even raise her arms to defend herself, both wrists were caught and deftly tied before her. She looked up, way up, at the man towering over her, but she couldn't see his face, as his back was to the light of the moon. All she could see was the dark outline of his head and massive shoulders.

Frantic, she tried to use the only weapon left to her disposal. Her feet. But trying to kick him was a total waste of effort. In her hoop, it only made her look clumsy and ridiculous, and much to her horror, only brought a contemptuous laugh from the man. As he whirled her back around once again, she felt the tip of a knife thrust against the small of her back, and heard him rasp in her ear, "Now, walk, and don't try anything. I have no compunctions about killing a woman."

Felicia didn't doubt the man's word. She had

never been so terrified in her life. Despite the fact that her legs were shaking, she walked down the path, until she was jerked from it and pushed through the woods, stumbling on thick roots that protruded from the ground. Thoughts ran wildly through her head. Why had this man abducted her? What did he want with her? Did he intend to rape her? That was frightening enough, but then what? Would he kill her?

When they reached a horse tied to a bush deep in the woods, the man stopped her, and for a moment that seemed like a lifetime, peered down at her from his great height. Then he sheathed his knife and, moving with the swiftness of a cat, threw up her skirts. Thinking to defend herself from rape despite her terror, she swung her arms at him, but he only batted them aside with a disgusted grunt and yanked the tab that held up her petticoat. It and her hoop fell to the ground in a heap, and her skirt came tumbling back down. Before Felicia could even realize that ridding her of her awkward hoop had been his only purpose, he had jerked the reins free, caught her by her waist, and tossed her on the back of his horse. Straddle-legged, she hit the hard saddle with such force that she saw stars. Then her abductor swung into the saddle behind her, and picked up the reins.

As the horse picked its way through the dark woods, Felicia sensed that this was her last chance to escape. She tried to jump off, but she might as well have saved her energy. The arm holding her tightened around her like a steel vise.

"Try that one more time, and I'll kill you," the man whispered, his mouth so close to her ear that she could feel his warm breath. "Do you understand?"

At that moment the presence of lethal danger was so powerful that Felicia was afraid to even breathe, much less move.

"I asked if you understood?"

Felicia swallowed hard and nodded her head.

"Good. Now be still. We've some ground to cover."

The man kneed the horse, and the animal bolted and tore through the woods, twisting and turning. The trees flew by, and Felicia held her breath, terrified they might ride right into one of the huge oaks in the darkness and break their necks. A wave of relief swept over her when they reached the clearing beside the river.

As the man turned his mount downstream, Felicia wondered who her abductor was, and gathered enough courage to look over her shoulder. From where she sat, all she could really see was the man's neck and his strong chin. Then, sensing her gaze on him, he looked directly down at her. Felicia sucked in her breath sharply. She recognized those black, piercing eyes. The spy Tarleton and his men were at that very moment seeking, the man who had inadvertently saved

47

her from Tarleton's attentions was here and very much alive. A little thrill ran through her, before she remembered her precarious position and wondered why he had abducted her.

As if reading her mind, the spy smiled. It was not a friendly smile or a reassuring one, but a smile so menacing that it clearly boded her no good. A shiver ran over Felicia, as she wondered bleakly what her fate might be.

Chapter Four

Felicia and the spy who had abducted her rode for hours through the countryside, across soggy rice fields, through deep woods, then over more rice fields. As the night progressed, Felicia put her worries about her fate behind her for one much more pressing. Unaccustomed to riding astride, her bottom was taking a terrible beating, and the insides of her thighs were rubbed raw. Her entire pelvic area ached, her head throbbed, and she was so weary, she could hardly keep her eyes open. To add to her discomfort, there was a heaviness in the air that made breathing even more difficult, especially with the gag in her mouth.

Somewhere during the night, flashes of lightning began to appear on the horizon, coming closer and closer as the approaching storm seemed determined to outrace them. Thunder rolled ominously, then crashed. Felicia felt the splash of a raindrop on her face, followed by another and another, then she jumped as a tremendous bolt of lightning rent the dark sky, forked, and forked again, briefly illuminating the entire countryside. A split second later, her abductor veered his horse sharply from the narrow road they had been following. It wasn't until they had almost collided with a small, dilapidated building, that she realized he must have seen it in the flash of lightning and planned to take refuge from the storm there. Knowing that her agony would soon be ended, she would have cried out for joy, if it had not been for the gag.

The spy leaped from his horse, then caught her around her small waist, and swung her down. Felicia didn't need to be urged inside. The sky seemed to have opened up at that moment, and the rain came pouring down. Despite the discomfort the movement caused her, she ran the short distance and ducked inside the door. Her captor, leading his horse behind him, followed her.

Felicia stood in the darkness and looked around her. A strong musty smell hung heavily in the air. Then, in a flash of lightning, she saw where one end of the structure had collapsed. She also saw something that identified the building to her. A row of heavy stone jars. She knew then that this was an abandoned willowing house, where the rice grain was separated from the chaff and stored, until it was time for it to be moved to the boats for transportation.

Felicia couldn't see a thing in the inky blackness that followed, but she could hear the spy moving about the building through the sound of the pounding rain. A few moments later, a flicker of light appeared, as he worked with his flint and steel to set fire to a pile of rice stubble that he had scraped together on the dirt floor. For a few moments he totally ignored Felicia, as he nursed the meager fire, feeding bigger and bigger splinters of wood that he broke from some of the half-rotten lumber lying about. When the fire was going well, he rose and faced her.

For a long moment, he just stared at Felicia, his face so devoid of expression that his rugged features might have been made of stone rather than flesh and bone. But such was not the case with his eyes. Those piercing, black orbs seemed to reach out across the distance that separated them, and hold her pinned to the spot. Even when he strode quickly towards her, Felicia couldn't move, despite her fear and the powerful urge she felt to run for her life. She watched, mesmerized by his compelling gaze, her heart pounding in her chest. Then, as he stopped before her and his hands rose, she did flinch, thinking he meant to strike her.

Hawk shook his dark head in disgust at the fear he saw in Felicia's eyes, then reached behind her head, and quickly released the cloth gag. He watched as the fearful look on her face turned to one of surprise, then said, "You needn't have worried. I don't beat women. Nor am I going to rape you, as you seem to have thought earlier."

Felicia should have been relieved on both counts, but relief wasn't what she felt. The contempt she heard in his voice was like throwing salt in a raw wound. Suddenly her fear disappeared, and a blind fury seized her. "How dare you!" she shrieked.

It was Hawk's turn to look surprised. What had happened to the fearful woman standing before him?

"How dare you abduct me, treat me so roughly, threaten to kill me, then tell me I shouldn't have worried! Is this some silly game you're playing? If so, I don't think it's funny!"

"This is *not* a game and *not* meant to be funny!" Hawk answered in a hard voice. "And when I told you I would kill you if you didn't obey me, I wasn't threatening. I meant it."

"You'd kill me, but you wouldn't *beat* me?" Felicia asked in disbelief. "What kind of stupid reasoning is that?"

"Only a coward beats a woman."

"And it wouldn't be cowardly to *kill* a woman?"

"In your case, no. It would have been an act of self-preservation."

Hawk turned his back on her, infuriating Felicia even more so, for it seemed terribly rude. As he walked to his horse, Felicia followed him and said, "I demand you take me back!"

Hawk ignored her, and calmly removed the horse's saddle and saddle blanket.

"Didn't you hear me?" Felicia shrieked. "I said, I demand you take me back!"

He turned, and once more Felicia felt the full impact of his black gaze. "I'm going to tell you this just once," he said in a low voice that was deadly calm, and for that reason all the more menacing. "Don't scream at me. I can't abide a woman who screams. And don't make demands of me. As my hostage, you're in no position for that."

Felicia had a tendency to be hotheaded and impetuous, but she wasn't a fool. At that minute she was very much aware of the man towering over her, of the broad expanse of his chest and shoulders, of powerful muscles in his upper arms straining against the linsey of his hunting shirt. She knew he could break her in two, if he so chose. That alone was enough to give her pause, but she knew he was also a desperate man, which only made him all the more dangerous. As she struggled to bring her outrage and anger under control, she wondered for what purpose he would take her hostage. There was only one she could think of. "Do you think taking me hostage will secure your escape, that the dragoons won't follow you, for fear of what you might do to me?"

There was no response to her question. Only that dark gaze bearing down on her.

"But they won't even guess you've taken me," she continued, hoping to reason with the man. "They'll never dream it was *you,* because they think you were miles and miles away at the time, far up-country. That's why they rushed off the way they did, to try and catch you. So you see, you can flee without fear. And you don't need me. I'll only slow you down."

The black eyes flashed. "I'm *not* fleeing! That's not why I took you hostage."

"Then why?"

A snarl crossed Hawk's lips as he answered, "Because you're Tarleton's woman, and—"

"Tarleton's woman?" Felicia interrupted in astonishment. "What makes you think that?"

"I saw him with you that day in Camden. Then, that night, I heard the women who brought the guards their food say he was courting you."

"Oh, those stupid townspeople!" Felicia exclaimed. "I was afraid they would misconstrue what they saw. That was just a silly rumor! Colonel Tarleton and I are just acquaintances."

"Acquaintances?" Hawk asked in a brittle voice. He scoffed. "Do you really expect me to belief that, after what I saw with my own eyes."

"Saw what?"

"The two of you running off into the woods, then kissing passionately."

"Kissing passionately?" Felicia asked incredulously, then flushed in embarrassment that someone had witnessed it. "No, it wasn't at all like that," she said quickly. "We weren't kissing. He was kissing *me,* but I was trying to get away from him."

Hawk laughed harshly the second time, saying, "Like hell you were! You couldn't get close enough to him. I saw you squirming, rubbing yourself against him. I'm no fool. I know lovers when I see them."

Felicia was totally dumbfounded by his accusation. My God, she thought, he was even worse than the townspeople at jumping to conclusions. "No, you're mistaken! I wasn't squirming. I was struggling! We're not lovers. We're not even friends. Despite what you saw — or think you saw — the Colonel and I—"

"Don't waste your breath denying it!" Hawk interjected. "And don't play me for a fool. You're Tarleton's woman. There's no doubt in my mind about that. And when he realizes I've taken you hostage, he'll come for you."

"Then it's *him* you want?"

"Yes, it's him! You're just the bait. You see, I planned on catching Tarleton on the way to the ball this evening. I heard him promise to come that day in Camden, and had a perfect ambush set up along the road, a place where I could drop down from a tree on top of his coach. Then it would have been just a simple matter of knocking out the driver. But Tarleton didn't come alone," Hawk informed her with disgust.

"He had a score of his dragoons with him. I knew I couldn't ambush him there, not armed with just a knife. So I climbed a tall tree in those woods, where I could see over everything, hoping to catch him alone sometime during the evening, or if not that, on his way back to town."

Felicia knew Tarleton had arrived at the ball in the company of some of his dragoons, guests from the elite fighting unit that her brother had invited. Everyone had been surprised. Like the spy, they had thought the colonel would hire a coach, particularly in view of the fact that he was such a dandy. One wouldn't have thought he'd risk getting his immaculate uniform dusty.

Unaware of her thoughts, Hawk continued. "When I saw you two going into the woods alone, I thought that might be my chance to call him out, so I followed. I was just getting ready to make my move, when his dragoons came on the scene, and he slipped through my fingers once again."

"Call him out?" Felicia asked in surprise. "That sounds like you mean to fight him, not murder him."

"I do. To the death! But my knife wasn't up to taking on four swords. That would have been suicide. That's when I decided to take you hostage. Make him come to me."

"Don't you think you're going to rather drastic

measures, to get revenge for what he did to you?" Felicia asked, drawing her own conclusions. "You must have realized when you took up spying how dangerous it was, that you'd be beaten or worse if you got caught. There's no reason for you to take it so personally, no more so than if Tarleton shot at you in battle. That's just the wages of war."

"I'm *not* a spy! And his beating me has nothing to do with this."

"Not a spy?" Felicia asked in confusion. "But they caught you lurking about his headquarters."

"I was. But it wasn't information I was looking for. It was him."

"To challenge him?"

"Yes. And kill him."

"But why?"

A mask seemed to drop down over Hawk's face. The cold, forbidding look might have given anyone else pause, but Felicia was spurred on by a burning curiosity. "Look, you made me a part of this. It wasn't something I asked for. If you plan to use me to lure Tarleton, I think I have a right to know why you have such a vendetta against him."

Hawk was grimly silent for so long that Felicia didn't think he would respond. Then his expression was no longer cold. His dark eyes came alive, as if a fire had suddenly ignited in them, burning with unadulterated hatred as he answered in an intense tone of voice, "He murdered my father."

Felicia was so shocked that she was momentarily speechless. Then she blurted, "Murdered him? Tarleton? How . . . ? Why?"

"Haven't you heard of what happened in the Waxhaws wilderness on the border of North Carolina?"

Felicia searched her memory, then answered, "No, I haven't."

"I find that hard to believe," Hawk answered in a cutting voice. "The news of the massacre spread like wildfire all over the Carolinas. I've heard that even some of the Tories were sickened by what Bloody Ban did there."

"Bloody Ban? Are you talking about Colonel Tarleton?"

"Yes, Bloody Ban! The Butcher! No Quarter Tarleton! He's known by all those names, and rightfully so. He murdered those men in cold blood."

"What men?" Felicia cried out in exasperation. "I still don't know what you're talking about."

Hawk gave Felicia a long, piercing look, then said in an incredulous tone of voice, "You really don't know, do you?"

"No, I don't! And I would appreciate it, if you would enlighten me."

There was a pause before Hawk answered, "All right, I'll tell you. But sit down. This may take a while."

Felicia didn't particularly relish the thought of sitting. Her backside was still terribly sore. But she was also very weary. Gingerly, she seated herself, then feeling a little braver in the stranger's company, held out her hands and asked, "Would you please untie me before you begin?"

Hawk had been about to sit himself. He paused in mid-crouch and looked at her for a long measured moment. Then, having put his suspicions aside, he rose, stepped across the small fire, and quickly untied her wrists.

"Thank you," Felicia muttered, rubbing her wrists where the rawhide bonds had cut off the circulation.

Instead of the usual response, Hawk nodded his head curtly, determined that he wouldn't show the mistress of his enemy even a cursory politeness. Felicia watched as he sank to the ground, coming to rest with his long legs crossed before him, the movement so effortless and graceful she couldn't help but wonder at it.

Without any preamble Hawk began his story. "About two weeks after the fall of Charleston, Tarleton and his men caught a group of Virginia militiamen coming to the aid of the city in the Waxhaws wilderness. The Virginians hadn't heard Charleston had surrendered. Despite the fact that they were on foot and outnumbered, the militiamen turned back Tarleton's first charge, and his horse was shot out from under him. On the next charge, the Tories broke the

59

Virginians' lines. Colonel Buford, the militia's commanding officer, knew there was no hope of winning against a superior force. He ordered his men to lay down their weapons and raise a white flag. But Tarleton was furious about his horse being killed, and refused to honor the surrender. He shot the flag-bearer in cold blood, and yelled, No quarter! No mercy! to his men. Those among the Tories that were dismounted opened fire and charged with their bayonets, while the mounted men plowed into the huddled, defenseless Virginians with their sabers. For fifteen minutes they stabbed and hacked the patriots. No one was spared. Not even the wounded. They were stabbed again and again. Finally it ended, but not because Tarleton called a halt. No one seems to know why. Maybe by then the Tories' lust for blood had become too much for even them. But when it was over, there were 113 dead, and 150 so badly wounded they were left to die on the field. My father was one of them, and Tarleton was the man who sank his blade into him over and over."

Felicia had listened to the story in horror. Knowing that it had been a massacre perpetrated on Americans by Americans made it all the more horrible. She had heard bits and pieces about the bitter and bloody civil war that was going on between the loyalists and rebels, but nothing this sickening, nothing this senseless. And why had she not heard anything of the massacre until now, if the news had spread like wildfire across the Carolinas? she wondered. Had her father known and not told her and her mother, thinking the story too bloody and shocking for their tender female sensibilities? But surely her father wouldn't have allowed her brother to join Tarleton's group, much less encourage Tarleton's attentions on her, if he had known the truth. Not her father. He had too much honor, too much integrity. So he must not have known. Their plantation was very isolated. They often missed out on pieces of the news, or didn't hear about them for months. Then there had been the Battle of Camden, a major victory that probably overshadowed any other stories going around. No, her father hadn't known, she decided, and thank God, Robert hadn't taken part in the dishonor. He hadn't joined the legion yet. But what was her brother involved in now? she wondered uneasily.

"You've been mulling over what I told you for a very long time," Hawk commented.

"I didn't know about it. I'm sorry it happened," Felicia answered in all honesty. She looked him directly in the eye, and then said, "But I still don't condone your vendetta against Tarleton. You can't be sure he was the man who killed your father."

"But I am sure. It was cold-blooded murder. One of the survivors told me. He was left on the field for dead. He saw it all."

Felicia was having trouble seeing Tarleton as a cold-blooded murderer. Oh, she knew he was a killer, all soldiers were, but they killed dispassionately, with no personal animosity. No, it seemed to her that the stranger seeking Tarleton out to kill him and avenge his father's death was much more premeditated and cold-blooded.

"All right, so Tarleton killed your father," Felicia said, deciding to once again try reasoning with the man, "but that doesn't give you the right to seek him out to kill him. That would be just as senseless as the other, and two wrongs don't make a right."

"I should have known you would defend your lover," Hawk replied contemptuously.

Felicia shot to her feet. "He's not my lover, and I'm not defending him! I just think revenge is pointless. It won't bring your father back."

Hawk rose slowly to his full, impressive height. Then, standing before her, he crossed his arms over his broad chest and said, "It is not just a matter of revenge. It is more. It is a matter of honor. A matter of seeing justice done. And it is for me, his son, to do. It is my people's way. The law of the clan."

There was something majestic about the way the tall, dark stranger stood before her, something that placed him out of the ordinary realm. "Who are your people?" she asked.

Just a hint of a smile crossed Hawk's lips, only whetting her curiosity more. As he remained silent, Felicia wondered why he persisted in being so secretive. Having to pull every bit of information from him was tiring. "You told me your father was from Virginia. But you don't talk like a Virginian."

"My father lived in Virginia. I did not say I did."

"Then where are you from?"

He motioned to the west and answered vaguely, "Over the mountains."

He was one of those rugged mountain men, Felicia thought in awe, one of those fearless, fiercely independent men who braved the Indians and the wilderness to cross the dangerous Appalachians, mountains whose heights had not been breached by any white man for hundreds of years, until men of his particular cut had come along. Felicia's eyes slid over the coarsely woven hunting shirt with its capelike, fringed yoke, the skintight buckskin pants, and knee-high moccasins. Yes, she thought, he was dressed like one of those mountain frontiersmen. Even the wicked-looking knife that hung from his belt fit to a tee. All he needed to complete the picture was a long rifle in one hand, and a shot bag and powder horn slung around his neck. But Tarleton had undoubtedly taken those from him when he had captured him.

Felicia remembered what the man had said about avenging his father's death being his people's way, the law of the clan. If it was true that he was a mountain man, that also fit, for she had heard that they were mostly rugged Scots-Irish, that hadn't left their ways behind them in Europe. Just as they had been in Scotland before they fled the British to Ireland, they were still wild highlanders who believed in an eye for an eye and a tooth for a tooth, who held strangers at bay, who still practiced clan revenge, and who fought at the drop of a hat. If the man before her was one of them, she could save her breath trying to reason with him. She could talk till doomsday and not sway him from seeking his revenge. It was in his blood.

Wanting to know more about this rugged stranger, Felicia asked, "What is your name?"

"Hawk."

"Hawk who?"

"Just Hawk."

"No, what's your surname—your last name," Felicia added, in case he did not understand what surname meant.

"I have none."

"But everyone does!" Felicia objected, thinking he was just being secretive again.

"*I* don't!" Hawk replied in a hard voice, then gave her a look that clearly warned her that any further questions would not be welcome, and might possibly be dangerous.

Yes, he's a Scot, all right, Felicia thought. A stubborn, closemouthed, wild Scot, who lived by his own backward, savage code. Imagine, taking a hostage to lure someone into a life-or-death duel for the sake of revenge! No civilized person would do that. He was still living in the Middle Ages.

Hawk was unaware of Felicia's uncomplimentary thoughts, and had he known, wouldn't have cared less. Her opinion of him meant nothing. All that mattered was his quest for justice. He led his horse to the back of the building and tied it there, to prevent it from wandering away during the night. As he walked back from the shadows, he swept up the saddle blanket, then spread it on the ground beside the fire, saying, "You can sleep on that."

Felicia looked down at the blanket with disgust. It was none too clean, and even from where she stood, she could smell the horse sweat on it. She glanced around and saw nothing that could be used as a pallet. Realizing it was that, or sleep on the ground, she sighed deeply in resignation, and sat down on it.

As Hawk settled down beside her, Felicia shot him a startled look, a look that only intensified as he rudely grasped one of her ankles, quickly circled it with the rawhide he had used to tie her hands, then looped the other end around his buckskin-clad ankle and tied it.

"That will keep you from trying to escape during the night," he explained. "And don't try to untie it. I'm a light sleeper."

With that, Hawk stretched out his long body

beside her, with his back toward her, and his dark head pillowed on the crook of one arm. For a few moments, Felicia stared at that broad back, thinking that she could never force herself to lie down beside the coarse barbarian. But she quickly discovered she was wrong. The ordeal she had gone through that evening had exhausted her both mentally and physically. She reclined, then rolled to her side.

For several minutes, Felicia lay staring out into space, wondering bleakly how she had gotten herself into this terrible position. If only she'd had the courage to refuse to walk to the river with Tarleton, but she had foolishly let him manipulate her. That she had known what he was doing made it all the worse. Damn him, and damn her pride! This was by far the worst predicament she had ever let it get her into, and she had a strong foreboding that before it was over, she would pay a heavy price for her freedom.

It was with that fear in mind that Felicia slipped into an uneasy sleep.

Chapter Five

Felicia spent a restless night, and was the first to awaken the next morning. Lying on her side, she could see through the collapsed end of the willowing house, and knew that the sun was just rising by the pearly light it was casting over the countryside. Then, as the first beams of sunlight appeared, making the raindrops on the trees in the distance look as if they were sprinkled with glittering diamonds, the birds in the area began to sing their hearts out.

At any other time, the sights and sounds of a new day dawning might have brought gladness to Felicia's heart, but not this morning. She had just spent the most miserable night of her entire life and ached all over from sleeping on the hard ground, and there was a chilling dampness in the air, for the fire had burned out long ago. Felicia knew the frontiersman was still asleep. She could hear the deep, regular sounds of his breathing behind her. Damn him, she thought. How dare he be so comfortable, while she was so miserable, but then the hard ground was probably his usual bed, crude backwoodsman that he was. And he undoubtedly didn't feel the cold either. If only she knew how to light a fire with flint and steel. Then Felicia realized that wouldn't do her any good either. She couldn't get up to light a fire, not tied to him the way she was. Never in a million years would she have dreamed this would happen to her, Felicia thought, that she would spend the night tied to a virtual stranger in an abandoned shack. Even more remarkable was that nothing of a sexual nature had happened. Of course, no one back home would believe that—when and *if* she ever got free—and undoubtedly her father had alerted the entire countryside to her disappearance by now. She needn't have worried about Tarleton possibly tarnishing her reputation. The bastard lying next to her had ripped it to shreds. Damn him!

Thinking to awaken the object of her anger, Felicia rolled over. She barely smothered a gasp of surprise, for she had not expected to come face-to-face with Hawk. She took the opportunity to study him more closely. Asleep, he didn't appear as dangerous-looking, and Felicia realized, with something of a start, that with his high forehead, straight, almost aristocratic nose, prominent cheekbones, and strong chin, he was really quite handsome, in a rugged, manly way. Even the darkness of his skin, which she attributed to his outdoor life, enhanced his masculinity, for Felicia thought nothing made a man look more unmanly than a pale, pasty complexion. Then she noticed the frontiersman's lips. The day before, they had been compressed, had looked thin, hard, even cruel, but with his mouth relaxed, they had a softness, a sensuality about them that made Felicia wonder what they would feel like on hers. The unexpected thought made a shiver of pure delight run through Felicia, before she recovered her senses and jerked her eyes away, feeling utterly shocked at her outrageous behavior.

She found herself gazing at a lock of hair that had fallen across the man's forehead; it was as black as a raven's wing. She had never seen hair so inky dark, just as she had never seen eyes so deeply black. A strange urge seized her, the desire to touch that lock, to push it back from his forehead. Then, before she could even react to this equally shocking impulse, she knew without a shadow of a doubt that the frontiersman had opened his eyes. She could feel them on her, boring into her. Suddenly, his closeness, his bearing, everything about him seemed to be smothering her. She bolted to a sitting position, and said in a voice that was strangely breathless, "Stop staring at me like that! Didn't anyone ever tell you it was rude?"

"Indeed?" Hawk answered in a calm, unruffled manner. "Then you should scold yourself. You were staring first."

A guilty flush rose on Felicia's face before she denied it, saying, "I was doing no such thing!"

Hawk sat up, saying in a disgusted voice, "Another lie? I'm beginning to wonder if you ever tell the truth."

"I'm not lying! I was just . . . looking, not staring, the way you were," she ended with an accusing tone of voice.

"And why were you looking so long and so hard?"

My God, Felicia wondered, how long had he been lying there awake, while she all but devoured him with her eyes? "I was just wondering when you were going to wake up," Felicia quickly fabricated. "Besides, I've never lied to you. You had no right to say that."

"You denied you were Tarleton's lover," Hawk reminded her.

"That was no lie! It was the truth." Felicia looked Hawk straight in the eye. "He won't come for me, you know. You're wasting your time. He won't come, because I mean nothing to him!"

"I told you, you can save your breath," Hawk said in exasperation, then bent and untied the bond around their ankles.

"But—"

"No buts! You're only lying to protect him."

Felicia seethed silently while Hawk rose, walked to his horse, and brought it back to where Felicia was sitting. "I need that blanket you're on," he said.

"We're not leaving already?" Felicia asked.

"Yes, we are."

"But aren't you going to build a fire?"

"What for?" Hawk asked, reaching down to catch one arm, and lifting her to her feet when she made no effort to move.

It was just as she suspected, Felicia thought, *he* wasn't chilled. No, not the hardened woodsman. Well, she'd be damned if she'd admit that she was. "What about breakfast? Aren't you going to cook breakfast?"

Hawk threw the saddle blanket over the horse's back, asking, "Cook what? I don't have any food with me."

Felicia glanced around, then said, "There's probably some rice in the bottom of one of the stone jars. We could boil it."

Hawk finished saddling the horse before he answered. "In what? We don't have a pot."

Exasperated, Felicia asked, "What have *you* been eating?"

He shrugged his broad shoulders, answering, "Dried corn I stole from someone's corn crib, roasted meat I snared."

"Then snare something!"

"That takes time, and I want to be on our way. We have a good distance to cover before nightfall."

"Then you intend to starve me until then?" she asked acidly.

Hawk was becoming exasperated himself. Taking Felicia hostage hadn't been something he'd planned. It had been a spur-of-the-moment decision, something he wasn't prone to do, and he was already regretting it. She was much too demanding. "No, I don't intend to starve you!" he answered crisply. "We'll eat later." Seeing her about to object, he cut across her words, saying in a hard voice that brooked no argument, "Enough! I told you, you're not in a position to make any demands. You'll eat when I eat, sleep when I sleep, ride when I ride." He led the animal to the open area where the walls had collapsed, then stepped back, and commanded, "Now, get on!"

Despite the fact that she knew Hawk was her captor and she was powerless against him, Felicia still resented his dictatorial attitude. She shot him an indignant look, then walked to the horse and attempted to mount, but her long, full skirt was an encumbrance. Giving an impatient snort, Hawk caught her around her slender waist and tossed her onto the saddle.

As he mounted behind her, Felicia looked over her shoulder and said hotly, "That wasn't necessary! I could have done it myself."

"When? By next week?" Hawk replied sarcastically, then gave the animal a swift kick.

Any response Felicia might have made was

smothered by her gasp, as the animal leaped forward and ran off. She grabbed the saddle horn to steady herself, then grimaced as her bottom bounced on the hard leather. *I'm not going to be able to endure an entire day of this,* she thought bleakly, but grimly she held her silence.

Hawk took the same narrow road he had followed the night before. Felicia knew there was little hope of running into someone who might alert the authorities. The road was obviously a private one, probably once used to transport rice from the fields, for in no place was there any sign of the planking that was used on the public roads in low places. And it appeared that it had been a long time since it had been used, for it was almost overgrown with weeds.

An hour later, the road petered out, and Hawk followed a trail that skirted a rice field. Felicia glanced around anxiously, hoping to gain sight of someone, for surely they would investigate when they saw a woman in a ball gown riding double with a frontiersman. Then, in the distance, she saw the plantation house, or rather what was left of it. It was nothing but a blackened shell sitting starkly against the blue sky.

Hawk had been aware of Felicia looking about, and knew she had been hoping someone would see them and try to rescue her. "You didn't think I'd be stupid enough to take you through an area where there was any possibility of us being seen, do you?" he asked in con-

73

tempt. When Felicia refused to answer, he said, "That's one of the plantations your lover and his men burned down. This entire area is littered with them. He even tried to set fire to the fields, but they were too wet to burn. Why he even bothered is beyond me. With no slaves, no tools, no wagons, no horses to even pull them, the owner couldn't possibly harvest anyway, providing he himself survived the raid."

Felicia could have pointed out that there were many loyalists who had also had their plantations burned in this war, that they, too, had suffered, but she didn't. She strongly suspected that Hawk was trying to goad her into an argument. His anger was so great it was almost palpable, and for that reason, frightening. She held her tongue.

Felicia had been wise in refusing to rise to the bait Hawk had thrown out. Every time he saw the blackened destruction Tarleton and his cohorts had wrought on the length and breath of South Carolina, he became incensed. But it wasn't just simple anger at his enemies. Only a part of it had anything to do with the British and this war. The emergence of his strong feelings was much more complicated than that, for the sight brought back painful and disturbing memories from a previous time long ago.

Three hours later, Hawk and Felicia were still riding in silence beside deserted rice fields overgrown with weeds, and enough time had passed that Hawk's anger had subsided. Felicia was too uncomfortable to notice, or care. Her bottom was numb, the insides of her thighs burned something awful, and the hot summer sun beating down on them was taking its toll. Felicia could feel perspiration gathering, then trickling beneath her armpits, between her breasts, and on the insides of her thighs. It was a miserable feeling to which she was totally unaccustomed, but what was even more unbearable was the feel of sweat on her head beneath her high, pomaded hair. Several times, she reached up, shoved her fingers through the gooey mass, and scratched.

Watching her, Hawk finally commented, "Can't you take that down? It's so tall I can barely see over it."

"I'd love to take it down, but I can't!" Felicia answered irritably. "It's glued together. It has to be washed to be removed, and it's beginning to itch something fierce."

"Then why do you wear it like that, if it's so uncomfortable? Not to mention how silly it looks."

Felicia was in total agreement, but she wasn't about to admit it to him. "It's fashionable!" she retorted, then added, "But that's something an *uplander* wouldn't understand."

Hawk knew Felicia was flinging an insult at him when she called him an uplander. South Carolina was divided into two geographical areas: the coastal low country where the wealthy plantation owners lived, and the mountainous upper country where the poor common people lived. Both groups held the other in contempt. But Hawk wasn't going to let the uppity lowlander bait him. He ignored her comment, and turned his horse towards a timbered area in the distance.

"Where are we going?" Felicia asked.

"There's probably a stream in those woods."

"Where I can wash my hair?" Felicia asked excitedly.

Hawk wasn't about to admit that he was going to accommodate his unwilling captive in any way, for he was very well aware that she considered herself much above him, and that irritated him to no end. "I hadn't considered that. I was thinking of finding water to drink and something to eat." He paused to give Felicia time to absorb the import of his words, that her comfort didn't matter to him, then said, "But if you hurry . . ." His voice trailed off.

"Oh, I will," Felicia promised, then frowned, thinking it sounded as if she were groveling. But she didn't care, she decided. She'd do anything to relieve herself of at least the misery of her sticky hair.

As soon as Hawk had stopped the horse beside a wide stream they found in the woods and lifted Felicia down, she hurried away.

"Where are you going?" Hawk asked.

"Over there to wash my hair," Felicia answered, motioning downstream.

"What's wrong with right here?"

"Surely you don't expect me to wash my hair in my gown? I'll get it all wet."

For a moment Felicia feared that Hawk expected her to do just that, or worse yet, strip to her thin chemise in front of him. Then he said, "I assume you're not going to be so foolish as to try to escape."

Felicia glanced around at the dark woods all around her, knowing full well she couldn't escape if her life depended upon it. In the first place, she had no earthly idea where she was. Why, she'd get lost, and there were wild animals in the woods. It would do her no good to get away from her abductor, only to become the victim of a bear or panther. Besides, even if she did try to brave it, escape would be hopeless. Undoubtedly, the frontiersman was an excellent tracker and would easily find her. "For once you're correct. No, I'm *not* that foolish!" she answered flippantly, tossed her head, and turned.

Hawk watched as Felicia flounced away and shook his head, thinking he must have been temporarily addled when he took her hostage. He had always heard that lowlanders' women were simpering creatures frightened of their own shadows, manageable women who were easily bent. But not this woman. There was nothing meek or docile about her. Not only was she demanding, but sassy and impertinent, certainly much more of a handful than he had bargained for. But the deed was done, and there was no turning back. He would just have to make the best of it, until she'd served her purpose.

Chapter Six

After leaving Hawk, Felicia went just far enough in the woods to assure herself that she was out of his sight, quickly removed her gown, and tossed off her satin high-heeled slippers. Dressed in her chemise with its deeply ruffled three-quarter-length sleeves and silk stockings, she waded into the water until it was waist deep and stood for a moment, relishing the soothing feel of the cool water on the chafed area on her thighs. Deciding that she might as well make the most of it, since she was going to get wet all over anyway, she waded in a little further, then dunked herself fully, holding her breath until the water could soften the gel that held her piled tresses together. Then she emerged and set to work seriously, trying to scrub the pasty substance out, massaging her scalp with a vengeance, and dunking over and over.

When she finally deemed her chestnut tresses as clean as she was going to be able to get them without benefit of soap, Felicia turned and headed to the bank. It was then that she saw Hawk through the leaves of a low-hanging willow, wading in the water several yards away from her. Terrified that he had seen her in her wet chemise, clinging to her body and hiding nothing, she covered her breasts with her arms and hurried to the bank. Taking refuge behind a tree trunk there, she peeked around it, then realized he was much too intent on trying to spear a fish with the long stick he had sharpened to have noticed her.

Deciding to take no chances that he might still come upon her, Felicia donned her gown and looked down at it in dismay. As wet as it was getting from her dripping hair and soaked undergarments, she might as well have worn it to wash her hair. Then, spying a sunny spot a short distance away, she picked her way through the dense woods, being very careful where she stepped; for she knew this was a good haven for snakes.

For almost an hour, Felicia sat in the sun, running her fingers over and over through her long hair to dry it, expecting Hawk to come looking for her at any minute. But in the end, it was she who went to him, drawn by the drifting aroma of fish being grilled over an open fire.

Hawk was crouched by the fire when Felicia came from the woods. He looked up before she even entered the clearing, and noted her jaunty stride and the sparkle in her greenish gold eyes. Then his breath caught in his throat, as the sunlight hit the long chestnut hair, falling in glorious disarray all around her shoulders. He hadn't realized it had so much red in it, nor had he noticed its luster. Looking at it in the bright noonday sun almost hurt his eyes. Then Hawk noticed something else. Felicia's still damp gown clung to her full, thrusting breasts like a second skin. He could even see the faint outline of her rosy nipples. All told, the vision she presented was both beautiful and seductive.

Thinking that Hawk was looking at her so hard because she had taken too long, the lightheartedness Felicia had been feeling since ridding herself of the sticky goo on her hair, disappeared like a puff of smoke. Even looking forward to eating was ruined by the sight of those dark eyes boring into her. She came to a dead halt, and said defensively, "I hurried as fast as I could." She raised one arm and passed her fingers over her scalp, saying, "As it is, it's still damp."

The movement made the breast on that side of Felicia rise, and look as if it were threatening to tumble from her low-cut bodice. Hawk's eyes were glued to that soft, milky globe, as erotic fantasies popped into his head. Then he felt a familiar heat flood his pelvic region. Horrified that his body might betray him, he jerked his eyes away and rose to his feet. Motioning to a flat rock near the fire that he had used in lieu of a grill, he said in a voice made harsh by his sudden, unwanted desire, "That's your fish, and don't dally in eating it."

He whirled around and started walking to where he had tethered the horse in a grassy patch in the woods. Felicia thought his harshness hateful, and shot his broad back a resentful look. Then her eyes widened, and she blurted, "What happened to your back? Your shirt is covered with blood."

Hawk came to a halt, looked over his shoulder, and frowned. "One of the wounds must have opened again, when I speared those fish."

Felicia had completely forgotten about Hawk being severely beaten. He hadn't been acting at all like an injured man. Why, he had even tossed her on the horse a few times. "Oh, yes," she muttered. "I forgot about that."

Hawk sent Felicia a look of pure disgust, wishing *he* could forget. Every time he moved he felt a stab of pain. "You go ahead and eat," he instructed her. "I'm going to walk down to the creek, and see if bathing it in water will stop the bleeding."

As Hawk walked away, Felicia grimaced. She knew her words must have sounded terribly insensitive. She hadn't really meant it that way. Even the enemy deserved some compassion. But on the other hand, she could not make herself apologize either, not after the way the frontiersman had been bullying her.

For some time after Felicia had finished eating her share of the fish, Hawk didn't return, and since he had made a point of going around a bend in the creek, she didn't follow, for fear he had stripped and gone into the stream naked. When she saw him walking towards her, she knew that must have been exactly what he had done, for he was carrying his wet shirt that he must have washed, while his pants and moccasins were as dry as a bone. As he approached, Felicia stared at his broad, muscular chest. As deeply tanned as his face, it seemed to be all hard planes and ridges, and there was just a smattering of dark hair that lay between his flat male nipples, then tapered to a fine line and disappeared beneath his buckskins. Felicia had grown up on a plantation, and was accustomed to seeing men bared to the waist, but somehow Hawk's impressive chest and broad expanse of shoulders seemed more manly. A strange excitement filled her, and a warm curl formed in the pit of her stomach.

When Hawk reached her, he turned his back to her, saying, "It's still bleeding, isn't it?"

Felicia felt the sight of Hawk's back like a dash of cold water, shocking her from what had been the beginnings of sexual arousal. It was crisscrossed with angry, red welts, and in several places there were strips of skin that had been lain open, a few of the lacerations covered with scabs, but others still oozing blood, and one particularly deep one bleeding freely. The gorge rose in her throat.

"Well?" Hawk prompted. "Is it bleeding or not?"

Realizing the bleeding wound lay in the curve of his back, where he couldn't clearly see it, Felicia swallowed and answered, "Yes."

"I thought so. I need something to bandage it," he said, turning to her. Then, eyeing her voluminous skirt, Hawk added, "A piece of that will do."

Rip her beautiful gown to cover this brute's back? Felicia thought in horror. "The devil it will!" she retorted. "I'm not ripping my gown. If you want something to bandage your wound, use *your* shirt!"

"I need my shirt, and you've got enough material in that skirt to bandage an entire army. Rip some off from the side there, where it's dragging on the ground. You won't even miss it."

Felicia didn't even have to look down to know he was talking about the material that formed the pannier on her gown, usually taken up by the hoop he had stripped from her the night before. The excess material lay spread out on the ground on both sides like trains, and she had stumbled because of it several times already. Felicia realized she wouldn't miss it, would probably be better off without it, but she still couldn't bring herself to deliberately tear it. This dress was one of her favorite ball gowns, and had cost her father a pretty penny.

Hawk had no such qualms. Before she realized what he was about, he had whipped his knife from its scabbard, yanked up her skirt, and sheared off several yards of material. Once she had recovered from her surprise, Felicia looked down in horror and viewed the damage he had done. In his haste, he had not only cut off the excess material, but a good deal of the rest of the skirt on that side, baring the ankle and lower calf of one shapely leg. "Look what you've done, you big lout!" she cried out angrily. "You've ruined my dress! It's all lopsided now."

"If you wanted it done neater, you should have taken the opportunity I gave you," Hawk answered, totally unruffled by her outburst and her insult. "You should know by now not to challenge me."

Indeed! Felicia thought in cold fury. He thought himself lord and master with his superior strength. God, she would give anything for a weapon at that moment, she thought. But not a knife. She'd probably cut herself with the naked blade. The use of a knife took skill and practice. No, she wished she had a pistol. Then, she'd show him. She'd blow his bloody head off!

Felicia continued to seethe silently as Hawk sheathed his long knife, then tore the material into long strips. Shoving them into her arms, he said, "Now, wrap them around me, so we can be on our way."

Felicia's greenish gold eyes narrowed and glittered, reminding Hawk of a mountain lion that had once jumped him. His own dark eyes narrowed dangerously. "Don't defy me," he warned.

"Or else what?" Felicia threw back, looking the very picture of defiance.

"Or else I'll cut the other half of your skirt off." He paused, then added, "But perhaps a little shorter."

Felicia knew he wasn't making idle threats. He was perfectly capable of cutting her entire gown to pieces. The bastard! "Turn around!"

Despite the suppressed fury in Felicia's voice, Hawk turned. He knew he had won that confrontation.

As Felicia bandaged Hawk's back, she got an even better look at it. She knew one particularly deep wound would leave a scar for life, as well might several others. "Considering how deep some of these are," she commented, thinking out loud, "they've healed remarkably well. You must have a good constitution."

"My fitness had nothing to do with it. It was just fortunate that I picked the same place to hide the night I escaped as an old slave woman, otherwise I would have bled to death. She mixed up a poultice of herbs and put it on my back."

"A slave woman?" Felicia asked, her curiosity aroused. "A runaway?"

"No. She came from one of the plantations that Tarleton raided and burned to the ground. She managed to escape to a nearby swamp, before the slaves could be rounded up and marched off. She'd been living there for several weeks in a little deserted trapper's hut. I would have died if it hadn't been for her, if not from loss of blood, then infection. She nursed me and cared for me, until I was strong enough to leave."

"Yes, Colonel Tarleton told my father the guards had been taken by surprise, because no one thought you had the strength to escape," Felicia remarked.

Desperation had given him the strength, Hawk thought. He had been desperate to escape. But not so he could live. He had expected to die. But he had been determined he wouldn't die at the end of a rope, for his people considered it the most degrading, shameful death a man could suffer.

"That slave woman must have come from the West Indies, if her poultice worked that well," Felicia continued, unaware of Hawk's thoughts. "The slaves that come from there seem to have a way with healing herbs."

"No, she wasn't from the West Indies. She was Indian."

Felicia wasn't surprised to learn that the slave was Indian, particularly if she was old. Indians had been often captured and enslaved during earlier colonial times. But only women and children were kept here in America. The men were shipped to the West Indies, where they couldn't run back to their tribes. Over the years, the practice had been pretty much discontinued, in favor of using African slaves. Indians were simply too resistant to make good servants, nor did they adapt as well to civilization. They missed their wild, free way of life so much, that many simply mourned themselves to death. "It's a good thing she didn't know you were a frontiersman, or she wouldn't have helped you," Felicia commented.

A closed expression came over Hawk's face. "Why do you say that?"

"Well, there's certainly no love lost between you. You're constantly at war with the Indians."

"Not all Indians. Indians are like white men. There are enemies, and there are friends."

"Are you saying that you have friends that are Indians?" Felicia asked, her voice heavy with disapproval.

"I do."

There was an undercurrent in Hawk's voice and something about the rugged frontiersman's entire demeanor—a certain tension—that made Felicia sense she was treading on dangerous ground. She prudently decided to change the subject.

"Colonel Tarleton said he searched the entire countryside, but couldn't find any trace of you.

That was why he was so ready to believe you had left the area."

Hawk frowned. That was the second time in just a few moments that she had referred to his enemy by his military title and not his first name, as he would expect a lover to do. Were they really not intimate, or was she just trying to throw him off? "Tarleton couldn't find the end of his nose in the dark," Hawk answered with contempt. "He and his men went all around us, and never got within fifty feet of us."

By that time, Felicia had circled Hawk's body three times with the bandage. Deeming it enough to stay the bleeding, she tucked in the free end, then stepped before him and asked, "If that's true, how do you expect him to find us? Or anyone for that matter," she added as an afterthought. "That rain last night was bound to have washed out our tracks."

"He'll know where to find me. My letter will give him explicit instructions."

Letter? Felicia thought in surprise, then came to her own conclusions and said, "I won't write a letter for you." Her golden green eyes flashed with fierce determination. "And you can't force me to! I won't be a part of this . . . this insanity!"

"Who said I was going to ask you?" Hawk rejoined calmly. "I'll write my own letter."

"You can write?" Felicia asked in utter astonishment.

"Well enough. And read and cipher. You see, I'm not quite the lout you think I am," he answered, then turned and began kicking dirt over the fire to smother it.

No, he wasn't a complete lout, Felicia was forced to admit. She had noticed other things about him that she hadn't expected of an uneducated backwoodsman. His speech for one thing. It was just a little too refined. Apparently there was much more to the frontiersman than first met the eye. She stared at him curiously as he walked to his horse, then brought it back to where she stood.

Hawk motioned for her to mount. Felicia looked up at the hard saddle and made a decision. She bent, picked up the other side of her skirt, and viciously ripped off the excess. Rising, she saw the stunned expression on Hawk's face, then said, "If you can use my gown to cover your back, then I can use it to pad that saddle. I'm not used to riding astride, nor is my . . ." Felicia paused in mid-sentence. She couldn't really think of an appropriate term for her tender bottom to use in mixed company. In frustration, she threw decorum out the window and blurted out the first thing she could think of, something that just jumped into her head that she had once heard her brother say. ". . . my arse as hard as yours!"

With that, Felicia folded the material several times, slammed it onto the saddle, then, much to Hawk's surprise, mounted, throwing her leg over the back of the saddle, as if she had been doing it that way all of her life.

Hawk mounted behind her and picked up his reins. As they rode off, he admitted that he hadn't been paying much attention to her comfort. She'd been gently raised, and he'd been treating her like one of the tough women on the frontier. Then he reminded himself that she was both a Tory and Tarleton's woman. She was the enemy, his hostage, and he'd be damned if he'd treat her as if she were some honored guest. But he had to admit to a grudging admiration for her spirit. And she was full of surprises. Who would have thought a lady would make any reference to her bottom, much less call it an arse. That sounded more like something a tavern wench might say. A smile crossed his lips.

"Where are we going?"

Felicia's question tore Hawk from his musing. "To a place where I can find some writing materials, and where you'll be safe while I'm gone to post the letter."

Felicia wondered what he meant by safe. Safe for her, or him? Once more she pondered her fate. She knew it was foolish, that it was pointless to even argue it any further with the stubborn frontiersman, but, perversely, she couldn't resist saying, "Tarleton won't come, you know. This entire escapade has been a waste of time and effort. You mark my words."

Hawk knew a challenge when he heard one. "We'll see."

Felicia heard the supreme self-confidence in Hawk's voice. She glanced over her shoulder. She would have given anything to be able to wipe that smug smile from his arrogant face.

Chapter Seven

Riding away from the stream, Hawk took a narrow trail through the woods. Although Felicia couldn't actually see any incline, she sensed the ground was rising. There was also a change in the forest around them, as more pines appeared, and less maples and oaks were seen. Felicia welcomed the change of scenery. It was cooler here in the shade of the woodlands. Combined with her newly padded seat, she was much more comfortable — until she became acutely aware of something else. Hawk's disturbing presence.

Felicia didn't know why she was so conscious of him, if it was because she had been too miserable that morning to notice, or because he was half-naked. Hawk hadn't put his shirt back on, but had placed it over the back of the horse behind the saddle to dry, and Felicia felt every brush of her back against his hard chest. The constant pressure of his bare muscular arms against hers, as he held the reins before them, seemed to be burning her skin right through the material of her sleeves. She closed her eyes and clenched her teeth, but that gave her no relief. Then she was plagued by a mental vision of what his manly chest had looked like. Even his hands seemed to have taken on a strange appeal. Large and deeply tanned, with long, slender fingers, they looked both powerful and incredibly graceful, capable of enacting both brute force and, she sensed, intense pleasure. Felicia was in a quandary. She had never been so aware of a man's sexuality before, not even when Tarleton had held her so close to his hard body and kissed her so intimately. All she had felt then had been revulsion and anger. But now, with Hawk's powerful masculinity bearing down on her, she felt an excitement, a tingling, a strange breathlessness. Even the rugged frontiersman's scent was unsettling, a faint muskiness mixed with wood smoke and leather that made her heart beat faster.

Felicia wasn't the only one experiencing discomfort. So was Hawk. When she had walked from the woods looking so beautiful and provocative, she had awakened his awareness of her as a desirable woman. Not that Hawk hadn't known from the beginning that she was beautiful. His pain from the whip hadn't blinded him to that fact. But he had been so full of contempt for any woman who would consort with Tarleton, that he had thought himself immune to her appeal. Besides, he had always been a man firmly in control of his emotions, and that included, first and foremost, his sexual appetite. Now he knew such was not the case, not by a long shot. With the impediment of Felicia's lofty hairstyle removed, he could clearly see the tops of her luscious breasts in her low-cut bodice, and, in the deep valley between them, a beauty mark that was driving him wild. Her newly shortened gown, hiked up as she sat astride the horse, gave him a tantalizing view of her shapely calves and slim ankles. Even when Hawk forced his eyes straight ahead, he wasn't given a reprieve from her tormenting presence. He could feel her hair between them on his bare chest, soft, silky, and incredibly arousing. Heat seemed to radiate from her, carrying with it a dizzying, womanly sweetness. It took every ounce of Hawk's iron control to keep his manhood from responding, a concentration that played on his nerves.

For several hours they rode like that, silent and painfully aware of each other, the sexual tension so thick between them it could have been cut with a knife. Then suddenly they rode into a clearing where everything was blackened and charred, the trees, the shrubs, even the ground. Both welcomed the unexpected distraction. Felicia was the first to speak, asking, "What do you think caused the fire? Lightning from that storm last night?"

"No, it's not that recent, otherwise it would still be smoldering." Hawk pivoted the horse, then pointed to a wide area of blackened ground that stretched out into the distance. "I think the fire spread to the woods from that field that had been set ablaze."

"Another burnt plantation?"

"Yes, an indigo plantation."

Felicia had sensed they were moving upland, and this proved it. The growing of indigo (producing a blue dye used in printing calico and coloring silks and wools) was relatively new to the Carolinas, having been introduced only a little over thirty years before, and generally occured farther inland, past the low-lying rice belt.

Hawk rode the horse over to the edge of the field, stood in his stirrups, and peered into the distance. "There's something still standing over there. Let's have a look."

Felicia was amazed at his keen eyesight. She couldn't see a thing, not even the blackened shell of a plantation house.

Hawk raced the horse over the field, kicking up a cloud of black soot that hung in the air behind them. By the time they reached where the plantation buildings had once stood, the horse's legs, underbelly, Felicia's shoes and Hawk's moccasins were covered with the dark grime. As they came to a halt among piles of charred timbers, Felicia saw what Hawk had spied. It was a half-burned corncrib. She felt a keen disappointment, and said, "I was hoping it might be the smokehouse, and we'd find something to eat."

"Even if it had been, there wouldn't have been any meat left," Hawk answered bitterly. "They always take that with them."

Felicia knew by the way Hawk had said *they* that he thought this had been done by loyalists, perhaps even Tarleton and his men. Remembering how peculiar he had acted at the sight of the last burned plantation, she held her tongue, refusing to be baited.

Hawk swung down from the horse, saying, "But they did leave something we can eat."

As he began picking up cobs of corn scattered about the ground, Felicia said in disgust, "We can't eat that. That's cattle fodder. It's as hard as a rock."

"You can if you're hungry enough," he replied. "And by tonight, you might be that hungry."

"You can snare some meat," Felicia answered.

"Maybe, and maybe not. A lot of it has been scared out of this area. There's nothing more terrifying to a wild animal than fire, you know."

Felicia didn't. She didn't know a thing about wild animals, except they could be dangerous. But she did know she couldn't eat that hard corn. The rugged frontiersman might, but not her. She'd break a tooth on it.

She looked about her, then finding what she thought she was looking for, dismounted and walked to it with determination. Seeing her rummaging about a pile of blackened timbers around what appeared to be a collapsed chimney, Hawk asked, "What are you doing?"

"From the size of this hearth, I thought this might be the cookhouse, and if so, maybe I can find a pot," Felicia answered, tossing a stone aside. "Then we could soften that corn by boiling it."

"Better yet, find a corn grater," " Hawk suggested. "Then you can grate it into cornmeal."

Felicia knew she wouldn't find a corn grater here, not in a plantation kitchen. They got their cornmeal from the miller. Only the poor grated their corn by hand. But Felicia didn't bother to point that out to Hawk. Instead, she said, "You still need something to cook it in. A skillet or pot."

"Not necessarily. You can mix the meal with water, form little cakes out of it, and cook it in the coals of a fire. Haven't you ever heard of ashcakes?"

"No, I haven't!" Felicia answered testily. She had noted that Hawk had said *you* and knew he meant *her,* and she had no intention of cooking for him, much less laboring over grating cornmeal! She was his prisoner. If anyone was going to do the cooking, it should be him. Besides, she didn't know a thing about cooking, other than what she had observed on her brief visits to the plantation kitchen.

Then Felicia stubbed the toe of her slipper on something, something hard enough to make her grimace in pain. She reached down and pulled a long-handled, three pronged skillet from beneath a pile of charred embers. "Look!" she said excitedly. "I told you I'd find something!"

Hawk looked at Felicia. Her fancy ball gown

was covered with soot, and there was even a smudge on her cheek. Standing there in the rubble, with her arms black to her elbows, holding up a battered, grimy skillet, she didn't look at all like a lady. She looked totally disreputable, and breathtakingly appealing with her golden green eyes sparkling with excitement, and the breeze blowing her long, chestnut tresses about her. A powerful wave of desire swept over him. It was all he could do to keep from throwing her to the ground and taking her right there in the rubble. He whirled around, saying harshly over his shoulder, "All right, so you found a damn pot! Now mount up, so we can leave. We've wasted enough time."

Felicia couldn't imagine what had put Hawk in such a foul mood. She picked her way through the rubble, watching as he dumped the corn he had collected into his shirt, then tied it to the saddle horn. As he stood aside for her to mount, she asked, "What about the skillet? Aren't you going to tie it to the horn?"

"I have no need of a skillet."

"Well, I do! And you certainly don't expect me to hold it all of the way to where we're going?"

Hawk was riding the razor's edge of sexual frustration. "You can do whatever you want with the damn thing! Throw it away or keep it! Just don't bother me about it."

What Felicia would have liked to have done with the skillet at that minute was hit Hawk over the head with it, which, of course, she couldn't do. But she was determined she wouldn't throw it away, if for no other reason than because the testy frontiersman had seemingly taken such an intense dislike to it.

Realizing that she needed something with which to tie it to the saddle, she looked down at her dress. The sight took her somewhat aback, for she hadn't realized how grimy she had gotten. She considered tearing more off the bottom, but decided against it. Already, it left too much leg showing to be even remotely modest. Instead, she reached down, tore a lace ruffle from the skirt, slipped it through the hole at the end of the skillet handle, and tied it to the saddle horn on the opposite side of the corn. Then giving Hawk a go-to-hell look, she mounted.

Hawk didn't follow her. He knew that as aroused as he already was, he'd never hold his desire in check in the close proximity that sharing a saddle forced upon them. Instead, he took the horse's reins and led it around the piles of blackened rubble that had been the plantation's outbuildings.

Passing a particularly large pile of charred timbers, Felicia spied something, then cried out, "Look! There are bones under those timbers!"

Hawk stopped the horse and craned his neck to look.

Felicia could hardly force the question from her lips. "They're not . . . not human, are they?"

"No, they're bones of a horse. This was where

the barn stood, and if you looked closer, you'd probably find more than one skeleton in there."

"What makes you think that?"

"Because that's how the British do it. The animals are forced into the barn before it's set on fire—the horses, cattle, hogs, even the chickens. I've been told they make a hideous noise."

Felicia's eyes filled with horror. "Are you saying they're not killed first?"

"Tarleton isn't going to waste gunpowder on animals. Nor is he going to take the time to bash their heads in or slit their throats," Hawk answered in a tight voice. "Not that cold-blooded bastard!"

"But that's needless suffering, just out-and-out cruelty!" Felicia answered, tears glittering in her eyes. "Those animals weren't his enemy. They're not anyone's enemy. Are the rebels who raid the loyalist plantations doing that, too?"

"We're not rebels! We're patriots. And no, we don't burn animals alive. We might take them for food, but we don't destroy for destruction's sake, like Tarleton does. But then we don't have the same objectives. We raid to obtain food and supplies, or at the worst, to punish someone for being on the wrong side in this war. But Tarleton raids to terrorize. He looks for ways to be cruel, and flaunts them. He thinks the more cruel he can be, the more people will fear him, and that he can use that fear to conquer them."

At that moment Felicia felt very vulnerable for two reasons. First, she half expected Hawk to remind her that this was the same Tarleton who was her lover, and she didn't think she could have borne his flinging that hateful accusation in her face. It made her sick to think that she had even been civil to the colonel, knowing that he made animals suffer needlessly, just to prove how cruel he could be! She also feared that Hawk might accuse her of being callous, of showing more compassion for those animals than she did for the Virginians Tarleton had massacred; for she knew the frontiersman had seen the tears in her eyes, tears that hadn't been there for the humans. In truth, Felicia *did* have an especially tender place in her heart for animals. She felt humans often brought much of their misfortunes on themselves, while animals were innocents, so often used, or misused by man. But she knew Hawk, a hardened frontiersman, would never understand her feelings. No, even if she could explain that it wasn't callousness, he'd think her silly. Her parents always had.

Much to Felicia's relief, Hawk made no further comment. He didn't feel any was needed concerning Tarleton. It was obvious from her shock that Felicia had known nothing of his cruelty. As for revealing her tenderheartedness for animals, she would have been very surprised to learn that knowledge had touched a deep chord within him. As a child Hawk had been taught a deep respect for animals, to never kill one needlessly; and if it were necessary to kill for survival, to first ask its forgiveness. Because of his upbringing, he understood Felicia's feelings far better than many of her own people might have, and the insight into her unexpected sensitivity had generated a new appreciation for her.

As Hawk pondered what he had learned, the sexual tension he had been feeling drained from him. He mounted behind Felicia, and as they rode off, leaving the grim reminders of the war behind them, he wondered just what he had gotten himself into when he had taken her captive. He hadn't expected to be physically attracted to her. That in itself was bad enough. But he was also finding that there was more to her than met the eye. He had expected her to be spoiled, selfish, weak. Instead he had discovered that she was spirited, yet sensitive, both very appealing attributes.

Hawk didn't like what was happening. It would never do to be enamored with the lowlander. She was his bait, nothing more. Once she had served her purpose, he'd get rid of her, and the sooner, the better. She was beginning to make him very uncomfortable.

Chapter Eight

Determined to keep his vow to rid himself of Felicia as soon as possible, Hawk didn't dally the rest of that day. Their pause at the burned plantation was the last stop they made, and their evening meal consisted of several ears of dried corn, or rather, his did. Felicia stubbornly refused to attempt to eat the hard kernels, even after Hawk warned her that it would be that or nothing, for they wouldn't stop until they reached their destination. Felicia discovered he wasn't making empty threats. Long after the sun had gone down, he kept the horse going at a steady pace, and she knew there was no hope of them stopping because the animal was tired. She knew the sturdy bay Hawk had stolen was an everlaster — a breed known for its remarkable endurance — and that it could make sixty miles a day, even carrying double. And from the looks of things, Hawk was going to get every single one of those miles from the creature.

The canopy of leaves over them was so thick

that not even a star could be seen, and as Hawk wove their way through the inky darkness of the forest, Felicia was amazed at his night vision. She couldn't see a thing. With the total blackness wrapped around them like a shroud, the musty smell of rotting leaves heavy in the air, and the only sound that of the horse's hooves and a screech owl hooting somewhere in the distance, it was eerie. Felicia kept waiting for something to happen. Just what, she didn't know. Perhaps a wild animal or some hideous night monster might jump out at them. Her anticipation was so acute, that her stomach was tied in knots and her nerves were stretched taut.

As they traveled farther and farther and it got later and later, Felicia's exhaustion finally overrode the spookiness she had been feeling. She could hardly keep her eyes open. She began to nod off, her head lolling this way, then that, until Hawk took pity on her and pillowed it against his shoulder.

Felicia was drifting into the warm planes of sleep, when she was abruptly awakened by a man's voice calling out, "Halt! Who goes there?"

Felicia almost jumped out of her skin and looked wildly about her. Hawk, on the other hand, was totally unperturbed. He'd been expecting the sentry. "The name is Hawk," he said calmly. "I'm a friend, a fellow militiaman. And I'd appreciate it if you'd aim that rifle someplace else."

"Not yet," came the surly answer from the darkness. "Not until I know more about you. What regiment are you with?"

"Colonel Shelby's, from over the mountains. That's how I knew where to find your camp. I used to ride courier between him and Sumter."

"You talkin' about Isaac Shelby, the Indian fighter who took Thicketty Fort and won that victory at Musgrove's Mill?"

"That's right."

It was then that the sentry stepped from the darkness, and Felicia finally perceived his dim outline, for before that Hawk could have been talking to a tree, for all she could tell. "Kinda far away from your people, ain't you? I heard Shelby and his men went back o'er the mountains."

"That's true. Our terms of enlistment had run out, but I got separated from the others and captured," Hawk answered, seeing no reason to tell the sentry he'd left on his own personal quest for revenge. "That's why I don't have my rifle. The British took it away from me, along with everything but the clothes on my back. I stole the horse when I escaped."

The sentry eyed Hawk's buckskin pants and moccasins, then asked, "And the woman, who's she?"

"She's my hostage. She's a Tory."

Hawk felt Felicia stiffen, and prayed she keep her mouth shut. He'd told the sentry enough of

106

the truth. The man didn't need to know the full story.

The sentry stepped closer, then said, "Yeah, I didn't reckon she was your wench, dressed the way she is. By God, these lowlander women sure do get all gussied up, don't they? We've got some more of 'em here in camp with us. But they ain't Tories. They're refugees from those plantations Tarleton and his men have been raidin'. We've got orders to take any of 'em in that ask for help. That's who I thought you were when I first seen you ridin' up, some more lowlanders lookin' for refuge."

Hawk nodded in understanding. Since Charleston had fallen, and the British had started ravaging the land, the patriot refugees had fled to the militia, if they could find them, hoping the military would give them protection and care for them. It put a double burden on the militia, who were hard put to feed and clothe themselves. "Is there any particular place we should camp, or do I just pick a spot?"

The sentry shot Felicia a quick glance, then answered, "Well, if you aim to keep that woman with you, you need to pick a spot to the left of the camp. That's where the men with women and children are. The other side is for men only. Other than that, you can squat anyplace you can find a likely spot."

"Thanks," Hawk muttered, and nudged the bay forward.

"Sure hope you think about joinin' up with us, since your enlistment is done with Shelby," the picket commented as they rode past him. "We can sure use some good fightin' men."

"I'll think about it," Hawk answered absently.

About a quarter of a mile further, Felicia spied the camp. The fires scattered all about looked like fireflies from the distance, for almost every one had burned down to just the red coals by this late hour. When they entered the lightly timbered clearing, Hawk stopped just inside the fringes and dismounted, saying, "We'll stay here for the night. If it doesn't look like a good spot in the morning, we can always move."

Felicia was so weary, she could hardly summon the energy to dismount. As soon as her feet hit the ground, she staggered a few feet away, then dropped down on a patch of grass.

Watching her from where he was unsaddling his horse, Hawk frowned, then said, "If you'll just wait a second, I'll have this saddle blanket off, and you can have it."

Felicia was too tired to wait even a second. Besides, she knew the blanket was probably damp with horse sweat. The ground might be hard, but it didn't stink. "No thank you," she muttered, then fell into a deep sleep.

Hawk finished unsaddling the horse, then led it to a nearby stream, where they both enjoyed a much needed drink of water, before Hawk tethered the animal and set several snares. When he returned to where he had left Felicia, she was still in the same position, lying on her side with her head pillowed on the crook of one folded arm. Looking down at her, sleeping on the hard ground in her tattered, grimy dress, her only covering her long hair, Hawk thought she looked more like a street urchin than a grand lady. Then she shivered in her sleep, and instinctively curled her body into a tight knot to keep warm. Moved by pity, Hawk removed the corn from his shirt, then tossed the large linsey wraparound over her.

Hawk reclined beside Felicia. Looking at the placement of stars above him, he judged he could still get several hours sleep before the sun rose, and that would have to suffice. He had things to do before he could leave Felicia to post his letter to Tarleton.

Felicia was so exhausted, she slept until midday, right through all of the noise Hawk was making in building their camp. It was the sound of him felling yet another nearby tree that finally roused her. The next thing she noticed was the hot sun on her face. Then she became aware of something that brought her fully alert: his shirt covering her. But it wasn't the feel of the rough, nubby material against the sensitive skin of her half-bared breasts and neck that played havoc on her senses. It was the rugged frontiersman's scent that was imprinted in the material—exciting, intoxicating, and very male.

Felicia pushed the shirt from her as if it were on fire and sat up, looking wildly about her. Spying Hawk about twenty yards from her chopping down a tree, she stared at the powerful muscles in his back as he swung the ax, over and over. Despite the angry welts that crisscrossed the dark skin, she felt a warm curl in her stomach. Realizing what was happening, Felicia forced her eyes away. Her gaze fell on his buttocks. With his long legs straddled for better balance, the skintight buckskins looked as if they would burst each time those twin sets of muscles contracted. The sight was even more arousing than his back.

Feeling her heat rise even higher, Felicia muttered an oath in self-disgust and forced her eyes completely away from Hawk. It was then that she noticed the lean-to Hawk had built beneath the boughs of a spreading pine. Before it was a fire burning, and over that fire, on a spit, was a turkey roasting. Beside the lean-to was a pile of fresh-cut firewood.

Amazed at all that he had accomplished, Felicia rose and walked to the lean-to, then bent and peered inside. At one end was the pile of corn he had gathered the day before, and the blackened skillet she had found, along with the saddle and saddle blanket. But there were other things there, things Hawk hadn't had in his possession the day before—a water bag, a scuffed, leather hunting bag, a powder horn, and a long Pennsylvania rifle. Felicia couldn't imagine how he had obtained them, unless he had stolen them.

Hawk's stride was so light, that Felicia didn't hear him when he walked up behind her. She jumped when he said, "As soon as I get a little more firewood cut, I'll be leaving to post my letter. The turkey and corn should last you until I get back."

She turned to him and asked, "Where did you get these things?"

There was an accusing glint in Felicia's eyes that told Hawk what she suspected. He snorted in disgust, then answered, "I didn't steal them, if that's what you're thinking. The ax is borrowed. I traded a couple of rabbits and another turkey I snared for the water bag and the blanket. The rest cost me two bucks, with the meat still attached."

An outsider might have been confused by Hawk's last words, but Felicia was from the Carolinas and familiar with the term *buck*. It meant buckskin, and in this area where fur trading with the Indians had played such an important role in the development of the colony, the skins had a better monetary value than either British or colonial currency. Nor was their use only limited to the frontier. Many a Charleston merchant had paid his debts to his English creditors in bucks, for hats and coats made of the skins were a rage in Europe.

"Of course, I'm in debt for those bucks,"

111

Hawk continued before Felicia could respond. "I couldn't deliver the goods until I had a gun."

"Two bucks doesn't seem much for a rifle, a powder horn, and a hunting bag," Felicia remarked, thinking that for all practical purposes, he might as well have stolen them.

"It isn't, unless you're starving and you don't know how to hunt, or rather, where to hunt. You see, the big game around here has been scared off by so many people. Even men who are used to hunting aren't having any success. The game has moved further up-country. The planter I got that rifle from was more than happy to make the trade. He doesn't know that area, and he's afraid he'll get lost if he ventures too far by himself. Then he'd be leaving his family alone with no protection or means of support."

"How does he know he can trust you?" Felicia countered.

"He doesn't. He's taking a big risk, but that's what desperate men have to do sometimes to survive. Besides, he'll get his meat. I gave him my word, and I always keep my word."

"The word of a mountain man who's a horse thief, an abductor of innocent women?" Felicia tossed back sarcastically. "No, if that planter knew you as well as I do, he wouldn't take that risk, no matter how desperate he is."

There was no expression, fleeting or otherwise, to warn Felicia of what was coming. With the swiftness of a striking snake, Hawk stepped up to her, caught her upper arms in a death grip, and jerked her hard against his long body. His dark eyes boring into hers, he said in a low, menacing voice, "If you have any ideas of attempting to discredit me while I'm away, or trying to enlist anyone's aid, you'd better forget them. Everyone in this camp knows you're my hostage and a Tory. They think I used you as a shield to escape, that the letter I'm sending to Tarleton is going to your father, with instructions of where he can find you when I release you. No one here, including the lowlanders that you consider your people, has any qualms about me using the enemy to secure my freedom, not after the crimes that have been committed against them by Tarleton and his men. You're *not* an innocent woman I abducted. Here, you're the enemy, and your temporarily loss of freedom is nothing compared to what they've lost. Their homes, their property is gone forever. A few even lost loved ones, husbands and fathers who tried to resist. They're bitter and angry, and you'd be wise to keep your distance. And whatever you do, keep your mouth shut about being Tarleton's woman. As strong as their feelings are about that bastard right now, there's no telling what they might do to you."

Felicia hardly heard a word Hawk said, even though his discourse was a very serious warning and rather lengthy. Her full concentration was on the feel of his hard, muscular body pressed against hers, particularly where her breasts were flattened against his chest, bare skin to bare skin. She could see the sweat glistening on the powerful muscles of his shoulders, feel his heat, smell his heady scent. Never in her life had she been so painfully aware of a man being male, and she being female. She found it difficult to breathe, impossible to move. She couldn't even force her eyes from his. It was as if she were paralyzed, and time had come to a standstill.

Felicia knew by the change in pace of Hawk's powerful heart beating against her breast that he, too, was becoming aroused. No longer was it just a steady thud; his heart was racing like a wild tom-tom. And fast on the heels of that change, was another in the frontiersman's dark eyes, from blazing anger to smoldering desire, a hot look that made Felicia weak with longing. Her eyes dropped from his eyes to lock on his lips. She wanted him to kiss her, to feel those hard lips on hers, wanted it so bad her lips ached. And then, for just a minute as his head moved ever so slightly towards hers, she thought he was going to do it. A wild exhilaration ran through her.

When Felicia hadn't responded to his tirade, but had stood so still, Hawk became suddenly aware of the close proximity of their bodies. With a will of its own, his body had reacted. He was on the very verge of kissing Felicia, when he came to his senses. Almost viciously, he threw her away from him, then said in a rasping voice, "Remember my warning!"

Felicia had been so surprised by Hawk's unexpected action, that she would have fallen if she hadn't reached out and caught the side of the lean-to for support. Stunned, she watched as he whirled around, walked to where she had left his shirt, and swooped it up. He wrapped it around himself and tied the long sash around his slim waist, walked back to the lean-to, and picked up the saddle and saddle blanket.

"I've decided you've got enough firewood to last you until I get back," he announced with a determined look on his face.

"Then you're leaving *now?*" Felicia asked, feeling a tingle of fear at being left behind in a strange place to fend for herself.

"Yes."

"But what about your letter?" she asked, grasping at anything that might delay him a moment or two longer.

"What about it?"

"When are you going to write it?"

"It's already written. The same planter I bought the gun from loaned me the supplies. It's in my hunting bag."

As Hawk walked into the woods to where the bay was tethered beside a stream, Felicia followed. She watched bleakly as he saddled the horse, then asked, "How long will you be gone?"

"A few days."

"A few days?" Felicia asked in surprise, then commented sarcastically, "Where are you going to post this letter? Charleston?"

"When I get through posting it, I've some hunting to do, remember?"

Felicia's fear was quickly replaced with anger. How *dare* he go off hunting, and leave her whiling away her time in these primitive living conditions, she thought. She had her life to get back to! "Hunting?" she asked, her eyes flashing dangerously. "You're going to go hunting while I wait here, with nothing but a pitiful lean-to to live in, and not even a change of clothing? Damn you! Pay off your debts on your own time, not mine! What happened to fighting Tarleton, or have you forgotten about your revenge?"

When Felicia was angry, she was magnificent. Not even her tattered clothing and wild tangled hair could detract from her beauty, and Hawk was hard put to keep his eyes from her heaving, luscious breasts. Her excitement—even though it was generated by anger—was arousing him once again.

He brushed past her, saying over his shoulder, "No, I haven't forgotten! But it's going to take time for that letter to reach Tarleton. You know how slow the postal service is, even under normal conditions. I've instructed him to meet me in a week."

A week? Felicia thought in horror. She'd have to endure this horribly crude existence for that long? No, she didn't think she could stand going that long without her comforts, without even a change of clothing. Why, she'd be reeking by then!

Desperate, Felicia decided to try one more time to plead for her freedom. She ran to catch up with Hawk's long, swift stride, then said, "Please reconsider. If you take me back now, I'll tell my father you rescued me! He'll pay you a hefty reward."

Hawk whirled around so rapidly that Felicia bumped into him, and the look on his face was terrifying. "I don't want money! I want revenge!"

"Then figure out some other way to get your revenge, some way that doesn't involve me!"

"I tried that already. Tarleton never ventures far from his men, and I can't take on his entire regiment. This is the only way I can get him to meet me one-on-one."

As Felicia opened her mouth, Hawk cut off what she was about to say with, "No! Save your breath! You're involved in this, whether you like it or not. You'll get your freedom when he shows up for that meeting, and not one minute sooner."

Hawk picked up the hunting bag and powder horn and slipped them over his head. Then, swooping up the long rifle, he mounted the bay. Looking down from the saddle at Felicia, he said, "You can keep the water bag. It might save you a few trips to the stream. You'll find a knife beside it. It's small and not very sharp, but it ought to be good enough to cut up that turkey or saw some kernels from that corn. Keep the fire going at all times, so it won't burn out. You should have enough wood to last you until I get back. If not, there are dead branches lying all over the place. It will give you something to do."

Felicia was so furious that she said, "And what if I'm not here when you come back?"

"You will be," Hawk answered calmly. "Every sentry will be on the lookout for you. Until I personally take you out of here, you're my prisoner." Hawk gave Felicia a calculating look, then said, "Besides, if you weren't foolish enough to try escaping earlier for fear of getting lost, you won't now. If there's one thing I've learned about you, you're not stupid. You know you wouldn't have a ghost of a chance out in those woods by yourself."

Felicia didn't like having the truth thrown in her face. "You bloody bastard! Someday, you'll pay for this!"

Hawk turned his horse and rode away. "Did you hear me?" Felicia yelled at his back. "You'll live to regret this! I swear you will!"

Hawk made no sign that he heard Felicia screaming at him like a irate fishwife, but he knew her words were true. He wasn't *going* to regret taking her as his hostage. He *had* been regretting it for some time. She was a spoiled, foul-tempered shrew, enough to try any man's patience, but for some unexplainable reason, she held the most compelling physical attraction. It was as if he had lost all control over his body. Hawk knew what would happen if one of his Cherokee brothers found himself with a hostage like Felicia. He'd slake his lust on her, then, if she didn't behave, kill her. But Hawk found he couldn't do either. Nor could he let her go and lose his chance at getting his revenge. His clan honor would never allow that.

Chapter Nine

The time that passed after Hawk left Felicia seemed incredibly long to her. She had never been totally alone before, without a soul to even talk to, and she quickly learned to heed Hawk's warning to stay to herself. He had barely ridden from the camp when she became aware of the hostile looks coming from the others — lowlander and uplander alike — and those that were the most hateful came from her own class, since it was the wealthy planters, and not the poor militiamen camped there, who had suffered the loss of their homes. Felicia realized with dismay that it was just as Hawk had said. No one would help her in this camp. She was the enemy. If she made any attempt to communicate with them, she would be snubbed, at best. And at worst? Would they attack her? she wondered, feeling a tingle of fear. Felicia prudently kept her distance.

The loneliness might have been more tolerable, if Felicia could have found some physical activity to keep her occupied, but, in truth, she really didn't have to fend for herself. Hawk had seen to her needs before he left. The lean-to was a better shelter than what most of the people in the camp had, for the majority just slept in the open; and while her diet of corn and turkey might be boring, it satisfied her hunger. After observing a farm woman, who had followed her husband to war, scouring her pot with sand, Felicia took the blackened skillet she had found to a deserted spot by the stream and scrubbed it until it shone. Then she painstakingly cut the hard kernels of corn from the cobs with the dull knife Hawk had left her. But once those two chores were finished, she was at a loss for finding something more to do, other than feed the fire by throwing a log on now and then. So she sat in the deep shadows of her lean-to, where she wouldn't be so visible, and observed the others.

Felicia had never thought she would see the day when lowlanders and uplanders would live side by side, with no sign of the usual contempt they showed one another. What surprised Felicia the most was the uplanders' willingness to help the refugees, and this was especially true with the women. Raw-boned, their faces as tanned and leathery as their men, the tough farm women helped the planters' delicate women build fires, chop wood, lug water. They taught them how to cook over an open fire, wash clothes in a creek by pounding them on rocks, and care for their wounded and ill. It wasn't at all unusual to see a camp follower give what little food she had to a lowlander's hungry child, or walk one of their tearful infants when its mother was so weary she could hardly stand. Despite the fact that they were ostracizing her, Felicia felt sorry for the plantation women. Bewildered by what had happened to them, and exhausted by just trying to live day by day under such harsh conditions, they were totally out of their element. Nor did they know when or if they would ever be able to return to their way of life. At least the farm women knew where they stood in that matter. Their homes, simple and austere as they might be, hadn't been destroyed, and very likely wouldn't be. The little farms simply weren't productive enough to be of any threat to the British. The farm women were in the camp by choice, not driven there by dire circumstances.

Watching the two radically different groups, Felicia wondered what would have happened if their positions had been reversed. True, the rich plantation owners had been giving aid to the militia in food and supplies, but would they have gone to such lengths to help the uplanders had it been the farmers' homes that had been destroyed? Felicia fervently hoped her class would show just as much compassion, but deep down, she felt an inkling of doubt.

While the days passed slowly for Felicia, the nights seemed to last an eternity. The other campsites were far enough away that she really couldn't see anything, other than a dark shadow silhouetted against a fire now and then. Felicia had always been a little afraid of the dark. For that reason, she burned a candle by her bedside. Alone and feeling very isolated, the darkness that ordinarily seemed somehow threatening, took on greater dimensions. She could hear every small sound in the forest behind the lean-to, the rustle of leaves, the crack of a twig, the drop of a pine cone, and knew they had been caused by some night creature. Through the cracks between the logs, she could sometimes glimpse the glow of their eyes, or see the tremble of the bushes they brushed past. Reason told her that no wild animal would come close to her camp, as long as she kept the fire burning brightly, but the same fire that should have offered her consolation cast eerie, dancing shadows over the thick black woods, and made her imagination work overtime. For that reason, Felicia slept very little. She was either straining her ears to listen or her eyes to see, or up to put another log on the fire.

On the morning of the fourth day, Felicia awakened feeling more exhausted than usual, for that night had been even more terrifying for her, due to the presence of sheet lightning in the distance. Not only had the pulsating sky added its eeriness to that of the flickering fire-light, but she had been afraid it would rain at any moment and extinguish her light, leaving her totally vulnerable to whatever was out there.

Bringing herself to a sitting position and gazing out at the campsites in the distance, Felicia became suddenly alert. Something about the man walking in her direction from the other side of the camp seemed familiar. It wasn't his clothes that caught her eye. Most of the militiamen wore linsey wraparound shirts, buckskin breeches, and high moccasins. Nor was it the horse that the man was leading that made her stare so hard, for bays were common in this camp. No, it was the man's walk that Felicia recognized. No one but Hawk had that light, graceful walk, a walk so effortless that it made him look as if he were floating on air. Nor did any man carry himself with such utter self-confidence, as if he commanded all he surveyed. A shot of sheer joy ran through Felicia, stunning her with its intensity.

As Felicia watched Hawk threading his way around the scattered campfires, she told herself that she was only happy to see him because it meant she would soon be released, that what she felt had nothing to do with the exciting frontiersman himself. But as he came closer and closer, her eyes hungrily took in the sight of him: his black hair, glistening with bluish highlights in the bright sun, his rugged features, his towering height, and magnificent physique. Another thrill ran through her, and Felicia was reluctantly forced to admit that she found Hawk the most attractive man she had ever met. She wondered how that could be. She knew other men who were more handsome, who were polished, charming, mannerly, who were fascinating conversationalists, yet none drew her as this bold, arrogant mountain man. Was his appeal sheerly physical, she wondered. She couldn't deny he reeked masculinity, making all the other young men she knew look like kittens compared to a lion. He wore his maleness like the vibrant mantel of a king, for all to see and imposingly proud. But why was she so suddenly aware of a man in a physical sense? That sort of crude behavior was for tavern maids and their likes. Was it because she had left civilization behind that she was more vulnerable, for there was no denying that he brought out shameful primitive instincts in her. Just looking at him was making tingles run through her, and bringing a peculiar warmth to her insides.

Despite his effect on her, Felicia had enough presence of mind to come to her feet just as Hawk stepped up to the lean-to. For a moment, the two silently stared at one another.

As Hawk's dark eyes swept over Felicia, he noted that her dress was dirtier and had several new rips in it, tears which he assumed must have occurred when she walked through the thorny underbrush to the stream for water. She had also either lost or deliberately removed the red heels on her dainty slippers, as they were as flat as his moccasins. Having scrutinized her from head to toe, Hawk was glad to see that no harm had come to Felicia in his absence. To his dismay and disgust, he had worried about her the entire time he had been gone, even though he knew she should be safe in the camp from both wild animals and the roving bands of thieves that preyed on refugees. That's why he had left her there. There was safety in numbers. Still, there had been a little nagging fear that one of the others might do something vindictive, or that she might draw the attention of one of the women-starved soldiers from the other side of the camp. After all, Felicia was a beautiful and desirable woman, he thought, his gaze making the return trip and then coming to rest on her face. Even her grimy appearance couldn't hide that fact. And if she could arouse him against his will, she would play havoc on other men with less restraint.

As Hawk stared at her in silent admiration, Felicia felt very ill at ease, convinced he must think she looked terrible, which was how she judged her appearance. As his eyes flicked upward to her hair, she self-consciously reached up and tried to cover the bow she had made, using silk stocking to tie the long, unruly locks back from her face. Seeing just a glimmer of a smile as Hawk recognized what it was, her anger came surging forward, and she said hotly, "Stop your bloody gawking! I didn't have anything else long enough to use, as you very well know!"

Yes, she's none the worse for wear, Hawk thought wryly. She was just as foul-tempered as when he had left her. He shrugged his shoulders, drawing Felicia's attention to their remarkable width, and commented lackadaisically, "I'm surprised you didn't rip off more of your dress."

"If I keep ripping pieces from my dress, I'll soon be naked."

The suggestion was all it took for Hawk to mentally visualize Felicia in the nude, and his eyes darkened with passion. Felicia knew what he was thinking, but for the life of her, she couldn't summon the outrage she ordinarily would feel. In the first place, she knew she had brought it upon herself, by mentioning nakedness in front of a man. No lady did that. Besides, a sudden weakness had invaded her, a feeling that was not at all conducive to anger. She pretended not to have noticed her slip of the tongue or his hungry look, and finished with, "As it is, I'm in rags."

Hawk forced his mind away from the tantalizing fantasy he had been entertaining, and said, "I remembered what you said about not having a change of clothes." He placed his rifle against the lean-to, turned to his horse, and removed a double saddlebag from behind the saddle. Seeing Felicia staring at his new possession quizzically, he explained, "I did some hunting for the innkeeper to buy this and a few other things." Opening one bag, he reached into it and pulled out a bundle of clothing, saying to Felicia as he passed it to her, "Among them, these."

Felicia quickly unrolled the bundle and saw that it contained a worn linsey dress, a petticoat, and a triangular neck scarf. "Where did you get these?" she asked.

"At the inn where I posted my letter. I asked the innkeeper's wife if her daughter might have some old clothes I might purchase, in exchange for some fresh meat. I knew you couldn't wear hers. She must weigh two hundred pounds."

Felicia held the dress up against her. Its length and waist seemed to be all right, but the bodice looked decidedly small. She strongly suspected she wouldn't be able to completely lace it over her breasts, "How old was this daughter?"

"About twelve."

"Why, she's just a child!" Felicia commented, thinking, no wonder the bodice was so small.

"Not out here, she isn't. She'll probably be married in a year or two."

Felicia handed the dress back, saying, "I can't wear a child's clothing. It's too small for my—" She came to an abrupt halt, realizing she had

128

almost made another embarrassing blunder by saying breasts. "It won't fit," she finished lamely.

Hawk knew exactly where the garment wasn't going to fit. He was very well aware of Felicia's luscious breasts. The memory of them had caused him the loss of a few hours' sleep over the past few nights. "Look," he said, trying to be patient but firm, "there aren't many full-grown women out here with your height and small bones. These country women come from sturdy stock. You can either choose to have a dress where the length and waist fit, or a garment that you can wrap around you twice that drags on the ground. Now, if you're worrying about not being able to lace the bodice to cover your breasts, that's why I brought a woman's neckerchief for your fichu."

Felicia had never in her life heard a man say breasts, not even her own father. A flush rose on her face, then deepened when she noted Hawk's eyes slide to that part of her anatomy, linger for a moment, then rise to meet hers.

Seeing she was still hesitant, Hawk asked, "Do you want the clothing or not? If not, I'm sure there's someone here that can use it."

Undoubtedly there was, Felicia thought. Like her, many only had the clothes on their back, garments that had been reduced to rags. "No, I'll keep them," she replied hastily, withdrawing her hand and the clothing. At least it would

129

give her something to wear while her clothes were drying, she thought. At the prospect of wearing clean clothes, Felicia found she couldn't wait to get out of the filthy rags she was wearing. She whirled around, saying over her shoulder as she walked off, "Excuse me. I have some laundry to do."

"Wait!" Hawk called.

Felicia turned and watched as he pulled a bar of hard, yellow soap from his saddlebags. Walking up to her, he handed it to her. "Here, take my soap. It might help."

Felicia was happy to get the harsh lye soap. She knew not many of the women had soap of any kind, for she had observed them doing their laundry. Felicia accepted the soap and hesitated. She hated to thank the frontiersman. He was the one who had put her in this terrible predicament. Yet, she knew he didn't have to buy her clothes or offer his soap to her. She struggled with herself while Hawk stood and patiently waited, then muttered grudgingly, "Thank you, for both the clothes and the loan of the soap."

Hawk had wanted to put Felicia in a position where she would have to thank him, thinking he would enjoy seeing the uppity female brought down a notch or two, but when she did, it was Hawk's turn to feel uncomfortable. He had told himself that he wouldn't go out of his way for his hostage, yet he had. She hadn't really needed the clothing. She'd be going back to her home in just another day or so. So what if her garments were dirty? Putting up with a little dirt for that length of time wouldn't hurt her. He had never in his life bought anything for a woman. *Any* woman! With these disturbing thoughts in mind, Hawk couldn't bring himself to say "you're welcome." He nodded his head curtly, then turned and walked away.

At any other time, Felicia might have been upset at Hawk's abruptness and lack of courtesy, but she was anxious to get away herself. She made a beeline for the stream. Upon reaching it, she was relieved to see that no one else was there, for she had already decided that if she found the stream deserted, she'd risk a bath. It was something she hadn't dared to do before, even though she had seen some of the other women doing it. Not only did bathing in the nude outdoors seem indecent, but pointless, if she was going to have to don her filthy clothing again.

Felicia stripped off her clothing with a speed that would have astonished her maid, and with the bar of soap in hand, waded into the water until she was about knee deep, then vigorously scrubbed herself. The lye soap refused to lather, but Felicia didn't care. She could feel the layers of dirt washing away. Then she waded farther in and washed her hair. She was just returning to the bank, when a group of women appeared.

131

She knew by their hateful glares that they had recognized her, and wondered if she shouldn't just dress and leave. She could always come back later to do her dirty laundry.

But Felicia was tired of hiding and cowering. It was almost as if she had washed her fear away with her dirt. Calmly she dried off and dressed, noting that, just as she had suspected, the bodice would not completely lace over her full breasts. Tying the neck scarf around her shoulders, she picked up her dirty clothes and soap, and walked to the bank, defiantly glaring back at the women as she washed her laundry. For a while, it looked as if that was all she was going to have to do, show the women she wasn't going to be intimidated by their looks. Then, when Felicia had just finished wringing out her laundry, she saw three of the women coming towards her, and knew by the angry gleam in their eyes that they weren't coming for a social visit. They were carrying big sticks.

With her heart thudding in her breast, Felicia came to her feet and faced them. Looking them directly in the eye, she crouched in a fighting stance, and said, "So you want to fight? All right, come ahead! I'll take on all of you, but one at a time, and no sticks. You don't need them. You've got hands and feet and teeth and nails, just like I do. Unless you're too cowardly to fight one by one."

Standing there with her long chestnut hair

hanging in wild abandon around her shoulders, with her golden green eyes spitting sparks, and with her teeth and nails bared, Felicia looked very determined and very dangerous. Almost simultaneously the women came to an abrupt halt, and glanced nervously at one another. Each woman knew that one on one, Felicia would tear them to pieces. Nor could they bring themselves to attack her as a group, since she had pointed out how cowardly that would be.

Felicia knew she had won the confrontation, but the women didn't know how to gracefully save face, and they were as proud as she. If they were to all get out of this awkward predicament, she would have to give them an out. She threw up her hands in disgust, and said, "I haven't got time to stand around here, while you make up your minds." She scooped up her wet laundry and turned her back to them, flinging over her shoulder as she flounced away, "When and if you decide, you know where to find me. I'll be more than happy to oblige."

Felicia was feeling proud of herself, as she walked through the woods carrying her dripping laundry. She had faced up to her enemies and walked away the victor. Fleetingly, she wondered if Hawk, too, would have been proud of her. Then she remembered that she and Hawk were on different sides of the fence, that those women weren't *his* enemies. If he had seen the confrontation and had any feelings about it, it

133

would probably be disgust at how poorly the other women had presented themselves, she admitted.

This realization brought on a pang of deep disappointment, so intense that it bewildered Felicia. What was wrong with her, she wondered. She didn't give a damn what the frontiersman thought of her. He was nothing but a barbarian, a crude, uncivilized half-savage. His opinion of her meant nothing.

But secretly—so deep down that she wasn't aware of it—Felicia wanted Hawk to admire her, admire her in all ways.

Chapter Ten

Hawk was at the campsite when Felicia returned from the woods after washing her clothing. His breath caught in his throat at the sight of her, for she looked even more beautiful in the plain homespun clothing than she had in her rich attire. As she spread her wet laundry over several bushes to dry, Hawk continued to observe her and wondered how that could be. Then he realized that she was a woman whose beauty didn't need rich colors, flounces, ruffles, and ribbons to enhance it. If anything, those things were a distraction from her natural loveliness, drawing one's attention away from her creamy, flawless complexion and striking green eyes, the perfection of her features, the lushness of her lips, the tantalizing arch of her dark eyebrows, the vibrant, breathtaking color of her hair. Even her inherent gracefulness was more apparent in the simple garment, as were her feminine curves, for the limp petticoat did nothing to hold the dress away from her body, nor did the skirt have nearly as much material as her ball gown. The worn linsey molded her shapely thighs with each seductive sway of her hips, and every movement seemed to emphasize her tiny waist and the curving thrust of her breasts beneath the modest neck scarf.

Hawk felt his body responding once more against his will, and knew he had made yet another mistake. All he had accomplished by making Felicia more comfortable, was to make himself more miserable. He should have left her in her rich trappings. Not only was she less desirable, but even as ragged and grimy as her clothing was, they served as a reminder of who she was: a rich Tory, Tarleton's lover, Hawk's means of attaining vengeance. Keeping his mind on his mission was going to be more difficult, and he had only himself to blame.

Seeing Felicia turn, Hawk jerked his eyes away and forced them to focus on the skillet he was holding over the fire. Felicia smelled the contents of the frying pan before she saw it, and cried out in delight, "Bacon? Is that bacon I smell?"

Hawk refused to look up, knowing what he would see — Felicia looking even more beautiful in her simple happiness. As it was, the joy he heard in her voice was playing havoc with his senses. He had never dreamed that pleasing someone could bring so much personal pleasure, and Hawk had purposely obtained the bacon for

Felicia. But at that moment, Hawk didn't want Felicia bringing him pleasure in any shape, form, or manner. He was too vulnerable. Nor would he ever admit to her that he had wanted to please her, by bringing her meat that was better suited to her genteel palate. "Yes, I was tired of fresh game."

It never dawned on Felicia to question Hawk's motives. His explanation seemed perfectly reasonable to her. She sat on a log she had pulled up in front of the lean-to that served as her chair, then glanced about, and saw the other things Hawk had traded for strewn on the ground. There was another blanket, a small burlap sack of cornmeal, a big hunk of johnnycake, a dozen or so luscious-looking peaches, and two crude wooden bowls and spoons. Felicia was as delighted to see the last as she was the bacon, for although the eating utensils were a far cry from the china and silverware she was accustomed to, they were a step up from eating with just her bare fingers. "Did you get these things from the innkeeper, too?" she asked.

"Everything but the peaches," Hawk answered, picking up one of the bowls and sliding a few slices of bacon onto it with his knife. "I helped myself to those from some farmer's orchard I passed."

Hawk handed Felicia the bowl, and any further questions she might have asked were forgotten, as she quickly picked up a piece of bacon and bit into it, savoring the familiar taste. She ate every piece of bacon in her bowl, before she picked up the johnnycake and sank her teeth into it. Despite the fact that it was cold and dry as a bone, she thought it tasted wonderful after her monotonous diet of turkey and boiled corn.

Hawk served himself, sitting on the ground across from Felicia. As they ate in silence, he was feeling quite comfortable with just Felicia's companionship, when she rose, then bent to pick up a peach. As she did so, her hair, which she had left hanging free so it could dry, spilled forward, looking to Hawk like a fiery waterfall in the bright sunlight. He sat perfectly still and stared. Then a small puff of wind caught a long tress and blew it across his cheek. It was just a light, fleeting brush, but Hawk felt it like a bolt of lightning. He was still stunned, when Felicia sat down and took a big bite of the peach. As juice ran everywhere, Felicia laughed, then licked a trickle of juice at the corner of her mouth before it could run down her chin. The sight of her pink tongue flicking out, combined with her delighted laugh, seemed incredibly erotic to Hawk.

At the first sign of the heaviness that flooded his pelvis, Hawk tossed his bowl aside and slammed to his feet. His unexpected action caught Felicia so by surprise that she jumped. Then seeing him swoop up his gun and walk rapidly away, she called, "What's wrong?"

"Nothing!" Hawk called back over his shoulder, through clenched teeth.

"Then where are you going?"

"Hunting!" came the curt reply.

Stunned at his abrupt departure, Felicia could only stare at his broad back and wonder if she had done something to anger him. She had the distinct impression that he couldn't get away from her fast enough. Yet she hadn't the slightest idea what she had done that could have offended him.

Two days later, Felicia still didn't know if she had offended Hawk in some way or another, but she did know he was deliberately putting distance between them. His absence was conspicuous, and yet she knew he wasn't *really* gone. She saw him several times, delivering game to others in the camp, but the only time he came to their campsite was late at night, when he apparently thought she was asleep. Even then it seemed he was avoiding her, for he never came into the lean-to where she pretended to be asleep, but remained by the fire. By morning, he was gone. Felicia was glad for his presence at night, for then she felt safe from the darkness and could sleep, but his ignoring her hurt. Even if she hadn't been secretly attracted to him, she would have been a little piqued. Felicia was accustomed to being pursued by eager admirers. Her female vanity was taking a tremendous battering.

Felicia was on her knees preparing her pallet in the lean-to on the third night, when she heard a loud thump at the back of the structure. Not knowing what had caused it, her heart raced, then she almost jumped out of her skin as Hawk stepped before the lean-to and said, "I brought more firewood. It's just a couple of logs, but it will be enough to last through the night."

He towered over her, the fire as a backdrop outlining the magnificent breadth of his shoulders, his narrow waist, lean hips, and long legs. His presence seemed to fill the entire forest, and Felicia felt a bolt of sheer happiness run through her. Then, as he stood stock-still, seemingly waiting for some response from her, Felicia's resentment at his absences overrode her pleasure at seeing him. She'd be damned if she'd thank him, she thought, if that's what he was expecting. No, hell would freeze over first, she vowed furiously. She nodded her head curtly and purposely turned her back to him.

Had Felicia been able to see the expression on Hawk's face, she would have known why he had stood so still, but his face was in shadow. She had completely forgotten that she had removed the neck scarf in preparation for sleep, and that her breasts in the too-tight bodice and gaping laces were all but totally bared to him. He had stood rooted to the spot by the sight of those luscious twin mounds, with their rosy nipples peeking at him from the edges of the material. Felicia turning her back on him broke the spell, and none too soon. A moment longer, and his iron control might have snapped. He whirled around and beat a hasty retreat.

Felicia turned and was stunned to find Hawk had disappeared as suddenly as he had appeared. Feeling very disappointed, she reclined and pulled the blanket around her, more for the security it gave her than the heat. But just like all the other nights, she couldn't sleep. Every little sound was magnified, even the crackling of the logs in the fire.

It was several hours later when Hawk finally made his customary nightly appearance, a time lapse that seemed an eternity to Felicia, for the loss of sleep over the past nights had taken its toll on her. Since Hawk's return, she hadn't been able to fall asleep until he came to the campsite. She breathed a sigh of relief and watched him through lowered eyelids as he reclined on the opposite side of the fire, then, feeling her world had finally been put to rights, she fell into an exhausted slumber.

Hawk's avoiding Felicia hadn't been her imagination. Keeping a safe physical distance between them was his way of handling his unwanted desire for her; he was simply putting temptation out of his reach. During the day, it worked. He had complete control over the situation, and Hawk was a man accustomed to being in total

141

control of his life. But every night, he had come to her—not driven by lust—but by a need to give her his protection. At first, Hawk had refused to acknowledge it, telling himself that he was simply going to *his* camp to sleep by *his* fire, a comfort which was *his* right. But the argument didn't ring true. Hawk had slept without the benefit of a fire too many nights to need that comfort. Hawk was finally honest with himself and admitted to this strange compulsion, something that filled him with just as much self-disgust as his lust, and totally baffled him. Wanting her, he could understand. She was beautiful and incredibly seductive, a woman to tempt a saint, and Hawk wasn't a saint. He was a healthy male with a very normal sexual appetite. But he couldn't understand his wanting to care for her and protect her. She was beginning to unearth feelings in him that Hawk found very threatening, but still, even after the earlier incident that evening, Hawk had come, drawn like the moth to the fire.

Later that night, Hawk was awakened by the sound of thunder. Lightning flashed over and over, and the smell of rain hung heavy in the air. Hawk knew the storm was approaching rapidly, and wondered if he should seek the shelter of the lean-to. He didn't particularly relish getting soaking wet. Even under normal conditions, buckskins had a tendency to be clammy, but when wet they were miserable and took days to dry out. That's why frontiersmen didn't wear buckskin shirts, unless as a jacket in the winter. The pants, however, were a necessity because of the thorny underbrush of the forest.

Another crack of lightning rent the dark sky, silhouetting a towering thunderhead over the treetops. Hawk glanced at the lean-to and saw that Felicia was still sound asleep, despite the loud noises of the storm. He wondered if he should risk it, or continue to keep his distance and live with the consequences. Suddenly Hawk was filled with self-disgust. He was a man who prided himself on fearing nothing, yet he was running from a woman—a sleeping woman, no less! Why, in her condition she was as lifeless as a sack of cornmeal, and probably just as desirable.

It was the splatter of several large raindrops on the fire, making a sizzling sound, that finally galvanized Hawk. He'd be damned if he'd sleep in the rain with shelter right next to him, the lean-to *he* had labored to build. He jumped to his feet and made a run for it. He had barely settled down when the rain came in earnest, a deluge that drowned the fire within seconds and threw the campsite into total darkness, except for an occasional flash of lightning.

Hawk lay on his side with his back to Felicia several feet from her and pillowed his head on the crook of his folded arm, but he couldn't sleep, and not because of the sounds coming

143

from the storm. Her scent, sweet and provocative, drifted across the distance and filled his nostrils, having an almost aphrodisiac effect on his senses. The memory of her exposed breasts flashed through his mind and remained there, as if it had been seared into his brain. Much to his utter disgust, he felt himself responding to the stimuli.

Felicia had been so exhausted that she hadn't even heard the noises of the storm, but when the fire was extinguished and the cold damp air hit her, she shivered and subconsciously groped in the darkness for the blanket she had earlier tossed aside. Not finding it, for Hawk had unknowingly laid on it, she instinctively sought the warmth of his body. At the feel of her pressing her soft body against his back, Hawk sucked in his breath sharply and jerked away.

It was his sudden movement that awakened Felicia. She shot to a sitting position and looked around her wildly, seeing nothing but total blackness. Her heart raced, for she sensed the presence of someone—or something—in the shelter with her. Her terror was so great that Hawk could almost smell it. He sat up and said, "There's nothing to be afraid of. It's just me, Hawk."

Felicia focused her eyes in the direction the voice came from, but all she could see was a dim outline that could have been anyone. But she knew it was him. Not only did she recognize his voice; she could smell his distinctive scent. "What are you doing in here?"

"What do you *think* I'm doing?" Hawk answered irritably, hating himself for feeling defensive. Dammit, this wasn't her personal boudoir. "I'm trying to keep dry."

It was then that Felicia noticed the rain and the thunder. She looked out of the shelter and said in a stunned voice, "Why, it's raining!"

"No, it's pouring," Hawk replied dryly.

"When did it start?"

"About thirty minutes ago." Feeling a drop of rain, Hawk looked up at the top of the lean-to, then said, "Move over a little. The roof above me is leaking."

Hawk moved before Felicia could and found himself chest to chest with her. The feel of her half-bared breasts pressing against him seemed to be scorching him right through his shirt, and once again, the memory of what they looked like flashed through his mind. Hawk clenched his teeth, trying to summon the will to move away, but her scent was even more powerful, surrounding him like soft, seductive arms and drowning him in her tantalizing sweetness. A groan that was part despair and part desire escaped his throat, before his arms went around her and his mouth came down on hers in a fierce kiss.

When Hawk's hard, male body had come into contact with hers, Felicia had been just as aware as he. Thrills coursed through her in anticipation

145

of what he might do next. She held her breath, not daring to move a muscle, a terrible yearning for him to kiss her filling her. Then, as he lowered his head, her heart leapt with gladness.

There was no tenderness in Hawk's kiss. He meant to punish her for arousing him against his will. His kiss was hard, demanding, almost brutal, as he pushed her to the ground and lay half over her. His lips grinding on hers frightened Felicia, but just for a moment. Then a sudden wildness seized her, and impetuously she slipped her arms around his neck and parted her mouth.

The last thing Hawk had expected from Felicia was surrender, but he quickly recovered from his surprise. He also forgot his anger at her as a wave of exhilaration swept through him. He softened his kiss, his lips brushing hers teasingly back and forth, making her moan with desire, before his strong tongue plunged deeply into her mouth, plundering her sweetness.

Felicia's senses were reeling dizzily at Hawk's hungry, demanding kiss. She was so enthralled with what he was making her feel, that she was just barely aware of his fingers working at the laces on her bodice. Even when he totally bared her breasts and his warm hand took possession of one mound, she felt powerless to move. As Hawk broke the torrid kiss and blazed a trail of searing kisses down her throat, then across her chest, she lay perfectly still, feeling as if she were submerged in thick molasses. Then, as his lips touched her aching nipple and his warm, wet tongue brushed across it, she jerked, at both his shocking intimacy and the bolt of mind-boggling, intense pleasure it brought her. She thought for a moment to stop him, but an incredible weakness had invaded her and she was tingling all over. She gave herself up to the wonderful sensations his lips and tongue and artful fingers were invoking. Her breath came in rapid gasps; her heart pounded so hard she feared it would burst. She threaded her fingers through the thick hair at the nape of his neck, and arched her back to give him better access, holding him to her.

The sound of Felicia's moans and the taste of her lips and breasts had excited Hawk to a feverish point. His aroused manhood strained painfully at the tight confines of his buckskins. In a effort to give himself some relief, he shifted his lower body. But the movement brought his hot, throbbing flesh up against the junction of Felicia's rounded thighs, and realizing how close he was to that part of her that he longed to bury himself in, he lengthened yet another inch.

Through her whirling senses, Felicia felt his hard length pressing against her, so hot he seemed to be burning her right through their clothing. Suddenly, she became aware of the animal-like sounds she had been making, of her bared breasts, of her sprawled legs. My God, what was she doing, letting Hawk take such intimacies with her? she thought in horror.

Frantically, she pushed at his shoulders, saying, "Stop! Stop it!"

His senses dulled, Hawk raised his head and looked at her with glazed eyes. His surprise at her sudden turnabout enabled Felicia to twist away from him. As she sat up and began to lace up her bodice, her hands trembling so badly she could barely manage it, it finally dawned on Hawk that she had called an end to it. He came to his knees, caught one arm in a viselike grip, and jerked her towards him, asking in an angry voice, "What silly games do you think you're playing with me? First you're willing, then you aren't?"

Felicia was ashamed at the way she had behaved, but she couldn't admit to it. "I wasn't willing. You forced yourself on me."

"Like hell I did! Do you think I'm a fool? You were embracing me, moaning, begging for more!"

Felicia couldn't deny his accusations. A hot flush rose on her face. Trying to think of some explanation, *any* explanation, she said, "I was still half-asleep. You caught me by surprise. I didn't know what I was doing."

Hawk's eyes narrowed as a sudden thought came to him. He threw her away from him, and said in a hard voice, "Or *who* you were doing it with? Is that it? You thought I was Tarleton, your lover, sneaking into your bed in the dead of night?"

"No, I didn't think that!" Felicia responded indignantly. "I told you, we're not lovers!"

Another suspicious thought came to Hawk. He cocked his head and asked, "Or maybe you thought to seduce me, distract me from our meeting later today, and that way save your precious lover's life? You must think yourself damn good, if you thought to occupy me for that long."

Felicia hadn't realized this was the day they had been waiting for, the day she would finally be set free. She was so stunned that she hesitated in her response. Then, as she opened her mouth, Hawk cut off her words, asking, "What changed your mind? Why did you decide you couldn't go through with it?" Then, remembering how he had moved right before her sudden capitulation, he caught her wrist and shoved her hand between his legs, asking, "Is *this* what frightened you? Did you discover I was too much man for you?"

Felicia could feel his erection beneath her hand—rock-hard and pulsating with a life of its own—and he did feel enormous. She shivered, an involuntary response that was both fear and excitement, before outrage came to her defense, and she jerked her hand away. "No, I decided that I couldn't sink that low."

Hawk couldn't miss the contempt in her voice,

and asked, "To make love to any other man, or just me?"

"Just you," Felicia answered, wanting to insult him just as badly as he had insulted her.

Hawk thought he knew why. Because he was a commoner and much below her. He wondered what she would think if she knew his real bloodlines, and knew that Felicia would scorn him even more. A cold fury filled him. He rose to his feet and stepped from the lean-to. Standing there in the pouring rain, he said, "It's just as well you changed your mind, because your sacrifice to save your lover wouldn't have changed mine. There isn't a woman in this world that could. Tomorrow, I'm going to kill Tarleton. Then you'll be free." His eyes swept over her with such utter contempt that Felicia felt like cringing. "I'll have no further use for you."

With that, Hawk turned and strode angrily away through the pouring rain, leaving Felicia to deal with a mixture of conflicting emotions, among which was a strange disappointment that had nothing to do with knowing she had denied herself the pleasure his lovemaking would have brought her. Deep down, she dreaded his walking out of her life forever.

Chapter Eleven

By the next morning, Felicia's fierce pride had come to the surface. The only emotion that remained from the boiling cauldron of confusing feelings she had experienced the night before, was outrage at Hawk's insults. She convinced herself that she couldn't wait to get away from him, and when he came from the forest leading the bay, she met him with a coldness that could have frozen hell. Then, determined to take nothing from him when she left, she shoved the clothing he had given her into his hands with utter disdain.

Hawk was cool and aloof himself, as he saddled the horse and then broke camp. He didn't even offer to help Felicia mount, something which took some effort on her part since she was once again wearing her ragged ball gown with its voluminous skirt. When she was finally in place on the saddle, Hawk swung up behind her with a lightness that irritated her all the more for its ease. As they rode from the camp, she railed silently against him, deliberately feeding her anger, for it was the only way she keep could her mind from his disturbing nearness.

It was midday when Hawk brought the horse to a stop in the middle of the path. Felicia looked at the dense forest all around her in surprise, for she had thought the meeting place would be in a clearing. Hawk's arm slipped around her small waist, and he lifted her down from the saddle. Thinking he was going to leave her there in the middle of the forest, she finally broke her silence and asked in an alarmed voice, "You're not going to leave me here, are you? I'll never find my way out of these woods."

Hawk heard the fear in her voice and, despite his anger at her, felt a twinge of compassion. "No, I'm not leaving you here," he answered, hoping his voice sounded appropriately disgusted. "I just needed you out of the saddle, so I could stand on it and make a jump for that low-hanging limb. This tree is going to be my lookout post, just in case your lover doesn't heed my warning about coming alone and tries to set a trap for me. You can see for miles and miles around from there."

Felicia watched as Hawk came to his feet on the saddle, then crouched, and made a flying jump for the branch. She gasped, thinking he had missed, but before she could hardly blink her eyes, he had one knee wrapped around it and was pulling himself up. Higher and higher he climbed, as agile and graceful in that as everything else he did. And when a limb wasn't within reach, he took daring leaps through the air, leaps that left Felicia weak-kneed with fright. Finally Felicia could no longer see him through the thick canopy of leaves. Then, from high above her, she heard Hawk call, "Might as well sit down. This will take a while. He's not due for three hours."

But it turned out they waited for much longer than three hours. It was almost dark when Hawk finally gave up the wait, and descended from his lofty perch. When he dropped to the ground in front of her, Felicia saw his face was as dark as a thunderhead.

"I didn't expect Tarleton to come because his honor demanded it of him. That bastard doesn't have any," Hawk said in angry scorn. "But I'd heard he was a man of daring, a man who lived for the fight. For that reason, I thought he would accept my challenge, or at least try to capture me. It appears he's an even bigger coward than I thought."

Despite the fact that she had said over and over that Tarleton wouldn't come, Felicia was a little surprised. She knew he wouldn't come for her—he held no responsibility for her—but she also knew how badly he wanted Hawk. And if Tarleton didn't come himself, she had thought the officer would tell her father about the letter, and *he* would have come to rescue her. "Are you sure there was no one there?" she asked in disappointment. "Maybe he was already waiting at the meeting point when we rode up. Maybe he arrived early."

"No one is there," Hawk answered in an emphatic voice. "I could see the clearing and the entire countryside surrounding it from up there."

No one came for her at all? Felicia thought, both bewildered and hurt.

Hawk saw the expression on her face and, having no idea she was thinking of her father, assumed she was hurt by Tarleton's lack of concern for her welfare, only confirming his suspicions that they had been lovers. But instead of feeling any pity for her, Hawk was elated that she had found out just how cold-blooded Tarleton was. He wanted any admiration or tender feelings she might have felt for the officer permanently destroyed, a secret desire that had nothing to do with avenging his father. There was a new aspect to Hawk's desire for revenge. In reality, Tarleton had become a new adversary to Hawk, a rival for possession of the woman Hawk wanted.

Felicia felt so miserable that it took a while for her to notice Hawk watching her closely. "I thought my father would come," she muttered, still in a state of shock. "Surely Tarleton must have told him about your letter, knowing how worried my parents must be over my disappearance."

Hawk was so convinced Felicia had been hurt by Tarleton's seeming desertion, that it never occurred to him that she had been thinking of her

154

father all along. It did seem strange, he admitted to himself, then began to seriously ponder the puzzle. The only reason he could figure for Tarleton not passing on the information, was he didn't want Felicia's father to know he was such a coward. But that would have been terribly irresponsible for an officer, even Tarleton.

"You'll take me back home now, won't you?"

Suddenly Hawk thought he knew why Tarleton hadn't come, or why he hadn't bothered to tell Felicia's father that he knew what had happened to her. The colonel hadn't, because he fully expected Felicia to be returned shortly to her family. Tarleton hadn't taken his note seriously, and that infuriated Hawk even more than thinking the Englishman had ignored his challenge simply out of cowardice. The bastard thought he was bluffing, that when he didn't show, Hawk would release his hostage! Furious at Tarleton, he answered, "No, I won't take you back!"

Felicia was stunned at Hawk's adamant answer, and the determined glitter she saw in his dark eyes. Thinking he might be fearing a trap, she said, "Then just take me someplace near a village and release me."

"I told you I wouldn't release you until I had avenged my father."

"No, that's *not* what you said! You said you'd hold me hostage until Tarleton came, that I was the bait. Well, it didn't work. He's not coming!"

Hawk wouldn't give Tarleton the satisfaction of

releasing Felicia. He could imagine how the cocky bastard would laugh at him, thinking he'd won the showdown and made Hawk look the fool. No! Hell would freeze over first! Hawk vowed. He'd told the bastard that if he didn't come, he'd never see Felicia alive again—and he wouldn't. Let the Englishman live with that burden on his conscence. Let him think his arrogance had brought about her death.

"Did you hear me?" Felicia asked, when Hawk made no response. "He's not coming! There is no point in holding me any longer."

"No, you are still my hostage. It is the way of my people. When someone is killed in battle, it is the right of his relatives to take a captive from the enemy to replace him. I am exercising my rights. You are my captive."

Felicia was shocked. She'd never dreamed that the Scots were that vindictive. "Then you're going to hold me a prisoner forever?"

Hawk had been following Cherokee tradition when he had decided to keep Felicia as his blood-for-blood captive. Usually that type of captivity was for life. Sometimes the captive might be adopted into the tribe, but they were never exchanged as prisoners of war or returned to their tribe. But forever was a long time, particularly to saddle himself with a woman with Felicia's fiery temperament, and Hawk had not yet admitted to himself that he had a motive other than vengeance for wanting to keep her. All of his life,

Hawk had been torn between his Indian and white blood, for more often than not, their codes of honor were at odds with one another. Hawk's way of dealing with that dilemma was to take whichever rule appealed to him at the time, thereby making his own unique code, and that is what he did at that moment. "No, not forever. Just until I have avenged my father."

"How can you avenge your father, if Tarleton won't come to you? If he won't accept your challenge?"

"Then I will go to him," Hawk answered with maddening calmness.

"But you said you couldn't do that," Felicia argued in exasperation, "that his men were always about."

"I will have to arrange for us to meet in battle, when it is every man for himself. Then he will *have* to fight me. When he is dead, I will release you."

"What if he kills you?"

"He will not kill me," Hawk assured her, and Felicia believed him, for there was a fiercely determined gleam in his dark eyes.

Hawk walked a few feet away, caught the reins of the bay that had been grazing on a small patch of grass, and led it to Felicia. Knowing that he expected her to mount, Felicia looked about wildly, wondering if she should make a run for it, then realized, as she always had before, that it would be foolish. Nor did she bother to plead with the frontiersman. She knew Hawk well enough to know that when he got that stony look on his face, nothing on earth would change his mind. She might as well try to move a mountain, or try to stop the sun from setting. Sighing with resignation, she climbed back up on the horse.

As Hawk led the horse through the darkening forest, Felicia asked, "Are you taking me back to that camp?" She dreaded the prospect of more boredom and terrifying nights.

Once again, Tarleton had thrown all of Hawk's plans astray. If things had gone as he had expected, he and Felicia would be on their way to her father's plantation, not traveling west. He considered her question for a moment, then remembered how he had worried about her while he was gone, and answered, "No, I'll take you to a safer place, where I can leave you with friends while I am gone."

Felicia fervently hoped those friends would be friendlier to her than the last people he had left her with. "And where is that?" she asked apprehensively.

"Over the mountains."

As far as Felicia was concerned, Hawk might as well have said he was taking her to the ends of the earth, or hell. Why, she might never see civilization again, she thought in horror, might be forced to spend her entire life in the company of a bunch of half-savage Scots on the dangerous frontier. But Felicia was not completely terrified at what lay ahead of her. Deep down, the secret part of her that hadn't wanted Hawk to leave her life, was absolutely ecstatic.

Chapter Twelve

Over the next few days, Hawk and Felicia traveled through more forests, moving in a northwesterly direction, and following streams and rivers that crisscrossed the area like a giant spiderweb. Occasionally they passed farms where corn and perhaps a small plot of flax was grown between massive girdled trees, the bare weathered limbs looking like huge bones against the blue sky. Several times they were seen, but other than a glance, no one paid any attention to them, not even at those times when Felicia was wearing her ball gown. She knew trying to enlist their aid in escaping Hawk would have been just as hopeless as in the army camp. They were closemouthed mountain people, whose credo was live and let live. They couldn't have cared less what Hawk did, as long as it didn't affect them.

At first the farms they passed had a look of permanence about them. Beside the log cabin there was a barn, an orchard, a smokehouse and chicken coop, a pigpen, fences to keep the wild animals out. But the higher they climbed in the foothills, the rockier the ground became, and the poorer the farms, until in some instances, the cabins didn't even have four walls, and there was only a small plot of corn to be seen, more than likely overrun with weeds and being rooted by pigs that ran wild. Felicia had been horrified that anyone could live in such miserable conditions, and feared that Hawk might be taking her to just that kind of existence, before he explained that the people who lived in those "half-faced camps" were wanderers who made their living hunting, and never settled permanently anywhere.

Then, as they left the staircase of foothills and climbed into the mountains, they seemed to have left all civilization behind. For days not another human being was seen, and Felicia didn't know if Hawk had deliberately taken a trail that went through a deserted area, or if this eastern section of the Appalachians was so wild and rugged that no one had tried to settle it. Felicia had always pictured mountains as being jagged, with bare peaks that jutted into the sky. Nothing could have been further from the truth. The Appalachians were heavily wooded. In some places spires of sunlight knifed down through the trees, while in other places the forest was so thick, it was dark as night and as silent as a tomb, for no songbirds came to these deep woodlands, where there wasn't even enough light for underbrush to grow. It was in these areas that Felicia saw giant trees that she would have never dreamed existed: chestnuts, sugar maples, yellow buckeyes, and poplars eighteen feet in diameter and a hundred to a hundred and fifty feet high.

Virgin forests so ancient they could be called primeval weren't the only thing Felicia saw for the first time. Scattered among the dense woodlands, they came upon open areas covered with a wild tangle of rhododendrons, azaleas, mountain laurel, blueberry and huckleberry bushes. Hawk explained that the areas were believed to have been caused by a fire started by lightning, or perhaps a landslide, and were called balds by the mountain people, except for those areas where the rhododendrons with their ropy trunks and glistening leathery leaves were so thick that they couldn't be penetrated and were appropriately called hells.

Appearing just as suddenly and unexpectedly as the balds were bogs fed by underground springs (where the bay's legs sunk a good foot in the ice-cold water) and the steep mountain valleys where you could look down the perpendicular, rocky walls and see far below a river twisting and turning in its narrow canyon bed, frothy white with rapids. There were strange lights at night, a brownish glow that appeared for a few seconds, then burned out, then reappeared faraway, then faded away, then glowed eerily in yet another place, lights which Hawk assured her were harmless and thought mystical by the Indians.

When they climbed higher, they reached the evergreen forests of mostly hemlock and spruce. Eventually even the hemlock disappeared. Looking about her, Felicia remarked, "The ground seems awfully bare here. Except for those ferns and mushrooms, nothing seems to be growing, yet there seems to be enough light."

Hawk was impressed with Felicia's observation. Because of his Indian heritage, he had a close rapport with nature, and nothing in his surroundings escaped his attention. But he hadn't expected a white woman—particularly a white woman of Felicia's exalted class—to notice.

"It's not the lack of sunlight that prevents things from growing," he answered, "but something in the spruce trees' leaves when they rot on the ground."

Again Felicia looked about, then said, "Well, at least we'll have something different to eat tonight, with all these mushrooms."

"No, don't get any ideas like that in your head. These mushrooms are poisonous."

"How do you know that?"

"Because of their color. Some are a pure white and some are orange, both are lethal if eaten."

"You can tell if things are poisonous by their color?"

"Yes. Be particularly wary anything with yellow and red bands or stripes, such as insects or snakes."

"Where did you learn all these things?"

Hawk shrugged his shoulders and answered, "From my people."

Felicia frowned. The way he said "my people" always seemed evasive in some manner. "The mountain men?"

Hawk didn't want to lie. It was something strictly forbidden by both the frontiersmen and his tribe. In that respect, the two codes were in agreement. Then he remembered that the Cherokee were mountain people and smiled. "Yes."

They had only traveled a short distance further when Hawk said, "We'll make camp at the top of this mountain. It's the highest summit in these parts. From here on, it's all down hill."

While Hawk was unsaddling the horse, then building a fire, Felicia walked to the very tip of the mountain and looked out at the breathtaking view. The rounded hills rolled out all around her for miles and miles like green waves, and were covered with a thin blue haze. Far down among the mountains, she could see long emerald valleys with lazy meandering rivers, then off to the left spied a spectacular waterfall, seemingly leaping from the side of one mountain, the river down below it shrouded in misty rainbows. The sight of several lazy clouds drifting across the horizon caught her attention, and she watched the settling sun tint their bottoms a rosy color, until a lavender twilight enveloped all. Feeling awed by what she had seen, Felicia turned and walked back to the camp, the spicy fragrance of spruce heavy in the evening air.

When Felicia woke up the next morning, the woodland was covered with its usual morning mist, leaving the long needles of the trees dripping water. Remembering the beautiful sunset the night before, the first thing she did was walk to the same lofty spot and look out. The low-hanging clouds around the tops of the mountains looked like a misty sea, soft and pearly, then turned to a faint pink as the sun rose higher, then flame-colored, before the sun came over the summits in a brilliant golden ball, and the sky turned blue, and the clouds became white again.

She was still feeling a little spellbound when she became aware of Hawk standing beside her. She had no idea how long he had been there, and wondered if he had sneaked up on her with that silent walk of his—as he so often did, frightening her half out of her wits—or perhaps she had just been too engrossed with the view to notice. She started to make some comment on how beautiful the sunrise had been, but feared the hardened frontiersman would laugh at her. Undoubtedly, he never paid any attention to scenery simply for the sake of its beauty, but only thought of how he could utilize the land and everything that came from it. Instead she said, "I was just wondering how these mountains came to be."

"The Cherokees have a myth about how these

mountains were formed. Would you care to hear it?"

Story-telling didn't seem to fit the frontiersman's image either. Why, he had hardly said a word since they had left the low country, and he had sat behind her on the horse as stiff as stone; when he rode at all. The majority of the time he led the horse, leaving her to stare in silence at his broad back. And now he was offering to tell her a tale? Even if her curiosity hadn't been aroused, she would have agreed, if for no other reason than to relieve her boredom. "Yes, I would."

Hawk looked out over the mountains and said, "In the beginning, all things dwelt in the sky. There was no earth, only water, an endless ocean. Eventually, the sky became overcrowded with people and animals, so the leaders sent a water beetle down to the ocean to seek land. The beetle dived down to the bottom and brought up some mud, which grew and grew until it became earth. But the earth was too soft for the people and animals to inhabit, so the leaders sent a great buzzard, the grandfather of all buzzards, down from heaven to dry the soft mud with the beating of his huge wings. As he flew over Cherokee country—this land . . ." Hawk made a sweeping motion with his hand ". . . the buzzard became very tired, sinking so close to the surface that his wings struck the soft earth and formed the ridges, mountains, and valleys you see."

As he spoke, Hawk's voice had taken on a

husky timbre and his facial expression had soft-ened. Why, he loves these mountains, Felicia thought in amazement. When he had finished, she asked, "Did your Indian friend tell you that story?"

Hawk wondered if he could count his mother as a friend, then answered, "Yes."

"He's Cherokee?"

Hawk didn't bother to correct Felicia on the sex of his friend. He nodded.

"You said this was Cherokee country," Felicia remarked, looking nervously around her. "I thought the Indians had been pushed further west."

Pushed was the appropriate word for it, Hawk thought, feeling a twinge of bitterness. Pushed further and further west by the greedy, land-hungry whites, always forced to give up more land with each peace treaty. "They have been, but at one time the entire southern Appalachians was Cherokee territory. Many of the older mountain men still call these ranges the Cherokee Mountains."

"I'd always heard that the Cherokee were the most savage Indians on earth, the most cruel and warlike. I wouldn't have thought they would be so fanciful."

Hawk automatically stiffened at Felicia calling his people savage and cruel, but he knew if he was too defensive, he'd give himself away. He chose his words very carefully. "It's true the

Cherokee are fiercely protective of their homes and honor. They pride themselves in fearing no man, scorn cowardice in any form, and waging war has always been a part of their lives. But they are just as human as anyone else. They laugh, they dream, they feel pain, they cry, and yes, they weave tales. Story-telling is their favorite pastime, but it serves another purpose than just entertainment. It's the only way they can pass down the history of their tribe, since they have no books or written word."

And no Bible, Felicia thought as Hawk turned and walked away. But how similar their account was to the great flood, even with a bird playing an important role, except in their story it was a buzzard who dried the earth, and not a dove who brought back a green twig. Was it possible that their Great Spirit and her God were one and the same? It was a profound thought, and without Felicia even realizing it, it was the first step in Felicia's accepting Hawk's mixed blood.

That afternoon, there was a heaviness in the air that strongly suggested rain, and not just the usual sultriness felt in the mountains at that time of the year. Hawk kept an eye out for a place that would offer some protection, then spied a huge tulip tree with a cavelike opening in the bottom of its trunk caused by a fungus. He brought the bay to a halt, and announced, "We'll make camp here."

"So early?" Felicia asked in surprise.

"Yes. It feels like rain, and we'll need time to prepare. You can sleep in that hollow tree."

As soon as she dismounted, Felicia walked to the tree and carefully peeked in, half expecting to see some wild animal that used it as a lair to come tearing out. Seeing it was empty, she stepped inside and looked about. The circular chamber was so tall, she could stand with room to spare, and so large, she couldn't even touch the sides when she spread both arms. The floor was soft and spongy, and the smell, while pungent, wasn't disagreeable. It reminded her of their carpenter's shop back home.

As she stepped back out into the open, Hawk asked, "Well, did it pass your inspection?"

"Yes, it looks like it will be quite comfortable and quite dry." She paused, thinking of him sleeping in the open, for Hawk had not built another lean-to since they had left the army camp. They had slept on opposite sides of the fire. Felicia thought her taking all of the shelter for herself a little selfish, then heard herself saying, "It's really big enough for two."

Not a word was spoken. Their eyes met across the pile of wood Hawk had collected, and each knew the other was remembering the last night they had shared a shelter. Hawk watched the pulse beat in Felicia's throat quicken, and she watched his eyes turn dark with passion. They both waited with breathless anticipation for the other to make the first move. It was Felicia who finally broke eye contact. Horrified at how brazen her observation must have sounded, she glanced away and said, "That is, if you want to share it. It doesn't seem fair, your getting wet, while I stay perfectly dry."

Hawk didn't know if Felicia was backing down, or if she hadn't meant the suggestion as an invitation to something more than a means of keeping dry, as he had thought. Regardless, he was glad she had clarified it, for he was determined he wouldn't force her to submit to him, although his Cherokee blood persistently urged him to do just that, as was his right as captor. He wanted her. There was no doubt about that. Even deliberately putting distance between them wasn't keeping his desire at bay. He had lived with a perpetual ache in his groin ever since that night of the storm. Not even believing she had been Tarleton's lover could cool his ardor. He wanted her more than he had ever wanted any woman, but he wanted her willing. Knowing that she thought herself so far above him, he would accept no less. She would have to meet him on equal ground. "We'll see how hard it rains," Hawk answered, knowing full well that he'd float away before he'd subject himself to the torment of lying beside her and not being able to touch her.

To the secret part of Felicia that hadn't wanted to leave Hawk, his answer sounded like a half-

170

promise. That night, despite the comfort of a soft springy floor, Felicia couldn't sleep. She kept listening for the sound of rain, plagued by memories of Hawk's fiery kisses, and the marvelous sensations his mouth at her breast had brought her, every nerve in her body strung tight with painful yearning. But rain didn't come, and by morning, Felicia's secret desire was no longer secret. She was forced to come face-to-face with an incredible, shocking truth. She wanted Hawk to make love to her, not just relive the pleasures he had brought her before, but discover the entire realm of lovemaking at his hands; for she sensed that the rugged frontiersman was just as exceptional as a lover as he was in everything else; and she wanted him.

Chapter Thirteen

Late the next afternoon, they came upon a cabin perched precariously on the side of a steep mountain. After days of seeing no sign of civilization, Felicia was stunned by its sudden, unexpected appearance. Then, as Hawk purposely guided the horse towards it, she felt a sinking feeling, thinking that the isolated cabin might be where he planned to leave her. Why, there wasn't an outbuilding in sight, or even a cornfield. For the first time since he had captured her, Felicia felt real despair. Tears came to her eyes.

Hawk brought the bay to a standstill in front of the cabin, and swung from the saddle, saying, "I've a friend who lives here. I'm sure he'll give us enough cornmeal to last us until we reach a trading post. I used the last of ours this morning. Maybe we can get another rack of bacon from him, too."

Realizing that this wasn't their final destination, a tremendous wave of relief rushed over Felicia. She dismounted, then almost fell into a sunken wooden tub beside the cabin. Becoming aware of a stench coming from the pit, she wrinkled her nose and asked, "What in heaven's name is *that?*"

"It's a tanning pit. Josh makes his living hunting deer and trapping."

Hawk knocked on the door, then, when there was no answer, opened it and walked in. Felicia followed, asking "Should we just walk in like this, when he's not home?"

"Josh won't care. I told you, he's a friend. Besides, even if he wasn't, it would be all right. It's considered frontier courtesy to leave the door unlocked when you're away. That way, anyone in need of temporary shelter is free to use it."

"What about stealing? Don't you worry about that?"

"Most people don't have anything worth stealing, and certainly not Josh, except his traps, and he caches those when he's not using them."

"Is that where you think he's gone, out laying his traps?

"Not at this time of the year. It's still too warm for good furs. He's probably hunting deer."

"When do you think he'll be back?"

Hawk shrugged his shoulders. "Who knows. He could be back by nightfall, or gone for days. We'll wait awhile and see."

Felicia looked around curiously. She had never been in a log cabin before. The entire building wasn't as big as her bedroom, and the floor was packed dirt. The only furnishings were a small table, a bench made from split logs, and a planked bed built into one corner that was padded with skins. On one wall were pegs from which various articles of clothing hung, on another, frames used to dry beaver skins, and on the wall beside the small stone fireplace, shelves that apparently served as the trapper's cabinet. There wasn't a window in the place. The only opening was the massive wooden door. However, light spilled through the cracks between the logs in many places, where the clay chinking had fallen out.

They waited until dusk, but Josh didn't appear. "I guess he's not coming back today," Hawk commented. He looked about him, then said, "Well, we might as well spend the night here." Glancing at the fireplace and seeing there were already several logs in it, he reached into his hunting bag and pulled out his flint and steel. Handing them to Felicia, he said, "Here. You get a fire started, and I'll tend the horse."

"I don't know how to start a fire," she objected.

"Not even in a fireplace?"

"No. We had servants for that."

The disgusted look that came over Hawk's face made Felicia feel as if she were an inch tall. She knew he thought her spoiled and totally useless, but she wanted him to value her. Yet, she knew there was no hope in that. She was as totally ignorant in managing simple household tasks on the frontier, as the mountain women would be playing hostess at a state dinner in the governor's mansion. Then, spying a wooden bucket sitting by the door, she smiled and said, "But I can carry water, if you'll just tell me where the stream is."

Her offer totally surprised Hawk, but he didn't refuse to accept it. Carrying water was a woman's chores both in his tribe and on the frontier. He nodded, then answered, "You'll find a stream out back. You can't miss the path to it."

Felicia had seen the look of surprise in Hawk's eyes, and it pleased her. She almost skipped to the bucket, picked it up, and stepped outdoors. Just as she was rounding the corner of the cabin, she heard Hawk call, "Watch out for wild animals. They like to water at dusk."

Felicia faltered in her step and stumbled. She looked about at the long shadows falling all around her, and hesitated. Then, realizing how demeaning going back on her word would look to Hawk, she gathered her courage and carefully made her way down a worn path. Much to her relief, there were no animals at the stream. She knelt and quickly filled the bucket to the brim.

On the way back to the cabin, Felicia found out just how terribly heavy a full bucket of water could be. It took both arms to carry it, and even then she sloshed almost half of it out, soaking her linsey skirt and petticoat from the knees down. By the time she reached the cabin, her back was aching from the unaccustomed strain. She sat the bucket down beside Hawk where he was tending the fire, hoping for praise of some kind, but to her utter disappointment, he made no comment.

They ate in silence, then Hawk rose, saying, "You can have the bed. I've already laid your blanket on it. I'll sleep outside."

Hawk was barely out the door, when Felicia rose and walked to the narrow bed in the corner. Bending slightly, she tested it with one hand and heard the rustling of the cornhusk mattress beneath the buckskin padding. She started to sit, then became aware of her damp skirt and petticoat. She knew sleeping in them would be miserable. She glanced at the closed door and decided that she had enough privacy to sleep in her chemise. Why, it would be sheer heaven, she thought, sleeping in a bed with no long skirt to encumber her.

She removed the kerchief from around her shoulders, then slipped off the linsey dress and petticoat. Wrapping her blanket around her, she walked to the corner of the cabin where Hawk had placed the saddle and looked around, thinking to find his saddlebags with her ball gown and chemise. But the bags were not there. She walked to the fire and looked about the cabin, her brow furrowed in puzzlement. The door suddenly

176

opened and Hawk walked in, carrying an armful of firewood.

When Hawk had left, pulling the door to behind him, Felicia had assumed he had retired for the night. She had not realized he had used all of the wood in the small wood bin to make his fire, or that he had planned to replenish it for her use during the night. His sudden, unexpected entrance startled her, and she lost her hold on her blanket. As it fell, she quickly regained her senses and grabbed it, holding it tightly across her breasts, but not before Hawk got a tantalizing glimpse of her nakedness.

Felicia knew he had seen her when his dark eyes blazed with unconcealed desire. She watched, pinned to the spot by that hot gaze as he kicked the door to with the heel of one moccasined foot, then walked towards her. Even when he bent and dropped the logs into the bin, she couldn't move, for he still kept eye contact.

Hawk stepped up to her, so close she could feel his heat and smell his heady essence. His breath fanned her face, as he said, "I brought you firewood, in case you got cold during the night, but you're not going to need it."

Felicia was shocked at how breathless she felt. Her words were a mere whisper. "Why not?"

Hawk's smoldering gaze moved slowly down her body and then back up, stripping her with his eyes and bringing a warm flush to her skin. Then, as his eyes once more met hers, he answered in a husky voice, "Because tonight I'm going to keep you warm."

There was no doubt in Felicia's mind what Hawk meant. She knew if she was going to object, this was the time to do it, this was the place to stop him. But she didn't want to stop him. She wanted him so bad she ached, her lips, her breasts, even the secret place between her legs. It was a yearning so powerful it overrode all decorum, all reason. She leaned towards him and muttered, "Yes, oh, yes."

Hawk could hardly believe his ears. For just a moment, he stared at her in disbelief, then seeing her golden green eyes glowing with a warmth of their own, any doubts he might have had flew out the window. He reached up and untied the rawhide string he had given her that held back her hair; as it fell about her shoulders like a silken curtain, and the fire behind her picked up its reddish highlights, he sucked in his breath and said softly, "Your hair is beautiful, so incredibly beautiful."

As his hands slid down the length of her hair—something that Hawk had been longing to do for days—Felicia was amazed. This was a Hawk she had never seen, never dreamed existed, a gentle Hawk. He pushed a lock of her hair back behind her ear, then traced the delicate shell of flesh before one slender finger trailed along her jaw, then lightly stroked her full lower lip, making it tremble with longing. Then he cupped the back of her

178

head and lifted it, his warm lips on hers softly playing, coaxing, wooing, before the tip of his tongue brushed her bottom lip, slowly back and forth, back and forth. His unexpected tenderness had a devastating effect on Felicia. An incredible weakness washed over her. Her bones seemed to melt. She dropped the blanket between them, and her knees buckled.

Hawk caught her and swept her up into his powerful arms. In two swift strides, he reached the narrow bed and placed her on it. He would have pulled back to drink in the beauty of her nakedness, but Felicia wrapped her arms tightly around his neck and brought him down over her, her eyes hazy with passion, lifting her mouth to his.

Hawk didn't disappoint her. His mouth covered hers, his tongue probing, then feverishly exploring the warm recess of her mouth as his hands swept over her bare, heated skin. Then, to his utter surprise, Felicia jerked her mouth away and said, "No! Stop!"

Hawk's hot passion turned to cold fury. He raised his head, his black eyes flashing, and said in a hard voice, "It's too late to object!" He jerked her legs apart and shoved his groin against her, so she could feel the rigid proof of his arousal. "Do you feel that?" he asked, grinding himself against her. "Well, I'm not going to be denied again. Not again!"

The feel of Hawk rubbing his erection against

her made Felicia's passion spiral. It was all she could do to remember what she had been objecting to. "Not *no!* I meant not here," she explained breathlessly. "This bed stinks."

It was then that Hawk became aware of how badly the bed reeked. He had not been as close to the covers as Felicia, and had not smelled the strong body odor that lingered on the skin padding, testimony to the fact that his trapper friend had a strong aversion to bathing.

He glanced over his shoulder and saw the blanket Felicia had dropped before the fireplace. He rose, swooped her back up into his arms, and carried her to it. This time, when he lay her down, he was quicker than she. He sat back on his heels and hungrily took in the sight of her nakedness, his hot eyes lingering on her breasts and then on the reddish curls at the apex of her rounded thighs.

Felicia was painfully aware of Hawk's devouring her nakedness. She felt terribly vulnerable. She was just on the verge of making some effort to cover herself, when he looked up. The sight of his black eyes blazing with passion took her breath away, then filled her with an excitement that matched his. She raised her arms and drew him back down to her.

A primitive groan escaped Hawk's lips as his mouth captured hers in a deep, ravishing kiss that gave full rein to his passion. Felicia's senses swam as Hawk's artful tongue slid in and out of her mouth, mimicking the intimate act that would follow, her heart racing, her breath coming in short, ragged gasps, the burning ache between her legs slowly building. She moaned in protest as he broke the searing kiss, then waited in breathless anticipation as he dropped a trail of fiery kisses down her throat and across her chest, descending inch by inch until Felicia thought she would scream in frustration before he reached his ultimate destination. As his tongue lazily circled one throbbing nipple, then flicked it while he rolled the other between his thumb and forefinger, she gasped in pleasure, quivering all over.

Felicia was awash in shimmering warmth that ebbed and flowed as Hawk's ardent tongue and mouth played at her breasts, the aching between her legs becoming a fierce burning. One hand swept the length of her body, then caressed her thigh, before it slipped between her legs and intimately cupped her womanhood. Felicia felt just a fleeting moment of shock at his boldness; then, as his fingers slipped through the soft moist folds and found the burning core, stroking and circling, a strangled cry escaped her throat, as wave after wave of exquisite sensation washed over her, making her feel as if a liquid fire was rushing through her veins, burning her clear to the soles of her feet, before the spasms shook her, robbing her of all thought.

Felicia's response to his ministrations, and the

feel of her hot and wet and throbbing had pushed Hawk's passion to the breaking point. While she was still floating on a cloud of warm sensation, he sat back and quickly stripped off his shirt and moccasins, then tore at the lacings of his buckskins with impatient hands before he slipped them down. Trembling with need, he rose over her, his knee nudging her legs apart, positioning himself between her soft thighs.

Still dazed, Felicia opened her eyes and saw Hawk kneeling over her. Slowly her eyes roamed over his ruggedly handsome features, the breadth of his shoulders, across his magnificent chest, wondering briefly when he had removed his shirt, before following the fine line of dark hair that narrowed as it crossed his tightly muscled abdomen, then flared again at his groin. Her eyes widened, seeing that bold, rigid flesh, looking even more enormous than it had felt the night he had made her touch him.

Felicia only had a split second to react before Hawk slipped his hands beneath her buttocks and lifted her, a split second to feel fear before she felt him entering her, stretching her, his searing, throbbing heat matching hers. A sense of wonder filled her as she felt her secret place stretching to accommodate his massive size, a wonder that became intense anticipation as he seemed to hesitate.

Through his reeling senses, Hawk felt the thin membrane that barred his penetration. His mind flashed warning signals, but his passion was riding too high, too hot, too fierce to be denied. With a will of its own, his body continued its onslaught, tearing the membrane before Hawk slid into Felicia's tight, moist void, filling her completely and then some.

Felicia cried out as a sharp pain tore through her loins, then relaxed as Hawk muttered incoherent, soothing words, his hands caressing her, his lips dropping soft kisses over her face and neck and shoulders, while he waited for her to become accustomed to the feel of him inside her. The pain faded to a dull ache, then a burning need once again, when Hawk took one nipple into his mouth and started to suckle it. When he began to move inside her, slowly and sensuously, stroking nerve endings that had never been touched before, Felicia's eyes once again filled with wonder, as a barrage of new sensations began to assault her senses. As he moved faster and faster, deeper and deeper, her body became an agony of intense anticipation. She wrapped her legs around his hips, making him gasp in pleasure and bringing him deeper, meeting him stroke for stroke. Her senses spun dizzily; a roaring filled her ears; every nerve in her body was strung tight, her skin feeling as if it might burst. Suddenly Hawk groaned and stiffened above her. She felt the hot spurt of his seed deep inside her. Then, as he collapsed over her, his hot breath rasping in her ear, the wondrous sensations she had been feeling fled, leaving her strangely disappointed.

As Hawk slowly drifted down from those rapturous heights, his mind, once more in control, slowly whirled in disbelief. A virgin?

He raised his head and glanced over his shoulder, then saw the telltale bloodstains on Felicia's thighs. Raising himself on his elbows, he glared down at her and said in a hard voice, "You were a virgin."

Felicia was still in a daze. "What?" she muttered.

"Dammit! You were a virgin!"

Felicia didn't like the accusing tone of Hawk's voice. "Don't use that tone of voice to me!" she answered angrily, "As if I've lied to you or something. Of course, I was a virgin. I told you Tarleton and I weren't lovers!"

Hawk didn't like the idea of making love to a virgin. It made him feel somehow responsible. That's why he had always limited his sexual involvements to experienced women. Yet, deep down, there was a exhilaration in knowing he had been the first, not just the first over Tarleton, his enemy, but the first over any man. Then, as a sudden suspicion took root in his mind, he said, "If you think this is going to change anything, you've made a gross error. I'm still holding you hostage until I get my revenge on Tarleton. You may not have been his lover. Not yet. But the way you were acting that night on the pier, it was just a matter of time before you would have been."

Felicia was shocked that Hawk had accused her of using her body to gain her freedom. She angrily pushed away and sat up, saying, "You insulting bastard! Do you really think I'd sink that low? That I'd use my body like some common trollop?"

Hawk had come to know Felicia better than he realized, and deep down, he didn't really believe she would play the role of a whore, for any reason. "Then why did you do it?" he asked.

The blunt question hit Felicia like a kick in the gut. She realized at that moment that it was more than just physical attraction that had made her give up her virginity to Hawk. Like it or not, she was becoming emotionally involved with him. But she couldn't admit that to him. Nor could she come right out and admit that she desired him. Lust was so . . . so unladylike.

"I was just curious, that's all."

"Curious?"

"Yes!" Felicia answered defensively. "I wanted to know what all the whispers were about, all the innuendo." She shrugged her shoulders, trying to give Hawk the impression that she was unimpressed, then said, "And now my curiosity has been satisfied."

Hawk didn't know why Felicia had allowed him to make love to her, but he seriously doubted that it had been simple curiosity that had motivated her. If so, why had she picked *him* to initiate her, and not some man before him. "And that's the end of it?"

Damn him! Felicia thought. Why does he always have pry into everything so deeply? "Of course, that's the end! I told you, my curiosity has been satisfied."

For Hawk it wasn't as simple as that. Now that he had had a taste of her passion, he wanted her even more. "How can your curiosity be satisfied, when you, yourself, haven't known satisfaction?"

"What are you talking about?"

Hawk leaned forward, so close that Felicia could feel his warm breath fanning her face, as he said, "I'm telling you that you haven't begun to scratch the surface of what lovemaking is all about, that you would have to know more—much more—before you could make any judgment." Hawk paused, then his voice dropped to a husky timbre, as he asked, "Does that renew your curiosity?"

His closeness sent Felicia's desire spiraling once again. She knew by the warm look in his eyes that all she would have to do was say yes, and he would make love to her again. But she couldn't do it. She felt she had to stand by her story, as flimsy as it might be, if she were to retain any respect from both him and herself. She turned her back to him and pulled the blanket up around her nakedness, saying coldly, "No, it doesn't. I'm just not interested anymore."

Hawk remembered how avidly Felicia had responded to his lovemaking, and knew she wasn't being truthful with him. Regardless of what had motivated her, she had enjoyed it, enjoyed it too much to suddenly have no interest. Hawk leaned forward, caught her chin in his hand, and turned her head to face him. "For tonight, we'll let it be. But for the record, I happen to think you're lying." His dark eyes bored into hers. "And someday, I'm going to prove it to you."

Leaving her with that tantalizing promise to ponder, Hawk rose, picked up his clothing, and walked to the door, giving Felicia an excellent view of his magnificent backside before the wooden panel opened, then closed behind him.

Chapter Fourteen

Hawk waited until mid-morning the next day, just in case his friend might make an appearance, then helped himself to a sack of cornmeal and a side of salted bacon, leaving his calling card behind on the trapper's table so Josh would know he had been there — a hawk's feather he had found in the woods.

Hawk chose to lead the horse through the forest and not ride behind Felicia, and he was even more taciturn than usual. Felicia was glad he seemed to be ignoring her. She needed time to mull over what had happened the night before, and try to sort through her mixed emotions. A part of her was mortified at the shameful thing she had done, while another gloried in the knowledge that Hawk desired her. The two warred all day, with nothing being resolved by the time Hawk chose a site to make camp that afternoon. And just to complicate matters, she couldn't identify the new, deeper feelings for him that were slowly emerging.

As soon as she had dismounted, Felicia made her way into the woods to relieve herself, then, still preoccupied with her thoughts, wandered aimlessly around, strolling for some time beside a twisting, shallow mountain stream that gurgled over and around lichen-covered rocks, while the trees around her cast longer and longer shadows. Finally becoming aware that it was growing late, she tried to retrace her steps, but when she reached the point where she had come upon the stream, she couldn't remember which direction the camp lay in. It was then that she realized she was lost. Reason told her to stay where she was and Hawk would find her, but with the light fading from the sky, all Felicia could think of was her fear of the dark. Impetuously, she struck off through the woods in a blind search for the camp, then suddenly walked into a clearing.

She stopped and looked about her, wondering if she climbed a tree, she could see their campfire. Then, gazing up at one tall pine, she froze in terror. Coming down the tree, rump first, was a huge, black bear.

The bear jumped the last few feet and landed on the ground with a thump that shook the earth, then turned and saw Felicia. As it rose on its hind feet to its full height, it looked monstrous to Felicia. She opened her mouth to scream, then heard Hawk's voice off to one side, saying in a low, urgent voice, "Don't scream! You'll frighten it. Frightened animals behave rashly. And stand still. Perfectly still."

Felicia barely managed to stifle the scream while it was still in her throat. Carefully she rolled her eyes to one side, and saw Hawk standing about a hundred feet away at the edge of the clearing. Then she focused her attention on his long rifle. Instead of being raised and pointed at the bear, as she expected, the weapon was dangling casually from one hand. "For God's sake!" she cried out. "What are you waiting for? Kill it!"

"Sssh! Keep your voice down!" Hawk cautioned. "And don't panic. There's no need to kill it. Despite everything you've probably heard, bears aren't fierce creatures that attack on sight. As a rule they engage in a lot of mock heroics to try and frighten their enemies away, and that includes man. Unless it's a sow with cubs, that is. They're dangerous as hell. But this is a male, so just stand still and don't show any fear."

Felicia looked back at the bear. It was making a big to-do about sniffing the air. Then the hair on its hackles rose, and it stared at her, its black eyes glittering, and Felicia couldn't believe it wasn't dangerous.

"It's going to make a mock charge," Hawk warned. "Don't move, and don't scream."

The words had hardly left Hawk's mouth, when the bear came down on all fours, then charged. Felicia's heart raced in fear. Every instinct told her to run for her life, but she held her ground, praying Hawk knew what he was talking about, but deep down still doubting it. No one could have been more surprised than she when the bear came to a sudden halt.

"See? I told you he's all bluff," Hawk said. "Just hold your ground."

Felicia didn't feel at all assured that the bear was just bluffing, not the way it was angrily slapping its big paws on the ground and sending clods of dirt and grass flying. When it began snapping its big jaws, its long, wicked teeth gleaming in the light, she was so terrified she felt weak-kneed and a cold sweat broke out on her forehead. As it let out a bloodcurdling roar and charged again, she knew she had to be looking death in the eye, that at any second she would feel sharp claws and teeth ripping her apart.

The bear came so close that Felicia could smell its fetid breath, then it veered sharply and tore off through the woods, leaving in its wake a trail of broken underbrush. Stunned, Felicia stood and stared out into space, her heart still beating wildly in her chest.

Hawk walked up to her and said quietly, "You did well."

Felicia had been waiting for days for Hawk to praise her about something, but when it finally came, all she could do was stare at him. Then, as reaction set in, she shrieked, "Are you insane? I was terrified! Why, I could have been killed!"

Hawk knew Felicia had been terrified, but nonetheless, she had held her ground. In his estimate, it had been a true test of courage, for he seriously doubted if any frontier woman he knew would have done as well. Most would have panicked and ran, and a few might have even fainted. Felicia had both surprised and pleased him, but Hawk didn't want her to know just how proud of her he was. That's why he worded his praise so mildly. As for her being killed, she had never been in that much danger. Hawk knew bears and their nature, much more than any of the frontiersmen who mistakenly thought them so ferocious, and even if this one had gone against its usual temperament and really attacked Felicia, Hawk could have put a bullet through its brain in a matter of seconds. His gun had been loaded the entire time. "But you weren't killed," Hawk pointed out. "It ran away, just like I said it would."

Hawk's pointing out what was obvious didn't make Felicia feel any better. She had just had the most terrifying fright of her life. "Still, you had no right to put me through that. No right! You could have just killed it."

"I told you," Hawk answered in an adamant voice, "it wasn't necessary to kill it, and I don't kill without reason."

"But it was just a bear, a wild animal!"

No, particularly not a bear, Hawk thought, for

they were considered sacred by the Cherokee. It was permissible to kill one in self-defense, or in a bear hunt which the medicine man had approved of for the purpose of attaining the bear oil used for tribal and religious ceremonies. But he couldn't tell Felicia his real reason. She already thought him much below her because he was a frontiersman. He knew she would scorn him even more, if she knew he was half-Indian.

He chose his words carefully. "Some men might have killed it, but I don't kill *anything* without reason. Such needless waste is a crime against nature. I hate it, and I won't do it. It's my . . ." Hawk hesitated. He didn't want to say people, for fear Felicia would ask more questions. "My way."

Hawk turned and walked away, and Felicia had no choice but to follow. Again she wondered at his firm resolve. He was undoubtedly the most intense man had she ever met. Then, once her fear and subsequent anger had subsided, her love of animals came once again to the surface, and she was glad he hadn't killed the bear. But perversely she wouldn't tell Hawk that she approved of his decision. Letting him think that she was angry at his putting her life in danger was his punishment for scaring her half out of her wits, even if he didn't know, or care, that he was being punished.

That night, Felicia waited for Hawk to make

good his threat of the night before. She was still struggling with her conflicting emotions, and in all honesty didn't know how she might respond, whether she might repulse his amorous advances in outrage, or welcome them. It turned out that Hawk made no move towards her, and Felicia was left with a keen disappointment that only confused her all the more. Was she let down because she hadn't gotten the opportunity to give him a scathing rebuff, she asked herself in bewilderment, or was she so miserable because she had wanted him to make love to her? Damn him! she thought. He was making mincemeat out of her emotions.

The next day they rode from the mountains into a deep valley of rolling hills and followed a fast-flowing river that twisted and turned, widened and narrowed, and was filled in many places with white rapids and small staircase waterfalls. Felicia thought this place was the loveliest she had seen so far, at least just to take a leisurely ride through, for although it was wooded, it was not as heavily wooded as what they had left behind them, and she could actually enjoy the scenery, instead of looking into a wall of trees. For a long while, she contemplated the vista in silence, then finally asked Hawk, "How long is this valley?"

Hawk shrugged his broad shoulders and answered, "Well, it runs from western Pennsylvania to Georgia, so I'd guess several hundred miles, but we don't call it a valley out here. We call it the trench, because it seems to form a natural dividing line between the Appalachians."

"Then that's still the Appalachians over there?" Felicia asked, nodding to a mountain range of purplish peaks capped with clouds in the distance.

"Yes."

"Are all of the mountains out here covered with that haze?"

"Yes, they all have a smoky look about them, but more so in the fall. And some have a more bluish cast to them, like that range back there," Hawk answered, pointing to a ridge of mountains to the east and north of them.

"Isn't that where we came from?"

"No, Virginia is on the other side of those mountains. We crossed from North Carolina."

"And this river? What's its name?"

"At this point, it's called the Holston, a little farther northeast, the Watauga, and at yet another branch, the Nolichucky. Where I'm taking you is a settlement on a creek that flows from this river."

Well, if he had meant to take her to a place she couldn't escape from, he was certainly attaining his goal, Felicia thought wryly. Not only had she gotten lost the day before, but she didn't even know the general direction they had come from, nor she had ever heard of any of the rivers. He might as well have taken her to another continent.

They came to a raft made of logs, parked in a grove of cottonwoods beside the river, the trees' silvery leaves fluttering in the breeze and making a soft, whispering noise. There was no one tending the ferry, so Hawk pulled them across the water, using the heavy rope strung from huge oaks on both sides of the river. Shortly thereafter, they left the main channel of water and followed a twisting creek, passing rocky pastures where fat cattle grazed. In the distance, perched on a hillside, Felicia could see a lone cabin here or there. For a while, they followed several two-wheeled carts loaded down with corn and pulled by oxen, until Hawk became impatient with their slow pace and passed them. A few minutes later, Felicia spied the gristmill they were headed for, a two-storied building made of logs that was built across a swift stream; the creaking wheel that turned the huge grinding stone inside hung in the water from the floor of the mill and looked like a huge paddle in a butter churn.

"There's a station up ahead," Hawk announced. "We'll stop there and pick up a few things."

"What in the world is a station?"

"That's what we call a fort out here. There's a trading post inside."

Felicia craned her neck, and at the top of a tall

hill, saw a palisade made of logs with a two-storied blockhouse at one corner. "Is that it?"

"Yes."

She looked at the clearing all around it and only saw two cabins sitting amongst the tree stumps. "Are the rest of the homes inside the walls?"

"There are three or four, I'd guess."

"That's a settlement? Six homes?"

"No, the settlement includes the cabins we've been passing and all those strung further along the creek. Probably fifty or sixty in all. Frontier settlements aren't towns. They're a collection of farms and homesteads, sometimes miles apart, roughly centered around a station they can go to for refuge in case of an Indian attack."

They climbed the hill to the stockade, passing several women laboriously lugging buckets of water up the steep incline from the creek. "Why didn't they build the fort closer to the stream?" Felicia asked.

"For two reasons. First, they need that height when they're fighting Indians, and second, no one builds too close to streams in this country, not the way they flood when it rains. In hill country the water has nowhere to run but down."

As they got closer to the fort, Felicia studied the blockhouse. About thirty feet square and made of logs, the second story jutted out from the first about three feet, and both stories had three-inch loopholes cut into the walls from which the frontiersmen could shoot their long rifles without exposing themselves to the enemy. The clapboard roof was hipped, and had an open watchtower built into its peak. Even after Felicia had observed all this, she still stared, thinking there was something different about the building, until it finally dawned on her and she voiced her thoughts out loud, saying, "That's it! That's what is different from the cabins. The outside walls are flat, and the pointed ends at the corners have been cut off."

Again Hawk was surprised at Felicia's observation. He wouldn't have thought she'd notice. "Yes, the logs have been squared and the ends sawed off. It's done so the enemy can't get a foothold and climb to the roof, then jump down into the stockade. If you look closely, you'll also see there's no caulking between the logs. It isn't needed. The logs are notched so perfectly that there are no cracks between them."

"The settlers should build all of their homes like that," Felicia commented. "It looks much neater, and it must be much easier to heat in the winter," she added, noting the stone chimney at the back of the blockhouse.

"That's true, but notching those logs that perfectly and squaring them by hand is tedious and time-consuming. It simply isn't practical for homes."

As they rode through the gate and into the station, Felicia looked about. The cabins had been built side by side along the palisade, so that their back wall was actually the wall of the fort, while their chimneys all faced the center of the fort, something she assumed was done to conserve wood, until she saw a lookout standing on one of the roofs and realized that the cabins were built that way so that their roofs could act as a parapet during an attack.

As they rode to the back of the dusty fort where the trading post was located, Felicia noted that the men were dressed exactly like Hawk, except they wore hats made from braided cornhusks and most had beards. There were only two women visible, and they were standing before the entrance to the blockhouse off to one side, so engrossed in their conversation that they didn't even notice Hawk and Felicia. The only differences between what they were wearing and Felicia's attire were the women's dingy aprons and limp sunbonnets, and the fact that they were barefooted while Felicia still wore what was left of her ragged slippers.

As they passed one of the cabins, Felicia noticed a hollow log sitting upright before it, and asked, "What is that log used for? I've seen one in the yard of almost every cabin we've passed."

"That's a hominy block."

Felicia had heard of hominy, but she had never seen it or eaten it, nor had the slaves on her father's plantation. Only the very poor ate hominy. "It's made from corn, isn't it?"

"Yes, parched corn that's so dry and hard the kernels have to be soaked in lye water before they can be removed. Then it's put in that block and pounded with a huge wooden pedestal to knock the hulls off."

Soaked in lye water? Felicia thought, wrinkling her nose. "Does it still taste like corn?"

The Cherokees didn't have hominy either, and Hawk had never developed a particular liking for it. "Not in my opinion. The soaking makes the corn swell several times its size, and leaves it tasting rather bland, probably because the germ seed as well as the hull is removed. However, it will fill your belly."

They came to a stop at a hitching rail outside of the trading post and dismounted. Next door, the sound of the blacksmith pounding on a red-hot horseshoe he was shaping rang in the air with each beat of his heavy iron mallet. Spying Hawk, the burly blacksmith stopped what he was doing, wiped the sweat from his brow with his forearm, and called out, "Welcome back, Hawk! Caleb stopped by a few days ago, looking for you. He said those U-rods of soft iron you were waiting on arrived on the last pack train. I told him I'd pass on the message the next time I saw you. You're welcome to use my forge, if you want."

Hawk waved back and called, "Thanks!"

As they walked into the trading post, Felicia wondered at the strange conversation, then almost tripped over a bag of cornmeal in the dim interior, breaking her train of thought. Again she looked around curiously, for she had never been in a trading post either. As musty as it was dim, the aisles were so crowded with piles of furs, sacks of meal and dried beans, barrels and kegs of almost every conceivable size, that they could hardly make their way to the back of the store where the counter and proprietor were.

While waiting for the owner to finish his business with another frontiersman, Felicia looked at the wall behind the counter and saw that it was covered with merchandise hanging from pegs: wicked-looking knives, powder horns, bullet molds, long-handled pots and pans, skillets of every size, bellows, sickles, harnesses and other leather goods, a few flintlocks, and more. It seemed almost every inch of the wall was occupied, and off to one side on the floor were several plows and huge black kettles.

As the frontiersman concluded his business transaction, he turned and walked away, giving Hawk a nod and Felicia a curious glance as he passed. The owner walked up to Hawk, offered his hand across the counter to him, and said, "Glad to see you got back safe and sound, Hawk. Shelby said you stayed behind for some personal business." He shot an expectant glance in Felicia's direction.

Hawk knew the merchant expected him to introduce Felicia, but he had no intentions of doing so. As far as he was concerned, the less people knew of why he had brought her west with him, the better. Shaking the man's hand, he looked him directly in the eye and asked, "Do you still have that gun I gave you to sell for me?"

The merchant didn't take offense at Hawk not introducing the strange woman to him. Mountain people were often fiercely protective of their privacy, and he had learned long ago to take his cue from them, no matter how curious he was. And he *was* curious to know who the stunning beauty was, and what she was doing here. It was obvious she wasn't a farm lass. Her face was sunburned, and the skin on her hand was as smooth as a baby's bottom. "Nope. I sold it a day or two after you left. Got a good price for it, too. Do you want payment in currency, or just added to your credit?"

Hawk was disappointed. The gun he had acquired after his had been taken from him by Tarleton's men, couldn't begin to compare in either balance or accuracy. "Just add it to my credit."

"You know, Hawk, I could sell one of your guns any day. No matter how hard up a man may be, he still needs a good flintlock, and rifles like yours are hard to come by in these parts. So anytime you have more to sell, you just let me know. I'll be glad to handle it for you."

Felicia frowned. Hawk's guns? Is that how he made a living, she wondered. Peddling guns? But

Felicia couldn't see Hawk as a peddler. It just didn't fit his image.

While Felicia had been musing on those thoughts, Hawk was thinking his. What the merchant had said was true. The possession of a good rifle was critical to survival on the frontier, and no settler came west or stayed there without one, but despite their importance, Hawk wasn't getting the kind of money he had been back east for his guns, and he'd worked too hard making them to throw his profit to the wind. The mountain farmers simply didn't have the funds, and he could ill afford a middle man. He preferred to sell his rifles himself. "I'll keep that in mind," he answered noncommittally, then, gazing at an assortment of tomahawks displayed on the wall, said, "Let me have that tomahawk in the middle there. I lost mine back east."

"Sure thing," the merchant answered, reaching for the small ax with the stone head. "Why, I bet you've been feeling downright naked without one. A man ain't a man out here without his tomahawk, rifle, and scalping knife."

Felicia had wrinkled her nose in distaste when Hawk had asked for the tomahawk. She knew all of the frontiersmen carried them, but they seemed such barbaric weapons. But she had had no idea that the long, vicious-looking knives they carried were used for scalping. My God, she thought, a shiver of revulsion running over her, these men were no better than the savages they fought.

Hawk saw the expression on Felicia's face, and had a good idea of what she was thinking. It only confirmed what he had suspected: that she would be totally repulsed if she knew of his Indian blood. A fury came over him, for Hawk was prouder of his Indian blood than his white. Shooting her a hard look, he picked up the tomahawk as the merchant slid it across the counter, and tied it to the hand-woven belt on his right side, opposite his knife.

"Anything else?" the merchant asked.

"Yes, give me a barrel of gunpowder and ten pounds of lead."

While the shopkeeper gathered the items, Felicia pondered over the puzzling look Hawk had given her when he had donned the club. There had been something defiant about it, almost as if he were daring her to say something, and yet she had the strangest feeling it was something more than the tomahawk that he was challenging her about, but she hadn't the slightest idea what that something was.

As they walked from the trading post, Felicia thought in bewilderment that Hawk was not only the most intense man she had ever known, but also the most perplexing.

Chapter Fifteen

When Hawk and Felicia had ridden into the fort earlier, the blacksmith had been the only one to notice them. Everyone else had either had their backs to them or were preoccupied with other things. Such was not the case when the couple rode out. Everyone took note, and Hawk called himself a fool for thinking they could ride in and out inconspicuously, when Felicia's glorious chestnut hair shining in the bright sunlight was so utterly conspicuous. He had hoped not to draw attention to her. The reason for her being here was a very private matter to him, something that he had no intention of telling anyone but his closest friends. Nor had he wanted to subject Felicia to the scorn the frontiersmen showed every outsider, but particularly a low-lander. The less people who knew of her presence, the better it would have been for everyone. But the damage had been done. Now the settlers knew she was here, and their curiosity had been aroused, and while they were closemouthed and aloof to strangers, when it came to their own, they could be terribly nosy. But it wasn't himself that Hawk was worried about being questioned. The settlers stood in awe of him, and, except for a few select friends, pretty much kept their distance. No, it was the old friends that he hoped to leave Felicia with that Hawk was concerned about. Now, because of his carelessness, Daniel and Sarah would be besieged by inquisitive neighbors, only making their job of holding Hawk's trust all the more difficult.

While Hawk was acutely aware of everyone staring at Felicia, she didn't even notice their curiosity, nor when the looks changed to admiration or envy, depending upon the sex of the beholder. She had been engrossed the entire ride across the fort with a pack train that was departing. As they followed the sturdy packhorses walking single file and loaded down with trading goods through the opening in the palisade where the heavy gate had been pulled back, she asked, "Do the horses always wear those bells around their necks?"

"They always wear them, but when they're passing through territory where Indians might be lurking, the clappers are tied, so they can't ring. Otherwise, they're left untied, so the horses can be found in the forest if they break their hobbles and wander away during the night, or to announce their arrival in the next settlement, where the train will pick up more horses and trading goods," Hawk answered, feeling much more relaxed since they had left the fort and stares behind them.

Felicia could see that the better part of the trading goods were furs. The little horses were loaded down with stacks of skins so high, she wondered how they could possibly carry that much. But there were at least a score of horses with sacks over their backs, and another score or so with bushels and barrels tied to their sides. "Is that corn in those sacks?" she asked, since that seemed to be the major crop grown in the mountains.

"A few sacks, yes. But they're not trading goods. The corn is carried to feed the horses, when they get into the deep forests where no grass grows. The rest contain ginseng roots. I understand there's a big demand for them in China, where they use them for medicines."

"And the bushels and barrels? What's in them?"

"The larger barrels contain bear oil, the medium, potash, the thick black crust left from boiling ashes that we call black salt out here. It's very valuable back on the coast, used for dyes, tanning, making soap, glass, paper. The smaller barrels contain maple syrup, and those kegs, corn whiskey."

Felicia's brow furrowed. "Do you mean rum?"

"No, this is made from corn mash, not molasses, and it's much more potent, or so I've been told. It's also much more practical for shipping than corn. A packhorse can carry four bushels of corn or two kegs of whiskey, which is equivalent to twenty-four bushels of corn."

"So these people ship their corn in the form of whiskey?"

"If they have a still, and enough corn to spare after feeding themselves and their animals. The main purpose of the crop is for fodder in the winter. A lot of cattle go to the coast from this area. This settlement alone sends at least one cattle drive a year back east."

The pack train veered off to the right, the tinkling of the sturdy, little horses' bells fading in the distance, until nothing more could be heard of them. Hawk and Felicia passed a few more isolated farms, then rode for several hours without seeing any sign of civilization. Finally, coming around a bend in the stream they were following, Hawk brought the bay to a halt, and said, "This is it. This is my friend's farm."

Felicia looked up the hill and could just see a cabin through the woods. Hawk swung down from the saddle, saying, "I'm going to leave you here by the stream, while I go and talk to them. That way, if they want to refuse to let you stay with them while I'm gone, they won't be put in the awkward position of having to do it front of you."

Felicia was surprised that Hawk was so considerate of his friends. Again, it didn't seem to fit the image of ill-mannered frontiersmen that she had always imagined. As he walked up the steep hillside, she wondered what would happen to her if his friends *did* refuse? Would Hawk leave her someplace by herself, or take her back? Neither appealed to her. And if they did agree, just who *were* these friends? Were they men, or a family? She fervently hoped they were the latter. Being left alone with a couple of wild mountain men was just as terrifying as being left alone.

It was a good thirty minutes before Hawk returned—so long that Felicia had considered dismounting and stretching her legs. He came alone. Watching him coming down the hill with that lazy, graceful walk that was so much a part of him, Felicia was filled with apprehension, for as usual his facial expression revealed nothing. Finally, she couldn't stand the suspense any longer, and called out, "Well? What did they say?"

Maddeningly, Hawk didn't answer until he reached her, then calmly announced, "They agreed." His expression hardened as he said, "But I want something understood from the very beginning. My friends aren't servants. They're taking you in as a favor to me. You won't be waited on or pampered. You'll be expected to earn your keep."

It wasn't so much what Hawk was saying that rubbed Felicia the wrong way, as his dictatorial attitude. "I will do no such thing!" she threw back. "I didn't ask to come here. Nor did I come of my own free will. I'm a prisoner, remember? A prisoner of war! My needs should be taken care of without me having to lift a finger."

Hawk stepped closer, his hard chest pressing against her knee. "There are places in this world where prisoners of war work harder than anyone else, where they are virtual slaves," Hawk said in a steely voice, thinking of the Cherokee. "Here, everyone works, man, woman and child. It is the law of the frontier, the law of the mountains. If there is one thing that cannot be abided among these people, it is laziness. You will work. Otherwise, you will not eat. Do you understand?"

Felicia hardly noticed Hawk's words. She was acutely aware of the power radiating from him, of the angry glitter in his black eyes. A tingle of fear ran through her, for he looked very dangerous and very determined. Instantly, she regretted her rashness. She should have known better than to challenge him. But it galled her to have to back down. She refused to give him the satisfaction of an answer. Instead she tilted her head haughtily, then nodded curtly.

Hawk knew Felicia had agreed only under duress, and then with great reluctance. He thought her the most stubborn woman he had ever met.

Even when she was forced to back down, she still clung fiercely to her pride, somehow always managing to rob him of the pleasure of his victory. Under other circumstances, Hawk would have admired her tenacity, but not when she pitted her strong will against his. Then all he could feel was exasperation.

"I'll also expect you to show my friends the respect they deserve. You may think them common and much beneath you, but I won't have you treating them that way. They're honest, hardworking, good-hearted people, so mind your manners."

Felicia gasped indignantly, hardly believing her ears. The big bully, the rude, arrogant frontiersman was lecturing *her* on manners?

Hawk chose to ignore Felicia's response to his last dictate, caught the reins of the bay, and led the horse up the hill, wondering if he was doing the right thing in leaving her with his friends. The couple had been very good to him over the years. He'd hate to repay them for their kindness by giving them a problem to handle in his absence, and he had learned Felicia could be a handful. At the time he had made the decision, he had been thinking only of Felicia's safety, and, in truth, this was still the only place he could possibly leave her for that period of time. God, he hoped Felicia put a tight rein on that haughty pride of hers and behaved herself. He wouldn't tolerate having his friends insulted.

211

Felicia had been nursing her resentment at Hawk all the way up the hill, but when they reached the clearing at the top, she forgot it and looked about curiously, seeing a good-sized cabin flanked with a towering sycamore on one side and a big kitchen garden on the other. Behind the house, she could barely make out a barn and several smaller buildings. On the opposite side of the hill, the cornfields, surrounded by a fence made of split rails, stretched out over a gently rolling terrain for several acres, the long narrow leaves of the plants fluttering in the breeze. At the rocky bottom of the hill, beside what Felicia assumed was the same stream they had followed, a herd of cattle grazed.

But it was the corn that had caught Felicia's attention. "Why is that corn still green?" she asked Hawk. "It was dried up in every other field we've passed."

Because his back was to her, Felicia couldn't see the pleased smile that came over Hawk's face. "That was summer corn you saw. This corn is a special variety that matures in the fall. If you look very closely, you can see the dried stubble of the summer crop between the new plants."

Felicia squinted her eyes, but her vision was simply not as good as Hawk's. She took his word that the stubble was there. Had she known more about corn, she might have asked further questions, but corn was the small farmers' crop, not the big planters'. Her eyes left the cornfield and swept over the expanse of the farm, this time coming to rest on the small orchard off the opposite side. All in all, she found the place reassuring. It was one of the largest and best cared-for she had seen, including those in the piedmont area back in the Carolinas. Her spirits rose.

A movement off to one side caught her attention. She turned her head and saw a man and woman stepping from the cabin. Had the woman not been wearing a dress and a sunbonnet, Felicia would have sworn the two were identical twins. Both were tall, big-boned, reed-thin, their faces deeply tanned and their skin weathered and leathery-looking. Both had piercing blue eyes and lank, mousey brown hair streaked with gray, hair that seemed as lifeless as their expressionless faces, and made Felicia wonder if all mountain people were so dour and stern-looking, if they never laughed, or even smiled. At the thought of being left behind with these two sour-looking creatures, Felicia's rising spirits quickly fell.

Hawk helped Felicia dismount and, still holding her elbow firmly in his hand, as if he were afraid she might bolt, led her to the couple. "Felicia, these are my very close friends, Sarah and Daniel MacTavish." To his friends he said, "This is Felicia Edwards."

Felicia waited to see if either would offer their

hand, or smile. Neither happened. She forced a smile to her face, and said, "I'm pleased to meet you."

The twinkle Felicia saw come into Sarah's eyes stunned her with its unexpectedness. Then, as quickly as it had come it was gone, as Sarah turned to Hawk, and said in a stern voice, "Shame on ye, Hawk. Maligning this lass. Why, there's nothing wrong with her manners." She turned back to Felicia, and said "We're pleased to meet ye, too. Now come in, lass, come in."

Before Felicia followed Sarah into the cabin, she shot Hawk a furious glance, wondering what other ugly things he had told the couple about her. As she stepped inside the home, she looked about with great interest. Like the trapper's cabin, it was only one room, but it was much bigger, much cleaner, and had a puncheon floor and a loft at one end. There was a table made of split logs with benches on both sides, several three-legged stools scattered about, and a rocking chair before the stone fireplace, while a built-in bed occupied one corner and a spinning wheel, a loom, and a butter churn the others. Again, clothing was hung on pegs, but there were also several sheaves of dried Indian corn decorating the wall, giving the cabin a homey touch, and hanging beside the fireplace and above shelves that served as cabinets, there was a bellows and an assortment of pots and pans and skillets, all scoured until they gleamed in the light.

It was then Felicia realized that the light wasn't just coming from the open door. There was a window at both sides of the cabin.

Seeing the look of surprise on her face, Sarah said, "I know it ain't usual to have windows in these cabins, but I got so tired of it being so stifling in here in the summer, that I told Daniel I'd just as soon get killed by an Indian as go through that misery another summer."

"Is that why there are no windows in the cabins? Because of Indian attacks?" Felicia asked.

"Aye. Ye don't want to give those heathens any way they can sneak in the cabin with ye. Them and wild animals. But nothing can't get in here, not with those heavy shutters Daniel built. Once ye pull them across the windows and bolt them down, ye're just as snug as a bug in the rug. Too snug sometimes. Daniel always insists on closing them at night. But at least I get some relief in the daytime."

Felicia looked around her, then asked, "Where did Hawk and Mr. MacTavish go?"

"To take Hawk's horse down to the barn. Reckon they'll stay down there for a while. Man talk, ye know."

Sarah walked to the fire and stirred a pot there, saying, "I reckon ye're hungry. Supper will be ready in a little while. Ain't nothing fancy, though. Potpie and corn pone."

As Sarah busied herself, Felicia felt very awkward and useless. It was these feelings, rather than Hawk's lecture, that made her want to do something to help. But she had no idea of what she could do. She finally asked, "Can I help in some way?"

"I reckon ye can set the table. The trenches, noggins, and tableware are over there on those shelves."

Felicia had never before seen the square wooden trenches or cups made from gourds. She placed them and the wooden spoons and crude forks on the table. She noted that there were no dinner knives.

Sarah turned from the fire, looked at the table, and said, "I reckon my dishes look pretty pitiful to ye. I used to have a nice set of pewter, but one year when the Indians were on the warpath so bad, Daniel had to melt them down for bullets. Never did get another set. Wasn't really no need to, since it's just us here."

Sarah dropped the long-handled spoon she had been using, walked across the room, and picked up a jug. Placing it on the table, she asked Felicia, "What would ye like to drink?"

"Do you have any tea?"

"Tea?" Sarah repeated, her long, bony nose wrinkling in distaste. "Hell and damnation, I wouldn't have none of that foul stuff in my house, nor will anyone else in these hills! That's why we couldn't understand those Boston folks getting so riled up about the Crown raising taxes on it, and stirring up all that trouble. It ain't fit for nothing but hog slop!"

Sarah's outburst took Felicia somewhat aback. Seeing her stunned expression, Sarah said, "Sorry, lass. I didn't mean to get so carried away. I've got buttermilk, this corn whiskey here," she tapped the jug, "and water. Had some sweet apple cider until a while back, but we ran out of it, and the apples ain't quite ready for picking yet."

The thought of buttermilk made Felicia's stomach feel queasy, and the potent whiskey was out of the question. "I'll have water."

The two men returned. Hawk gave Felicia a questioning look, as if to ask, "Have you behaved yourself?" Felicia shot him a go-to-hell look in return, then the three sat while Sarah dished the potpie—a stew with meat, vegetables, and small dumplings—into their trenches.

As they ate, Felicia noted that both Sarah and Daniel drank corn whiskey, but Hawk had water. She wondered if he had an aversion to the corn mash drink for some reason or the other, for she couldn't imagine him not drinking anything alcoholic. That was unheard-of in the colonies, where rich and poor, male and female, freely partook of the ales, rums, brandies, hard ciders, beers, and wines. Even she had been accustomed to an after-dinner drink of peach brandy every evening.

The conversation at dinner was stilted, something that Felicia attributed to her presence. After discussing how the weather had been and speculating on what it might be the next day, then Sarah giving Hawk an account on how many eggs her chickens were laying, and Daniel telling him how many hogs he planned on butchering that fall, the group fell silent.

While Felicia helped Sarah clear the table and wash the dishes, something she had never dreamed of doing, she was acutely conscious of Hawk watching her from the corner of his eye, as he and Daniel talked in front of the fire. Finishing their chores, Sarah walked to the fireplace, took a corncob pipe down from where it lay on the mantel, then proceeded to stuff it with tobacco from a small leather pouch. Felicia assumed she was preparing it for her husband, until Hawk picked up a candle, held the wick to the fire until it caught, then held it to the pipe that Sarah had placed in her mouth.

"Thank ye, Hawk," Sarah said, after she had gotten the pipe burning, then sat in the rocking chair. Rocking and puffing, she murmured, "Ah, there's nothing more relaxing than a good smoke before bedtime."

"Aye," her husband agreed, picking up a clay pipe from the mantel and handing it to Hawk, then taking another for himself.

As the three smoked, Felicia tried to hide the shock she had felt when she had seen Sarah smoking a pipe, by concentrating on watching Hawk with his. But even though she had never seen Hawk smoke before, it looked natural on him, and her eyes kept straying to Sarah.

"Do ye smoke, lass?" Sarah asked.

"No," Felicia answered, trying very hard to hide the fact that she felt highly insulted by the question.

"Do ye dip?" Daniel asked in his gruff voice.

Felicia jumped in surprise, for the Scot had not said one word to her until then. "Do you mean snuff?"

"Aye."

This time Felicia wasn't insulted. Dipping snuff among the gentry, male and female alike, was so popular that the jewelers made a heavy profit on the sale of jeweled snuffboxes, but Felicia found it as disgusting as the practice of powdering hair. "No, I don't."

Felicia noticed that her answer seemed to please the Scots. They almost smiled. Almost. Then Sarah said, "If ye'd like to give smoking a try, ye can use my pipe. It draws easier than those clay ones Hawk and Daniel are using."

Felicia almost said, "no, thank you," then remembered that Sarah had been kind to her. Even offering the use of her pipe had been generous, and Felicia didn't want to hurt the older woman's feelings. She amended her answer to a simple, "Thank you," which carried no commitment one way or the other.

Sarah nodded and rocked in the creaky rocker, back and forth, back and forth, puffing on her pipe, while the two men stood leaning on the mantel and staring down at the fire, seemingly doing more thoughtful chewing on the pipe stem than actual smoking. Felicia had a feeling that this was a ritual that had been enacted between the three very often. They seemed so comfortable with their shared solitude, and Felicia found herself envying them in some strange way.

The minutes ticked by; the sweet aroma of burning tobacco filled the air. Finally, Daniel removed his pipe, bent, and knocked the remaining ashes from the bowl by hitting it lightly against the stones on the inside of the fireplace. He placed the pipe back on the mantel, and said to Hawk, "I'm going to make my nightly rounds."

"I'll join you," Hawk answered, knocking the ashes from his pipe.

As the two men walked to the door, Felicia noted that while Daniel was tall, Hawk towered over him by several inches, and his exceptionally broad shoulders made the older man's look almost pathetic. Yet Felicia knew that while Daniel was thin, he wasn't frail. Where in the world had Hawk gotten those muscles on his shoulders and arms, she wondered.

"Hawk?" Sarah called softly when the two had reached the door.

Hawk turned, and there was something about

his expression as he looked at Sarah that brought a peculiar yearning to Felicia, something more than just the hint of a smile on his sensuous lips. Then she realized that it was his eyes. The same black eyes that could penetrate like an arrow, glitter like splintered ice, flash like lightning, and smolder like coals in a fire, had a velvety softness she had never seen before, a look that made her heart twist strangely, a look she would have given her soul to have bestowed on her.

"Are ye going back east tomorrow?" Sarah asked.

At the prospect of Hawk leaving her, Felicia felt her knees go weak, as if her bones had suddenly turned to water. She sank to the bench beside her, her heart suddenly racing. She never had a chance to decipher what her strange reaction meant, only that she knew it wasn't fear of being left behind with Sarah and Daniel that prompted it. And the strange weakness left her the second she heard Hawk say, "No, I thought I'd stay a few days and give Daniel a hand."

"Aye, we'd appreciate that. Ye're a good man."

Hawk showed no reaction to Sarah's praise. He turned and ducked his head to keep from hitting it on the doorjamb, as he stepped outside.

"Are ye tired, lass?" Sarah asked.

"A little," Felicia admitted.

"Well, ye can go to bed anytime you like. Ye can sleep up in the loft, in Hawk's old bed. Except, it ain't a bed. 'Tis just a cornhusk mattress lying on the floor, covered with some blankets.

"Where will Hawk sleep, if I take his bed?" Felicia asked.

Sarah had wondered if there was something going on between Hawk and Felicia. She was much more astute than her husband, and more attuned than most to others' feelings. She had sensed the electric undercurrent flowing between them, seen Hawk casting hungry looks in Felicia's direction when the lass wasn't looking, witnessed the anxious expression on Felicia's face when she had asked Hawk if he was leaving the next day. Felicia's question had sounded maidenly to Sarah's ears, and led her to believe that nothing had happened between the two—yet. "He can sleep in the barn, on a pile of straw. It will be as comfortable as that bed of his."

Felicia seriously doubted that Hawk would care where he slept, as much as he had been sleeping on the hard ground. But the barn seemed so faraway, and she would miss his nearness. She rose from the bench, saying, "Well, I think I will retire."

Sarah rose from the rocking chair and placed the cold pipe back on the mantel, saying, "I'll get ye a candle. There's a small, sawed-off stump up there ye can put it on. Give you a little light while ye're undressing."

"Oh, I won't be undressing. I'll sleep in my clothes."

"No one can see ye up there, lass, if that's what ye're thinking."

"Still, I wouldn't feel right sleeping in just my petticoat. You see, there wasn't any shift with these clothes Hawk bought me. I guess because they belonged to a young girl, and the chemise I was wearing when Hawk took me is in his saddlebags, along with my ball gown," Felicia added, for fear Sarah would get the wrong idea.

"Then that's all the clothing ye've got?" Sarah asked in surprise. "The clothes ye're wearing and yer ball gown? Ye've no nightgown?"

"No. I guess Hawk didn't think it was necessary."

"Aye, Hawk knows nothing about clothing a woman, that's for sure. But then, even married men don't," Sarah added with a disgusted sigh. "Why, I reckon Daniel still don't know the difference between a shift and a petticoat after all these years. Aye, men are a lot better at taking clothes off a woman, than knowing what to put on her."

Felicia was just a little shocked at Sarah being so candid, but she was in total agreement with the older woman's observation, remembering how quickly and deftly Hawk had stripped her of her hoop the first night, then her bodice that night in the lean-to. Then her mind pondered

223

something Sarah had said. She had never even considered that Hawk might be married. She was immensely relieved to know he wasn't, but refused to delve into why she felt that way.

Sarah picked up a tin candle holder, then lit the candle in it. She handed it to Felicia, then walked to one wall and snatched a garment from the peg there, saying, "Ye can borrow one of my gowns, until we have time to sew ye one. I'm sure it's going to swallow ye, as little as ye are. And ye'll be needing another dress, too. A ball gown won't do for the chores we'll be doing."

It appeared that Sarah also expected her to earn her keep, Felicia noted, but Felicia didn't resent it coming from the older woman. Just as she hadn't wanted to insult Sarah, she didn't want to be a burden on the Scots. Obviously, they worked very hard to eke out a living on this land. Nor did she have a bone to pick with them. Hawk was the one who taken her freedom away. They were only helping him as a favor. Suddenly that struck her as curious. Why a favor? Why not out of clan honor?

It was a thought that Felicia was not able to pursue at that time. Sarah caught her arm and led her to the ladder, saying, "Climbing a ladder in a long dress carrying a candle, takes some getting used to. Why don't ye climb on up, and I'll hand ye the candle and gown."

Holding her skirt up with one hand, Felicia

4 FREE BOOKS

TO GET YOUR 4 FREE BOOKS WORTH $18.00 — MAIL IN THE FREE BOOK CERTIFICATE T O D A Y

Fill in the Free Book Certificate below, and we'll send your FREE BOOKS to you as soon as we receive it.

If the certificate is missing below, write to: Zebra Home Subscription Service, Inc., P.O. Box 5214, 120 Brighton Road, Clifton, New Jersey 07015-5214.

FREE BOOK CERTIFICATE

4 FREE BOOKS

ZEBRA HOME SUBSCRIPTION SERVICE, INC.

YES! Please start my subscription to Zebra Historical Romances and send me my first 4 books absolutely FREE. I understand that each month I may preview four new Zebra Historical Romances free for 10 days. If I'm not satisfied with them, I may return the four books within 10 days and owe nothing. Otherwise, I will pay the low preferred subscriber's price of just $3.75 each; a total of $15.00, *a savings off the publisher's price of $3.00.* I may return any shipment and I may cancel this subscription at any time. There is no obligation to buy any shipment and there are no shipping, handling or other hidden charges. Regardless of what I decide, the four free books are mine to keep.

NAME

ADDRESS _____ APT

CITY _____ STATE _____ ZIP

( )
TELEPHONE

SIGNATURE _____ (if under 18, parent or guardian must sign)

Terms, offer and prices subject to change without notice. Subscription subject to acceptance by Zebra Books. Zebra Books reserves the right to reject any order or cancel any subscription.

climbed up the shaky ladder to the loft. Then she knelt at the edge and took the candle Sarah held up to her. Holding the flickering light up, she looked about her, then walked to the back of the loft and placed the candle on the stump she found there.

"Ye forgot the gown."

Felicia turned and saw Sarah standing on the ladder and holding the gown out to her. Felicia accepted it and shook it out. It, too, was made of a rough tow-linen, but with bits of lace on it and spotless; it was much prettier than Sarah's stained and tattered butternut dress. "Oh, I can't wear this. It's too pretty."

"Aye, 'tis my prettiest nightgown. 'Tis my party dress."

"You wear nightgowns to parties?" Felicia asked in a shocked voice.

"Aye, we do. We sure don't want to wear our everyday dresses to something special. Our gowns and undergarments stay a lot whiter and prettier." Sarah winked suggestively, then added, "Since they get taken off, if there's going to be anything happening but sleeping."

Felicia wasn't accustomed to such frankness, and she blushed. Sarah saw it and was pleased with her innocence. Mountain people were very candid about sex, sometimes to the point of being lurid, and while Sarah didn't mind making a suggestion here and there, she didn't like the bold manner of some of the lasses.

Aware of the older woman's eyes on her, Felicia said, "Thank you, and I'll be careful not to tear it."

After Sarah had gone back down the ladder, Felicia stripped off her clothing and donned the gown. Just as Sarah had predicted, it swallowed her. Then she sat down on the cornhusk mattress, blew out the candle, and stretched out, convinced she wouldn't be able to sleep in the strange surroundings and without Hawk nearby. But after sleeping on the hard ground for weeks, she found the mattress incredibly comfortable. And even more comforting, the blanket she was lying on and the one she had pulled up to cover her, held Hawk's scent. She fell into a delicious slumber, wrapped in his familiar heady essence, and dreamed of being held in his powerful arms.

Chapter Sixteen

When Felicia descended from the loft the next morning, she found the cabin empty. She stepped outside and looked around, then saw Sarah standing beneath the huge sycamore at one side of the cabin, stirring something in a big, black kettle that hung on an iron spit over a fire. Felicia walked up to her and said, "Good morning," then glanced down at the pot and saw that it was laundry Sarah was stirring.

" 'Morning," Sarah answered, then, picking up her apron with one hand, wiped her brow. "There's some corn mush sitting on the back of the fire in the house, if ye're hungry. Just help yerself. Sorry I don't have any milk for it. The cow ain't been milked yet this morning. But there's a jug of bear oil on the table ye can pour on it, or maple syrup if ye prefer. 'Tis what Hawk always has."

"Thank you, but I'm not hungry right now. Maybe later."

"Suit yerself. Do ye want to wash up? There's a

bucket of water and a washbasin on that bench in front of the cabin. Ye can take it inside if ye want privacy, but that ain't necessary. The menfolk are gone."

Back home, Felicia had always bathed in the morning, but on the trail, she bathed whenever the opportunity presented itself. She really didn't feel the need to wash up, particularly since she had no clean clothing to put on. She wondered if Hawk had left his saddlebags in the barn or taken them with him, then wondered how long he would be gone. "No, I think I'll do that later also."

"Aye, I prefer to do my bathing in the evening, too," Sarah responded, assuming that was what Felicia had meant when she said later. "Don't make much sense to do it in the morning, not if ye're going to get all hot and sweaty during the day."

Felicia was in total agreement with Sarah's logic, but she had never had to do hard labor where she got sweaty and dirty. It appeared that her bathing habits were going to have to change. "You said the men are gone. Where did they go?"

"Out in the woods to dig some wolf traps. A particularly mean pack of those mangy critters have been giving the whole settlement trouble for some time now, killing livestock. Got one of our calves a few weeks ago. Why, they even dragged off a little girl in broad daylight, even though

228

they're supposed to be night creatures. What they found left of her wasn't worth burying. Just makes me sick every time I think of it."

Felicia was horrified. "Why don't the men around here mount up a posse and go after them?"

"Ye mean track them down and kill them with guns?"

"Yes."

Sarah shook her head. "That's not how to hunt wolves. They're too smart. They hide. And they ain't afraid of guns. Daniel told me he once saw a wolf take six bullets without it stopping him. Nay, the only way to get wolves is trap them. Even the bounty hunters do it that way, and that's how they make their living."

"Then why can't you just lay traps?"

"Ye can't catch a wolf with a steel trap. He'll chew his leg off to get free. Nay, the only way to get those mangy critters is to dig a deep pit, then conceal the opening with sticks and leaves so they won't see it. That's where Hawk beats every other man in these hills. He knows just how to build those traps so they won't collapse under the weight of nothing heavier than a wolf, while Daniel is always finding possums and foxes and raccoons in his. But then I reckon building wolf traps is just in Hawk's blood."

Felicia thought it an odd statement, then was distracted by Sarah saying, "Hell and damnation, I sure will be glad when the weather cools off a little. Even under the shade of this tree, 'tis hot as blazes by this fire."

"I could stir for a while," Felicia offered.

"Nay, there's no use in both of us getting soaking wet with sweat." Sarah paused, then said, "But there is something ye can do for me. Fetch the cow, so I can milk her when I get through here."

"You mean, fetch her from the barn?"

Sarah laughed, then said, "Nay, lass, from the woods. We let her roam free so she can graze on the grass there. Ain't no sense in wasting our corn to feed her, except in the winter."

Felicia looked at the woods all around them, then asked, "Where will I find her?"

"Well, she could be almost anywhere, but ye won't have any trouble finding her. She's wearing a bell. Just follow the sound."

Felicia cast a nervous glance once again at the woods, then asked, "What if I get lost? What if I can't find my way back?"

"Ye don't have to worry about that. She knows the way home. Ye can follow her. Just pick up a stick and give her a couple of whacks on the rump. She'll know what ye want her to do."

"But what if she won't go home?"

"She will, particularly this morning. She's used to being milked earlier than this, and her tits are probably aching something fierce. Why, ye may have to run to keep up with her."

Felicia was still a little leery about going into

the woods—after getting lost just a few days before—but she didn't want to refuse doing something that Sarah apparently considered a simple chore. She turned and walked into the woods, keeping an ear out for the sound of a bell and trying to forget the grizzly tale Sarah had told her about the wolves attacking a child in the broad daylight. Following what looked to be some kind of path, she walked deeper and deeper into the forest, then jumped in fright when a fat sow and her pudgy piglets ran across her path. Watching the pigs as they rooted in a pile of leaves, making very rude sounds with their long snouts, Felicia realized they were tame. Apparently the MacTavishes let their hogs run free, too.

Then Felicia heard the sound, a faint clanging of a bell. She followed the sound, twisting and turning through the woods. She found the cow, a brown-and-white-spotted bovine that was as bony as her owners, beside a pool of crystal clear water nestled at the foot of a hill.

The cow raised its head from where it was grazing, and mooed what Felicia assumed was a welcome. But at that moment Felicia was more interested in the beautiful pool. Since she couldn't see any stream, she assumed it must be spring-fed. She stepped closer, and saw that it was shaped like a bowl and about six feet in diameter, its sides and bottom made of pure rock. Hearing a tinkling sound, she spied the small waterfall that cascaded down the rocky hillside, disappearing behind the brush, then reappearing in a rocky outcrop, then disappearing once again. She looked up, but from where she stood, the water seemed to be coming from out of nowhere.

The cow gave another long moo and then trotted off, without Felicia having to even pick up a stick. Felicia would have loved to stay by the pool for a few more moments, but followed, knowing if she didn't, she might never find her way back.

By the time Felicia and the cow reached the farm, Sarah had finished her washing and was draping it over the zigzag (or worm) fence to dry. As Felicia walked up to her, Sarah said, "Well, I see ye found her."

"Yes, and an absolutely lovely pool."

"Surrounded by trees, at the foot of a hill, with a little waterfall?"

"Yes."

" 'Tis what we call a sink out here, and where I take my weekly baths."

Felicia wondered why weekly and not daily, but she didn't ask. She knew the common people weren't much on bathing. "Where does the water come from? A spring at the top of the hill?"

"Nay, from a stream up there. A part of it just left the main channel and tumbled down and made that hole in the ground. Of course, it took years and years for that to happen. At least, that's what Daniel said."

As Sarah spread another garment on the rail, Felicia recognized her ball gown. A quick glance to the side and she saw her chemise. "Where did you get those?" she asked in surprise.

"Hawk gave them to me this morning. I was supposed to give them to ye, but they looked like they could use a good washing, so I just dumped them in the kettle with everything else."

They had needed a good washing, Felicia realized, seeing her chemise was almost white again. "I guess I didn't get them very clean, washing them in streams the way I did."

"Nay. The only way ye can really clean clothes is to boil them. But I don't imagine ye've done much of that in yer lifetime."

There was no scorn in Sarah's voice. It had been just a simple, matter-of-fact observation. "How much did Hawk tell you about me?" Felicia asked.

Sarah shrugged her bony shoulders and answered, "I imagine everything me and Daniel need to know. Hawk never hid anything from us."

"Do you hate me because I'm a . . ." Felicia hesitated, not wanting to call herself a Tory. It was a degrading Irish word for outlaw that the rebels had picked up to show their contempt for loyalists. That was why she always felt so insulted when Hawk called her one. But she knew that's what Sarah would call her, a Tory.

"Hate ye because ye're a lowlander?" Sarah asked, when Felicia's question trailed off. "Nay. 'Tis not yer fault ye were born rich and pam-

233

pered, no more than it was my fault that I was born dirt poor. The Almighty decided that. It's what ye do with yerself that matters."

Sarah's simple answer made Felicia feel humble. "Thank you, but I didn't mean that. I meant, do you hate me because I'm a Tory?"

"Of course not! Until a few months ago, Daniel and I were Tories ourselves, along with most of the people in these mountains. We never were in favor of this war. We weren't worried about taxes, like the people back east. We had nothing to tax, or any use for those things that were taxed, like that silly tea I was talking about last night. All we cared about was surviving in this wilderness, and protecting ourselves from the Indians. That's why we were loyal to the Crown. The British sent us soldiers, built forts to protect us, made treaties with the Indians, kept the savages under control, or at least tried to. When the rebellion started, the British had to withdraw their soldiers to fight in that war. The rebel government offered us no protection. We were left at the heathens' mercy. They went on the warpath, and these hills ran with blood. The entire frontier was ablaze. There's peace now, but it's not an easy peace. Everyone feels like they're sitting on a powder keg about to blow up."

Felicia had never known where the mountain people stood on the war. She had assumed they were rebels, since they were so fiercely independent. She started to ask a question, but the cow interrupted her by giving a loud, plaintive moo that told her mistress of her distress. Sarah turned to the miserable animal and gave her a whack on her bony rump, saying, "All right. Get to the barn with ye. I'm coming."

As the cow trotted off to the barn with Sarah following, Felicia fell in beside the older woman and asked, "Is that why you changed sides, because the British deserted you?"

"I didn't say we changed sides. Daniel and I ain't rebels either. We just stopped being loyal to the Crown."

"But why?" Felicia persisted.

"It wasn't the British pulling their troops out. We knew that might happen, and it was something that couldn't be helped. We blamed the rebels for that. Then we found out the British were stirring up the Indians, giving them guns and ammunition to use against us, even leading them in their raids sometimes. We know that's always been the way of things here in America — the British using the heathens against their enemies — but it didn't set well with us. We weren't their enemies, like those Frenchies in the last war were. We'd been loyal, despite our Scots' blood. We weren't rebels, and they knew it. Hawk said they did it in hopes the Continental government would send troops to protect the frontier, and that would weaken their armies back east. But the rebels didn't send any troops. They didn't have any to send. We fought the heathens by ourselves. I reckon that's when we decided we didn't want nothing to do with either side. The British turned on us, and the colonials left us to our fate."

Felicia had never been aware of the precarious position the frontier had been left in because of the war, and she could understand their bitterness towards both governments. "Under the circumstances, I can't blame you for not wanting to side with either, but what I can't understand is why Hawk fought for the rebels."

"Hawk does his own thinking. Always has. I was just telling you how Daniel and I feel."

"I presume you know he plans on killing Colonel Tarleton, to avenge the death of his father."

"Aye, he told us all about that. 'Tis fitting justice. An eye for an eye and a tooth for a tooth."

A part of Felicia had yet to accept her fate, and had still been hoping for a way to escape. Since learning that Sarah and Daniel were neutral in this war, she had considered the possibility that they might help her. But Sarah's answer wasn't encouraging. If she and Daniel didn't support Hawk because of their shared political beliefs, they did because of their Scottish heritage, which preached a vengeance that came straight from the Old Testament. But did they actually approve of Hawk's keeping her captive?

"How much did Hawk tell you about my part in this?"

"Everything, I reckon." Sarah stopped in her

tracks, gave Felicia a long, speculative look, then said, "Hawk said ye and that officer who killed his father are betrothed."

"That's not true!" Felicia retorted hotly. "Tarleton and I were just acquaintances. I told Hawk that, over and over, but he refused to believe me. He kept me as bait to lure Tarleton to a meeting with him, then when the colonel didn't come, he said he intended to keep me a prisoner until his father's death had been avenged; that it was his people's way to claim a captive to replace a lost relative. Is that true?"

"Aye, 'tis true."

Felicia's frustration at having no control over her life since Hawk came into it came to the surface, and she threw all caution to the wind, saying, "I know you Scots are vindictive people, but don't you think that's carrying things a little too far?"

Thankfully, Sarah didn't take umbrage. She laughed and said, "Aye, we're vindictive, quick to avenge an insult, clannish, wild, hot-tempered, bullheaded, all those things people say about us, but Scots don't keep captives to replace the lives of relatives. Not even back in the old country, where we did take hostages for ransom. When Hawk told you that, he wasn't talking about us. When he said 'his people,' he was talking about his mother's people. It's their rules for vengeance he's following, not ours."

Felicia was very confused. She had assumed

Hawk's parents had come from the western, mountainous part of Virginia and were Scots-Irish. "Then who *were* his mother's people?"

"The Cherokee," Sarah replied calmly, then, seeing the shocked expression come over Felicia's face and the color draining from her complexion, said, "Hell and damnation, lass! Didn't Hawk tell ye that?"

"He said his father was from Virginia," Felicia muttered.

"Aye, he was. And Hawk's mother was a Cherokee princess. Hawk's half-Indian."

Chapter Seventeen

Still shocked by the news that Hawk was half-Indian, Felicia stood as if frozen to the spot, trying to fully digest what Sarah had revealed to her. Felicia had called him a half-savage without realizing he actually was one. A half-savage! No wonder he had been so defensive about Indians, knew their myths, had such an extensive knowledge about wild animals and nature, and was such an excellent woodsman. No wonder he seemed so intense, so complicated. She had been trying to figure out a white man, while he was part Indian.

Felicia tried to fire up an anger at Hawk for deceiving her, but it didn't work. She remembered the times he had referred to "his people," and everything else he had said. Not once had he lied to her. She had made her own wrong assumptions, and in being so sure she was right, had ignored dead giveaways. Now she could see the Indian influence in his features, and where he had gotten his black, black eyes and light walk. Now she knew why he had no last name. Then she recalled the night he had made love to her, and walked arrogantly away from her in all his naked male glory. His taut buttocks and long legs had been as bronze as his upper torso. Yes, she admitted grudgingly, she should have guessed, or at least been suspicious.

A million questions about Hawk besieged her. She looked about her, then, realizing that Sarah and the cow had gone into the barn, followed them. Sarah was sitting beside the cow on an inverted wooden bucket, her head resting against the bovine's side as she milked it. Felicia rushed up to her and asked, "How did Hawk's father meet his mother? Were they married? Where is she?"

Sarah sat bolt upright on her improvised stool, as rigid as a board, and interjected before Felicia could ask another question, "I ain't telling ye nothing else! Said too much already. Ye have questions to ask about Hawk's parents or him, ye ask him."

"But —"

Sarah whirled about, almost kicking over the milk bucket. "I said, no more, lass. And I mean it! But I have got one more thing to say." Her eyes bored into Felicia as fiercely as Hawk's ever had. "Hawk can't help how he was born, any more than ye or I can. Like I said earlier, it's what a person makes of himself that matters, and

Hawk's the finest man I've ever known. He's loyal, honest, hardworking, steady as a rock, caring. That last may come as a surprise to ye, but Hawk has always been real considerate of Daniel and I. There ain't nothing he wouldn't do for us, and there ain't nothing we wouldn't do for him." Sarah paused, giving Felicia a moment to absorb everything she had said, then continued. "Now Hawk is doing something he feels he has to do. He's a man who takes his obligations very seriously, and Daniel and I respect him for that. It don't matter to us if it's Indian obligations, or white, we aim to support him. Ye can stay here with us — we already promised Hawk that — but I'm warning ye, we won't tolerate ye looking down on him because he's half-Indian, or insulting him."

Felicia had already scorned Hawk as being much below her, and he had overcome her contempt. She realized that knowing he was Indian didn't change anything. Hawk was still the same man she had come to recognize as exceptional, the same man who attracted her wildly. "I don't like what Hawk is doing to me, keeping me a prisoner. I can't deny that, and I won't try to hide it. But I don't look down on him because he's part Indian, not now that I've gotten to know him."

Felicia held her breath, for fear that she had given away too much. She'd die of embarrassment if Sarah guessed she had been intimate with

Hawk. But Sarah wasn't even thinking along those lines, when she answered, "Aye, 'tis like I said. A man should be judged for himself. I'm glad to hear ye judged Hawk right, lass. It will certainly make things easier on all of us. I'd surely hate to have to turn the cold shoulder on ye. I'm enjoying having a woman's company, and someone to talk to. I reckon I haven't chattered this much in years. Daniel never has been much for talking. All Scotsmen are that way, until they get liquored up. Then they're loud and wild. Seems there's no in-between," Sarah finished, then turned her attention back to her milking, clearly telling Felicia that was the end to their conversation.

The last explained why Sarah had been so talkative and open, Felicia thought. She'd been lonely, and was making up for lost time.

"Do ye know how to churn butter?" Sarah asked over her shoulder.

"No, I don't," Felicia admitted.

"Well, today ye're going to learn. And when ye're through with that, I'm going to teach ye how to make potpie and corn pone." Sarah turned halfway in her seat, looked Felicia directly in the eye, and asked, "Do ye have any objections?"

Again Felicia wondered if Hawk would appreciate her more, if she wasn't so useless. She wanted him to admire her so badly, not just her beauty, but her accomplishments. Obviously, he couldn't care less how well she danced, how knowledgeable she was about music and the arts, how pretty her embroidery and handwriting were, how well she played the role of hostess; and Felicia was forced to admit that those things did seem pretty worthless compared to what the frontier women did. "No, I don't object. This may sound strange, but I'd like to learn everything you can possibly teach me."

As soon as the words were out, Felicia held her breath, for fear Sarah would ask why, since Felicia would be going back to her spoiled existence and have no need of those things. But the Scotswoman was much more astute than Felicia gave her credit for. She strongly suspected Felicia's motives, and approved. But Sarah had a little more in mind than simply helping Felicia become more attractive in Hawk's eyes, something of a more permanent nature. From the moment she had laid eyes on Felicia, Sarah had liked her, and Sarah was an excellent judge of character. She had decided then that she would groom the young woman to become wife to the man Sarah loved second only to her husband. Hawk. Not for one minute had Sarah believed Hawk's story that he was exercising his Cherokee prerogative in keeping Felicia hostage. Daniel might have fallen for it, but she knew it was a bunch of hogwash. Nay, Hawk was exercising his *male* prerogative. He wanted Felicia, but the damn fool wouldn't admit it, and Sarah was a firm believer that every man should have a worthy helpmeet.

Sarah hid a sly smile, picked up the bucket of milk, and answered, "All right, lass, I'll teach ye. I'll teach ye everything. But just remember, ye asked to be taught. It ain't going to be fun and games." Sarah rose, then winked, saying, "But from then on, it's up to ye."

As Sarah walked to the barn door, Felicia stared at her back, wondering what she had gotten herself into, and what in the world the Scotswoman had meant by that last cryptic remark.

For the rest of the day, Sarah kept Felicia busy. Not only did she learn how to churn butter, how to start a fire, and the rudiments of frontier cooking, but swept the floor with a crude broom made of reeds, then mopped it with a rag and a bucket of water on her hands and knees. When those chores were finished, she sat at the table grinding a whole sack of dried corn, with a hand grater made from a circular piece of tin nailed to a block of wood, scraping a little skin from her knuckles along with the corn.

Rubbing her aching shoulder muscles, Felicia asked Sarah, who was shelling peas across the table from her, "What do I do with the cobs?"

"Put them back in that sack, along with these shells. We'll take them out and toss them in the pigpen and chicken pen."

"I thought I saw the pigs out in the woods."

"Aye, but we like to lock them up at night, when all the predators come out. They root around in the woods all day, then every evening come home for the slops."

"I'm surprised you let them run wild in the woods like that. There must be a lot of poisonous snakes out there."

"Aye, we've got our share, but that's why hogs do so well out here. Snake bites don't bother them. They're too fat. Poison stays right there under the skin."

After Felicia and Sarah had fed the pigs and locked them in, they gathered the laundry from the worm fence. Picking up Felicia's ball gown, Sarah shook her head and said, "We'll have to start sewing you another dress first thing tomorrow. This poor thing is almost threadbare, except for the lace. 'Tis still very pretty," she observed, fingering the lace almost lovingly. "Ye can use it for your nightgown."

"That won't be necessary. If we're going to make me another dress, I can use my chemise to sleep in."

"Nay, ye'll need a gown, and soon. Fall is coming, and it gets a mite cold up there in that loft. Ye can't wrap your feet in a short chemise to keep them warm."

At the mention of feet, Sarah glanced down at Felicia's, and said, "While we're talking about clothes, why don't you shed those slippers? They're even more threadbare than this dress."

"Then I wouldn't have anything to wear on my feet."

"Hell and damnation, lass! Go barefoot, like I do."

Felicia could never go barefoot in front of someone, particularly outdoors. Why, that would be almost as bad as being naked. It would be too unladylike, too uninhibited, too . . . wanton. But she didn't want to admit that to Sarah, for fear she would take offense. Instead, she said, "Oh, I don't think I could do that. My feet are too tender."

Hearing the sound of hoofbeats, the two women turned and saw Daniel and Hawk riding up to the barn. After they had dismounted, Daniel walked towards the women, while Hawk led the animals into the barn.

As Daniel sauntered up to them, Sarah asked, "Did ye get the traps made?"

"Aye, and we're hungry as bears," he answered in his gruff voice.

"Supper's about ready, but ye ain't coming into my house until ye've washed up and put a clean shirt on," Sarah said sternly, giving Daniel's filthy clothing and grimy hands and face a once-over. "And ye scrape the mud off those moccasins, too," she added. "Felicia just swept and mopped."

Daniel shot Felicia a surprised look, then turned and grumbled as he walked away, "Aye, woman, I know, I know."

As soon as Daniel was out of hearing, Sarah turned to Felicia, and said, "Here, let me have those clothes. I reckon if ye still have questions to ask, this is the best time to catch Hawk alone. But don't dally too long. I'm a mite hungry myself."

Taking the clothing from Felicia's arms, Sarah turned and walked off. For a moment, Felicia stood on the spot, torn by conflicting emotions. Her curiosity about Hawk's parents and past had only grown throughout the afternoon, but she feared confronting him. She knew with a certainty that he wasn't going to like her probing. She had already learned that Hawk was a very private man. But Felicia was determined that she wasn't going to be left in the dark any longer. Squaring her shoulders, she whirled around and walked to the barn.

When she stepped into the dim building, she saw that the horses had already been unsaddled and were standing in a stall, munching a pile of dried cornstalks lying on the ground. But Hawk was nowhere to be seen. A chicken flew from the loft, making her jump in fright, then hurried past her. She looked up, thinking Hawk might be up there, then heard his voice off to one side, asking, "Are you looking for me?"

Felicia jumped and turned to face him. Hawk stood beside a barrel on which a bucket of water was sitting, bared to the waist, his wet skin glistening in the light coming from the open barn door. "Yes, I am," Felicia muttered, unable to tear her eyes away from his magnificent chest.

"Your timing was opportune. I was just getting ready to strip off my buckskins."

A spontaneous tingle of excitement ran through Felicia, then met a cold death when Hawk continued, saying, "You should knock before you enter. This is my bedroom, you know. Unless you're accustomed to entering men's bedrooms unannounced."

Felicia's anger came to her defense. "You know better than that!"

Hawk picked up a piece of tow-linen that served as his towel, and began drying his chest, answering lazily, "Yes, I guess I do know better. You *were* a virgin, weren't you? A virgin wouldn't do that." His dark eyes bored into hers. "But then, it wouldn't really matter if you walked in on me naked, would it? You've seen me that way before."

What in the world was wrong with him, Felicia wondered. Why was he being so insulting? It was almost as if he were deliberately trying to anger her. "Will you please stop talking about that? I came here to find something out!"

"Oh? What?"

"Sarah told me you were half-Cherokee." Seeing Hawk's black eyes flash, Felicia quickly added, "Don't be angry with her. She didn't mean to divulge anything. She thought you had told me."

"And you're here to confirm it?" he asked. "Yes, I'm half-Cherokee."

There was a dangerous, cutting edge to Hawk's voice that should have warned Felicia away, but she ignored it. "No, I didn't come here to confirm it. I believe Sarah. But why didn't you tell me?"

"Why? What difference does it make? I would still have taken you hostage." His dark eyes narrowed as he asked, "Or are you talking about that night in the cabin? If you'd known I was a half-Indian, you wouldn't have let me touch you? Are you sickened by the thought that you've been made love to by a savage? An animal!"

Knowing that Hawk was half-Indian made no more difference to Felicia as a lover as it had as a man. "No! That has nothing to do it! I just want to know why you didn't tell me. You didn't lie to me, but you weren't completely honest with me either. You knew I didn't suspect. Are you ashamed of it?"

"No!" Hawk answered emphatically, then asked in a challenging tone of voice, "Should I be?"

"Dammit, what's wrong with you?" Felicia asked in exasperation. "Why are you acting so hateful? I didn't come here to pick a fight with you. I only came to get the answers to a few questions."

Felicia had no idea that Hawk was feeling the edge of sexual frustration, that the minute she had stepped into the barn, he had become aroused, that her power over him angered him. And now, her knowing that he was an Indian left him feeling vulnerable and defensive. "You got the answer to your question. Yes, I'm part Cherokee."

"No, I didn't get the answer! Not to all of my questions. I'd like to know more about you, about your parents, about your past."

Hawk had no idea that Felicia was falling in love with him, that she wanted to know more about him in the hope of understanding him better. He thought her curiosity insensitive and insulting. "What do you want to know? Am I a bastard? Yes!"

Felicia was so shocked at Hawk's calling himself a bastard and at his fury, that she could only stare at him.

"Now what do you want?" Hawk asked angrily. "The titillating details? All right! My father was a young Virginian who went west one summer to help survey the mountains as a lark. The surveying crew made their headquarters in my mother's village. They were lovers that entire summer. Then he went back east, and I was born. That's it! The explanation of how I came to be half-Cherokee." Hawk paused for a split second, then said, "Now get out! You've got your story."

Hawk's explanation of the circumstances of his birth hadn't begun to touch the tip of the iceberg of what Felicia wanted to know. More questions spun in her head, and she opened her mouth.

"No!" Hawk cut her off before the question could even cross her lips. "That's all I'm going to tell you—ever! Now get out!"

Felicia had never seen Hawk look as furious and dangerous as he did at that minute. Despite her curiosity, she realized it would be prudent to forego any other questions. However, she couldn't just turn and walk out. She sensed she had unearthed painful memories. She wanted to take him in her arms, soothe him, but knew that to make any move of that nature at this time would be sheer folly. She said simply, "I'm sorry, Hawk. I didn't mean to upset you."

As Felicia turned and walked from the barn, Hawk couldn't believe his ears. The uppity lowlander had actually apologized! Also, she had shown no scorn when he had told her the truth of his birth. Could it be possible that it really didn't matter, he wondered.

Then another dark thought came to him. Maybe it didn't matter, because she didn't care enough for it to matter. Hawk felt himself sinking into despair. He could bear her scorn, but not her indifference.

Chapter Eighteen

Later that evening, Hawk appeared at the cabin, hurriedly ate his supper, and left, without saying a word and deliberately avoiding so much as a glance in Felicia's direction. If Sarah and Daniel thought his behavior unusual, they were gracious enough not to show it. As soon as the dishes were done, Felicia excused herself and went to bed, thinking she could use some private time to mull over everything she had learned about Hawk; however, she was so weary from her physical exertions, that she fell asleep almost as soon as she reclined.

The next morning, Felicia was awakened by the sound of roosters crowing. She dressed and climbed down the ladder from the loft, but again the cabin was empty. Remembering how hard she had worked the day before, she ate a bowl of corn mush sweetened with maple syrup before she went outside, knowing that if Sarah worked her near as hard today as she had the day before, she was going to need the nourishment. It was the first time Felicia had eaten the sweetener made from the sap of maple trees, and thought the pleasant taste much lighter than the molasses she was accustomed to.

Going outside, Felicia found Sarah in the kitchen garden beside the cabin. After the two had exchanged a greeting, Felicia looked about her, thinking that the kitchen garden that the slaves tended back home looked nothing like this. There the vegetables had grown in neat rows, with the viny plants carefully staked, but here in Sarah's garden, everything grew at random on hills of mounded dirt with cornstalks serving as stakes. Peas, beans, squash, melons, pumpkins, and potatoes all twined happily about each other, and poking from the ground and through the leaves of these plants, she could see the distinctive feathery leaves of carrots and the broad leaves of turnips. Catching a bright spot of yellow from her side vision, she turned and looked up into the biggest sunflower she had ever seen.

Seeing the stunned expression on her face, Sarah laughed and said, "I reckon ye've never seen a garden like mine."

"Well, no, I haven't," Felicia admitted. "I've never seen so many vegetables crammed into such a small space, much less flowers mixed with vegetables."

"Hawk taught me how to do this. Everything we grow for our table is here. 'Tis how the Cherokees farm, plant everything on big hills so they can't wash away every time it rains. Hell and damnation, I lost more gardens that way every spring. Then, in the summer, they'd burn up! But Hawk taught me how to water them by flooding these trenches between the hills. Before that I was trying to lug water to each plant and killing myself. And when he told me to plant everything all together, I thought he was touched in the head. But he explained when I mixed them up like that, I'd never have to worry about wearing out the soil. And ye know, he's right!" Sarah exclaimed, still amazed that it worked. "Every year, my vegetables grow just as tall and thick as they did the year before, even my tobacco, and ye know, nothing wears out the soil faster than tobacco."

Felicia nodded in agreement. She knew the crop that had made Virginia the richest colony in North America was notorious for completely depleting the soil in just a few years. That's why the majority of tobacco farmers never built beautiful plantation homes, like those in the Carolinas and Georgia, where rice and indigo were raised. When the land was worn out, the tobacco men simply bought more land and moved on. Big plantation homes were impractical. "Wouldn't it be easier to just buy tobacco? I understand the plants get well over six feet tall," Felicia commented, looking about the junglelike garden for the big tobacco plants.

"Not the Indian tobacco I plant. It has smaller leaves and tastes much milder." Seeing Felicia look up once more at the giant sunflower—as if she were afraid it might attack her at any minute—Sarah said, "That sunflower is one of the Cherokees crops, too. They grow them for their seeds. When they're roasted, they taste just like nuts."

"I didn't realize the Indians did that much farming, other than growing corn," Felicia remarked. "I thought they were mostly hunters."

"Nay, they're good farmers. Or they used to be. Hawk said many of the eastern tribes are losing their farming skills, what with buckskins bringing such a good price. The braves would rather hunt than farm."

"The men farm?" Felicia asked in surprise. She had always thought it was the women who performed that chore, that the men thought it beneath them.

"Aye, they prepare the fields and help with the planting. They leave the tending and gathering to the women. But when the game plays out from them doing too much hunting, they have to move on and leave their fields behind. Hawk said he's seen entire fields where the vegetables are just rotting and the corn going to seed, because the Indians deserted them to follow the game. And those were big tribal fields, fields that took those heathens years and years to clear." Sarah shook her head, saying, "That's a shame. Can ye imagine all that work going to waste?"

Sarah's comments about Hawk and the Indians reminded Felicia of one of the questions that had baffled her since she had learned of Hawk's true bloodlines. "I was always under the impression that the frontiersmen hated Indians with a passion."

"We do."

"Then how did you and Hawk come to know one another, and become friends?"

There was a wary look in Sarah's eyes, as she asked, "Did Hawk tell ye about his parents?"

"Yes, he said his father was a Virginian who went west with a surveying team as a lark, that he and Hawk's mother were lovers that summer, then his father went back to Virginia. That's all he told me. He didn't say anything about his mother being a princess."

Sarah laughed and answered, "Nay, he wouldn't tell ye that, because that's *my* way of explaining her high position in the tribe. Indians don't have kings and queens and princesses, but his mother wasn't just any ordinary maiden, either. She belonged to the Wind Clan, the family that the Cherokees pick their leaders from. That's why Hawk is named after a bird, because it's a creature of the wind, and his mother chose Red Hawk, because Cherokees revere birds that soar high in the air. They think the things closest to the heavens and the Great Spirit are the holiest of all creatures."

"Then his name really is Hawk?" Felicia asked in surprise. "It's not just a nickname?"

"Nay, 'tis his real name. We just dropped the Red."

"And the Cherokees actually have clans, just like you Scots?"

Sarah laughed. "Aye, that surprised me, too. But they have only seven, while we must have hundreds of families that claim kinship. And they're just as clannish as we are. Hawk said the Cherokees sit with their own clan at all the tribal ceremonies, and that they could only marry within their own clan. Of course, each Cherokee village had a Wind Clan, so that left them a lot of choices." Sarah paused for a moment, a thoughtful look on her face, then said, "I reckon there are a lot of things we Scots have in common with the Indians. We're proud, independent cusses, tight-knit, stubborn, stern, stoic, vengeful, and . . . aye, violent," she admitted with her usual candor.

And perhaps that was why the Scots-Irish had been the only people able to dig in and stay in these mountains, because they were so much like the Indians themselves, Felicia thought. Which brought her right back to her original query. "You still haven't answered my question. How did you come to meet Hawk and become friends?"

"He came to live with us, after his mother died."

"Died? Of what?"

Seeing the closed expression coming over Sarah's face, Felicia said, "No, please don't refuse to answer my questions. I'm not just being nosy. I want to know more about Hawk, who he really is. I want to understand him better."

Sarah thought that Felicia understanding Hawk better could only be to his benefit, and she suspected she knew why the lass was so interested. Yet, she still didn't want to reveal any confidences. She compromised, saying, "I'll tell ye nothing about his early life with the Cherokees, nor any more about his mother. That's his place to tell ye those things. But I see no reason why I can't tell ye about his life with Daniel and me, since I was a part of that, and it's my story."

"Oh, please do," Felicia answered fervently.

"All right, but we'll work while I talk. I can't abide wasting time. 'Tis sinful. Help me pick these beans."

"I'll be glad to, but I've never picked beans before. Is there anything I need to know?"

"Nay, except try to find beans that are about four inches long. They're the most tender."

As Felicia turned and began searching through the twisted vines on one corn stalk, Sarah deftly

258

picked beans from another stalk, saying, "After Hawk's mother died, when he was ten years old, the resident trader in his village—Ivan MacKensie—and the chief of the tribe decided Hawk would be better off with his father's people, and should go live with them. Hawk didn't want to leave the Cherokees. It was the only life he had known, but his chief ordered him to leave, and he was a good Indian, so he obeyed."

Felicia didn't mean to interrupt, but she was so curious, she had to ask, "Why did the chief order him to leave? Did they not want Hawk in the tribe because he was half-white? Or was it because he was illegitimate?"

"Nay. There are quite a few half-bloods among the Indians, offspring of white traders and pack-horsemen. The Indians accept them completely, regardless of whether the men married the women or not. Hawk said there isn't even a Cherokee word for bastard. He didn't even know people were scorned for things like that, until he came to live with the whites."

"Then why did his chief tell him to leave?"

"I don't know. That's something ye'll have to ask Hawk. But I do know it was Chief Little Carpenter, and he's highly respected by both the Cherokees and the whites, thought to be real wise. Anyway, to get back to how me and Daniel came to know Hawk, MacKensie was a personal friend of ours, and he asked Daniel and I if

259

Hawk could stay with us, while he searched for his father in Virginia. Ye see, this wasn't too long after a long and bloody war with the Cherokees, and feelings were running high against them both here and in Virginia. He was afraid Hawk would draw undue attention, for the lad was as wild and savage as they come. Daniel didn't think much of the idea, but there was something about Hawk that tore at my heart, so I talked him into agreeing."

Sarah dropped the beans she had picked into a small basket sitting on the ground, then continued, "Everyone in the settlement told us we'd made a mistake, that Hawk would murder us in our sleep some night, but he wasn't any danger to us. He resented being here — we knew that — but he obeyed us. I reckon 'cause Little Carpenter told him to. He was a strong, strapping lad and a hard worker, to say nothing of how well he hunted. It turned out he was a big help around here, and eventually he came around, so that he didn't keep so much to himself. I reckon he finally learned to trust us, just like we learned to trust him."

"But wasn't this MacKensie looking for Hawk's father, so he could live with him?" Felicia asked.

"Aye, but it took awhile for MacKensie to track down Hawk's father. He wasn't with the surveying company any more, and they didn't know where he'd gone. It turned out, he'd become a highly respected, wealthy tobacco planter, and he'd also married. Up until then, he hadn't even known that Hawk existed, and he felt he couldn't take the lad into his own home, or even acknowledge him, for fear of what the backlash might do to his family, or how it might affect Hawk. His wife was one of those overly righteous women, not at all the type to take kindly to a child born on the other side of her husband's blanket, to say nothing of him being half-Cherokee. The planter asked if we'd keep Hawk a few more years, until the lad was old enough for him to make arrangements for Hawk to be apprenticed, and we agreed. By then, we had gotten to appreciate Hawk for himself, and were fond of him. We knew he'd never be suited to the life of the planter, and thought it just as well things turned out like they had. But we wouldn't take the money that he offered us to keep Hawk. Hawk was like family. Besides, Hawk always more than earned his keep."

Felicia remembered the three smoking by the fire, and how they had seemed so at ease with one another. It was a companionship that surpassed friendship, just as the look Hawk had given Sarah that night had. Now Felicia knew why she would give anything to have him look at *her* like that. It was a look that spoke of love, of genuine caring. "How long did he live with you?"

"Five years, which was longer than we'd agreed

261

to. Of course, we didn't mind. You can always use an extra hand on the farm, and by then Hawk was doing the work of two men. Besides, we hated to give him up."

"What happened? Didn't the planter want to keep his end of the bargain?"

"Nay, he had all the arrangements made by the time Hawk was twelve, but Hawk didn't want to go east. He said he didn't see any reason for that, that he didn't need a trade, that he could become a farmer, like us. Daniel and I didn't agree. We didn't want to see him having to scratch a living out of these mountains the rest of his life, not when he could have a better life. So we argued back and forth about it for three years, Hawk against us, his pa, and MacKensie." She shook her head. "Hawk can be mighty stubborn when he puts his mind to it."

"Yes, I know," Felicia remarked dryly. "I'm surprised you finally changed his mind."

"We didn't! MacKensie had to go back to Hawk's chief to enlist his help, and Little Carpenter was in firm agreement with us. If the lad was going to live in the white world, he wanted him to get as much learning as he could. He summoned Hawk and ordered him to go. And me and Daniel are sure glad he did. Hawk not only learned a valuable trade, but how to read and write. He even came back talking better."

"Just what trade did he learn?"

"He's a gunsmith," Sarah answered proudly. "And his pa did right by him, too. Apprenticed him with the best German gunsmith in Pennsylvania. It must have cost his pa a pretty penny. But, lass, it was worth it. Ye should see the guns Hawk makes. They're plumb beautiful. Hawk gave one to Daniel, but he won't use it. He's afraid it's going to get scratched. He won't even hang it over the fireplace with the others, for fear the heat might damage it. He keeps it wrapped in a blanket under our bed. Hawk says he's just being silly. That he made the gun for him to use. But Daniel says he can't bear to use the gun for everyday use, even though it shoots better than his old one. So he just uses it for shooting matches. Hits that nail on the head every time. Remind me to show it to ye sometime."

Felicia remembered what the blacksmith and innkeeper had said to Hawk. Now that she knew he was a gunsmith, their words made sense. And it also explained Hawk's broad shoulders and muscular arms, since he undoubtedly spent some time over the forge shaping the barrels for his guns.

Sarah picked up the basket, saying, "I reckon we've got enough beans here."

Felicia felt ashamed of herself. She had gotten so engrossed with everything Sarah had been telling her, that she had only contributed a few. "Is there anything else we need to pick?" she asked, thinking this time she'd pay better. attention.

"Nay, this will do for today," Sarah answered, shouldering her way through the lush garden.

As they walked back to the cabin, Felicia asked, "How long is a gunsmith's apprenticeship?"

"Seven years."

"Then Hawk came back after he finished his apprenticeship?"

"Nay, he stayed east for a few years longer. Daniel and I never expected him to come back. We knew he'd make better money on his guns there. But he said he missed the mountains. I reckon he's like us highlanders. He's got them in his blood."

"And he's been living with you ever since?"

"When he's around, but he ain't been around much. Shortly after he arrived, Isaac Shelby talked him into joining the militia he was getting together to fight the Chickamaugas, who were on the warpath at the time. Then when he got back from that war, it wasn't too long before he joined up with Shelby again to fight in the one against the British."

Felicia came to a dead halt. "Chickamaugas?" she asked in surprise. "Aren't they Cherokees?"

"Renegade Cherokees that have formed their own tribe. They moved south and joined up with the Creeks."

"But I'm surprised that Hawk would fight

against his own people."

"I don't think he would have, if they hadn't been renegades. Their leader is Dragging Canoe, Little Carpenter's son, who disobeyed his father and made war on the whites, and Hawk has some pretty strong feelings about that."

"What feelings?"

"That's another question for ye to ask him. But ye'll have to wait until tonight. He and Daniel went down to the pasture to mend some fences. They won't be back until then."

Felicia turned, looked down the hill to where the cattle were grazing, and could barely see the two men in the distance.

Later that afternoon, the two women were busy making soap beneath the big sycamore tree. Felicia relieved Sarah in stirring the smelly concoction of rendered fat and ashes in the big black kettle over the fire. Turning the big stick over to the younger woman, Sarah said, "Now, remember to stir it in the same direction, so it will come."

Felicia nodded, having no idea what "come" meant, but wishing it would happen soon. Between the heat of the day and the fire, she was wringing wet. "I think this evening I'll walk to that pool I saw yesterday and bathe. Do you think I'll have any trouble finding it?"

"Nay, just follow that path back there," Sarah

265

answered, motioning vaguely to her left. She walked a few steps further away and craned her neck, then said, "I wonder who that is down there, talking to Daniel and Hawk."

Felicia craned her neck, too, expecting to really have to strain her eyes. However, the two men had moved closer to the cabin as they mended the fences, and she could clearly see all three frontiersmen. Noting that Hawk towered over the two men, Felicia asked, "Did you ever meet Hawk's father?"

"Aye, he came for Hawk, himself, to take him to Pennsylvania."

"That must be who he gets his height from," Felicia remarked.

"Nay, 'tis from his mother's side. The Cherokees are unusually tall, well-built people. According to MacKensie, they're the finest-looking tribe in North America, and he should know. He's traded with all of them at some time or another."

"Then Hawk did have a chance to get to know his father a little?"

"Aye. They spent a few weeks together."

"Hawk said he was told of his father's death by a man who witnessed it. How did that man know about Hawk, if his father never acknowledged him publicly?"

"That was MacKensie. He left the Cherokees after the big Indian War in '76, and went to live in Virginia. He and Hawk's father were in the

266

same militia."

"Is that why Hawk became a rebel? Because his father was one?"

"Nay, it didn't have nothing to do with his father. He picked up his rebel beliefs while he was in Pennsylvania, but he didn't join in the fighting until Charleston fell."

The two women fell silent, Felicia stirring and Sarah still gazing intently at the three men in the distance. Sarah wished she could make out who the third man was, but she couldn't distinguish his features. She had an uneasy feeling that he was the bearer of bad news.

Chapter Nineteen

At the bottom of the hill, Daniel had thought the same as Sarah, when he saw the man riding down the narrow road towards him, as if all the demons in hell were after him. As the man's horse came to a skidding halt, rearing as the bit in its mouth was painfully jerked backward, Daniel caught the reins and asked the rider in alarm, "What's wrong, Jed? The Cherokees on the warpath again?"

"Nay," the lanky frontiersman answered, swinging down from his mount, "but I'm expecting that to happen any day now, with the British stirring them up even more since their army invaded the south. Nay, 'tis not the Indians, for a change. The threat is coming from the other direction this time, and Shelby and Sevier are getting an army together to deal with it."

"The other direction?" Daniel asked. "Are ye talking about o'er the mountains?"

"Aye. The British are bringing the war to us, or threatening to."

"Who's threatening?" Hawk asked. "Cornwallis?"

"Nay, his right-hand man, Major Pat Ferguson."

"Why would Ferguson threaten the people out here?" Hawk asked.

"I ain't got time to explain. Shelby can answer any of yer questions later." Jed turned his full attention to Daniel, and said, "Shelby wants to know if he can use yer barn tonight for a meeting with the local men. Yer farm is most central, and he don't have time to visit everyone. If ye agree, I'll spread the word."

"Aye, 'tis agreeable with me," Daniel answered.

"Thank ye, Daniel. Shelby knew his man when he said he could count on ye." Jed mounted his horse and put his heels to its flank, then called over his shoulder as it galloped away, " 'Til tonight, then!"

Daniel turned to Hawk, and asked, "Do ye know of this Major Ferguson?"

"Yes, when I was with Shelby we fought his army twice at Cedar Springs, and beat them both times."

"Is he really Cornwallis's second in command?"

"Cornwallis relies heavily on both him and Tarleton, but many think Ferguson is the more able of the two. He's a Scotsman who came up from the ranks and is known for his toughness, which explains his being nicknamed the Bulldog. He relies more heavily on proven military tactics

269

than Tarleton, who leans towards bold, reckless maneuvers. But don't underestimate Ferguson. He's no ordinary lobsterback officer. Like Tarleton, he's trained his own Tory rangers, who are just as bloodthirsty and brutal as Bloody Ban's." Hawk paused for a thoughtful moment, then said, "But I can't imagine why Ferguson would threaten the people out here. You're not Whigs, at least not enough of you that it should matter."

"Aye, 'tis not our war," Daniel agreed. "But we'll find out what's really going on tonight, when Shelby comes. Until then, we've work to do."

Later that day, when the two men walked into the cabin, Sarah looked up at them from where she was doing some mending, and asked, "What are you doing here? It's not dark yet."

"Aye," Daniel answered, "but we need to eat early, so Hawk and I can clear out the barn a bit before Shelby and the others arrive. He's called a meeting of the local men tonight in our barn."

The color drained from Sarah's face. "Are the Indians on the warpath?"

"Nay, 'tis the British threatening us."

"The British?" Sarah asked in surprise.

"Aye," Daniel answered, then seeing her open her mouth, quickly added, "Nay, woman. Don't ask any more questions. That's all Hawk and I know. Ye'll have to wait until after the meeting to learn more."

As Sarah left her mending and walked to the

pot of stew cooking over the fire, Hawk asked, "Where's Felicia?"

"She's down at the sink, taking a bath."

"Taking a bath?" Daniel asked in surprise. "Why, it ain't even Saturday!"

"Ladies bathe more often than we do," Sarah answered, feeling defensive in Felicia's behalf. "And don't ye say nothing to her about it. She worked hard today. She earned it."

The three ate, with Daniel grumbling about how unhealthy frequent bathing was, while Hawk smiled in amusement and Sarah shook her head in disgust at his ranting. The men had been gone a good thirty minutes when Felicia returned. As soon as she walked in, she asked, "Is something going on? I saw four men riding up to the barn."

"Aye, there's going to be an important meeting here tonight. Something about the British threatening us. All the men from around these parts are gathering with Colonel Shelby."

"Isn't that the man that Hawk fought with?"

"Aye, he's a big leader out here. Everytime there's danger, he gets together a militia." Sarah paused, then said, "Something big is brewing, and I ain't waiting until after the meeting to find out what. Hurry and eat, lass. We're going to that meeting."

By the time Felicia had eaten, it was dark, and she was just as anxious to find out what was going on as Sarah. As the two women walked towards the barn, Felicia remarked, "I'm surprised

271

your men let women come to their meetings. Back home, women aren't allowed at the town councils."

"We ain't allowed, either, not usually. That's why they go out in the barn, so they can be real secretive. Silly men. We always wheedle it out of them anyway."

"But you said *we* were going to the meeting," Felicia objected.

Sarah smiled slyly and answered, "Aye, we are. We're going to sneak out back and listen in. Of course, if ye're afraid of getting caught, ye can go back to the cabin and wait."

Felicia had been liking Sarah more and more, finding her straightforwardness refreshing, and admiring her remarkable endurance and strength, but what the older woman was suggesting was something that made Felicia feel as if they were kindred spirits. She laughed and said, "Sarah, you're a woman after my own heart. No, I'm not going back to the cabin and wait! If you're game, I am."

"Then let's slip into the woods, where we can't be seen going in behind."

A little later, Sarah and Felicia squeezed through a tall bush behind the barn and peered through a crack in the logs. The barn was well lit with candles, and Felicia could see that there were at least thirty men present, sitting on over-turned buckets and barrels, on the ground, on the top rungs of the horse stalls, while others

272

stood and lazily leaned on their long guns. Their ages stretched from youths with peach fuzz on their chins, to old men with long gray beards, men of every possible size and body shape, many smoking pipes and all taking a swig from the jugs of corn whiskey that were being circulated. All except Hawk, Felicia noted, spying the tall frontiersman at the back of the crowd, and watching as he passed the jug from the man on his left to the man on his right.

Then a powerfully built, middle-aged man, dressed in the same worn clothing as the others, stepped to the top of an overturned barrel and said in a loud, authoritative tone of voice, "All right, men! Let's get down to business."

The hum of conversation that had filled the barn died down, until the sound of a pin being dropped could have been heard. "You all have an idea of why I called you here, and I'll try to fill you in on what's been going on," Colonel Shelby began. "About two weeks ago, Cornwallis and his army marched from Camden for Virginia. He separated his army into three columns, Cornwallis taking the easternmost route through North Carolina, Colonel Tarleton and his men, the middle, and Major Ferguson's army, the westernmost. Both Tarleton and Ferguson have been laying waste the ground they've covered, burning and pillaging every patriot's property in their path. You already knew that. But what most of you didn't know was that Ferguson isn't just raiding the big plantations anymore. He's operating in the hill country, and his men have been looting and burning every little Whig farm in the area, farms just like yours, and they've been doing it just for the sheer meanness of it. Not only that, a few of those farmers weren't even Whigs! They were just dirt-poor, hardworking, God-fearing men trying to stay neutral, like a lot of you."

Shelby watched the frowns coming over the men's faces, then continued, "Some of the mountain men closer to the North Carolina border heard about what was happening and didn't like it. It was just a little too close for comfort for them. They organized and started bushwhacking Ferguson's patrols. Ferguson didn't like having the shoe on the other foot one bit. He told some Whig refugees he turned loose to give us a message from him, and I'm going to tell you exactly what he said. Ferguson said if those ambushes didn't stop, he was going to cross the mountains, hang every last one of us, and lay waste the country with fire and sword."

Shelby's words were obliterated by a howl of outrage. He waited until the uproar subsided, then said, "I knew you'd be mad as hornets. So was I. And I'm not sitting still for it. That's why Nolichucky Jack and I are getting together an army to go over the mountains and teach Ferguson a lesson. We sent word to Will Campbell in Virginia to join us with his militia, if he can.

274

Every man counts. Ferguson has well over a thousand men."

"You asking us to join up for six months?" one man asked, "Like regular militia?"

"No, I know a lot of you men can't afford to be gone that long. Besides, with the Cherokees always threatening to go on the warpath, that would be pure suicide. No, we're just going to go over the mountains and make Ferguson eat his words. Those of you who want to stay, can, and those who feel they have to get back, can come home. And I know a lot of you can't even go. You have things more pressing here. Don't feel bad about that. I understand. Besides, someone needs to stay around to keep an eye on the heathens."

"When are you leaving?" another man asked.

"I'm leaving tonight, to do some more recruiting." His eyes slowly moved over the solemn men. "Go home and think it over. If you decide to join up, meet me at Sycamore Shoals in two days. That's our rendezvous point. But remember if you come, to bring your own horse, weapons, ammunition, canteen, blanket, and food. Any man who's served with me knows what that is. A bag of corn sweetened with maple syrup. You can fight on that for weeks. Anything more will just weigh you down."

"Aye," one grizzled old-timer commented, "we ain't like those redcoats, carrying one hundred and fifty pounds on their backs. We move!"

"We certainly do, Jonas," Shelby agreed, then added, "And don't forget to wear a sprig of evergreen in your cap or hat. In battle, even with all the smoke, it's as good as a uniform."

Shelby stepped down from the barrel, signaling that the meeting was over. Preoccupied with their thoughts, the men filed out of the barn with hardly a word, each knowing that if he decided to go, he would have to leave the next day. Shelby walked over to Hawk, and said, "I heard you were back. Sorry you didn't get your man."

Shelby was the only man in Hawk's regiment who knew what personal business had detained Hawk in South Carolina. "He managed to slip away from me, but I'm not through with him yet." Hawk cocked his head and asked, "When did you say Cornwallis and his army pulled out of Camden?"

"The middle of September. I'm not sure about the exact date." Hawk wondered if that was why Tarleton hadn't answered his summons, if the officer had already left Camden when the letter arrived.

"Are you joining me, Hawk?" Shelby asked. "I can sure use a sharpshooter like you."

"I'm afraid not, Isaac. Ferguson isn't my priority. Tarleton is."

"I understand that, but bear in mind that Tarleton is covering Ferguson's right flank. Ever since they began their march, those two armies have never been more than fifty miles apart. And they'll know we're coming, certainly if I can gather the size army I want. Their blasted Tory spies will keep them informed. I'm hoping that Tarleton will come to Ferguson's aid, and we can bag both birds with one shot."

Shelby saw the light come to Hawk's dark eyes, and knew what he was going to say even before he announced, "I'm coming."

Shelby clapped him on the shoulder, and said, "Excellent!" then turned to Daniel and asked, "What about you? Are you coming?"

"I'm still thinking on it," Daniel answered.

Shelby nodded his head, extended his hand, and said, "Thanks for the use of your barn, Daniel. I hope I'll see both of you at Sycamore Shoals."

As the three men walked towards the open barn door, Sarah whispered to Felicia, "Come, lass. And hurry! We need to get back to the cabin before the men do."

As they hurried through the dark woods, Felicia asked, "Who is Nolichucky Jack?"

"John Sevier. They call him that because he lives on the Nolichucky River. He and James Robertson were the first to bring settlers into these mountains, and they're both important men out here."

Sarah and Felicia hadn't been back in the cabin more than a few minutes when Daniel walked in, strode to the fireplace without so much as a glance in their direction, and removed one of the

277

rifles hanging above the mantel. As he set it and his powder horn in the middle of the table, Sarah asked, "Are ye going hunting in the morning?"

Daniel turned and said calmly, "Nay, I'm going to war."

Sarah was so shocked that she was momentarily speechless. Then she exclaimed, "Are ye touched in the head? That's not our war!"

" 'Tis now." As Sarah just stared at him, Daniel continued, "Hell and damnation, woman! You heard what Shelby said." Seeing the surprised expression coming over Sarah's face, Daniel nodded his head and said, "Aye, I know ye listened in. Hawk spied ye two through the cracks. Ye know what eagle eyes he has. And ye know me well enough that I won't sit still for any man threatening me or my property. This farm ain't much, but it's all I got, and there ain't no man going to destroy it, red or white."

"Then wait and see if Ferguson really comes," Sarah suggested. "He may be just threatening."

"Nay, woman! When he sent that message, he was daring us to come, and no true Scotsman turns down a dare. Ye know that! I'm bound to fight him."

Sarah spread her feet and put her fists on her hips, saying angrily, "So you and Hawk are going to go off and leave us two women here all by ourselves, with no menfolk at all?"

"Ye've been left alone before, and ye can shoot a gun as well as I can."

"I ain't talking about protecting myself! I'm talking about the work. That corn is almost ready for picking, there's hogs to be slaughtered, and wood to be chopped for winter. I can't do all of that by myself. Ye're needed here."

"Stop fretting, woman! I'll be back in enough time to do all that."

"Well, ye better be. 'Cause I ain't picking one ear of corn or chopping one log. I'll use the shingles for firewood, if I have to!"

Daniel gasped. The shingles had been planed by hand from a log, a long and tedious chore. "Ye wouldn't do that, would ye, woman?"

"Aye. I would."

There was a determined gleam in Sarah's eyes that told Daniel she wasn't making idle threats. "I'll hurry back," he promised fervently.

Sarah nodded her head curtly, then glanced at the door and asked, "Where's Hawk?"

"Back at the barn," Daniel answered, gathering the things he would take the next morning. "He said he wanted to get to bed early, since we'll be leaving before daybreak. And I think that's a good idea. As soon as I've laid out everything, we'll go to bed early, too."

And that's exactly what they did, since Daniel was lord and master of his home, or at least, Sarah let him think so. And since the couple went to bed early and their bedroom was in the corner of the cabin, Felicia was also forced to retire. She couldn't even keep a candle burning, for fear the light would disturb their sleep.

But Felicia couldn't sleep. Even long after she heard the two snoring below — Daniel loud and rumbling and Sarah soft and regular as a clock — she tossed and turned. She couldn't bear Hawk going away to war without at least telling him goodbye. Her feelings for him, still unidentified, were simply too strong. Felicia knew she would never wake up early enough to see the two men off in the morning, and she hadn't thought to ask Sarah to wake her.

Turning over once more, Felicia noticed something through a slight crack in the logs. Sitting up and peering closer, she realized that there was still a light in the barn. And that had to mean Hawk was still up.

A thought came to her. She could go to the barn and tell Hawk goodbye. But did she dare? she wondered. Go in the dead of night, after he had clearly told her the barn was his bedroom, off-limits to a lady? And then there was that threat he had made the night he had made love to her: that someday he would prove she was still interested in him. In view of those things, it would be terribly brazen on her part.

But Felicia really had no choice. She was motivated by two powerful needs, the need to tell Hawk goodbye before he went to war, and the need to have that terrible aching deep within her satisfied. One was emotional, and the other was very physical, and either way, Felicia knew she had to go. If she didn't, and Hawk didn't return, she'd never forgive herself.

She rose, removed the chemise she slept in, then slipped on the linsey dress. Not even bothering with the neck scarf, she backed down the ladder, then crept across the cabin, and carefully slipped the heavy, wooden bolt on the door back. Stepping outside, she quietly pulled the door to and turned.

For just a split second, Felicia hesitated, then, taking a deep breath to fortify her courage, ran to the barn, her long hair flying about her in wild abandon, as barefoot as the day she was born.

Chapter Twenty

Felicia ran into the barn, then stopped and looked about her. Hawk was nowhere in sight. Noticing that the light seemed to be coming from the back of the building, she started walking in that direction. Hawk's bay, standing in the horse stall nearest her, whinnied a welcome, a soft sound that seemed like a trumpet blast to Felicia's ears. Sudden doubts assailed her, and she was on the verge of turning around and fleeing when Hawk stepped from an empty stall right in front of her, his appearance so sudden that Felicia jumped in fright.

"What are you doing here?" he asked.

It wasn't the sight of his magnificent bared chest that held Felicia to the spot this time, or his hard, accusing question, but rather his penetrating gaze. Then, as his black eyes swept slowly down her length and back up in a devouring appraisal, she was too weak to move. Finally regaining some semblance of composure, she muttered, "I came to say goodbye, since I'll probably be asleep when you leave tomorrow."

Hawk's dark eyebrows arched; then he snarled slightly and asked, "Goodbye? You have a lot of confidence in Tarleton's ability, don't you?"

Felicia hadn't been thinking of Tarleton killing Hawk, for there was no doubt in her mind that if the two met in a one on one confrontation, Hawk would be the victor. But Hawk was going away to do battle with an army, where bullets would be flying everywhere, to say nothing of cannon shot; and that made Felicia acutely aware that Hawk, although very capable, was not invincible. He could be killed as easily as the next man. She had come to try to heal the breach between them, and he was only behaving hatefully again. A sudden anger filled her. "Why do you always do that?" she demanded. "Find another meaning to my words? I wasn't even thinking of Tarleton. I just wanted to show my . . ."

"Concern?" Hawk prompted, when Felicia's voice trailed off.

There was a strong hint of sarcasm in Hawk's voice that only angered her more. "Damn you! You are without a doubt the most currish man I've ever met! Yes, *concern!*" Then, seeing the astonished look coming over his face, she continued, saying in exasperation, "For God's sake, Hawk, I don't hate you! I hate the way you trampled on my rights and robbed me of my freedom, but I don't hate you as a person. And I certainly

283

don't want to see you dead. I just came to . . ." Felicia couldn't bring herself to wish him good fortune, not when he might very well be fighting her brother and their mutual friends. "To wish you a safe return."

Hawk wanted desperately to think Felicia cared, at least a little, but the Indian part of him—the part that had been scorned so much over the years—was still suspicious. "Why? Are you afraid if I get killed, you'll never be reunited with your people?"

Felicia had been angry, but now she was furious. It seemed that no matter what she said or did, he had some caustic retort. She'd put aside her pride to come here, but she'd be damned if she'd crawl. "You're impossible! Rude, argumentative, stubborn. Believe any damn thing you like. To hell with you!"

Felicia was always beautiful, but in her fury she was magnificent, with her eyes flashing golden sparks, her cheeks flushed with anger, and her proud, lush breasts heaving in agitation. Even the reddish highlights of her long hair falling in abandon about her seemed to have taken on more color, surrounding her face and shoulders in a flaming aura. She looked fierce and wild and very desirable, and Hawk was filled with a sudden, overwhelming need to taste her fire, to tame it, to place his brand on her soul forever. As she turned to run from the barn, he caught her shoulder and whirled her around, then brought her soft body flush against his hard one with such force, it knocked the breath from her.

Locking both arms about her in a tight embrace, Hawk muttered, "I'm sorry."

It wasn't Hawk's apology that made the anger drain from Felicia as if a plug had suddenly been pulled from a whiskey keg. It was the smoldering look in his dark eyes, a look that made her bones melt and her heart race. The she felt it—the stirring of his manhood where it pressed against her groin and upper thigh, growing thicker and thicker, lengthening inch by inch, hardening like a rock as the blood rushed into it.

Hawk knew that Felicia was just as aware of the changes in his body as he, and what it meant. "Do you want to leave?" he asked in a thickened voice, wondering if he *could* let her go at this point, or if his physical demands would be too much for him to overcome. He wanted her so desperately he was on the brink of ravishing her, of taking her by seduction, by force, by whatever it took.

Felicia was in no more control of her body than Hawk. There was a terrible burning between her legs. Then, as he lengthened yet another magnificent inch, she felt a scalding moisture slip from her. A flush rose on her face at her body's brazen signal of its readiness. "No," she whispered, "I'll stay."

Hawk felt a surge of sheer exhilaration. He struggled to fight down the powerful urge to throw her to the ground and take her in a rush. He stood perfectly still until he regained control, then slipped both hands down to cup Felicia's delicious buttocks, and lifted her to her tiptoes, so that his bulging erection was pressed dead center between the apex of her legs, and her breasts were pressed against his bare chest.

With Felicia's arms wrapped around his shoulders, they stood chest to chest and groin to groin, gazing deeply into one another's eyes, seeing the awareness of the changes in their bodies there, as well as feeling them. Hawk's shaft grew longer and harder, the blood furiously pounding, while Felicia's breasts swelled and her nipples hardened and rose, mimicking his manflesh. Their hearts raced, and their muscles quivered in anticipation. Their breaths became shorter and shallower, until they made a rasping sound in the air. A faint musky smell surrounded them, the essence of desire on the cutting edge, making their nostrils flare as their excitement rose yet another notch.

Holding her firmly against himself with one hand, Hawk slipped the other around her and lifted her breasts from the gaping bodice, then bent and kissed one turgid, aching tip, making Felicia cry out softly as a bolt of flame seemed to tear through her loins. With his hot, wet tongue laving her breasts, she felt half-mad with passion. Every part of her was crying with need; her heart and head pounding, her breasts and belly stinging, her woman's place a throbbing fire.

Hawk raised his head from his feasting and nuzzled her throat, before whispering raggedly in her ear, "I'm about to burst my breeches for want of you. Have pity on me. Free me."

It seemed a shocking proposal, and terribly exciting. Slipping her hands from around his neck, she reached down. As her hands brushed over his erection as she struggled to undo the laces, Hawk sucked in his breath sharply, then sighed in relief when his manhood burst from the opening.

Felicia cried out herself when Hawk's erection was suddenly freed and seemed to jump into her hands, filling them with his rampant, throbbing maleness. Feeling suddenly very embarrassed and a little frightened at his immense size, she started to pull her hands away, but Hawk's covered them with his own, saying, "No! Hold me. Touch me."

As he taught her the movements, slowly sliding her hands up and down his hot, steely length, Felicia's reluctance and embarrassment were replaced with excitement, as Hawk shuddered and moaned and grew—unbelievably—even longer, his excitement arousing her even further. When he lifted his hands to fondle her breasts, and his fingers brushed over the tender nipples, her knees buckled.

Hawk caught her, picked her up, and, in several swift strides, carried her to the back of the barn where his makeshift bed was. Placing her on her feet beside the blanket thrown over a pile of hay, he supported her with one arm while quickly stripping her, then lowered her to the blanket. She watched with hooded, passion-filled eyes as he slipped off his buckskins, floating on a warm, hazy cloud and thinking what a magnificent specimen of manhood he was, with his broad shoulders, wide chest, bulging muscles, and sleek tendons, all encased in smooth, bronzed skin. She thought every inch of him beautiful, even the powerful muscle between his legs, standing long and proud, the ultimate testimony to his masculinity. Then, as he lowered himself over her, she spread her legs to him, anxious to have that powerful part of him deep inside her.

But Hawk didn't accept Felicia's silent invitation. Not yet. He knelt between her legs and stared at the junction between her thighs so intently, that Felicia blushed at his close scrutiny. Then he raised his dark eyes and, meeting hers, said, "Your hair is even redder down here, and your woman's lips look like dewy, pink rosebuds."

Felicia knew what made those throbbing lips so moist-looking, and flushed even deeper. Hawk leaned over her, his face so close she could feel the warmth of his breath, and asked, "Why do you blush when I compliment you? You're beautiful all over." He kissed the tip of her nose, saying, "Here," then her lips, "and here," then the tip of one breast, "and here," then her abdomen, "and here," then nuzzled the lush silky curls between her legs, "and here." His voice dropped several octaves, "And, God, you smell so sweet, so womanly, so enticing."

Felicia had hardly recovered from the shock of Hawk mentioning such an intimate scent, when she heard him mutter, "And does your honey taste as sweet, as intoxicating?"

The words didn't even have time to register, when she felt Hawk's tongue sliding over her swollen lips. "No!" she cried out, trying to clamp her legs shut.

But Hawk was not to be denied. Her scent was driving him wild, and the brief taste of her nectar was like an aphrodisiac. He held her legs apart while he ravished her with his tongue, her frantic twisting only serving to wildly excite him — and her — all the more.

Felicia was writhing under the exquisite pleasure of Hawk's making love to her with his mouth. Her pulses were pounding, her senses swimming, her blood flowing like liquid fire. She moaned and whimpered, quivering with delight, then gasped when his tongue dipped lower and shot inside her like a fiery dart. Still he continued his sweet-savage assault, bringing her over and over to the very brink, then retreating, until a fine sheen of perspiration covered her, and every nerve in her body felt as if it would snap. "Please, please," she began to beg, not knowing for sure what she was begging for, only knowing she couldn't bear much more of this torture. "I need, I need . . ."

Then Hawk was hovering over her, his face inches from hers, and she could smell her scent on his breath. "Need what?" he questioned huskily. "This?"

Felicia felt no pain when he thrust into her and buried his entire length deep within her. Rather, she felt as if she had suddenly been impaled on a lightning bolt, as every nerve in her velvety sheath seemed to explode. As his mouth came down on hers in a fierce, demanding kiss, and he began his movements, she was jolted with shock wave after shock wave of intense pleasure with each masterful stroke. New, incredibly exciting sensations seemed to be engulfing her from every direction, as his strong tongue moved in perfect unison with his hot, rigid length, in and out, giving and taking, until her senses seemed to be expanding as that terrible, urgent pressure inside her built and intensified. Then, for just a split second, time stood still, and a tingle of fear ran through her, for she sensed she was on the brink of a momentous discovery. Then, in a flash of blinding light, she was thrown upward into a swirling vortex, as her body convulsed in spasms of ecstasy.

Hawk had been determined to bring Felicia to total fulfillment this time. With an iron will, he kept his raging passion at bay, focusing his entire attention on giving her pleasure. When he felt her stiffen and knew she was on the brink of reaching her release, he broke his torrid kiss and raised his head, just in time to see her eyes fly open at the wonder of it. Then, with her rapturous cry in his ears and the feel of her hot spasms contracting on his own feverish, pulsating flesh, he followed her to his own white-hot, shattering release.

As Felicia drifted back down from those rapturous heights, her body still trembling, she opened her eyes and saw Hawk gazing down at her. She was still so awed by the experience she had just had, that she didn't even notice he was smiling with self-satisfaction. "You were right," she muttered. "I had no idea it was like that, so . . . so beautiful."

Hawk had expected Felicia to say satisfying, perhaps exciting or wonderful, but not beautiful. It was a word that seemed to imply something more than physical enjoyment, and hit him with the same impact that a kick in the belly would have, when he realized that the act of making love with Felicia took on a special meaning he had never experienced with another woman. He had never been so unselfish with his partner, nor had he ever experienced the strange satisfaction that making her happy had given him. Even his climax had been more intense.

"Is it always that way?" Felicia asked, totally unaware of the earthshaking thoughts Hawk was having. "Time after time?"

The feel of Felicia stroking his sweat-slick shoulders, combined with the husky timbre of her voice, distracted Hawk from his disturbing thoughts. He looked down at her luscious lips, still swollen from his torrid kiss, and his desire rose, along with his manhood, still inside her depths. Seeing her eyes widen as she felt him stir, Hawk kissed her lips lightly, then said, "Why don't I just show you the answer to that question?"

Felicia's heart quickened in anticipation. She found she couldn't refuse the prospect of feeling those exciting, wonderful things again. Why, he was offering her a taste of heaven. "Yes, why don't you?," she muttered, then boldly rubbed her breasts against the damp mat of hair on his chest.

Hawk gave her what she wanted, and more. He made love to her over and over, again motivated by a need to place his brand on her irrevocably, each time making her soar higher and bringing her to a more intense, mind-boggling release.

She was snuggled against him and dozing, when he whispered in her ear, "It's getting late. You'd better go back to the cabin, before Daniel and Sarah rise."

Felicia didn't want to leave. She could have lain in Hawk's strong arms forever. But she really didn't want the older couple to know that she and Hawk were lovers. Strangely, it had nothing to do with shame. What she and Hawk had shared had seemed so right. It was just that it was so new, so special, so very private.

They dressed, and Hawk walked with her back to the cabin. Before it, he dropped a kiss on her forehead, then turned to leave.

Felicia caught his arm and said, "Please be careful."

After that night, there was no doubt in Hawk's mind that he could command Felicia's passion, but even after her remark about his lovemaking being beautiful, he still had doubts on just how much she cared for him as someone other than a lover. Her caring at that moment seemed so genuine that it warmed him deep down, a warmth that had nothing to do with passion.

"I will," he promised, then took her in his arms and gave her a long, fierce kiss.

Felicia's senses were still spinning from that kiss, when Hawk turned and walked away into the darkness.

Chapter Twenty-one

In the days that passed after Hawk and Daniel left, Felicia found out just how terribly hard frontier life could be. It was no longer a matter of learning a few household skills so she could impress Hawk. It was a matter of survival, and not for one minute did Felicia consider leaving Sarah with the entire burden. Felicia had come to admire and respect the feisty Scotswoman too much for that. So when Sarah took over her husband's work, Felicia relieved the older woman of her chores, as soon as Sarah could teach her and she could perform the tasks.

Felicia did all of the cooking, and thanked God that it was simple fare: cornmeal mush or johnnycake for breakfast, corn pone for the midday meal, and potpie for supper. She also did all of the cleaning and laundry, as well as lugged the water from the stream, milked the cow, fed the chickens and the horse, collected the eggs, and slopped the hogs. She tended the garden, churned butter, made cheese from the clabber and candles from tallow. She even learned to work the spinning wheel, but the loom was much too complicated for her. The only thing that she excelled in was sewing herself a dress. Because of the embroidery her mother forced on her in her earlier years, her stitches were much finer than Sarah's.

By the end of the week, Felicia was exhausted. Every muscle in her body ached, and she thought she could sleep a week straight through, she was so tired. She awoke one morning and couldn't force herself to rise. She simply didn't have the energy left for one more day's hard labor. It just wasn't in her. She wasn't meant to be a frontier woman! She was cut from an entirely different pattern.

Memories of her previous life filled her mind, and for the first time since Hawk had made her captive, tears came to her eyes. She wanted to go back home to her soft, luxurious way of living, wanted it desperately. She couldn't endure anymore of this. She couldn't!

"Felicia? Are ye awake, lass?"

Felicia jumped at the sound of Sarah's voice coming from the cabin below, then answered, "Yes, I'm awake."

"Do ye think ye could help me a bit in the orchard today? The apples are ready for picking."

It was the final straw. At the thought of yet another backbreaking chore, the tears that had been threatening spilled down Felicia's cheeks. Then she heard the door open and close, and thanked God that Sarah hadn't expected an answer. For the love of her, she wouldn't have been able to force it through the lump in her throat. Then the tears came in earnest, with wrenching sobs. The crying jag was a luxury she really couldn't afford. When it was over, she felt even more exhausted.

Then Felicia remembered her great-grandmother, and the stories the old woman had told her about her bondage. Her great-grandmother had started her long day's work hours before the sun rose, and continued them well into the night, and they had certainly been as hard — or harder — than anything she was doing. Besides that, the poor woman had to fend off every male on the premises, from the other servants and field hands to the man who held her papers. And she had been beaten several times by her owner's jealous wife. At least Felicia didn't have those indignities to deal with. The more Felicia thought about her remarkable ancestor, the more determined she became to emulate her. If her great-grandmother could survive her ordeal, then she could hers, Felicia decided. The same blood ran in her veins; she was fashioned of the same bone and tissue. But more important, she had her great-grandmother's fierce will. Then, calling upon that resource, Felicia rose from her bed and dressed for the day.

It wasn't until midday that Felicia finished her more pressing chores and walked to the orchard. She found Sarah on a crude ladder made of hefty sticks tied to two poles, picking apples. Seeing her approach, the older woman said, "Pick up the ones that have already fallen on the ground, will ye, lass? Put the stunted runts in that basket to the side. We'll use them to make cider."

The ladder didn't look any too steady. What if Sarah should fall? Felicia wondered. Old people's bones were very brittle and prone to breaking. "Why don't I go up there, and you come down here?" Felicia suggested.

"Nay, lass. The bottom of this ladder isn't even, and it has a tendency to wobble a bit. Ye might loose yer balance and fall, but I'm used to it. Nay, if ye'll just get those on the ground, it will be a big help. Why, I reckon half are down there, after that big wind storm we had last night."

Felicia had been so exhausted, she hadn't even noticed the storm. Now she noticed that there were a few broken limbs along with the fruit. Then, taking note of the delicious odor of ripe apples hanging in the air, she asked, "May I have one?"

"Hell and damnation, ye can eat a dozen, if you like. But ye don't want to eat too many, for fear of getting the runs."

Felicia picked up an apple, checked to make

sure it didn't have any wormholes, then bit into it, savoring its crispness and sweet juice. Watching her, Sarah remarked, "Aye, there's nothing as good as a fresh apple. I could hardly wait until our trees were old enough to bear. The turnips just didn't ease my craving."

"Turnips?" Felicia asked in surprise.

"Aye, that's what we ate until the apple trees started bearing. Raw turnips. We grew a patch in the corner of the garden, just for that purpose."

As Felicia started picking up the apples on the ground and putting them into a basket, she remarked, "I think there's something wrong with the fireplace. It seemed to be smoking."

Sarah sighed in disgust, and said, "Oh, the blasted chimney probably needs cleaning again, and that means we'll have to let the fire die out, instead of banking it every night."

"How do you clean it? Are there chimney sweeps out here?"

Sarah laughed and said, "Aye, there are. There ain't a farm out here that doesn't have several of them living on the place." Seeing the puzzled expression coming over Felicia's face, she laughed and said, "We use chickens for chimney sweeps. Just drop them down the chimney, and all that wild flapping they do with their wings sweeps the soot away."

"It doesn't hurt them, dropping them all that distance?" Felicia asked, her love of animals coming to the fore.

"Nay, but I'll admit it upsets them. You've never heard such furious cackling in your life, when they come tearing out of the cabin as black as a raven, and I've known them not to lay eggs for a day or so after. Of course, that may have been out of pure spite."

Felicia couldn't help but laugh. "I can't say I blame them. I'd be indignant, too."

It was mid-afternoon by the time they had finished picking the apples. Felicia looked at the twenty or so bushels with dread, knowing that by the time they carried them down the hill to the cabin, her aching back would really be aching. She bent to pick up a basket, saying, "Well, I guess we might as well get it over with. They aren't going to sprout feet and walk down, are they?"

"Nay, lass. We'll bring the wagon up here and take them down."

"Are you talking about that old wagon that sits behind the barn? I didn't think it even rolled."

"Aye, it rolls. One wheel is a little warped, but it rolls. Do ye want to go down with me to hitch it up to the horse, or wait here?"

"I'll wait here," Felicia answered, thinking she'd welcome a few minutes of rest.

As Sarah walked down the hill, Felicia sat on the ground beside one of the baskets and helped herself to another apple. Just as Sarah was leading the horse from the barn, Felicia saw a wagon with two women drive up. The women talked to Sarah for a few minutes, then turned the wagon and drove back down the narrow, rutted trail they had come on. When Sarah appeared at the top of the hill a little later, Felicia asked, "Who were those women?"

"They live on farms around here. Said they dropped by to see if we'd heard any news from the menfolk, but that was just an excuse to nose around. Those two are the biggest gossips in the settlement. 'Twas ye they were really wanting to know about. Ye were seen at the station with Hawk. Word's spread all over these mountains that he brought a strange woman back with him."

"What did you tell them?" Felicia asked anxiously.

"Well, I figured ye wouldn't want them knowing the real story, that Hawk just yanked ye up and brought ye out here against yer will."

"No, I wouldn't," Felicia admitted. "It's rather humiliating."

Sarah nodded her head, making the limp brim on her sunbonnet bob up and down, then said, "Besides, if they knew the truth, they'd just look down on Hawk for acting like an Indian. Lord knows, he had to work long and hard enough to overcome their suspiciousness and scorn as it is. Couldn't see any reason in getting anything else stirred up. So I told them ye were a distant cousin of Hawk's, whose home back east got burnt down and family killed by those soldiers the menfolk went after. I told them Hawk had brought ye up here to live with us until ye could get in touch with some other kinfolk, when things kinda settled down a bit. That way, when Hawk takes ye back, they won't think it strange."

"And they actually believed I was Hawk's distant cousin?"

"Sure they did! They know his pa is a lowlander from Virginia, and he's bound to have kinfolk. And ye sure ain't one of us. One look at ye is all it takes to know you're a fine lady."

Felicia scoffed and asked, "And how would they know that? Look at me! I'm dressed the same as you, my hands are just as dry and red. Why, I'm even barefoot!" she added, looking down with disgust at her dirty feet poking from beneath the hem of her skirt. "Maybe they'd know if they talked to me, but not by just looking at me."

"Nay, lass, they'd know. There are some things that just can't be hidden. It's the way ye walk, the way ye hold yourself. Ye're gentry, not common folk. It stands out on ye like a sore thumb."

Sarah climbed from the wagon, and the two women loaded the baskets of apples onto its bed. As they rode down the hill to the cabin, Felicia asked, "How long do you think the men will be gone?"

"I don't know, lass. Another week, maybe another month. Maybe even longer. It's hard to tell with war."

"Have you ever been left alone before?"

"Aye, once when Daniel went to fight Indians."

"How in the world did you manage by yourself?"

"I didn't manage as well as I have this time. Ye've been a big help, lass. And then that was in the springtime, plowing time. I couldn't do that. It takes a man's strength to hold that plow down in the dirt. So we didn't have any corn crop that year. We almost starved to death that winter."

"Couldn't Hawk help you?"

"That was before he came. And if we'd known then what he taught us later, we could have still gotten in a fall crop."

"Then growing that fall corn came from the Indians, too, like how you grow your garden?"

"Aye. Hawk said the Cherokees have three corn crops, one in the spring, one in the summer, and one in the fall. But the fall crop makes the best grain. We tried to get others around here to put in a fall crop, too, but they didn't want to have anything to do with it 'cause it came from Hawk. They were just being mulish. Look at all the other things we learned from the Indians. Why we wouldn't have nothing to live in, if we hadn't copied their cabins, and most of the food we eat came from them. Why, our men have even taken to wearing buckskin breeches, and everyone wears moccasins in the winter."

"I thought Indians lived in wigwams," Felicia remarked in surprise.

"Not the Indians down here in the south. They live in log cabins, just like us, except Hawk said they have little separate cabins for cooking, to cut down on the heat in the summer. They call them hot houses."

Felicia was stunned. All of the plantations had separate kitchens. Had the colonists gotten the idea from the Indians? "You said the others were suspicious and scornful of Hawk. Did they ever try to hurt him?"

"Nay, they just gave him hateful looks. Of course, Hawk kept his distance, when he could. Anytime any of them came around here, he disappeared in the woods. He didn't trust them anymore than they trusted him."

"But that's changed now, hasn't it?"

"Aye, since he came back. In the first place, he looks more like a white man, since he let his hair grow and started wearing our clothing. Clear up to the day he left here, he dressed like an Indian, with his head shaved except for a scalp lock and their buckskins. You know they don't wear breeches. They wear leggins that come up to their hips, and a little flap of material over their privates, and in the summer, that's all that boy wore, his breechcloth. Except by the time he left, he wasn't a boy any longer. He was

303

coming into his manhood. "Twas downright embarrassing sometimes, him running around half-naked, particularly when we went to the station for supplies. The females couldn't keep their eyes off him. Besides being a fine-limbed man, Hawk's well hung."

Sarah glanced over and saw the red flush on Felicia's face. "Sorry. I didn't mean to embarrass ye. I keep forgetting ye're not a mountain woman. We talk pretty blunt. But the fact is, that Hawk looking more like a white man helped the others accept him better. And then he joined the militia against the Chickamaugas. A lot of the men came back saying they were sure glad he was on their side, he was such a fierce fighter. Even the ones who didn't go on that expedition are coming around, since Hawk's helped with a few barn-raisings and fixed a few of their guns for them for free."

"Then he's changed?"

"Aye, but there's still a lot of Indian in him, and that worries me."

Felicia ducked a low limb that hung over the path, then asked, "Why?"

" 'Cause if he stays out here, he's bound to fight Indians. That's the law of the mountains. And I don't know if Hawk can fight his own people. The Chickamaugas were renegades, outlaws among his people, too, so fighting them was different. But his own?"

The two women fell into silence, each pondering Sarah's question and bouncing hard on the wooden seat each time the warped wheel made another revolution. Then Sarah said, "That was why I was so glad Hawk wasn't here those bad years we had with the Cherokees. Seventy-six was so bad, we had to go to the station three times. Of course, it was Dragging Canoe and all of those younger, hotheaded chiefs that were stirring up everything, the same ones that eventually split from the Cherokees, but we didn't know that at the time. They were just Cherokees hell-bent on destroying us, and we were bound to kill them on sight. I don't think Hawk could have done that, and feelings were running so high at the time, there's no telling what the others would have done to him if he'd balked. Hanged him, I guess, since they know a Cherokee would rather die at the stake than suffer the degrading death of being hung."

Had that been why Hawk had been so determined to escape Tarleton, Felicia wondered, then commented, "I wondered if the fort had ever been attacked by Indians. Hawk told me there were fifty to sixty families in the settlement. It didn't seem big enough to hold that many people."

"It ain't. But then it don't have to. There's always those mulish cusses that won't leave their homes no matter what, and that's usually where they're found afterwards, too, in the smoking embers of their homes. Of course, there's those

305

times when ye have to fight from yer homes, if they catch ye by surprise, but if ye have a warning, it's pure foolish to stay. I sure dreaded going to the station though. It was terrible, so crowded ye could hardly move, particularly since everyone brought their animals with them. The gun smoke was so thick sometimes, ye'd think ye were going to choke to death on it, and it made yer eyes water and your nose run. Animals didn't like it either—with all the noise from the guns—and they made a terrible racket. Chickens squawking, cows mooing, pigs squealing, horses whinnying. Then there was the kids crying and the wounded moaning, or hollering when they had to have a bullet dug out of them. No matter how many times I heard that scream, it made my hair stand on end. Of course, ye couldn't sleep for all the noise, even if ye were used to sleeping on the hard ground with just a blanket. Besides all the noises, it stunk something awful, between the people and the animals. We always ran out of water before we did food. We'd go for a day or so, hoping the Indians would give up the fight. Then when our tongues were so swollen we couldn't keep them in our mouths, some brave soul would volunteer to make a run to the creek to try to bring back a couple of pails."

Felicia was appalled at the hardships the settlers had had to endure. "How long did that last?"

"A month was the longest we ever sat there, but that seemed like forever to me. Everyone was a little stir-crazy, men fighting at the drop of a hat, women ready to tear out each other's hair. Then, when we went home, we never knew what we'd find. Between '76 and '79, our place was burnt to the ground three times, everything, even the crops. 'Twas nothing left to do but rebuild and replant."

"How could you do that, over and over? Why didn't you just leave?"

"And go where?" Sarah asked in her usual forthright manner. "This is the only place we can get free land and own our own homes. You can't do that in Ireland, where me and Daniel come from when we first married. Hell and damnation, we were starving to death there!"

"You'd rather take your chances with the Indians?"

"Aye! I would!"

Sarah brought the wagon to a stop beside the barn, then turned in her seat, and looked Felicia directly in the eye. "We mountain people are stubborn. We're not leaving. Nothing is going to chase us off, not Indians, not hardships, not famine, not nothing man or nature can throw at us. We've dug in now, lass, and we're staying."

Yes, Felicia thought, the frontiersmen were a breed unto themselves, rugged, fierce, brave, tenacious, a people who would never move backwards, but always forward, forging and shaping a new nation from the wilderness. As she had come to know Sarah, she had come to admire her on a personal basis, but she had to admit to a grudging admiration for all of the people on the frontier. What they lacked in social graces and education, they made up for in guts, determination, and fortitude.

The two women unloaded the apples and put the baskets into the barn, for lack of a root cellar. As they walked back to the cabin, Sarah commented, "I don't suppose ye know how to shoot a gun."

"No, I don't," Felicia admitted. "Why?"

"All that talking about Indians got me to thinking, it might be wise to teach ye how to use one."

A shiver ran over Felicia at the thought of being attacked by a bunch of howling savages. "But what good will that do us? You've only got the one gun, and you'll be using it."

"Nay, ye forgot the gun Hawk gave Daniel."

"Daniel didn't take it with him?"

"And risk getting it scratched?" Sarah asked in mock horror. "Nay, lass, 'tis still here, under our bed. And I won't hesitate to use it, if I need to."

By that time, they had entered the cabin. Sarah walked straight to her bed, bent, and pulled out a long object enclosed in a blanket.

Carrying it to the table, she unwrapped it and said, "I've been meaning to show it to ye."

As Sarah uncovered the gun, Felicia's breath caught. She had been around guns her entire life, for her father and brother were both hunting enthusiasts and didn't spare any expense on their hobby, but she had never seen a more beautiful gun. The metal of the long barrel gleamed with a bluish luster, and the brass and silver inlays on the butt, stock, and patch plate, all intricately scrolled, gleamed in the light. Even the wood shone with a rich patina, and the butt, except for the raised cheekplate, was elaborately engraved. "I don't blame Daniel for not wanting to use it," Felicia said in an awed voice. "It's beautiful. Why, a gun like that would cost a small fortune back east."

"Aye. Hawk said the wood itself was prized, that it came from a tiger maple. They don't grow around here. See how it's striped. But that's not why Daniel treasures it so much. 'Tis that Hawk labored so hard over it for him. We've seen other guns Hawk has made. They're superior, too, but none as purely pretty as this one."

Felicia thought about the hours Hawk must have spent over the hot forge shaping the barrel, then carving the butt and stock, to say nothing of all the tedious engraving and scrolling. "Yes, it's truly a labor of love," she remarked, finding it hard to believe that the same sensitive man who fashioned this gun could be so fierce and unyielding.

Tears shimmered in Sarah's eyes. "Aye, 'tis that. Hawk's way of telling Daniel he loves him."

Almost reverently, Sarah wrapped the gun back up, saying, "I'll teach ye how to shoot with my gun. We won't disturb this one anymore, unless we absolutely have to."

Felicia fervently hoped that would never happen.

Chapter Twenty-two

A month later, Felicia had just finished making a batch of soap beneath the big sycamore, when Sarah walked up the hill from the fields and removed her damp sunbonnet. Fanning herself with it, Sarah sighed, "Whew! It's hot as hades today."

Felicia answered, wiping her brow with her dingy apron. "I thought we'd seen the last of the warm weather when we had that cold spell last week."

"Nay, 'tis just our usual Indian summer. We always have a warm spell before winter."

"Why do you call it Indian summer?"

" 'Cause the Indians always use it to get in one last raid before winter."

Felicia looked uneasily at the woods all around them, asking, "Always?"

"Nay, not always. I shouldn't have frightened ye like that. 'Tis just one of their favorite times of the year to go on the warpath. Besides, if anything was brewing, the men who stayed behind would alert us. With most of the menfolk gone, they're keeping an even closer eye on things than usual."

Feeling reassured, Felicia bent and examined the wooden tray of soap cooling on the ground. She frowned and said, "It's not hardening like that last batch we made. Did I do something wrong?"

"Did ye add salt right before ye poured it?"

Felicia sighed in self-disgust, answering, "No, I forgot. Now I suppose I'll have to restart the fire and melt it again."

"Nay, lass. We'll use it for washing."

"Why did I have to make it, anyway? We still have a lot left from that last batch we made."

"That's one thing I like to get ahead of before winter comes. I purely hate having to stand out here in the cold."

Speaking of preparing for winter reminded Felicia of something else. "I saw you in the cornfield a little while ago. Were you checking to see if the corn is ripe again?"

"Aye." Sarah paused and a downcast expression came over her face. " 'Tis ripe."

"How do you know?"

"The silk is turning brown, and I peeled back the husks and pinched a few kernels. The liquid is no longer clear. 'Tis milky, ready for picking."

Felicia looked down at the big cornfield. At that moment it seemed to stretch out forever. "Are we going to pick it?" she asked with dread.

"I don't know, lass. It would be a big job for

us. Daniel planted heavier than usual, thinking Hawk would be here to help him. He knew his enlistment would be up by then."

"Can't we just leave it in the field?"

"Aye, but it wouldn't be good for nothing but feed and hominy. That's our biggest and best grain crop out there, the one we use to make our whiskey, and our whiskey is the only thing we have to trade with, besides a couple of barrels of maple syrup that don't bring much. Our fall corn crop is so important to us, 'tis the only one Daniel takes to the miller to have ground. Ye know, that's costly. The miller takes a tenth of everything he grinds. That's why they're always the richest person in any community."

And the most resented, Felicia thought, remembering how even her father had complained about the high prices the miller had charged for his services. "Well, if it's that important, we'll just have to get out there and do the best we can."

Sarah grinned at Felicia's spunk, then said, "Aye, we'll give it our best, even though I told Daniel I wouldn't touch an ear. But we'll wait a few more days. Maybe the men will be back by then."

Felicia knew Sarah was worried about the men, just as she was. Both women had expected them back before then, but neither expressed their concern openly.

Just as Felicia was aware of her worrying,

Sarah was aware of Felicia's. Trying to distract the younger girl from her dark thoughts, she said, "Look out there, lass. Ye'll never find a prettier picture."

From their high point on the hill, Felicia looked out at the hills rolling off into the distance. Through a break in the low-hanging dark clouds, a brilliant shaft of sunlight streamed through to touch the multicolored forest below. "Yes, it is," she replied in awe. "I wish there was some way I could capture it, not just paint it, but catch it just exactly as it is at this moment."

"Ah, lass, ye're really dreaming now. But wouldn't that be something, if ye really could?"

"These mountains are absolutely beautiful in the fall," Felicia remarked. "I've never seen such vibrant reds and yellows and oranges. It's the maples, I guess. We don't have them where I come from."

"Aye, 'tis beautiful. The only thing prettier is spring, when everything is in bloom. When I have a minute or two, I like to pull my rocking chair out here under the tree and just rock and look. Even in the summer, I find it relaxing."

"You should build a veranda, like we do in the low country, or at least a covered porch to sit on," Felicia suggested. "It's so cool out there in the warm weather, that we spend the better part of our days on ours. Then you could just leave your rocking chair right there on the porch, except in the winter."

A dreamy look came over Sarah's face. "Aye, and I could sit out and watch a thunderstorm. I've always wanted to do that."

"Then have Daniel build you one."

"Nay, he wouldn't. He's a very practical man. We don't really need a porch. A place for just relaxing?" she scoffed. "Nay, he'd think it was silly."

"But he'd probably enjoy it just as much as you," Felicia pointed out.

"Maybe, but I'd never be able to convince him of that. He's even more stubborn than he is practical." For just a moment, there was a wistful look on Sarah's face. Then it was replaced with a determined one, as she said, "But Daniel ain't here today, and I'm calling a holiday. I'm going to get my rocker and spend the rest of the afternoon out here under the tree."

"Then we're not going to do any more work today?" Felicia asked in surprise.

"Nay. We deserve a little time off."

"In that case, do you mind if I go down to the sink? I've been dying for a long, leisurely bath."

"Nay. Ye do what you enjoy, and I'll do what I enjoy. The rest of the day is ours."

A few moments later, Felicia was walking down the path to the sink, carrying a bar of lye soap and a piece of tow-linen for a towel, thinking how wonderful it felt to have a few hours to just relax. It occurred to her that before she came to the mountains, she had never appreciated her free time, but then that was all she'd had, time on her hands to try and fill with some frivolous pursuit. Much to her surprise, she found the hard work she had been doing rewarding. It gave her a sense of self-esteem she had never experienced, and also made her feel physically better, once her body had become accustomed to it. It was just a shame that there wasn't a happy medium between the two extremes!

Hearing a furious chattering, Felicia came to a halt and watched two male squirrels fighting, or what they considered fighting. They chattered and flipped their tails angrily back and forth, as they charged down the trees headfirst, then tore across the ground, scattering crisp fallen leaves everywhere, before they scampered up the trunk of another tree to squawk at one another indignantly, then back down again. Felicia noted that despite all of their furious antics, they were very careful to keep at least one tree's distance, proving that they were mostly bluff. Finally the challenger gave up and bounded away, while the winner stood on his hind feet and gave a victorious cheering call.

Felicia continued down the path with an amused smile on her face, then, remembering the bear that had been mostly bluff, felt a wave of longing for Hawk so powerful it brought tears to her eyes. She was shocked at how much she missed him. She spent hours on end thinking

316

about him, reliving every moment they had spent together. She knew her life would never be the same again, that he had awakened something deep inside her, something much more than just passion; and the thought of going back to her former life and never seeing him again was unbearable.

When Felicia reached the pool, she undressed, twisted her long hair and arranged it into a knot on top of her head, and slipped into the waist-high water, skimming back the scarlet and gold leaves floating there with her hands. She washed quickly, then lay back against the stone rim and gazed up at the brilliantly colored canopy above her, still preoccupied with sorting through her feelings, but stubbornly refusing to admit to her love for the rugged frontiersman, who had come into her life so unexpectedly. The only sounds were the chirping of the birds and the tinkling of the little waterfall that fed the pool.

"Your skin is going to wrinkle if you stay in there much longer."

Felicia shot to her feet at the sound of Hawk's voice, and whirled around to face him. Seeing him standing beside the pool, she felt a tremendous bolt of sheer joy. It was then that she could no longer hide the truth from herself. She knew she loved him, and the realization brought another surge of intense happiness.

Quickly, she looked him over, to ascertain that he was not wounded or hurt. She had forgotten how tall he was, how broad his shoulders were, how robust and virile he looked, or how incredibly handsome he was, she thought, her eyes coming to rest on his face. Then she became aware of his devouring stare and remembered that she was naked. A flush rose from the tip of her toes to her head.

Hawk had wondered how Felicia had fared on the harsh frontier, and feared that he'd find her sickly-looking. She looked a little slimmer, from the conditioning of her muscles, but otherwise even more beautiful than he had remembered. After reassuring himself that she was fit, his eyes had locked on her proud, high breasts, the water drops on the pink nipples glittering like jewels in the dabbled sunlight. Then, noting her skin flushing, he looked up at her face, and said, "You're blushing."

"Yes, I am," Felicia admitted, belatedly crossing her arms over her breasts.

Hawk chuckled. "Why are you embarrassed? I've seen you naked before. And not just the top half. I've seen all of you."

As his eyes dropped, Felicia wondered how much he could see through the water. "That was different," she answered nervously.

"Why?"

"Because this is broad daylight, and I'm taking a bath. It just isn't . . . seemly," Felicia finished for lack of a better word. "Now, go away."

Hawk ignored her command and answered,

"Maybe you'll feel more at ease if I'm naked, too," He grinned. "I'll join you."

"No!" Felicia cried, but it was too late. Hawk was already stripping, and despite herself, she couldn't help but stare as he revealed each magnificent male inch. There was only one thing different from when she had seen him nude before. Unaroused, his manhood didn't look as blatantly intimidating, but she still found his male beauty exciting, and when he walked towards her, the hard horseman's muscles in his thighs rippling, she felt a warmth deep in her belly.

He waded into the pool and stood before her, his broad chest with its triangular pelt of dark hair at eye level. She could feel the heat from his body through the water, and was acutely aware of his nearness. Her mouth turned dry with expectation.

"Where's the soap?" Hawk asked, and Felicia felt a wave of disappointment. "There," she answered, pointing to the mushy bar lying on a rock to one side of the pool.

Hawk reached for the soap and quickly lathered his arms and chest, then his lower body through the water, never taking his eyes from her. Watching a man bathe seemed terribly intimate to Felicia, and she started to leave the pool.

"No! Stay where you are," Hawk commanded. He handed her the soap and asked, "Would you mind washing my back? It's hard for me to reach."

Hawk handed her the soap and turned his back to her expectantly. Hesitantly Felicia began to wash him, then discovering how much she was enjoying rubbing the powerful muscles on his shoulders and back and the feel of his sleek skin, more boldly and far longer than necessary. Suddenly, Hawk turned and took the soap from her hand, saying, "I think that's enough. I'm not *that* dirty."

He tossed the soap to the side of the pool and reached up to the top of her head. As he flipped the twisted hair there, Felicia cried out, "No! It will get wet!"

But it was too late. Her thick reddish tresses tumbled down, the ends floating in the water about them. Hawk smoothed his hands down the length of her hair, saying huskily, "I love the feel of your hair. It's so soft, so silky."

Felicia knew by the tone of Hawk's voice and the glitter in his eyes, that the bath was finished and they were moving on to other, more exciting things. He stood so close, she could feel his manhood brushing back and forth across her lower abdomen. She reached up and untied the buckskin queue that held his hair back, watching the lustrous black locks fall to his shoulders, then said, "I've always wanted to do that."

Hawk's eyes darkened yet another degree. He bent his head and licked a drop of water from one of Felicia's rosy nipples, making her feel weak with desire, before he righted himself and

320

asked in a ragged voice, "And is there anything else you've wanted to do?"

Felicia knew he was hardening and growing. His shaft was no longer brushing back and forth, but boring into her belly persistently, making her feel as if he were branding her there. Knowing she was arousing him just as much as he was her, gave Felicia the courage to answer boldly, "Yes, this."

She ran her hands through the wet springy hair on his chest, lightly rubbing her fingers back and forth over his flat, male nipples, until they were as hard as pebbles, then bent and licked one. Hawk sucked in his breath sharply, then swept her up in his arms and carried her from the pool. Felicia snuggled up to him, loving the feel of their wet feverish skin as they pressed against each other, and the exciting brush of his erection against her buttocks with each step he took.

He stopped at the side of the pool and dropped Felicia's legs, bringing her flush against his length. Cupping her buttocks to lift her, he slid his rampant weapon between her legs, moving it back and forth over her swollen, throbbing lips. As wave after wave of delicious sensation washed over her, Felicia could only cling to his broad shoulders with her face buried in the crook of his neck, dropping hot kisses on the skin there between delighted gasps and throaty moans. Hawk kept up his erotic play, sometimes stopping to circle the tight bud of her womanhood with

321

the velvety head of his erection, until Felicia couldn't stand anymore. She was burning for him and wanted him inside her desperately. She raised her head weakly and muttered, "Hawk?"

As if from faraway, Hawk heard her. He dropped his head next to her mouth to hear her words better. Then, as Felicia's small tongue shot out like a dart and probed his ear, he sucked in his breath sharply as he felt a bolt of fire course through his body to the very tip of his rock-hard shaft. Fearing he would spill his seed right there, he jerked his head away and struggled for control, a fine sheen of perspiration breaking out over his upper lip. When his raging passion had abated a little, he lowered Felicia to the ground, coming down over her as he did, then opened her legs and plunged into her tight, hot depths; they both gasped at the intense pleasure of their joining. Then he took her with a wildness, an urgency, a fierceness that both frightened and excited her, releasing all of the pent-up passion he'd been harboring since he had left her, until Felicia was lost, utterly lost in the devastation of his lovemaking.

Chapter Twenty-three

That night, as soon as the four had finished eating, Sarah said to her husband, "I know ye found that Ferguson fella and his army and beat them, but I want to know the details."

Daniel's brow furrowed, and he said in a stern voice, "Now, woman, war is men's work."

"That's hogwash!" Sarah retorted. "I've fought just as hard as ye against the Indians, and if that ain't war, I don't know what is. And if ye're going to go gallivanting around and leave me to run this place by myself for over six weeks, ye're going to at least tell me what ye were doing all that time."

"All right, woman! Stop your harping!" Daniel answered in exasperation. "I'll tell ye." He rose and walked to the fireplace, saying, "But let me get my pipe lit first."

As soon as the pipe was smoking, Daniel leaned against the mantel and asked, "Where do ye want me to start?"

"At Sycamore Shoals, I reckon," Sarah answered, walking to her rocking chair and sitting down. "I want to hear it all."

"That might take some time," Daniel pointed out irritably.

"I ain't going nowhere," Sarah answered stubbornly.

Shaking his head at his wife's annoying persistence, Daniel began by saying, "Well, I reckon there were about a thousand of us mountain men, including Campbell and four hundred of his militia from the Virginia mountains, and another one hundred and fifty or so Carolina men that had fled the redcoats earlier. We left Sycamore Shoals, and crossed the mountains three days later at Gillespie's Gap into North Carolina. By the time we reached Quaker Meadows, the Tories knew we were there and were reporting to Ferguson, and Whig spies were telling us about his movements. We headed for the border between the Carolinas where he was operating, and it looked like everything was going pretty good, until the men started quarreling and splitting into groups, according to where they came from. Shelby was afraid it was going to lead to serious trouble, that some of the men might turn around and go back home. He suggested Colonel Campbell be made commander, since he led the largest group and he was a regular militia officer. Thankfully the other leaders agreed. They were all a little jealous of each other, and a bit touchy."

324

Sarah rolled her eyes, thinking, if anything, her husband's words were probably an understatement. Any time mountain men got together for any length of time, it seemed they got into a brawl over something. They were all fiercely independent and terribly opinionated, and the leaders were the worst, fighting for authority like a bunch of hound dogs for a bone. It was nothing short of a miracle that the leaders managed to agree on one commander with a half-dozen of the ornery cusses around, all hungry for that honor.

Daniel took a long draw on his pipe, and then continued, "We pushed on, following Ferguson. As soon as he'd heard about us, he turned east towards Charlotte, where Cornwallis had his headquarters. We figured he was trying to get to the protection of Cornwallis's redcoats, and we were trying to catch him first. Then we'd have three times as big an army to whip. When we got to Cowpens—"

"Where?" Sarah asked.

"Now, woman, don't be interrupting," Daniel said in vexation, "or else I never will get this tale finished. That's just a big meadow where we fatten up our cattle before we drive them east, and the men have started calling it Cowpens. That night, after we'd eaten, we heard Ferguson was camped not too far to the east on a little, flat-topped ridge called King's Mountain by the local folk. It was raining something fierce, but Campbell and the other leaders decided we'd march that night. We left the weak and sick behind, and struck out through the rain. Kept right on going until noon the next day, when we reached the place. Campbell gathered us around at the bottom of the mountain, told us to give them Indian play, and for each man to be his own officer. We all put a couple of bullets in our mouths to relieve our thirst and make it easier to load, and attacked."

When Daniel came to a halt in his story, Sarah asked testily, "Is that all ye're going to tell us? Ye attacked?"

"And won!"

"Hell and damnation, I know that! I want to know about the battle."

"Have Hawk tell ye the rest," Daniel answered in disgust. "My throat is dry."

Sarah turned expectantly to Hawk, and he didn't disappoint her. Being Indian, he was accustomed to relating war tales, although the Cherokees pantomimed their stories in the form of a dance. Besides, he knew Sarah would badger him until she got every little detail from him. "We were pretty evenly matched," he began. "There were about nine hundred of them and nine hundred of us, and they had the high ground, which usually is an advantage, particularly since the sides of the hill were very steep. Ferguson was a believer in cold steel, in bayonet charges, and he sent several against us. But the hillside was covered with big boulders and trees, and we had plenty of cover to hide behind. We swarmed up the hill, giving our war whoops, moving tree to tree, and boulder to boulder, picking them off one by one with our long guns. When we got close enough for them shoot back with their muskets, they overshot almost to the man. They obviously weren't used to fighting in an uphill position. The entire mountain was covered with smoke and flame, then the Carolina patriots and Tories got close enough to recognize each other, and started yelling curses and taunts. By that time, Ferguson had lost at least a third of his men. But I'll have to hand it to him. He was a magnificent leader, riding recklessly everywhere, swinging his sword and blowing that big silver whistle that he used to give orders, trying to rally his men. If the rest of his force had fought like him, we wouldn't have won. Twice he had his horse shot out from under him, while he was plunging right into the midst of our men. His Tories began raising handkerchiefs on the ends of their guns to surrender, and he struck them down."

"Aye, 'twas a true Scot he was," Daniel added gravely. "Brave to the very end."

"Ye killed him?" Sarah asked, her voice almost accusing, for to her Ferguson had seemed the hero of the hour.

"Yes," Hawk answered. "One of Sevier's men shot Ferguson from his third horse and killed him. The rest of his men ran to the their baggage wagons for cover, but the battle didn't last much longer. Ferguson had been the driving force. From the first shot to the last, the battle had taken roughly a half of an hour."

"Aye, and some of Campbell's Virginians kept it going a little longer," Daniel added. "He had a hard time getting them to accept the Tories' surrender and stop killing. They were half-mad, yelling, 'Remember Buford! Remember Tarleton's no quarter!' "

"Tarleton!" Sarah exclaimed. "I plumb forgot about that devil. Was he there?"

That had been the question that had been foremost in Felicia's mind. If Tarleton had been at the battle, then it was likely her brother had. But she hadn't dared to ask, for fear that Hawk would misinterpret it as concern for Tarleton again. She saw the sharp look Hawk sliced her and schooled herself to show no emotion.

"No, he didn't show up," Hawk answered in disgust. "And he couldn't have been over thirty miles away."

"Aye," Daniel added, "the only thing we could figure, was he and Cornwallis didn't take us seriously. Like Ferguson, they just considered us nothing but rabble. Some of the prisoners we took said that's why Ferguson decided to make a stand and fight, that he said he could hold that mountaintop against God Almighty and all the rebels out of hell."

"So his entire army was destroyed?" Felicia asked, still maintaining her enforced composure and revealing none of her true feelings.

"Yes," Hawk answered, frowning at her calm acceptance of the news, "over three hundred were killed, and the rest captured, except for two hundred who were out foraging that escaped."

"Aye, and we only lost twenty-eight men," Daniel interjected, warming to the tale. "The news of the battle upset Cornwallis so badly he's retreated to Winnsboro, outside of Camden, and we were told that the Tories were so shaken by it, that they're deserting the British cause right and left."

"And how do ye know that?" Sarah asked. She peered at her husband suspiciously. "Just when did this battle take place?"

"October 7."

"October 7? That was over a month ago! Hell and damnation, where have ye been?"

"Well, someone had to help take the prisoners to General Greene," Daniel answered defensively.

Sarah scowled. "General Greene? Who's he?"

"He's the new commander of the southern army that General Washington appointed to replace that coward Gates. Nathanael Greene. And guess who his second in command is. Daniel Morgan!"

"Old Waggoner Morgan?"

"Aye. Now I reckon we'll get somewhere with this war."

"What do you mean, we?" Sarah asked. "Ye ain't a rebel."

"I am now," Daniel answered in a firm voice.

"Are you telling me ye aim to go back and do more fighting?" Sarah asked, a shocked expression on her face.

"Nay, not unless things get desperate. I did my fair share of fighting at King's Mountain. Besides, there ain't no fighting going on right now. Both armies have settled down for the winter."

Sarah turned to Hawk and asked, "Does that mean ye'll be staying with us until spring?"

"I might as well, since there is nothing going on over there." He shot Felicia a meaningful look, and added, "Tarleton isn't going anyplace."

Felicia had felt a jolt of happiness at Hawk's announcement; then, when he had thrown in his deliberate taunt to remind her he hadn't forgotten his vendetta, that joy died a quick death, as she realized that she had only attained a reprieve. Come spring, she would have to go through all the anguish of waiting and worrying again. Dammit! she thought in exasperation. Why couldn't he just let it go? But Felicia was very careful to show none of the turmoil she was feeling, giving Hawk a taste of his own medicine, and frustrating him with *her* stony expression for a change.

She rose from the bench and started collecting the wooden trenches. Seeing her, Sarah stood and said, "Well, I reckon ye're right, lass. Those dishes aren't going to wash themselves."

As the two women washed and dried the dishes in the shadowy corner of the cabin, Felicia pondered over everything she had learned. She had been shocked at how utterly total the frontiersmen's victory had been, and feared they had dealt the British a blow they might not completely recover from, particularly if the loyalists in the south were withdrawing their support because of it. The frontiersmen had done just what they had said they would: crossed the mountains and taught Ferguson and his army a lesson. But who would have dreamed that a bunch of wild mountain men—out to answer a careless threat made against them—could have such an impact on the war? she thought. Certainly not Ferguson, who grossly underestimated their fury and their unorthodox fighting skills, and paid the ultimate price for it. Certainly not Tarleton and Cornwallis, who were paying the price now by facing the rebels alone. But she could have warned the officers to tread more lightly. Since coming to live among these people, she had learned that they weren't someone to mess with. You didn't stir them up or agitate them, anymore than you did the savages that they had learned so well from. Living on the dangerous frontier, facing unbelievable hardships every day, the backwoods people had been forged in a fearsome furnace. They could be a fierce ally or a terrifying foe. Yes, she could have warned them.

But Felicia knew the military men wouldn't

have listened to her or anyone else. She seriously feared the British would lose this war, and the colonies would become a new nation. The pity was that the British would lose because of their own arrogance.

Chapter Twenty-four

The next day, the four set to work frantically picking corn, racing against time while they still had good weather; then that night, after they had eaten their evening meal, they sat in the barn and shucked it with a crude tool called a husking pin, tossing the shucks to one side to be used as cattle fodder during the winter, and putting the ears into sacks to be carried to the miller later. This continued day in and day out, and of all of the chores Felicia had had to perform since her arrival on the frontier, she found this job the most taxing. Working all day and half the night, along with sandwiching in her regular chores, she was so exhausted by the end of the third day, that she fell into bed without even removing her clothing.

On the morning of the fourth day, Sarah put an end to the double labor by saying to Daniel, "Felicia and I will help harvest the corn, but we ain't husking no more. We're both plumb worn-out."

"But we've got to get this corn to the miller, before any ice forms on the trail. Ye know that, woman."

"Aye, I know. But that don't mean ye have to work us all to death, both harvesting and husking. If we didn't do nothing but pick, we could have it done in a few days, then we could throw a husking bee."

Daniel frowned, then said, "Nay. If we do that, we'll have to furnish the whiskey. Why, they'd end up drinking half our profits."

"Stop being so tightfisted. It would only take a couple of jugs. We can spare that."

It was an argument that continued after breakfast and into the day, until Daniel finally relented under Sarah's persistence, saddled his horse, and went out to invite the neighbors for a husking party a few days later. Then the four picked like mad, until the day of the party, when Sarah and Felicia spent the entire morning making a huge kettle of potpie, roasting a haunch of venison and several hams, baking corn pone, and squeezing apples for juice for the children.

Around noon, Sarah said, "We'd better put our gowns on now. Our guests will be getting here soon."

"Gowns?" Felicia asked in confusion, then remembering, said, "You're not serious about wearing our nightgowns?"

"Aye, 'tis what we women wear to all our parties."

334

"I can't parade around here in front of God and everyone in my nightgown," Felicia objected.

"Sure ye can. If ye don't, ye'll be out of place. Everyone will think ye're acting uppity. Ye don't want them thinking that, do ye?"

"Well, no, but—"

"Good," Sarah said, cutting off any further objections Felicia might have made. "Wear the one we sewed all that lace from yer old ball gown on. Why, it's pretty enough to be a wedding gown."

"You wear your nightgowns for wedding gowns, too?" Felicia asked in horror.

"Aye. We can't afford special gowns for something that's only used once." She chuckled. "Besides, it simplifies things. That way the bride don't have to change into her nightgown when we bed her down in the loft."

"In the loft?"

"Aye. That's where the bride and groom spend their wedding night, in the loft of the bride's home."

"Isn't that rather embarrassing for the couple?"

"Oh, they don't do nothing." Sarah laughed again. "They can't! After the husband is put to bed beside his new bride by his friends, everyone keeps pestering them by bringing them food or insisting they have a swig of Black Betty."

Felicia assumed Black Betty was what the mountain people called their whiskey. "When do the guests leave?"

"They don't. They stay all night. No one is allowed to sleep. The fiddler keeps playing and everyone sings, 'Hang on 'til Tomorrow' at the top of their lungs. The celebrating lasts until the afternoon, sometimes longer. Why, when Daniel and I got married, we had a battle."

"A battle?"

"Aye, that's what we call weddings that last a few days. You see, with all that drinking, the men eventually land up fighting, if not the neighbors who weren't invited and were sneaking around the place up to no good, then each other. It's all just part of the fun."

It sounded wild and insane to Felicia. "What does the preacher have to say about all this?" she asked out of curiosity.

"Preacher?" Sarah asked in surprise, then said, "Nay, we don't have preachers at our weddings. The ministers are circuit riders out here. We might not see one for years."

"Then who marries you?"

"We marry ourselves."

"That's legal?"

"Of course, it's legal! We get marriage licenses."

Shortly thereafter, the guests started arriving, entire families, some riding double and triple on horses, others in wagons, a few even on foot. Each time a group arrived, they were greeted by Daniel, who directed the men and boys to the barn, and the women and children to the house.

336

Soon the little cabin was crowded with women, all chattering excitedly; and just as Sarah had predicted, they wore their nightgowns and showed off their little pieces of lace and ribbons proudly. Some were barefoot, a few wore moccasins, and several wore long, buckskin gloves that looked ridiculous to Felicia, but drew many "oohs" and "aahs" from the others.

A little later, Felicia and Sarah were placing food on the table, pushed to one corner of the cabin to make more room. Seeing several newcomers squeezing into the cabin, Felicia gaped, then gasped, "Look at those girls! Why, they're almost naked!"

Sarah glanced at the young women dressed in low-cut, sleeveless shifts and short petticoats. "Nay, lass. They're covered. 'Tis how the single girls dress for parties out here, to show off their full bosoms and shapely legs. You sure can't attract a man in a nightgown."

Felicia had to admit that the floor-length, coarse linen gowns that buttoned at the neck were modest, and shapeless. You could hide the worst figure in the world beneath them. But it seemed the girls had carried their dress, or rather undress, to the extreme. Their full breasts threatened to spill from the shifts at any moment, and each and every one of them exaggerated the swing of their hips, making the short petticoats sway, and revealing provocative glimpses of naked thigh. Felicia wondered, if they did that to show off their figures to the other women, what would they do to make the men take notice?

"When are we going to join the men in the barn?" Felicia asked.

"We ain't," Sarah answered.

"But I thought everyone takes part in a husking bee?"

"Maybe in the lowlands they do, but not here in the mountains. Here, it's for men only, and it always gets a little rough. That's why we women keep our distance and don't even watch. It's safer here than out in the barn."

"But how could a husking bee be dangerous?"

"The men divide up into teams and race each other, to see who can get their side of the corn pile husked first. There's a lot of cheating and drinking, and naturally, fighting."

A little later, while the women and children were eating, and therefore quieter than they had been, Felicia heard loud noises coming from the husking bee, the males cheering, shouting, cursing. Then, shortly before sundown, the men and boys came spilling out of the barn, the winning team carrying their captain on their shoulders, and Felicia noted that there were a good many cut lips, swollen eyes, and abrasions. However, no one seemed to carry a grudge. All were in rollicking high spirits, and while the men ate, the women passed the jug around, until almost everyone was inebriated to some degree. Laughter filled the air, the men's boisterous rumbles and the women's high-pitched shrieks, along with the telling of many crude jokes that made Felicia's face turn beet red with embarrassment.

Then a fiddler started to play, and the men and women filed out of the cabin and started dancing around a big bonfire that had been lit in the middle of the front yard; while the onlookers clapped their hands and tapped their feet in unison with the music, many of the women sitting on the men's laps, since there was a shortage of benches and stools. Dancing a wild two-step that would have shaken the floor had there been one, no one seemed to notice or care that there was a decidedly cool nip in the air.

Felicia saw Hawk standing at the back of the crowd on the opposite side of the fire, and knew he was cold sober by his stance. Everyone else was weaving to some degree, or leaning at a peculiar angle. Then she watched as one of the young women sashayed up to him, took his hand in hers, and said something to him. As the girl led him through the crowd, Felicia realized that she must have asked him to dance, then watched, feeling consumed with jealousy as Hawk whirled the girl around and around, and the female brazenly took every opportunity to rub herself against him.

It was just the beginning. From then on, Felicia was forced to watch as one bold female after the other engaged Hawk in a dance, and much to Felicia's disgust, she noticed the rugged frontiersman didn't appear adverse to their attention. He was grinning from ear to ear, and even laughed outright a few times. Therefore, when Felicia was asked to dance by an awkward-looking youth well into his cups, she agreed out of spite. The youth was incredibly clumsy, stepping on her feet several times, but Felicia kept up a good front, smiling through clenched teeth, even managing a gay laugh for Hawk's benefit, as he whirled one of his many partners past. To Felicia's satisfaction, the laugh caught Hawk's attention. Just before the youth swung her around, she saw the startled look on Hawk's face, and hoped that he might ask her to dance. But such was not to be the case. The fiddler decided it was time to go home, and the party abruptly ended.

Later, as she and Sarah were cleaning up the cabin, Sarah said, "That was a nice party. I'm glad we did it."

Felicia thought it a little loud and wild, then remembered that the frontiersmen led difficult lives, and deserved to play as hard as they worked. She certainly couldn't deny them the little pleasure they got from life. "Yes, it was," she agreed.

"The women were real surprised at ye. They thought ye'd be uppity."

Felicia had tried very hard to be sociable by smiling and making small talk, as well as complimenting the women on their children, even offering to hold an infant or two so the mother could dance, which was why she hadn't been asked to dance more often. "I don't think the younger women liked me very much," she commented.

"Oh, they're just jealous of ye and Hawk, that's all. Ye saw how they made over him. Why, every marriageable girl in these mountains would give her eyeteeth to be in yer place."

"And what place is that?"

"In daily contact with him. There ain't a one of them that wouldn't kill to have him courting them."

"Where in the world would they ever get an idea like that—that Hawk is courting me?"

"Well, they figure ye two being together so much, things are bound to happen."

"But they think I'm Hawk's cousin."

"Distant cousin," Sarah corrected. "And marriage between cousins is real common out here."

Marriage to Hawk? Felicia thought. It sounded wonderful, but unfortunately, not very likely. Felicia was wise enough to know desire and love were a world apart, and Hawk had said nothing of love. "Well, they certainly aren't very observant," Felicia answered bitterly, "otherwise they would have noticed he didn't dance with me."

"Ye didn't ask him."

"No, I didn't!" Felicia retorted. "I don't happen to believe in a woman asking. That's the man's role—to pursue. If Hawk cared for me, he would have asked me to dance. That's my point."

"To tell ye the truth, I'm surprised he danced. I don't recall ever seeing him do that."

Felicia didn't want Sarah to know how jealous

she had been, or that she felt hurt by Hawk's ignoring her. "Well, it hardly matters," she answered, trying to be flippant. "I'm just his hostage, that's all."

Sarah strongly suspected that Felicia and Hawk were lovers. She had noted their lengthy absence the day Hawk and Daniel had returned from war, and she hadn't missed the hungry looks the two gave one another, when they thought no one was looking. But she made no comment. Instead, she said, "I think I'll go with Daniel tomorrow, when he takes the corn to the miller. There are some things I need to pick up at the station, before winter sets in."

Sarah watched the light come into Felicia's eyes, as it dawned on her that she and Hawk would be alone. Just a hostage, my eye, Sarah thought, and bit back a laugh.

The next day, Sarah and Daniel had hardly disappeared down the trail, when Hawk walked into the cabin. Felicia had been anticipating his appearance with bated breath, but was still smarting from the night before. Out of sheer perversity, she told herself firmly that she wouldn't fall into bed with him, that she could ignore him just as coldly as he had ignored her the night before.

As he walked across the cabin, she pretended not to notice the look of purpose in his eyes, and asked, "What are you doing here? Don't you have work to do?"

Hawk paused. A frown crossed his handsome face. "Not anything that can't wait. I thought you would be glad to see me."

"I saw you a few hours ago, at breakfast!"

"Why are you angry with me?" Hawk asked. Then, remembering how he had deliberately set out to make her jealous, a grin spread across his face. "Is it because of those girls last night? You're jealous?"

"Jealous? That's ridiculous!" Felicia denied emphatically, too emphatically to be believed.

In two long, swift strides, Hawk was standing before her. "Now you know how I feel about Tarleton."

If Felicia had been in full possession of her senses, she would have realized that Hawk's admitting to being jealous of the British officer was revealing a lot about how he felt about her, but she was already under the devastating effects of his nearness. She was acutely aware of his body heat, his exciting scent. It took all of her concentration to remember what their conversation was about. "I've told you, there was never anything between us!"

"And there is nothing between me and those girls," Hawk answered in a low, husky voice.

Felicia meant to turn and walk away, but she found she was as helpless as a fly caught in a spider's web, as Hawk took her into his arms. When his lips covered hers, she melted into him, hating herself for being so weak. As his kiss deepened and he molded her softness to his long, hard frame, she forgot how to even think. All she could do was react, her tongue dueling provocatively with his, until they were both trembling with need.

They climbed the ladder to the loft and undressed one another with urgency, fondling and touching, their eyes feasting on the naked beauty of each other, until they sank to Felicia's low bed. Hawk entered her in one powerful thrust, sure of his reception, and Felicia welcomed him with a glad cry, wrapping her legs around his slim hips, wishing she could hold him a prisoner there forever. She moaned beneath him, matched his driving rhythm with her own, met him fiery kiss for fiery kiss, and shared a shattering release before they floated down, quivering, to a warm afterglow.

They stayed in the loft all day, while Hawk taught Felicia the many moods of love, taking her wildly, then tenderly, then with a playfulness she would have never dreamed the half-savage capable of. Neither was in a hurry to leave, for they knew not when they might have another opportunity to make love. Trying to prepare themselves for a long siege of abstinence, they gorged themselves on their lovemaking, and when Sarah and Daniel returned that evening, they were both sitting at the table, looking perfectly innocent.

Innocent to Daniel, that was, but not to Sarah's sharp eyes. She saw the radiant glow on Felicia's face and the happy shimmer in her eyes, sensed Hawk's calm contentment, both silent testimony to something more than just sated passion. Sarah no longer suspected their emotional entanglement. She knew it, and sincerely hoped the future would treat the young lovers kindly.

Chapter Twenty-five

The next morning when Felicia awoke, it was miserably cold in the loft. She peeked out between a crack in the logs and saw that there was a light frost on the ground. It appeared that what everyone had been waiting for and preparing for had come. Winter had arrived.

While the four were eating breakfast, Sarah said to Felicia, "As soon as we've cleared the table, we're going to start on some moccasins for ye. Ye'll freeze your feet off in what's left of those slippers of yers."

"That won't be necessary," Hawk announced quietly from across the table. "I've already made Felicia some moccasins, one indoor and one outdoor pair."

"But how could you do that?" Felicia asked. "You don't know my size."

Hawk didn't tell her that once after they had made love and she was dozing in his arms, he had measured her foot against his. "I guessed." He

346

rose from the table, saying, "We'll see if they fit. I'll get them."

A few moments later, Hawk reappeared, carrying two pair of moccasins. Both were lined with soft fur for warmth and comfort, but the outdoor moccasins were calf-high and made of a dark leather that Hawk explained had been smoked to make them more water-resistant, while the indoor pair came to her ankles and were make of the softest buckskin she had ever felt and were elaborately beaded. Running her hands over the beading admiringly, Felicia asked in awe, "You made these yourself, even the beading?"

Hawk was glad she was pleased with his simple gift. He had been half-afraid she would scorn them. He chuckled and answered, "I *am* part Indian, you know."

"I know, but I always thought the women made the clothing, or at least did all the beading."

"Beading is considered a means of self-expression among the Cherokee, along with painting, and is done by both sexes. And no brave would let a woman bead anything of his that has to do with war, not his bow, not his tomahawk, not his ceremonial breechcloth or arm bands."

"And sewing moccasins ain't women's work among us mountain folks, either," Sarah pointed out. "Daniel always makes his own moccasins, and every mountain man carries an awl for repairing them in his hunting bag. Those soft soles don't last very long, ye know."

347

"No, I didn't realize that," Felicia admitted.

"I'm making you a fur hat, too," Hawk informed her, "but it isn't finished yet."

"And I'll knit ye some mittens and stockings," Sarah offered. "I've also got an extra linsey-woolsey petticoat and a shawl ye can use. Then ye'll be set for winter."

Felicia remembered the shopping spree for a winter wardrobe her mother and she went on every year. They came home with boxes and boxes of dresses, furs, hats, muffs, cloaks, and shoes. But here in the wilderness, everything came down to the bare necessities. There were no frills, no extras. But then, they weren't really needed. She laughed good-naturedly and answered, "Yes, I will be. Thank you."

Two weeks later it snowed, and Felicia, who rarely saw it in the low country, was enthralled. As soon as the flakes had finished falling, she went for a walk, and Hawk went with her.

Standing in front of the cabin, Felicia looked about her. Everything was covered with white: the ground, the trees, the roofs of the cabin and barn and outhouses, even the rails of the worm fence, gleaming so brightly in the sunlight, it almost hurt her eyes to look at it, while the trunks of the trees, covered with thin ice, glistened. She turned and gazed out at the blue mountains stretching out in the distance, the bald spots on them covered with snow, and making them look as if they were covered with a blue and white patchwork quilt. Then, seeing a splotch of unexpected color, she asked, "What's that red over there, on the hill across from us?"

"It's the leaves of a red oak. Neither they nor the beech drop their leaves in the winter."

They walked to the stream at the foot of the hill, Hawk cautioning her to watch carefully for treacherous patches of ice on the way. The black rocks that nature had strewn across the brook were covered with snow, and there were ice crystals in the water around each rock, but the stream still flowed, its gurgle seeming all the louder for the lack of any other sounds. "Did all of the birds leave?" Felicia asked.

"Most flew away to warmer climates, but a few, like the whippoorwill, stayed. You won't hear them singing, though. Not today. It's too cold. They've got their heads buried beneath their wings."

Felicia looked entranced, and said softly, "It's beautiful. I didn't think anything could be more beautiful than these mountains in the fall, but this is. It seems so peaceful, so serene."

"The mountains are beautiful in every season, and each season has its own mood. My favorite is *kogeh*—spring—when everything takes on new life."

"*Kogeh?* That's Cherokee, isn't it?"

"Yes."

"And the other seasons? What are they called?"

"*Akooea,* summer. *Oolekohste,* fall. And *kora,* winter."

Felicia smiled. She had thought the sound of an Indian language would be harsh to her ears, but with Hawk's deep voice and his soft incantation, the strange words had had an almost musical sound to them. She glanced once more at the lovely winter scene around her, and asked, "How long will the snow last?"

"A few days. Then it will melt. Then it will snow again. Over and over. The only places it accumulates and really gets deep are the passes."

A shiver ran over Felicia. "You're cold," Hawk observed, then frowned and said, "That shawl isn't warm enough to be out here for any length of time. We'd better go back."

As they walked back up the hill, Felicia asked, "What do the Indian women wear for wraps in the winter?"

"Blankets now, but in the old days, they wore fur robes."

Their path led them past the barn. Hawk stopped Felicia before the door and said, "Come in for a while, and let me warm you." He took one hand, bent it at the wrist, and kissed it above the mitten, saying, "It's been a long time since we've been alone together."

Felicia glanced nervously towards the cabin. "They'll miss us," she objected.

"No, they won't. They'll think we're still walking."

"What if they should come out here?"

"They rarely come to the barn, since I do all of the milking and collecting the eggs now. And they sure won't come today. They both hate snow with a passion."

By that time Hawk had opened the door and pulled her inside. As he closed the door behind him, she remarked, "Why, it's almost as warm in here as in the cabin."

"It's the heat from the animals. I don't even need a fire."

He led her to the back of the barn where his "bedroom" was, and as he undressed her, he looked deeply in her eyes and muttered with sensual promise, "And now to warm you."

Later, Felicia lay snuggled up to Hawk's side and absently ran the tips of her fingers back and forth over the damp skin on his chest. Her eyes fell on an empty whiskey jug that had been left from the night Shelby had gathered the men in the barn. Remembering something she had been curious about, Felicia said, "I've noticed that you don't drink the whiskey they have out here. Is it just this strong mountain brew, or all liquor you dislike?"

"All liquor."

"Why? Did it once make you ill?"

"I've never had so much as a sip. I'm afraid to. I'm half-Indian, remember?"

"What has that got to do with it?"

"Indians have no tolerance for any kind of intoxicating drink, whether it be rum, or brandy, or whiskey, or beer. It makes them crazy."

Felicia laughed and said, "It can make white men crazy sometimes, too."

"But Indians get wilder and meaner and more dangerous. And it's more than just how they behave while they're under the influence. Indians have a particular weakness for it; they can't resist it. They're ten times more susceptible to becoming addicted to it than white men. And because of this, the white man's firewater is destroying the Indian. He craves it so much, he's given up his ordinary way of life to just hunt for skins to buy rum or whiskey; and the more he hunts, the more scarce the game becomes. Then he moves on, leaving his village and deserting the fields his ancestors cleared, that have fed his family for generations. Come winter, there's no food because there was no harvest, no game because the brave shot it all to skin for whiskey. He and his family are starving, and his brain is being slowly rotted by the vile stuff. The liquor has robbed him of his health, his ambition, his senses, and the thing every Indian values above all, his pride. That's why I don't even dare to take one drop, for fear it will get me in its evil clutches."

For Hawk, it had been a long discourse, and the most revealing of how he thought and felt as an Indian. Felicia wanted desperately to know more of Hawk's beginnings, of his life among the Indians, more of that part of him that he seemed to hold so closely, so secretively to himself. It wasn't simply a matter of curiosity. It was a part of her love, a need to know and understand all of him, so she could fully appreciate his beautiful spirit, as well as the magnificent body that brought them both such exquisite pleasure. She kissed his chest lightly, almost as if she were trying to reassure him that she would not harm him, then said, "Tell me more of your life with the Indians."

Just as she feared, Hawk stiffened. "What are you afraid of?" Felicia asked, half-angry that he might lock her out again. "What harm can that do?"

Hawk was not a man to admit to fear lightly, and yet he knew that it *was* fear that had motivated him. He feared Felicia would scorn or ridicule anything Indian about him. Yet, she had not done so. At least, not yet. "What do you want to know?" he asked tentatively.

Everything, Felicia thought, but answered, "Tell me about your childhood. Was it happy?"

"Indian children are the happiest children in the world, because they are so free to be themselves and so loved, not just by their parents and relatives, but by the entire tribe. By white standards the children might seem spoiled or undisciplined, but that's not true. There is no need for punishment, because the children have no fear or dis-

353

trust of adults. They know they are loved, and they want to please in return. Yes, I had a happy childhood . . . up to a point."

"When your mother died," Felicia surmised.

"How did you know my mother had died?"

"Sarah told me that was when you came to live with them, when your mother died. She didn't tell me anything else though. Was that when your happy childhood ended?"

"No, she died later. This happened when I was five. From then on my childhood was never carefree and happy again. That was the year the *U-nehka*—our name for whites—destroyed our village, along with fourteen other lower and middle Cherokee towns. They came in June, in what we call, *Da-tsalunee*, Green Corn Month, and by the time they left in September, *Dulu-stinee*, Nut Month, they had leveled every town, burned over fifteen thousand acres of crops to the ground, slaughtered all of our animals, and left over five thousand Cherokees starving."

Hawk paused, feeling almost overwhelmed by the haunting memories, then continued in a low tone of voice. "After our village had been destroyed, we wandered through the forest from town to town, looking for a place to live. Everywhere we went we found desolation, everything blackened and charred, sometimes still smoking. We found no place of refuge that winter. We lived in the deep forest in open lean-tos, huddling together for warmth—since there wasn't enough

354

small wood to burn—and tried to gather enough acorns and berries to survive. Every night, we went to sleep cold and hungry, with the sickening smell of burned flesh and charred wood still hanging heavily in the air, and with the sound of wolves howling in the distance. We never knew if we would be attacked by a pack during the night. They were particularly vicious that year. They had feasted on what they had scavenged from the embers, dug up many of the graves, and were made bold by the easy bounty they found. They seemed to have no fear of humans, or even the few fires we could light. And as if all that was not enough, it was one of the coldest winters we have ever had in these mountains. The *Ani-yun-wiga*—that is how we call ourselves—the principle people—were dropping like flies, if not from starvation, then from disease in their weakened condition. It was hardest on the old and the very young. I lost both of my grandparents and three cousins that winter."

When Hawk remained silent for so long, Felicia thought he had finished his tale. She was on the verge of asking more questions, when he continued, saying, "That spring, most of the surviving Cherokees stayed and rebuilt the lower and middle towns, but my mother and I, along with others in our clan, fled to the upper towns of the nation. They, too, had been attacked by the whites, but had managed to repulse them. We settled in Chota with others of our clan, and finally, through the efforts of Attakullakulla—known as Chief Little Carpenter to the whites—peace was made. But my mother never fully recovered from that terrible winter. She was almost an invalid, and I spent a good deal of my time caring for her, since she was very independent and refused to live with her brother after her parents had died. She felt he had enough to do to care for his family. When an outbreak of *oonataquara*—smallpox—hit our village, she was the first to succumb. Thank God, it was not as severe as the outbreak back in the thirties, that wiped out half of the Cherokee nation. It seemed to be of weaker nature, but not weak enough for my mother to throw off."

Felicia heard the sadness in Hawk's voice, and knew that he must have loved his mother very much. "I'm sorry," she said softly. "It must be difficult to lose someone so important in your life so young."

Felicia wasn't particularly surprised when Hawk made no comment. All men seemed to have trouble expressing grief. Their masculine image of themselves prevented them from revealing pain, and most certainly emotional pain. That was considered a weakness, and how much more so for one with Indian blood in him, who put such stock in showing courage and endurance. But surely their show of strength must be a burden at times, she thought, a terrible burden. And they brought it on themselves, for they were the ones who dictated this "manly" behavior. Stupid men!

"And what brought on that war against the Cherokee?" she asked.

"The same thing that always keeps the wars going between the whites and the Indians—vengeance," Hawk answered bitterly. "The whites kill Indians, the Indians avenge the deaths, the whites avenge those deaths, the Indians reciprocate, round and round."

"But some incident precipitated it," Felicia persisted. "What was it?"

"It will be the Cherokee's side of the story. Are you sure you want to hear that?"

Felicia didn't hesitate. "Yes, I would."

Hawk looked at her for a long moment, as if he were peering into her soul, then said, "During the French-Indian wars, the Cherokees were British allies. This was not something that was just a whim of the chiefs at that time. Unlike many of the other tribes, they didn't pledge their allegiance to the highest bidder, to whoever offered them the most guns and blankets and whiskey or the most promises. The Cherokees had made a treaty with the King himself, when Chief Little Carpenter visited Great Britain while he was still a *dunawaga-we-u-we,* a war chief. The treaty stipulated that the Cherokee would always be Britain's ally and that they would only trade with them and not the French or the Spanish, nor could they sell any of their land without British consent. In return, the King agreed to honor the Cherokee land and keep the white men out. From then on, Little Carpenter would hear nothing against the British. He became a peace chief and changed his name from Oukanaekoh to Attakullakulla. As the most powerful chief among the Cherokee, he was also the most influential. Although each town had its own war and peace chiefs, it was Little Carpenter that the entire nation looked to as their advisor and spokesman. And therefore, when the British wanted the Cherokee to aid them by attacking the Shawnees in the northwest territory towards the end of their latest war with the French, they went to Little Carpenter. The Cherokees agreed, if the English would build three forts in their country to protect their people from the French, while their warriors were gone. The forts were built and manned by Virginians, and the Cherokees went off to fight the Shawnees on the Ohio. It turned out to be a disastrous expedition. Before they even got out of the Virginia backwoods, their canoes were overturned during a storm, and they lost all of their provisions. They had to kill their horses for food, which left them on foot. They came across a farm and stole some horses and poultry. The Virginians they stole them from didn't know they were allies. They mounted a party, ambushed the Cherokees, and killed twenty-four of them before the others managed to escape. Then the settlers had the audacity to take the Indian scalps to the governor of Virginia, who paid a bounty for them, adding insult to injury. When the mistake was discovered, the Governor apologized to Little

Carpenter, but it was too late. The Cherokee code of honor demands that murders must be avenged, and in the eyes of the warriors who had been ambushed, the deaths of those braves were murders. They had been attacked without provocation by people who were supposed to be their comrades in arms. The warriors went on the warpath and killed twenty-four white settlers, before they got back to their home ground. Twenty-four," Hawk repeated for emphasis. "One for each brave that had been murdered. But the whites wouldn't leave it at that. The British military reciprocated and sent a battalion of Highlanders and four companies of Royal Scots into Cherokee country, and the entire nation went on the warpath at this breach of their treaty with the King, and put the forts the Virginians had built under siege. The Long Knives managed to take two of the forts back, but couldn't relieve Fort Laundon in the upper Cherokee country. The Virginians there finally surrendered and were allowed to march from Cherokee territory unharmed, but were forced to leave their ammunition behind. By that time the war in Canada was over, and the Cherokees wanted to make peace. But the British military's pride had been wounded at Fort Laundon, and they refused. That's when they sent the vengeful expedition against the Cherokee that destroyed my home."

Felicia didn't know what to say. The killing on both sides seemed so unnecessary, so pointless, but she would have to admit that if she were to place the blame at anyone's feet, it would have to be the white man's. They had started the war, then refused to end it when the Cherokee sued for peace, hell-bent on getting revenge for what they had brought on themselves. Yes, men were incredibly stupid. "It's a wonder that peace was ever made," she observed.

"Oh, it was made, and broken, and made again, and each time the Cherokee was forced to cede more of his land to the whites as part of the peace treaty. The Cherokee can't afford too many more wars. If he continues, he won't have any land left. Little Carpenter realizes that. He also knows that the whites vastly outnumber the Cherokee, that they can produce a never-ending stream of land-grasping whites. He was in England. He saw the hordes of people there. London alone had more people in it than the entire Cherokee nation. He knows the only way the Cherokees can survive is to make and keep peace. But the young hotheads like Chief Dragging Canoe—his own son!— refuse to listen. They keep the hate going, hot and heavy, stirring up the others. Fools! They can't turn the white tide back. No one can! They're only making it worse. If someone doesn't stop them, the entire Cherokee nation will be annihilated, the peaceful along with the renegades."

Now Felicia understood why Hawk had fought the Chickamaugas. He fought for the Cherokee nation, and if it meant severing a part of it that

360

was corrupting and threatening the whole, then so be it. It was like amputating a foot to save the body, a drastic measure, yet sometimes the only effective one. "You have a very great respect for Little Carpenter, don't you?" she remarked.

"Yes. He was the wisest and most respected chief the Cherokee nation has ever had."

"Was?"

"Yes. I understand he died earlier this year. He must have been at least ninety-five."

"Why did he send you away to live with the white man?"

"He thought the white man's life would be easier for me, since I could easily pass for one. Like I said, he'd lived for a long time, and watched the changes that had occurred over those years. Unlike the other chiefs, who discredited the strength of the whites, he knew better. He also recognized the white's insatiable greed for land for what it was. I think he knew what was coming for the Cherokees — years and years of turmoil, of almost constant war. He thought to spare me more of the horrors I had just gone through."

Hawk paused as the old doubts once again came to the surface, doubts that had haunted him over the years. He had always wondered if the wise, old chief had really acted in his behalf when he had sent Hawk away, or if Little Carpenter had felt he was not up to living the life of a Cherokee because of his white blood, that his character lacked something intrinsic and important to the

Indian way of life. It had upset Hawk deeply to think that Little Carpenter might have thought he would not make a good Cherokee, particularly since that had been his driving dream—his only dream—and to that day, Hawk still felt torn. He thought in Cherokee, even though he spoke fluent English and was proficient in writing the language that was his second tongue—something that not many whites could do—and many times it was his Cherokee beliefs that guided his decisions. Yet he had assimilated much of the white culture, and he could no more sever that from his nature than he could remove his Indian blood from the white in his veins. He was neither Indian nor white, but both, and doomed forever to walk in that shadowy in-between world.

"Hawk?" Felicia asked, breaking into his deep thoughts.

Suddenly Hawk felt terribly exposed. He realized that he had revealed much more than he had meant to, and feared Felicia would probe even deeper. He had told her things he had never told anyone. "No! No more questions!" he answered adamantly, then rolled over and gazed down at her face. "Talk can wait. We have more important things to do."

As Hawk began to drop soft, feathery kisses over her forehead and cheeks, Felicia knew he was closing the door on her, and felt a keen disappointment. While he had been telling her about himself, she had felt a closeness that far surpassed any physical intimacy they had ever shared. She lifted her arms and caressed his back, then gently ran her fingertips over the raised ridges there, thinking the wounds to his soul were much deeper, and wishing desperately that there was some way she could heal them, could take the pain from him and carry it as her own. Her love for him welled up inside her, a powerful wave of emotion that brought tears to her eyes. Her arms tightened about him convulsively, in an embrace so fierce that Hawk found it difficult to breathe. Then, when he entered her, she gave of herself so completely, so totally, so utterly unselfishly, that Hawk was to later left wonder what had precipitated the special magic of that loving.

Chapter Twenty-six

It turned out that Hawk and Felicia had more time to themselves than they had expected. Sarah and Daniel often disappeared into the little shack where their still stood, and busied themselves for hours distilling fermented corn mash in a peculiar-looking apparatus that consisted of a pear-shaped, copper kettle with a narrow neck that ended in a spiral of tubing called a worm. Because of Hawk's feelings about liquor, he wasn't asked to assist in the brewing, and Felicia's offer to help was turned down after Sarah saw how sickly the noxious odors were making her look. Therefore the young couple were left to their own devices much of the time. Sometimes Hawk went to the cabin and talked to Felicia while she did her chores, and sometimes she went to the barn, where he had set up a simple shop to repair the guns that some of the mountain men had brought him, and those times almost always ended in not just talking, but the two making love.

By silent, mutual agreement, any conversations about Felicia's being held hostage and the war were forbidden and that was fine with Felicia. She preferred to forget that there was any strain in their relationship, and just the thought of leaving Hawk and going back to her home left her feeling depressed. She was quite content in using the time to get to know Hawk better, but unfortunately, she was never able to draw any more from Hawk about his Indian life, something she felt the key to understanding his complex nature. But he did talk quite freely about his life with Sarah and Daniel, and the time he had spent back east. It seemed the German gunsmith his father had apprenticed him to was not only the best in his field, but a stickler for education, and it was because of him that Hawk learned to read and write and how to cipher. The gunsmith was also responsible for polishing Hawk's rough edges, although his "civilizing" was accomplished without Hawk having been aware of it happening. Over the years, by constant exposure to the gunsmith's upper- and middle-class clientele, Hawk picked up bits and pieces of their speech, their mannerisms, even their political views. He also developed a sweet tooth, for it seemed the gunsmith's wife was an excellent cook, and introduced him to the delights of griddle cakes, waffles, cookies, and cruellers—twisted sweet dough fried in deep fat—foods that Felicia had never even heard of, much less eaten.

One day, Felicia was in the barn, listening to yet another of Hawk's tales about his experiences up north, while he tinkered with a defective firing mechanism. She had discovered that he was an excellent storyteller — something that Hawk attributed to his Indian heritage — with a wealth of information. She had never been aware that there were so many differences in the customs and the people in the north and the south. Where she came from, the people were of English or French descent, but Hawk had been exposed to a hodgepodge of nationalities, as well as Quakers and two religious groups she had never heard of, Mennonites and Moravians. On this particular day, Hawk was explaining how the German and Dutch settlers on the Pennsylvania frontier built more substantial homesteads, using stone whenever possible for their houses, and building larger and sturdier barns; when the door suddenly opened and Daniel rushed in, followed by a breathless Sarah.

Both Hawk and Felicia jumped in surprise, and Felicia thanked God that they hadn't been occupied with something more intimate. "What's wrong?" Hawk asked.

"I've got an important letter for ye," Daniel answered, waving the missive in the air. "Caleb just rode it over from the station. It's from Shelby, and the man who delivered it said he was supposed to rush it to ye."

Hawk took the letter, broke the wax seal on it,

and quickly read it. Then, aware of the three watching him with bated breath, he looked up and said, "It's from Shelby, all right. He said if I want to get my licks in against Tarleton, I'd better get back east fast. According to him, Cornwallis has split his army between himself and Tarleton, and Tarleton is in hot pursuit of General Morgan and his men, hell-bent on catching the patriots and destroying them. Shelby said a big battle is inevitable, and soon."

"When in the devil did all that happen?" Daniel asked in surprise. "I thought Cornwallis had settled down for the winter!"

"According to Shelby, on New Year's Day. That would have been six days ago."

"Do you think they've already battled?" Daniel asked. "Morgan's army was in a weakened condition. They couldn't run too fast."

"I hope not!" Hawk answered, his dark eyes glittering dangerously. "But I'll soon find out."

"You're going, then?" Daniel asked.

"I am."

"The passes will be full of snow," Daniel warned.

"I know, but if that postal rider got through, so can I."

"You ain't going, are you, Daniel?" Sarah asked anxiously.

There was no hesitation. "Nay. I stay here."

If Hawk expected any differently, he didn't show it. He nodded his head and turned to

Sarah, asking, "Could you fix up a bag of corn and molasses, while I saddle my horse?"

Felicia had been stunned by the unexpected news and had listened in silence. When Hawk announced his immediate plans, she recovered enough to blurt out, "You're not leaving now, this very minute?"

For the first time since he had heard the news, Hawk looked at Felicia, then answered in a hard voice, "Yes, I'm going now. Every moment may make a difference."

"Aye," Daniel agreed, "ye miss a battle by a few hours, ye might as well miss it by a lifetime. I'll saddle yer horse for ye, while ye get yer things packed."

As Sarah rushed to the house to prepare Hawk's food, Daniel turned and walked to the back of the barn where Hawk's horse was stabled. Without another glance in Felicia's direction, Hawk hurried to pick up his saddlebags and started shoving things into them, making her feel as if an iron curtain had suddenly dropped between them. She longed to beg him not to go, for not only would he be facing the dangers of battle, but those of trying to cross the treacherous mountains in the dead of winter, but she knew her pleas would fall on deaf ears. From the moment he had heard the news, Hawk had changed from the person she had become so close to. This was the vengeful Hawk, the Cherokee, the man he held at arm's length from her, the man she had absolutely no control or influence over. She stood in the middle of the barn, wrapped in a cloak of misery, while the man she loved prepared to go to war.

When Hawk's horse was saddled and he had slung his blanket and saddlebags over the animal, the three walked in silence to where Sarah was waiting before the cabin. The old woman handed Hawk the buckskin sack with corn and molasses, waited while he looped the straps of it around his saddle horn, then hugged him, and said, "Take care of yerself. We'll be praying for yer safe return."

Hawk returned her hug with his free arm, saying, "Don't worry. *Asga-Ya-Galun-lati* will protect me. My quest is a righteous one."

Felicia didn't have to ask who *Asga-Ya-Galun-lati* was. She knew it had to be the Great Spirit, and that Hawk firmly believed what he had said. She just wished she could feel so assured of his safety. She watched while Daniel solemnly shook Hawk's hand, so deeply disturbed by Hawk's leaving that she felt physically ill. When he turned to her, she was so choked up with emotion that she couldn't say a word. All she could do was stare bleakly at him.

Sarah tugged on the sleeve of Daniel's shirt, saying, "Come on. Let's go inside."

"If ye're cold, go on in. I'll wait until Hawk has left."

Sarah rolled her eyes towards heaven, then

pushed her husband towards the door, saying in disgust, "Ye're undoubtedly the most thick-skulled cuss that ever lived. Give the young'uns a moment to themselves."

For a long moment after the cabin door had closed behind the older couple, Felicia and Hawk just stared at each other. A million things seemed to be whirling around in their heads, but not a word was spoken. Finally Felicia muttered, "I wish you wouldn't go."

Why? Hawk asked himself, still plagued by doubts. Did she still have feelings for Tarleton after all they had shared, or was her concern only for him? And how deep was that concern. Did she love him?

Hawk desperately wanted Felicia's love. Passion would no longer satisfy him. He wanted all of her. Her love, her respect, her very soul. But he didn't have the courage to come right out and ask. Nor could he tell her of his strong feelings. His fear of rejection was too strong. He waited for something more, then, when it didn't come, answered, "You know this is something I must do. It's pointless to discuss it." Then he embraced her tightly and gave her a fierce kiss.

Felicia was still reeling from that kiss, when he mounted and placed his long rifle over his lap. Bending from the saddle, he cupped her chin in his hand and lifted her head. For a long moment, his eyes drifted over her face, as if he were trying to commit each feature to memory. Then he said softly, "Goodbye," nudged his mount with his heel, and trotted off.

Felicia couldn't even force the word goodbye from her lips. She had been incapable of speech, since she had muttered she wished he wouldn't go. All the anguish she had been feeling had seemed to rise in her throat to form a huge knot. She watched as Hawk rode away, knowing it might be the last time she saw him alive. Desperately she longed to run to him, to tell him she loved him, to fall on her knees to beg him to stay, but she was powerless to move. It was as if her legs had turned to wood, and her throat was in a vise. Then she wished with all her heart that he would turn and look in her direction just once more. She stared as he wove his way around the barren trees on the hill across from her, steadily climbing higher and higher, trying to will him to do just that.

But Hawk didn't. He didn't trust himself to look back. He topped the hill and determinedly turned his mount to making the tricky descent on the icy ground. But if he had glanced back at that moment, he would known the answer to his torment. He would have seen the naked love on Felicia's face before she sank to the cold ground on her knees and broke into uncontrollable tears.

Later, after her tears had been spent, Felicia walked back to the cabin and let herself in. She knew her eyes were swollen and red, but she didn't care. She was beyond trying to hide her feelings from Daniel and Sarah any longer. Seeing her, Sarah wrapped her arms around her shoulders and led Felicia to her rocking chair by the fire. Seating her, she said, "You're as cold as ice. Sit here by the fire and warm up, while I get you a warm cup of cider."

"Perhaps the lass would like something stronger," Daniel remarked, surprising Felicia with the softness of his voice and the compassion she saw in his eyes.

"No," Felicia muttered, "cider will be fine."

Felicia was grateful when the two left her alone to recover, and busied themselves with other things in the cabin. She would have been terribly embarrassed if they had made a fuss over her.

By evening Felicia had recovered her composure, and thought Daniel seemed a little edgy. Felicia wasn't the only one that noticed. As soon as the two had settled down to their usual nightly smoke, Sarah said, "All right, Daniel. What's got you so jumpy?"

A startled expression came over Daniel's craggy face. Then he asked, "What are ye talking about, woman?"

"Don't start that foolishness with me!" Sarah said in exasperation. "I can read ye like a book, and ye know it. Now, what's bothering ye?"

Daniel shot a quick glance at Felicia, who was doing some spinning in hopes the activity would occupy her mind. "I'd hoped to wait until the lass had gone to bed."

" 'Tis bad news, then?"

"Aye."

"The lass is no child. She helped me hold this place together while ye were gone, remember? I reckon anything ye can say to me, ye can say in front of her."

Daniel glanced again at Felicia, and saw that she had stopped what she was doing and was waiting apprehensively. "Aye, I reckon ye're right. She's in this as much as us." He turned back to Sarah, saying, "That letter wasn't the only news Caleb brought. Before you noticed him and came out of the cabin, he told me the Cherokees are on the warpath again. Everyone is being alerted."

"At this time of the year?" Sarah asked in surprise. "The middle of winter?"

"Aye. The British must really have them stirred up."

"How come ye didn't tell Hawk that before he left?" Sarah asked.

"I said Cherokees, woman, not Chickamaugas. Maybe I shouldn't have done it, but I figured he'd be better off o'er the mountains, fighting the British, than here."

"Aye, ordinarily," Sarah agreed. "But there's the lass to think of. If he'd known they were on the warpath, he might not have gone."

"He knew that might happen when he brought her here," Daniel pointed out.

"Knowing something might happen, and it being a fact, are two different things. Besides, when he brought her here, he thought he'd bring this to an end sooner than he has. I don't think you should have done that, Daniel. I think he should have been told."

Daniel looked extremely uncomfortable under his wife's criticism, and Felicia took pity on him. "May I say something?" When she had the couple's attention, she continued, "I know why Daniel did what he did, because he didn't want Hawk put in the position where he would have to kill his own people. The British are his enemies. There's no doubt in Hawk's mind about that. He'll feel no remorse about it when it's over. But that wouldn't necessarily be so if he had to kill Cherokees. It might be something he couldn't come to terms with, and I don't want that to happen, either, particularly not because of me." She looked directly at Daniel. "I'm glad you didn't tell him."

Since he didn't know Felicia as well as Sarah, plus the fact that he was just naturally more cautious, Daniel had been holding back in forming an opinion of the girl. Not even seeing how deeply Hawk's leaving had affected her had swayed him, but Felicia's unselfishness in putting Hawk's feelings above her safety really impressed him. "Thank ye kindly, lass. I wouldn't want to do wrong by Hawk—he's like a son to me—but anyone can make a mistake. I hope I did the

374

right thing." He paused, then said, "And don't ye be worrying. We've gone through a lot of Indian uprisings since we moved out here. We'll make it through this one, too. Ye've my promise on that."

"Aye," Sarah joined in, "and don't worry about Hawk. He'll come back safe and sound. I'll promise ye that."

Felicia could only hope that the two promises could be kept, but without Sarah's, Daniel's was meaningless. Life without Hawk would be nothing but a vacant expanse of time.

Chapter Twenty-seven

The days that passed after Hawk had departed were tense for everyone on the small mountain farm. Felicia discovered what it was like to live with a constant fear of attack. She found herself repeatedly looking over her shoulder, particularly if she were outside, and listening closely for any unusual noises. Even nights offered no reprieve from apprehension, for although Sarah had told her that the Indians rarely attacked in the dark, that was usually the time someone would come to knock on their door and tell them to hurry to the station, because an attack was imminent. Then they would have to gather the things they had packed for that purpose and hurry through the darkness. By the end of the week, Felicia's nerves were strung taut, and her ears actually hurt from straining to listen.

When Daniel learned that Sarah had begun to teach Felicia how to use a gun, he continued the lessons, but he was a much harder taskmaster than

Sarah. He made Felicia practice every day, and her shoulder seemed to be perpetually bruised from the recoil of the long gun. But Felicia didn't resent his persistence. She was well aware that he was determined she must learn, because her life could depend upon it.

When a month passed and nothing happened, the three began to relax a little, but still kept up their guard. Often Felicia would see Daniel standing at the top of the hill, peering off into the distance. Sarah explained that he was looking for signs of smoke, which might mean a neighbor had been attacked. No news from the station arrived. They didn't know if it was because there *was* no news, or because all of the trails in the mountains were iced over and too dangerous to travel.

When spring arrived and the ground thawed, they heard the first report by way of a rider sent out from the station. The middle and lower Cherokees were still on the warpath, and had been raiding settlers along the North Carolina border, but thus far, there had been no attacks in their locality. As for the war going on in the east, there had been no news, since the routes were still snowed in and impassable.

Sarah and Daniel didn't feel reassured by the news. They feared the Cherokees might become more active with the warm weather. Daniel started his plowing with Sarah standing guard with her long rifle, while Felicia assumed all of the household duties.

One day, Felicia came out of the cabin for a

breath of fresh air. For a while she stood beneath the budding sycamore and admired the scenery, something she could do again now that the winter fog was gone. The hills that rolled off into the distance were ablaze with red azaleas and covered with a faint bluish veil, and in the forests closer to her, she could see the creamy blossoms of the towering chestnuts, and beneath them, the purplish red flowers of the redbud trees and the white of wild plums.

Sarah and Daniel walked up the hill from where he had been planting his corn. Daniel continued on to the cabin, but Sarah veered away and ambled over to where Felicia was standing and admiring the view. " 'Tis beautiful," Sarah remarked, leaning on her long rifle while her gaze swept over the colorful panorama.

"Yes, it is," Felicia agreed.

"It's even prettier when ye walk out into it. There are so many things ye can't see from a distance."

"I wish we could take a walk in the forest," Felicia said wistfully.

Sarah gazed out for a long moment, then said in a decisive voice, "Aye, that we will."

"But Daniel doesn't want us going into the woods," Felicia reminded her.

"I know. But if there were any Indians lurking around today, they should have attacked by now. It will be dark in a few hours. Besides, we'll take our guns with us."

Having one wish fulfilled reminded Felicia of

another. "Do you think we could possibly go to the sink for a bath, while we're at it?"

The prospect of a bath in the pool sounded just as delightful to Sarah, after months of bathing from a bucket. "Aye, lass, we'll do that, too." She turned and headed for the cabin, saying, "Hurry, lass. Let's get our soap and towels, and Daniel's gun. Now that I've decided on it, I can't wait."

When Sarah announced their plans, Daniel had a fit. But the poor man might as well have saved his breath. No amount of arguing, reasoning, then threatening could change Sarah's mind. He finally relented, making her promise to keep a close watch and fire her gun, if she saw anything suspicious.

A short while later, the two women walked into the woods. Felicia looked about in awe. Wildflowers bloomed everywhere in profusion, and looked like a crazy quilt made of blossoms. There were purple- and yellow-fringed orchids, orange trumpet creepers, blue purple monkshood, blue and purple irises, white violets, pink lady slippers, yellow buttercups, along with pale pink mountain laurel, red azaleas, pink, red, purple and white rhododendron. Color was everywhere, on the ground, on the bushes, on many of the trees, and there was every color and every hue imaginable present. "I've never seen so many wildflowers," Felicia muttered, looking from side to side and trying to take it all in. "It's like nature went berserk, and threw every seed she had out here."

"Aye, that's true. Every spring I find a flower I haven't seen before. There seems to be no end to them."

"Do they always bloom this early? We don't really get a lot of wildflowers until May."

"Here in the mountains they have to do it early, before the leaves come out completely on the trees and blot out the sun. Ye don't see too many summer wildflowers here, except in coves."

"Well, the flowering season might be short, but it certainly is spectacular. You're right, Sarah. Spring is more colorful than autumn." Felicia took a deep breath. The forest smelled wet and clean. Then she caught a whiff of something else. "What's that sweet smell?"

"It's probably coming from a magnolia, or one of the tulip trees. They're blooming, too."

When they reached the pool they took turns bathing, while the other stood guard. Neither cared that the water was cold. It felt so good just to immerse their bodies in the liquid and scrub away the dirt, that a few shivers was well worth it.

When they walked back through the woods, Felicia again admired the beauty all around her. She was in total agreement with Hawk. The forest was beautiful at all times, but the most beautiful during spring.

The reminder of Hawk brought tears to her eyes. She missed him and worried even more this time than the last, and knew it was because she had come to love him even more.

Sarah glanced across and saw the tears in Felicia's eyes, then said gently, "What's wrong, lass? Are ye thinking of Hawk?"

"Yes. He's been gone longer than the last time. I'm worried. Surely the battle is over by now."

"Aye, but not the war. Hawk feels strongly about the rebel cause."

Felicia should have been relieved to have a reason for Hawk's lengthy absence, but she wasn't. The war might last for years, and she didn't think she could stand much more of the agony she was going through, and the thought of not seeing Hawk for that long filled her with despair.

At the very moment Felicia was thinking about Hawk, he was thinking of her, something that had occupied the better part of his time since he had left her. On that particular day, Hawk was taking part in the retreat after the Battle of Guilford in North Carolina and feeling very low. Like Felicia, he feared the war might continue for years, yet he couldn't bring himself to desert the cause when the patriots needed every fighting man so desperately, nor had he been successful in his quest for vengeance. Tarleton—the bastard!—had managed to escape him again. His mind drifted back over the events of the past months.

After leaving Felicia, Hawk had crossed the mountains. The trip had not been easy. The passes had been filled with snow so deep, his horse had barely managed to plow through them, and he had been plagued by a pack of vicious wolves that trailed him for days, until they made the mistake of getting within rifle range and felt the lethal bite of his bullets. As soon as he had reached the eastern side of the mountains, he sought information about the location of Morgan's army, and was told they were nearing Cowpens with Tarleton and his army in hot pursuit.

Hawk rode nonstop for almost twenty-four hours, and reached the army positioned in a thinly wooded camp in the bend of the Broad River the night before the battle. No questions were asked when he presented himself to General Morgan, nor were any future commitments made on his part. All that mattered to Morgan was that he had an extra fighting man for the upcoming battle, and because Hawk had a horse, he was assigned to the cavalry under William Washington, George Washington's cousin. Ordinarily, Hawk would have preferred fighting with the foot soldiers. The rifle was his weapon of choice, and he was a crack shot. But Hawk knew he would have a much better chance at coming face to face with Tarleton on horseback, since the colonel led a calvary unit. Therefore he voiced no objection to relinquishing his rifle for a saber, although he had no experience with that weapon. He rationalized that he could probably swing the long blade as well as the next man, and if that didn't accomplish his goal, he could always fall back on his tomahawk or his scalping knife.

Morgan had about sixteen hundred men in his command, mostly militias from Virginia and Maryland. That night, Hawk sat and listened as the old Indian fighter, crippled by painful arthritis, limped among the campfires and encouraged his men to stand firm the next morning long enough to fire three volleys, saying, "Just hold your head up, boys, three fires and you are free." He told them how the girls would kiss them and the old folks would bless them, when they returned home. But despite all of the general's encouragement, Hawk felt the fear all around him. The patriots were untrained, and Tarleton and his dreaded cavalry legion's savage reputation had preceded them. It was then that Hawk realized why Morgan had picked that particular spot to turn and fight. With the unfordable Broad River behind them, there would be no fleeing the enemy, at least not far.

The next morning, Tarleton attacked. His force consisted of his dragoons, light infantry, five battalions of British regulars, and a small artillery unit, about eleven hundred men in all. The sight of British infantry line coming down on them with heavy tread and glittering bayonets was too much for the untrained patriot militia, and many of them turned and ran, but Morgan was there waiting for them, waving his sword and barring their way, shouting "Form again! Give them one more fire, and the day is ours."

While this was going on, Hawk sat astride his horse, chomping at the bit for action and wishing he had his rifle, so he could pick off a few of the redcoats, as some of the Virginia sharpshooters were doing. The sounds of battle filled the air: gunshots, cannons booming, wild Indian howls, curses, shouted orders coming from the officers, cries of pain from the wounded. Then, through the thick cloud of rolling smoke, Hawk spied Tarleton's cavalry riding towards them. He was off, even before Washington gave the order to charge, swinging his saber just as vigorously as the enemy riding down on them.

The two cavalries met with a clash of steel that rang out in the air even over the sounds of the cannons. All around Hawk men fell, either slashed or stabbed by his saber, or shot from their saddles by the continentals behind them who Morgan had rallied. Once, just briefly, Hawk caught sight of Tarleton out of the corner of his eye, but at that moment he was engaged in a fierce fight with another cavalryman. Suddenly, the British cavalry turned and fled, and fast on their heels, the British line broke and ran, with the Americans in hot pursuit. For almost a mile, the Americans chased the British, but much to Hawk's disgust, Tarleton's cavalry didn't make another charge, and he was left to fight his way through the panicked British line to try to reach the officer. It was the most frustrating experience Hawk had ever known. He could see Tarleton in the distance, furiously yelling orders at his horsemen to attack, but Hawk couldn't ride to engage his enemy in battle because his way was blocked by both fleeing redcoats and Americans, tearing after them with poised bayonets. The last Hawk saw of Tarleton was when his infamous legion turned and galloped from the field, followed by their leader. Hawk would have given chase along with some of Washington's cavalry, if fate had not intervened. A split second later, a cannon shot exploded nearby, killing his horse and sending Hawk flying through the air.

It was hours before Hawk regained consciousness from the concussion he had received, to learn of the patriots' victory. Except for about three hundred who managed to escape—Tarleton included—virtually the whole of Tarleton's force was killed or captured—a substantial portion of Cornwallis's army—along with Tarleton's entire baggage train of much-needed ammunition. If it had been possible, Hawk would have followed his sworn adversary even then, as Washington gave him one of the captured horses to replace his mount. But Hawk couldn't because of severe dizziness every time he so much as lifted his head, a condition that lasted for two days.

Hawk was just beginning to return to normal, when word arrived that Cornwallis himself had taken up pursuit, determined to give the rebels no chance to exult over their stunning and unexpected victory at Cowpens. Unable to desert his comrades in need, and hoping that Tarleton might be with Cornwallis, Hawk stayed with Morgan's army as they fled into North Carolina. The weeks that passed were sheer misery for the rag-tag patriots. Heavy rains mixed with snow turned the roads into a morass of mud and flooded the rivers and streams. Had it not been for General Greene ordering wheeled platforms on which improvised pontoons could be hauled, the Continental Army would have never made it across some of the swollen rivers. To their utter amazement, Cornwallis and his army followed. It was through spies that they learned the British General was so determined to catch and annihilate them, that he had resorted to drastic measures in an effort to lighten his wagon train to speed his pace. To his troops' horror, he burned his tents, blankets, personal baggage, even several hogsheads of rum, leaving his army stripped to the minimum of provisions and ammunition. Had it not been for the raging Dan River and the fact that the patriots had stripped it of every boat, Cornwallis might well have caught the rebels. But the flooding river stopped him, and he was forced to retreat to Hillsboro to resupply.

But the Southern Continental Army's reprieve from pursuit was short-lived. As soon as Cornwallis had restored his losses with reinforcements, he was hot on the patriots' trail again. In the weeks that followed, Hawk thought that the misery he now experienced was surpassed only by the winter he had spent in the forest after his Indian home had been destroyed. The army marched through a sea of mud in constant rain, slept without benefit of fires, cold, hungry, weakened by fever, and shaking with ague. The underfed horses were often too weak to pull the cannons, and the men had to substitute for them. The only thing that gave the patriots consolation was the fact that Cornwallis's army was suffering the same, his supply lines hampered by the rebel partisans between him and

Charleston, and the local loyalists refusing to give him any aid. For both the pursued and the pursuer it was a living hell.

Many of the men in the patriot army couldn't understand why Cornwallis wouldn't give up the chase. Surely, they argued, he must know that Greene was deliberately luring him farther and farther away from his supply bases. But Hawk understood. The Earl couldn't rest until he had avenged his defeat at Cowpens, and recovered the British prisoners. Cornwallis was just as single-minded in his vengeance, as Hawk was in his. Finally, judging that the time had come, Greene picked his spot and turned. What followed was the Battle of Guilford.

To Hawk it was the most senseless waste of lives he had yet to see. Predictably, the British advanced in a compact phalanx with fixed bayonets and kept coming, and kept coming, despite the lethal fire of the Virginia sharpshooters that mowed them down like a sickle mowed grain. Both armies were exhausted before they even engaged, but still they fought, back and forth, back and forth, until Cornwallis fired grapeshot through the ranks of his own redcoats and forced Greene to withdraw, leaving the British in possession of the field and a technical victory, much to Hawk's disgust. In his opinion the war was no closer to an end than it had been four years before, nor was he any closer to avenging his father. He'd seen absolutely no sign of Tarleton that day, and was left to assume that his hated adversary was not with Cornwallis, else he would have been in the thick of the fight, to give the devil his due.

Hawk was startled from his thoughts by the sound of a man asking, "Weren't you at the Battle of King's Mountain?"

Hawk turned and saw the man who had brought his horse up against his. The stranger was dressed in frontier garb just like him. "Yes, I was."

"I thought I recognized you. You fought like the devil himself that day. I'm with Campbell's militia."

"Campbell's here?" Hawk asked in surprise.

"Aye. Greene sent word and asked if he could send some men for the upcoming battle. We fought under General Henry Lee. That's probably why you didn't notice us. You're with Washington's cavalry, aren't you?"

"Yes," Hawk answered, then after a moment of silence, said, "Damn! I wish we'd won the other day! This war is never going to end."

"Well, I don't reckon we did so bad for ourselves," the man drawled. "According to Campbell, Greene said it didn't matter if we won or not, that as long as we kept rising up and fighting, they couldn't call us whipped. And the British sure can't afford many more victories like Guilford. According to our spies, they lost twice as many men as us, almost a fourth of their army. Cornwallis is retreating, you know."

"No, I didn't," Hawk answered in surprise.

"Aye, he's heading for the coast. Don't have enough supplies to hold the ground he took.

Damn, it's a shame we couldn't get together a force like the one we had at King's Mountain. A bunch of fierce mountain men. We could have whipped him once and for all."

"Why didn't Campbell get together a bigger force?" Hawk asked. "And now that I think about it, where in the hell was Shelby? Why didn't he come? The passes must be cleared of snow by now."

"Hell, Shelby couldn't bring any men for the same reason Campbell could only get a few together. Everyone is busy protecting the frontier."

Hawk sucked in his breath sharply, then asked, "The Chickamaugas are on the warpath again?"

"Nay! It's the Cherokees themselves. Lower, middle, and a few of the upper towns. It ain't been as bad as it was back in '66, but the weather is just turning warm. Who knows how bad it's going to get."

Suddenly, all Hawk could think of was Felicia's safety. He forgot the war, his revenge, everything. He wheeled his horse around, and as he galloped off, the Virginian called, "Where in the hell are you going?"

"Home!" Hawk called over his shoulder.

The Virginian shrugged his shoulders, not thinking that Hawk's abrupt departure was at all unusual. Men came and went at will in the Continental Army all the time, according to need. A man did what he had to.

Chapter Twenty-eight

Sarah and Daniel were in the field when Sarah spied the rider coming up the trail. Because he wasn't mounted on the bay he had left on, she didn't recognize Hawk until she could actually see his face. Then she let out a loud whoop, making Daniel, who was occupied planting corn, almost jump out of his skin in fright.

Daniel looked wildly around him, thinking the cry had come from Indians and expecting to see a war party tearing from the woods. Then, seeing Sarah run down the hill and the rider at the bottom of it, he dropped the stick he was using to poke holes in the ground for his seeds and ran after her.

Hawk had swung down from his horse before Sarah reached him, almost bowling him over. He returned her hugs and endured Daniel's enthusiastic slaps on the back good-naturedly, before Sarah pushed away from him and asked, "Is the war over?"

"No, far from it, I'm afraid," Hawk answered in disgust.

"Then you got yer man?" Daniel surmised.

A wave of fury swept over Hawk, making his dark eyes flash. "No, the bastard got away from me again." Seeing the two exchanging puzzled looks, he explained, "I heard the Cherokees were on the warpath. I thought I might be needed here."

Both Sarah and Daniel knew it wasn't their need that had drawn him back, but rather his feelings of obligation to Felicia. Much to Daniel's relief, Sarah didn't mention his deliberate omission in not telling Hawk of the Cherokee threat before he had left.

"Where's Felicia?" Hawk asked.

"In the cabin," Sarah answered.

Hawk looked anxiously in that direction, and asked, "She's well and hardy?"

It was Daniel who answered, "Aye, and getting to be a real fine frontier woman. Why, the lass can cook just as good as Sarah, and skin a deer faster than me! And if she keeps it up, she'll be a better shot than either of us."

As the three walked to the cabin, both Sarah and Daniel continued to praise Felicia's surprising accomplishments. Hawk thought that the woman they were extolling didn't sound a bit like the spoiled, headstrong girl he had abducted. Ordinarily, he would have been proud that the couple approved so hardily of her, but right now, all Hawk cared about was seeing her, and Sarah and Daniel were hard put to keep up with his rapid pace.

Felicia was carrying a long-handled, baking skillet from the fire to the table, when Hawk opened the door and stepped into the cabin. She was so surprised, she almost dropped the heavy skillet, then recovering, sat it on the table and, with a cry of joy, ran to him. She hugged him fiercely, not caring in the least that Sarah and Daniel were witnessing her show of affection, for she knew they realized she had strong feelings for Hawk. Then she lifted her head, waiting breathlessly for Hawk's kiss.

But it didn't come, even though Hawk wanted desperately to do just that. At that moment, his Cherokee upbringing had come to the surface, and he was following his tribe's dictate that men and women did not display affection before others. That was why courting couples did their wooing under the cover of a blanket, thrown over their heads. Instead, he said in a voice hoarse with yearning, "Come with me to the barn, while I tend my horse."

The disappointment Felicia had felt when Hawk hadn't kissed her was short-lived. Even if she hadn't seen the sensual promise in his eyes, she would have known the true meaning of his invitation. The barn was their favorite trysting place. Her heart raced in anticipation, and an urgency filled her.

Hawk felt the same urgency. As soon as they stepped outside and he closed the door of the cabin behind them, Hawk took Felicia into his arms and kissed her deeply, passionately, as if he wanted to crawl inside her, and Felicia gloried in it, not caring that she could barely breathe, that his embrace was so tight it hurt her ribs, or that his lips were bruising hers. She strained against him, wishing she could melt into him, become one with him right then and there.

Somehow or another, they finally made it to the barn. They didn't even wait until they reached Hawk's pallet before they began to strip one another, hands trembling with excitement between hot, fierce kisses. Another step, another fiery kiss, another piece of clothing fell to the floor. They tumbled naked into the straw, and Hawk entered her with one deep thrust—then froze. With the feel of Felicia's soft, pliant body pressed against his, her arms wrapped around him, the scent of her sweet fragrance in his nostrils, and her tight, wet heat surrounding him where he lay deep inside her, he felt an incredible sense of belonging, a feeling as if he had finally come home after a long, long journey. It was a feeling that Hawk hadn't known since he was a very young child, and he knew at that moment that Felicia was his soul mate, the woman the Great Spirit had created just for him, the woman he loved.

Beneath him, Felicia wondered why Hawk was so very still and looking down at her so intently. "What's wrong?" she asked.

Hawk wanted to tell her he loved her, but he couldn't. He was still afraid of rejection, something that, strangely, sprang from the deeply ingrained warrior within him. Openly admitting to such tender feelings — when he didn't know if they were returned — left him feeling too vulnerable, too wide open, too exposed, something his warrior's training would not let him risk.

"What is it?" Felicia prompted when he didn't answer her question.

"Nothing." Then, realizing that was a ridiculous answer, he said, "It's just that I didn't realize how much I missed you until now."

Felicia had hoped for more, much more, but for the time being, she would settle for that admission. She was acutely aware of the burning where their bodies were joined, and had more pressing needs. She pulled his head down, whispering just as her lips touched his, "I missed you, too. Terribly!"

For Felicia, Hawk's feverish lovemaking was more than just proof that he desired her. It was an affirmation of life, that he had come back to her whole and sound. As he led her up the glorious heights, she reveled in not only the breathtaking, electrifying things he was making her feel . . . and feel . . . and feel . . . but in the motion of his powerful muscles contracting and relaxing, the thud of his mighty heart against hers, the warmth of his body, the salty taste of his skin, the smell of his musky, exciting scent. He was man personified: powerful, magnificent, bold, every inch of him vibrantly alive; and she basked in his virility, his strength, and yes, for that moment, even his fierce domination.

After it was over, Felicia was loath to give him up even for a moment. When he started to lift himself from her, she clutched him tightly and locked her legs around his narrow hips, saying, "No! Stay with me."

Hawk didn't object. He loved the feel of her soft, heated skin against his, the smell of her womanly fragrance. He moved just enough to support his weight on his forearms, then nuzzled the crook of her neck before nibbling and kissing the soft skin there. Seeing a faded bruise on her right shoulder, he frowned and asked, "What happened? Did you fall?"

"No. That's from shooting Sarah's rifle. Daniel has been making me practice practically every day."

"That's right," Hawk answered, remembering Daniel's praise. "He said if you kept it up, you'd be a better shot than either he or Sarah."

Felicia laughed. "That's a gross exaggeration. I've become a fair shot, but I'll never be able to bark a squirrel, like Sarah."

Hawk smiled. Barking a squirrel took some shooting expertise. It required hitting the tree behind the squirrel, close enough to its head to cause death by concussion without striking the animal, since it was so small that the ball would all but destroy it. It had taken Hawk awhile to learn the knack himself. But Hawk still found it difficult to believe Felicia could load and fire a rifle, and do all of the other things Sarah and Daniel had praised her for. She was still continuing to surprise him, revealing virtues and strengths he had never dreamed were there. He wondered how much was still hidden and if he'd ever get to know her fully. He kissed the bruise gently, and said, "I'll have to make a pad for Sarah's rifle. I should have thought of it before now. I don't imagine it feels too good on her shoulder either."

Hawk completely forgot the rifle, being distracted by the sight of the beauty mark that lay in the deep valley between Felicia's breasts. He bent his head and licked it, muttering something about it being his little treasure. Then, so that the twin mounds on both sides wouldn't feel jealous, he kissed and laved each of them, his long black hair where it hung free brushing back and forth across her chest and rib cage, a featherlike caress just as exciting as what he was doing to her breasts. Felicia stroked the slick muscles on his back, cupped his tight buttocks, and massaged them.

Felicia heard his groan of pleasure and felt him stir where he was still nestled inside her, then grow, hardening and lengthening until he completely filled her. Their passion flamed anew, and he took her to paradise a second time.

Later, while they were dressing, Felicia took note of his horse. The poor animal had been left to its own devices and was munching on some corn husks it had found on the barn floor, still bearing the load of the saddle and Hawk's saddlebags.

"What happened to the bay?" she asked.

"He got killed by a cannon shot."

"While you were on him?" Felicia asked, her

heart suddenly leaping to her throat in fright.

"Yes. That's why I couldn't follow Tarleton, when he escaped from the battle. The explosion knocked me out."

Felicia felt so weak from Hawk's close call with death that she had to lean against the nearest horse stall for support. "So you found him?" she asked, wondering if her brother had been present, and if so, how he had fared.

Hawk was aware of how pale Felicia had become, and speculated over it. Did she still care about the officer? He found it hard to believe after her passionate response, and yet, he was leery. Thank God, he hadn't told her he loved her. What if she was still carrying a torch for the bastard? Was her only interest in Hawk that of a lover, someone to satisfy her passion? An intense jealousy filled Hawk, and out of pure spite he said, "Yes, I found him! And we beat the hell out of him, before he and that cowardly legion of his ran from the battlefield. But that's not the end of it. As soon as this Indian uprising is over with, I'm going back. I'll find him, if I have to search to the ends of the earth."

Felicia didn't question Hawk's sudden fury. She assumed it was just his frustration at not being able to get his revenge. She had no idea his vendetta against the colonel had become more personal. Her happiness at Hawk's return drained from her, as she realized that nothing had been settled, that she had the agony of waiting and worrying to go through still ahead of her, that all she had gained was just another reprieve. Her disappointment was so acute, it was more than she could bear at the moment. Tears welled in her eyes, and fearing Hawk would see them, she quickly turned.

But Felicia hadn't been quick enough. Hawk noticed, and just as he had misinterpreted her pale face, he misread her tears. A part of him told him to take her back, to let the damn bastard have her if she cared so much about him, but Hawk knew he couldn't. Not because of his pride, though. Tarleton laughing at him seemed insignificant to the real reason Hawk couldn't release Felicia. He loved her too much to let her go. She had become a fever in his blood, a fire in his loins, an ache in his heart, the light of his life. He couldn't bear to give her up. Not yet. Maybe someday, but not yet.

Over the next few months, Hawk continued to make love to Felicia, when the occasion arose and they could find privacy. He hated himself for it, yet he couldn't resist. His hunger for her seemed to be insatiable. It was as if he were trying to cram a lifetime of loving into what little time they had left.

Felicia was as hungry for Hawk, and gave of herself eagerly. Yet, she knew their relationship had changed. They no longer just sat and talked, as they had done before he went back to war, and she sorely missed that companionship, that special sharing. She told herself that it was because they didn't have the time they had had during the winter. This was a busy season on the farm. But her argument didn't ring true. She knew he was holding something back, something vital to their relationship.

One day, when she and Sarah were doing some sewing in the cabin, Sarah said, "Something has been bothering ye lately. Ye've been as quiet as a church mouse. Do ye want to talk about it?"

Felicia was reluctant to talk about something so personal, but she desperately needed to unburden herself, and she knew Sarah would never divulge what she said. "Yes, I have been upset. I just don't know where I stand with Hawk. What he feels for me, if anything."

"Feels for ye?" Sarah asked in astonishment. "Hell and damnation, lass, ye must know that. He can't take his eyes off ye. Why, sometimes I think he's going to eat ye up right there in front of me and Daniel."

Felicia knew that Sarah must know she and Hawk were lovers. The older woman wasn't obtuse, not by a long shot. "I'm not talking about passion," she answered frankly. "I'm talking about love."

"And ye don't think he loves ye?"

"No, I don't. He's never told me so. He's never said anything except he missed me, and that doesn't mean anything. All he might have missed is my body."

"Don't make too little of passion, lass. That goes along with the loving. And I wouldn't worry too much about him not telling ye. I don't know why it is, but men seem to have trouble saying the words. I had to pull it out of Daniel, and he only said it once. And every other woman I've talked to, agrees with me. It just seems to get stuck in their craw. Now, what could be so hard about saying, I love ye? Three little words? I don't know if they think love is weak, and that admitting to it makes them weak, but they couldn't be farther from the truth. Love is the strongest feeling there is. Nay, lass, I wouldn't worry about him telling ye. I'd go more by his actions."

"Well, there's that, too," Felicia admitted, her spirits sinking lower. "We used to spend a lot of time sitting and talking, but he hasn't done much of that lately."

Sarah shrugged, answering, "Maybe he ain't got that much more to say. Hawk never was one to talk yer arm off."

"No, it's more than that," Felicia persisted. "After it's over . . ." She flushed. "He seems moody, withdrawn."

"I'm surprised he doesn't just go to sleep. That's what Daniel does," Sarah answered candidly. Then, seeing the exasperated look on Felicia's face, she sighed and said, "Maybe ye're expecting too much of him. He is half-Indian, and they're very reserved. Maybe how he is acting is normal for a Cherokee. I don't know exactly how they treat their women, but I wouldn't imagine they spend a lot of time with them. At any rate, I wouldn't be worrying so much about it. He loves ye. I'd stake my life on that."

Felicia knew that Sarah had an almost uncanny wisdom, and the older woman certainly knew more about men than she did, particularly rugged frontiersmen, who were a breed unto themselves. She desperately hoped Sarah was right. Loving someone who didn't love you in return would be sheer torment, a living hell she could well do without.

Chapter Twenty-nine

Summer came with no sign of Cherokees. Having heard nothing about the uprising and not even knowing if it was still going on, Daniel risked a ride to the station to find out what was happening, since Hawk was on the farm to protect the women in case of an attack. The old man came back with the grim news that the Cherokees were still on the warpath, and grisly tales of other settlements having been razed.

"What about the war over the mountains?" Hawk asked, when Daniel had finished his report on the Indian hostilities.

"Cornwallis retreated to Wilmington, and picked up more men and supplies for his march into Virginia. That's where he is now, heading towards the Chesapeake Bay."

"Then he just marched off and left Greene and his army, without even securing the Carolinas?" Hawk asked in astonishment.

"Aye. I reckon he figured if he couldn't beat Greene, he'd just pretend he doesn't exist. Word is

Greene's back in South Carolina, and determined to push the British right back out into the sea."

And how long would that take him to do? Hawk wondered. He wished the Cherokees would settle down, so he could get back to his other business, that of avenging his father. Then, hopefully, he could get back to his life. Hawk didn't know just what that life might entail. He desperately hoped that Felicia might be a part of it, but was afraid to do too much dreaming along those lines. He knew only too well that shattered dreams could be very painful. He'd experienced that when he had been forced to leave his people.

A few days later, when he and Daniel were again mending fences, Hawk spied a trail of black smoke in the sky to the north of the farm. Almost as soon as he saw it, Daniel noticed also.

"Do ye think it's Cherokees?" Daniel asked apprehensively.

"I'm afraid so," Hawk answered, his look grave.

"Think we should pack up right now and leave for the station?"

"With them between us and it? No, we'd be fools to risk getting caught in the wide open, with no protection."

"Tonight, then?"

"Maybe. But I'm more prone to wait and see if someone comes from the station. For all we know, that could be what's burning, and there would be nothing to go to."

The four hurriedly prepared for a possible attack. Hawk and Daniel took the animals and hid them deep in the woods, so they wouldn't roasted alive if the Indians set fire to the barn. Then the four spent the rest of the day wetting down the cabin, so fire arrows couldn't catch, and stocking up on water and supplies, in case they would have to wait out a siege. Just as dusk was falling, the two men cut loopholes into the four walls, not daring to leave the windows unbarred. Then the four went inside, latched the front door and the heavy shutters on the windows, and waited.

It was the longest night Felicia had ever spent. No one slept. But not because they feared an attack — Cherokees did not fight at night — but because they wanted to be ready to leave in case someone came for them from the station. When that didn't happen and dawn crept nearer and nearer, they four became more and more apprehensive, knowing that if the attack came, it would likely be at sunrise, for the Cherokees believed the east to be the holiest of all directions, and preferred fighting when the all-powerful sun was in that hemisphere.

The sun came up and nothing happened, but they still didn't leave the cabin. They sat in the stifling heat, sweat pouring from their bodies, peering out of their loopholes until their eyes ached. Finally that evening they opened the windows and doors, and let in a welcome breath of fresh, cool air.

For the next few days, they left the animals in the woods and stuck close to the cabin. Then at mid-morning on the fourth day, Daniel spied smoke far to the south of them.

As the two men stood beneath the rustling syca-more, Daniel asked Hawk, "What do you think?"

"I think they've gone around us. They do that, you know, zigzag from farm to farm, so no one can predict where they'll hit next."

"Then you think the scare is over?"

"For the time being, yes."

"Thank God!" Sarah said fervently from where she had walked up behind them.

Hawk didn't comment, but he thought the same thing, not only thankful that no harm had come to the three people he cared so much about, but that he hadn't been forced to kill one of his own kind. He'd heard that some of the Overhill towns were taking part in the uprising, but didn't know if his former village was or not. He would have hated to come face to face with someone he knew person-ally, and have to kill them. Of course, it would have been a matter of self-defense, and he would have done it, but he knew with great certainty that he would have regretted it. He wasn't at odds with the Cherokee, like he was the British and the Tories. He knew in his heart that the Cherokee cause was just, that they were fighting for what was rightfully theirs. These were their mountains, their land, the land given to them by the Great Spirit. Again he felt the chaos of his torn loyalties.

Hawk stood on the hilltop staring out at space for a long time, deep in thought. From the cabin, Felicia watched him and sensed what was bother-ing him. She wished she could ease the turmoil he was feeling, but she knew there was nothing she could say. But there was something she could do, she decided, or try to do. Hoping he wouldn't reject her, she squared her shoulders with firm resolve and walked to him.

Hawk didn't notice when Felicia came to a stop at his side. Then, when she slipped her small hand into his, he was startled. He started to pull his hand away, but was stopped by a strange feeling. It was almost as if the confusion and pain were draining from him, leaving instead a sense of peacefulness. He didn't know what was happening, but he didn't fight it. His hand wrapped around Felicia's, and without even glancing at one another, they stood shoulder to shoulder, holding hands and gazing out.

Felicia had never felt as close to Hawk as she had at that moment on the hilltop, when she had shared his burden and hoped that it would mark a return to their previous relationship; however, nothing changed. Hawk acted as if the almost spiritual experience had never occurred, bewildering Felicia all the more.

The last day of July, Felicia and Sarah were busy in the cabin, performing one of the many steps required to make clothing from linsey, which had wool in it. The cloth had to be "filled" to keep it from shrinking, a process that consisted of soaking it in hot soap suds, then throwing it on the floor and stomping on it. As Felicia sat on a stool and pounded her bare feet on the wet material, she thought of all the work that went into making this homemade linen. First the flax plants had to be grown, then pulled, then placed in piles that were kept wet, so the hard core that formed the sheath protecting the useful fibers would rot. The stalks were then dried over pits with slow fires and stored until winter, when they were removed and broken on a flax break, placed on a scutching block to knock bits of the stalk from the fiber, then pulled through a hackle, a planed piece of wood that had been made into a bed of nails that removed the last of the impurities. All this before the fibers were even put on the spinning wheel, the long, glossy lengths bleached to become the better linen, and the brownish blond threads put aside for the coarser tow-linen. Then the threads were spun into yarn, that was woven into material on a clumsy frame loom. Felicia had never taken the time to wonder how material came to be, much less guessed at the tedious and time-consuming work that went into it. She realized for the hundredth time how many things she had taken for granted, and knew, if nothing else, that her time on the frontier had taught her how to appreciate even the most common and smallest of comforts.

By the time the two women had finished the chore, they had worked up a sweat. "I think I'll take a break to cool off under the sycamore, after I put this out to dry," Sarah commented. "Do you want to join me, lass?"

"No," Felicia answered, wiping the perspiration from her brow with the hem of her apron. "I have a better idea. I'm going to the pool."

"This early?"

"Yes. I'm hot and sweaty and miserable."

"But we still have work to do. You'll just get that way all over."

"I don't care. I'm going, if for nothing else than for a quick dip."

Since they'd seen or heard nothing of the Indians for weeks, Sarah didn't object. The only caution she did give was to say, "Be sure to take a gun."

Just as she had promised, Felicia didn't stay at the pool long, just long enough to refresh herself. When she walked back up the hill, she saw an unfamiliar horse standing before the cabin and wondered who had come to call. Then, when she stepped into the cabin, she was surprised to find not only a red headed stranger there, but that both Hawk and Daniel had come in from the fields.

Seeing her, the strange man, who had been sitting at the table across from Daniel and Hawk, came to his feet, then looking at Hawk in astonishment asked in Cherokee, *"Ishtama?"* Have you married?

"No," Hawk answered, then rose and said, "Felicia, I'd like you to meet an old friend of mine, Ivan MacKensie. Ivan, this is Felicia Edwards."

Ivan noted that Hawk offered no further explanation for the young woman's presence, making him very curious as to who the lovely girl with the breathtaking mane of hair might be. Remembering his manners, he stepped over the bench and walked to her, offering his hand and saying, "I'm pleased to meet ye."

So this tall, lanky Scotsman was the man who had been responsible for bringing Hawk to live with the whites, and reuniting him with his father, Felicia thought. She couldn't help but notice the horrible scar on his cheek that ran down his neck. Then, realizing Ivan was offering her his left hand, she saw his right shirtsleeve was empty and pinned against his chest, and wondered how he had lost his arm. "How do you do," Felicia responded with a smile, quickly averting her eyes before he noticed.

"Ivan brought us good news about the Cherokees," Sarah informed Felicia, as she walked from the cabinet where she had gone to get a jug of whiskey. "They've signed a new peace treaty."

"Aye, I was one of the commissioners that helped negotiate the peace," Ivan added.

"That's wonderful!" Felicia responded, a wave of relief washing over her.

"Sit down, lass," Sarah said, placing the jug on the table beside several cups. "We're going to have a little celebration. Are ye sure you won't join us and have a drink, just this once?"

"No, thank you. I'll have cider, along with Hawk."

After the group had toasted the peace and the three Scots had drained their cups of whiskey, Daniel said to Ivan, "We sure do appreciate ye riding all the way out here to tell us the news."

Ivan glanced sharply at Hawk, then answered,

"Well, I'll have to admit that's not why I came. A rider is circulating the area and doing that. I came because I heard Hawk was here, and I wanted to talk to him."

Guessing that Ivan was wondering what the status was with his avenging his father's death, Hawk said, "If you're wondering about that business we discussed the last time I saw you, I haven't been able to finish it yet. Tarleton got away from me twice. Then I heard about the Indian uprising and thought I ought to come back, in case I was needed here. But I haven't forgotten it. I planned on going back as soon as things settled down here. Have you got any idea where the bastard might be right now?"

Ivan squirmed a little in his seat, then replied "Aye, he's down around Charleston, trying to flush Marion and his swamp rats from the Santee area. Or at least he was, when I left Virginia a few weeks ago."

Hawk nodded. Because Ivan had personal friends in the Virginian government, including the governor, he knew the Scot had access to information that wasn't generally known. "How is the war going?"

A smile spread over the Scot's lips. "They don't know it yet, but they've lost the South. Greene's pushing them steadily back towards Charleston, and Cornwallis is marching towards Yorktown on the Chesapeake, with Lafayette and his army fast on his heels. And if things are going according to schedule, the French navy should be arriving any day now to blockade the bay. Cornwallis is trapped. He'll be forced to surrender, and Clinton can't hang on without him. It's just a matter of time before the entire war is over." Ivan paused for a thoughtful moment, then said, "And do you know what's so ironic about it all? The Battle of King's Mountain was what turned the tide in the South, and it wasn't even fought by regular militia. The British never did recover from that beating. I heard ye and Daniel took part in it. Congratulations on the excellent job ye did!"

Both men nodded in acknowledgement, neither really feeling comfortable with praise. Then Hawk said grimly, "Well, I guess I'd better get back to South Carolina, before Greene is successful in throwing the British completely back, and Tarleton gets shipped out. I'd hate to have to follow him. I never did trust those big leaky boats."

Ivan glanced around at the others, looking decidedly nervous, then addressed Hawk in a solemn voice, saying, "Before ye make any further plans, I need to talk to ye." Again he glanced at the others, before he added, "Privately, please."

Hawk thought it a peculiar request, but nodded his head curtly and rose. He walked from the cabin, with Ivan following, the expression on the Scot's face one of utter dread.

The two walked a good distance from the cabin, before Ivan ventured to say, "I saw Little Carpenter when I was visiting the Overhill towns."

Hawk came to a halt and said in surprise, "I thought he was dead."

"No, that's just a rumor going around."

"How is he?"

"Ancient-looking. My God, he must be nearing a hundred. Ye know those big scars he had on his face?" Hawk nodded. "Well, I couldn't even see them for the wrinkles. He wasn't strong enough to attend the peace proceedings, but he was spry enough to hold a long discussion with me, and there's certainly nothing wrong with his mind. It's as clear as a bell. He asked about ye."

"After all these years?" Hawk remarked in astonishment.

"Hawk, ye were very important to Little Carpenter, and not just because ye were distantly related. He thought highly of ye personally. And it's because of him and what he told me I had to do, that I made a point to find ye." Ivan paused, then said, "You see, I have a confession to make."

"About what?"

Ivan was clearly uncomfortable. He broke eye contact and took a deep breath to fortify himself, before saying, "I lied to ye. Tarleton didn't kill your father. Some other man did, while Tarleton was busy mangling my arm so bad with his saber that it was left hanging by just a few shreds of flesh. I hated that son-of-a-bitch with a passion for what he did to me. Losing a limb does something to a man. I wasn't whole anymore, and I knew I never would be, and all because of Tarleton and his mania. He didn't have to keep hacking at me. I'd already laid down my weapon and surrendered. It was just pure meanness on his part, and

412

if I hadn't raised my arm to protect my head, he would have decapitated me. I wanted him dead so bad, I could taste it. I promised myself if I survived, I'd get even with him, but with my fighting arm gone, I knew I'd never be able to get my own revenge on him—an ordinary man, maybe, but not a trained killer like him—so I lied to ye. I knew ye'd never completely given up yer Indian heritage, that ye'd go after him to avenge yer father and see justice done, that ye'd never give up. Now I realize what a grave error I made. I shouldn't have done it. It was terribly wrong to use ye, particularly in that manner. Little Carpenter made me see that." Ivan paused and raised his eyes. Because he couldn't read the expression on Hawk's face, he sighed heavily with remorse and said, "I suppose ye hate me now, and I can't blame ye."

What Hawk was feeling was utter shock. Never in a million years would he have thought his friend would lie to him. It was something strictly forbidden by both the Indian and the frontiersman's code, and Ivan had always kept both as faithfully as he had. When Ivan mentioned it, Hawk realized he should be angry—no, furious!—but strangely, that wasn't what he felt. When the full realization hit him that he *didn't* have to avenge his father, because he didn't know who his murderer was, Hawk felt as if a terrible weight had been taken from his shoulders. Until then he hadn't realized how heavily he had felt the burden of his obligation. It had been like a rock around his neck, dragging him down and keeping him from his life. Now he was free! A tremendous wave of relief swept over him.

But he still should be angry, Hawk thought with a deep scowl. Having the burden removed shouldn't have changed that. Then he realized that he couldn't be angry with Ivan for what he did, because if Ivan hadn't done it, Hawk would have never met Felicia, never known the heights of passion and the joys and happiness she had brought him, never known the quiet moments of contentment they had shared, never experienced the excitement of sparring with her, and yes, never felt the vexation and frustration she caused him. He treasured the time he'd had with her, because she'd made him come alive with feelings and emotions, and even if there were no future for them, he would never regret it. Never! And he had Ivan to thank for it.

Ivan watched in disbelief as a smile came over Hawk's face. "Stop worrying, old friend," Hawk said with a hearty slap on the Scot's shoulder. "I'm not angry with you. In fact, I'm grateful for what you did. It changed my life."

"I don't understand," Ivan muttered.

Hawk didn't want to take the time to explain about Felicia. "Never mind. That's all behind us now. But there is something you said I'm curious about, something about Little Carpenter making you see you were wrong?"

"Aye. I told him what I had done. I thought he would be proud of ye for being true to yer Indian heritage, but he was furious with me. I've never seen him that angry. Never!"

"Because you lied?"

"Nay, it was more than that. He said he knew he had given up an outstanding Cherokee when he sent ye away. He thought ye had the makings of a fine chief. He knew ye would have been an asset to the tribe. But for once, he put the needs of the tribe aside, and thought only of what was best for ye. He knew that the Cherokee time of power and glory was coming to an end, that it was the white man's sun that was rising, and he wanted ye to share in their bright future, and not the bleak one he saw for the Indian. He said he knew no man could be divided against himself, half of one thing, and half of another, but that he must be all of one, if he is to be strong. He chose the one for ye, and when he sent ye away, he wanted ye to turn yer back on the Cherokee part of ye and become a good white man, a just white man, to give yer all to them, just as he knew ye would have given yer all to the Cherokee, if he had chosen that life for ye. That was why he was so angry with me for reminding ye of yer Cherokee heritage. Out of self-ishness, I put ye in the position where ye would be once more divided and torn, where yer soul could find no peace. Oh, Hawk," Ivan ended with sincere regret, "ye really should hate me. I deserve no less. I lied to ye, used ye, and betrayed yer trust."

But Hawk still felt no anger. Instead, the old doubts he had been tortured by for so long had finally been put to rest. Now he knew for certain that Little Carpenter hadn't sent him away because he thought he was somehow lacking. The old chief had known he would have been a good Cherokee, would have given it his all. But Hawk realized that he *hadn't* been giving his all to his white life. He'd been holding back, feeling it was a betrayal to his Indian blood, and Little Carpenter was correct when he said a man divided within himself could not be strong, could not know true peace. The time had come for him to stop walking in that shadowy, in-between world and step into the light. But the choice must be his, and his alone. Then, and only then, could he be truly at peace.

"Hating you would be pointless, Ivan. Nothing would be gained by it. What you did was wrong, yes, but it's over. I survived with no ill effects. In fact, I'll be a better man for it."

Ivan wondered what Hawk meant by "a better man for it," but held his silence. The rugged frontiersman had been acting very peculiar, not at all like himself. He'd changed right before Ivan's eyes, yet the Scot couldn't quite put his finger on what was different. Then it dawned on him. There was a calmness about Hawk that he had never seen before, a calmness that bordered on tranquility. "Thank ye for forgiving me. I'd hate to lose yer friendship.

"I'd hate to lose yours, too," Hawk answered in all sincerity.

The two turned by mutual, silent agreement and started walking back to the cabin. "Will ye be going back east to fight in the war?" Ivan asked.

Hawk realized then that he was sick of war and

fighting, that he'd seen enough death, suffering, and destruction to last him a lifetime. His feelings came as a surprise. A good warrior thrived on fighting, lived for the battle. It was his means of attaining glory in this life, and his eternal reward in the afterlife. Hawk smiled, thinking he was more white than he had known. But still. he wanted to do some serious thinking before he made the final choice. "No, not unless the war turns around again."

When the two men reached the cabin, Hawk stopped and said, "Tell them inside that I'll be back shortly. I need to be alone for a few moments, so I can think."

"Well, then, I'll tell ye goodbye now," Ivan said, holding out his hand.

"You're not staying over until tomorrow?" Hawk asked in surprise.

"Nay, I'll be leaving as soon as I tell Sarah and Daniel goodbye." Seeing Hawk's quizzical look, he explained, "Ye'll have to tell them what changed yer mind about going after Tarleton, and I can't quite face them right now. Ye may have forgiven me, but I'm not so sure they will."

Hawk didn't think so either. Like Little Carpenter, they'd be angry, but not for the same reasons. They'd be angry because Ivan had placed him in unnecessary danger. He accepted the extended hand and shook it, saying, "They'll get over it. I'll see to it."

"Thank ye, Hawk. Ye're a good man. Next time ye're in Virginia, look me up. Ye know where to find me."

Hawk nodded, then turned, and walked away. Ivan watched him until he disappeared in the woods, thinking there were more changes about him than just an inner calmness. He'd never dreamed that Hawk would forgive him, could have sworn it wasn't in his nature. But he'd shown understanding and compassion. Thank God for the new Hawk. There's no telling what the old Hawk would have done to him. Aye, he very much liked this new man, Ivan thought. Instead of detracting from it, his new qualities just enhanced his remarkable strength.

Chapter Thirty

As soon as Hawk stepped inside the cabin an hour later, Sarah said, "Hell and damnation! Where have ye been?"

"Didn't Ivan tell you I was going for a walk?" Hawk asked, glancing around and noting that Daniel and Felicia were present also. That's good, he thought. He wouldn't have to tell his story but once.

"Aye, he told us," Sarah admitted grudgingly, "but we didn't expect ye to be gone that long, and we know something is wrong, or he wouldn't have rushed off that way."

Which explained why Daniel had not gone back to the fields, Hawk thought. He'd waited to find out what was wrong. "Ivan rushed off for fear you wouldn't be too happy with what he came to tell me. He had a confession to make. It seems Tarleton didn't kill my father. Some other, unknown man did. Tarleton was the man who crippled Ivan and almost killed him. Ivan lied to

419

me to get his revenge, since he knew he was incapable of doing it himself."

Daniel was the first to recover from the stunning news. He slammed to his feet, his face beet red with anger. "That son of a bitch! I'll skin him alive!"

"Calm down, Daniel," Hawk soothed. "That's exactly the kind of unreasonable reaction Ivan feared, and made him rush off the way he did."

"Unreasonable?" Sarah asked angrily, coming to her feet also. "Nay! Ye could have been killed!"

"I could have been killed at King's Mountain, or Cowpens, or Guilford courthouse, or at any of the battles I took part in before I even heard about Tarleton," Hawk answered with maddening calmness. "That's a risk you take when you go to war."

" 'Twas not war, when ye went after Tarleton that first time," Daniel pointed out. " 'Twas nothing but pure revenge. My God, man! Ye almost got hung. Ivan put ye at unnecessary risk. Besides, he lied to ye! That's unforgivable."

"No, only if he hadn't admitted to the truth," Hawk argued. "But he did, and that took a lot of courage. Besides, I don't believe that Ivan really thought he was endangering me that much. He has a very high regard for my fighting skills. I've forgiven him, and I want both of you to do the same. It's done and over, and hopefully forgotten."

Sarah and Daniel exchanged glances, neither as willing to forgive and forget as quickly as Hawk. But Hawk knew he could do no more along those lines at that moment. He turned his mind to the second announcement he needed to make, the decision that he had arrived at after much painful soul-searching. He was still reluctant to carry through with it. It would be easier to cut off an arm or a leg than to sever his life from Felicia's. But he no longer had any excuse to hold her hostage, and he didn't believe she would be willing to stay of her own free will. The much-dreaded time had finally come—the time to let her go.

He turned stiffly in his seat and faced her. Felicia had been just as stunned and just as angry at Ivan as Sarah and Daniel, but she had held her silence. It didn't occur to her that had it not been for Ivan's deception, she would never have met Hawk. The time for that realization would come later. Hawk touched her elbow to catch her attention, and Felicia had only a split second to wonder at the strange look on his face, before he said, "It was wrong of me to take you hostage. Even if what Ivan had told me was true, I had no right." Hawk knew he should say he was sorry, beg her forgiveness, but he couldn't do it. He had been wrong, but he couldn't regret it. He would always treasure the memory of their time together. "I'll take you back to your home the first thing tomorrow morning."

Hawk's announcement shocked everyone. The cabin was as silent as a tomb, as he rose and walked to the door. Just as he swung it open, Daniel recovered enough to ask, "Where are ye going?"

"To the barn, to repair my reins. I'll be needing them tomorrow."

"I'll go with ye," Daniel answered. "Maybe I can help."

After the two men had left, Sarah and Felicia stared at one another across the table. Finally, reaction set in, and Felicia felt tears welling in her eyes. Furiously, she tried to blink them back, then said in an agonized voice, "See? I told you he doesn't love me!"

Sarah reached across the table and caught one of Felicia's small hands. "Nay, lass. He loves ye. I *know* he loves ye! I *can't* be wrong about that."

There was a sharp edge to Felicia's voice that bordered on hysteria. "Didn't you hear what he said? He's taking me back!"

"Aye, and for the life of me, I don't know what's going on. He must be a little touched in the head. But I know he loves ye."

A sudden, unexplainable fury rose in Felicia. She jerked her hand away and jumped to her feet. As she headed for the door, Sarah asked in alarm, "Ye're not going to do anything foolish, are ye?"

Felicia whirled around, her eyes glittering with fierce determination. "No, I'm not going to do anything foolish! I'm going to do what I should have done a long time ago. I'm tired of him toying with my emotions, pulling me this way, then that, to say nothing of the way he makes my decisions for me. I'm going to find out where I stand with him, once and for all. And then I'm going to take control of my life—and do what I damn well please!"

As Felicia rushed through the doorway, she heard Sarah chuckle, then call, "That's my lass! Give him hell! 'Tis good for a man every now and then."

Felicia didn't walk into the barn, or run into it. She exploded into it, making both Hawk and Daniel jump to their feet in surprise. She glared at Hawk, but addressed Daniel, saying in a tightly controlled voice, "I'd like a moment alone with Hawk, if you please."

Daniel knew that Felicia was as mad as a wet hen, and was glad her fury wasn't aimed at him. He put down the reins he had been helping Hawk mend and quickly departed, pulling the barn door behind him.

For a long moment the two faced one another, Felicia silently seething and Hawk eyeing her warily. It was Hawk who broke the silence, asking, "You had something to discuss with me?"

The golden green eyes flashed, and Hawk could have sworn sparks flew from Felicia's fiery mane. "No! Not something to discuss. Something I'm going to *tell* you, for a change. And you'd better listen and listen good." Felicia crossed the distance between them in two swift strides, and stood so close to Hawk that he could feel the heat from her body. "I'm sick and tired of you disrupting my life. First, you yank me up and carry me off, ignoring my objections and trampling on my will—"

"I—"

"Shut up!" Felicia yelled, making Hawk jerk back from her fury. "I'm not finished!"

Felicia might have laughed at the astonished look on Hawk's face, if she had not been so furious. "And now, when I'm just getting used to this life, you have the unmitigated gall to think you can take me back and drop me back down into my old life, as if nothing ever happened! Well, it won't work. I won't go back. I *can't* go back!"

"Why not?" Hawk asked, holding his breath and hoping her answer would be the one he desperately wanted to hear.

"Well, I *could* say because you compromised me, but that's not it. Not totally." Felicia paused. Her fury was abating, and Hawk's staring at her with those dark eyes of his, as if he were trying to peer into her soul, was making her feel very nervous. How had she let her anger get her into this predicament, she wondered. Better yet, how was she going to get herself out? Well, she thought with bleak resignation, there was only one thing to do. Brazen it out. Stop beating around the bush and say it. "The truth is, I can't go back because I'd be miserable. I couldn't face life without you." She saw the look of expectancy coming over Hawk's face and hated it. "Damn you! I guess you're going to gloat over this. But the truth is . . ." The words came as if they had been wrenched from the depths of her soul. "I love you."

Hawk felt a tremendous surge of joy. He wanted to dance, jump up and down, shout at the top of his lungs. But he did none of those undignified things. He managed to control himself and simply reached for her.

"No!" Felicia said sharply, jumping back. "I bared my soul to you, and I'll be damned if I'm going to let you touch me until I know where I stand. Now, do you love me or not?"

"I do," Hawk answered without the slightest hesitation.

Felicia's spirits soared, but she refused to let Hawk know how happy his affirmation had made her. She had said the words, and she was determined to get the same from him. "That won't do. You'll have to say it."

"I'd rather show you."

A shiver ran through Felicia at the smoldering look in Hawk's eyes, a sensual look that promised heaven. It took all of her resolve to reject his proposal, and say, "No. I want the words."

A smile spread over Hawk's sensuous lips, a

smile that was so warm and loving it made Felicia's heart twist. "I love you."

The words were a soft caress, so beautiful to Felicia's ears that tears came to her eyes. "Say it again," she breathed.

"I love you."

Felicia closed her eyes and savored the moment. Then, after finally hearing the answer to the question that had tormented her for so long, she discovered herself face-to-face with another. What now? she wondered. Saying I love you wasn't a lifetime commitment, and that's what she wanted, wanted desperately. Well, she wasn't going to sit around and leave that question dangling in the air and making her life miserable, she decided. She'd buried her pride and made him admit he loved her. She'd just have to push for an answer to this one, too. After all, she had said she was going to take control of her life, hadn't she?

Felicia opened her eyes to find Hawk's lips just inches from hers. She gasped and jumped back, saying, "No! Not yet! There's still something else I need to know."

After admitting to their mutual love, Hawk's need to make love lay heavy on him. "What?" he asked in exasperation.

"Well, now that we've admitted we love one another, what are we going to do about it?"

"I had something in mind, before you interrupted me."

Felicia glanced down and saw the hard evidence of what Hawk had in mind straining at his buckskins. A thrill ran through her, before she jerked her eyes away and forced her mind back to her resolve. "No, I mean, when people tell someone they love them, something usually just naturally follows."

"Exactly!"

Becoming a little exasperated herself, she snapped, "I don't mean immediately! I mean in the future."

Hawk stood as still as stone and just stared at her. God, Felicia thought, he certainly wasn't making it easy for her. Surely she'd given him enough hints by now. "Damn you!" she cried out in utter frustration. "You can't be that thick-skulled! I'm talking about marriage."

When Felicia had said she loved him, Hawk had accepted it for what it was, an admission of how she felt about him. He'd been afraid to pursue it any further, despite what she had said about not being able to live without him. Marriage was a very serious step under any circumstances, but particularly in theirs, and he wanted to be sure she knew exactly what she was saying.

"You'd marry me, knowing what I am?"

"Of course! Why do you think I've been working my fingers to the bone, learning how to be a good frontier woman? I certainly haven't done it for the fun of it. I wanted to prove I was up to it, that I was good enough for you."

Hawk could hardly believe his ears. Good enough for *him?* And he had feared she wouldn't accept him on a permanent basis, because she thought him not good enough for *her.* "Have you forgotten my Indian blood?"

"No, but what's that got to do with it?"

"There are those who might scorn you, because your husband has Indian blood."

Her husband? Of God, that sounded wonderful! "Then the hell with them! I don't care what they think. I'm proud of your Indian blood. It's what makes you so very special."

Oh?" Hawk asked, his dark brows rising in surprise.

"Yes!" Felicia retorted. "As a matter of fact, I secretly think of you as my . . ." A flush rose on her face. "My magnificent savage."

Hawk smiled at her compliment, partly in amusement and partly in pleasure. But his doubts were put to rest, and the choice he had been leaning towards was finalized. With Felicia at his side, it would be easy to walk the white man's path. But he wouldn't completely put his back to the Cherokees. He wouldn't fight them; he wouldn't take their land, and he would do everything in his power to see they were treated fairly.

Felicia was unaware of his thoughts. "Besides," she continued, "I don't think it really matters that much, not as much as you seem to think it does. What you are is who you make of yourself, not who your parents, or grandparents, or great-grandparents were."

Hawk laughed, saying, "You're beginning to sound like a patriot."

"In what way?"

"Haven't you read the Declaration of Independence? That all men are created equal?"

Felicia hadn't read it. Her father had considered it treasonous, and refused to let a copy come into their home. All men are created equal? What a powerful thought. No wonder Hawk had been so attracted to the rebel cause, if this was any example of what they professed.

Felicia grinned, then admitted, "Well, maybe I am beginning to come around to your way of thinking. You'll have to tell me more. But not now."

She waited for Hawk to take the initiative and formally ask the question she wanted to hear, knowing full well he knew what she was expecting. But he just stood there, his grin growing wider and wider. Finally, her impatience got the better of her, and she asked, "Well, are you going to ask me or not?"

"If I don't, will you ask me?"

The smug look on his handsome face infuriated her. She tossed her head, making her long reddish tresses fly. "No, I won't! I've crawled all I'm going to."

The grin changed to a warm smile. "Well, in that case, will you marry me?"

It didn't sound like he was very enthusiastic about it, Felicia thought in disappointment. "Why should I?" she threw back.

"You're determined to wrench it all from me, aren't you?" Hawk answered with a chuckle. He stepped forward and caught her, then as she tried to back away, said, "No! This is something that needs to be said with you in my arms, with your heart against mine." She stopped struggling, and Hawk drew her close, then said in a voice filled with emotion, "I love you, Felicia, more than life itself. Marry me, share my dreams, my success, my failures. Stand by me, in good times and bad; nurture my seed and carry it beneath your heart, than bear it in love; lie by my side every night as long as we both shall live, and then be with me in eternity."

Tears flooded Felicia's eyes. "Oh, Hawk," she cried softly, "that was so beautiful." She looked into his eyes. "Yes, I'll marry you. And I'll do everything in my power to be a good wife and mother."

Hawk was wrapped in a warm cocoon of happiness. "Now, are you satisfied? Is there anything else you want from me?"

A devilish twinkle came to Felicia's eyes. "Yes, as a matter of fact, there is just one more thing I'd like to ask." She paused purposely and watched as a wary look came over Hawk's face, then laughed and asked, "Will you make love to me?"

The pent-up passion Hawk had suppressed came rushing to the surface. With a groan of exultation, he swept her up in his arms and carried her to the back of the barn, muttering against her throat, "That will be a pleasure, my love. I'm yours to command."

Chapter Thirty-one

When Hawk reached the empty stall where his pallet lay, he sat Felicia down on her feet, kissed her long and incredibly sweet, making her insides feel as if they were melting and her bones dissolving. Then they undressed one another, taking their time about it, their eyes caressing, their hands touching the other's heated skin almost reverently.

As Felicia stood naked before him, Hawk's breath caught in his throat. He could hardly believe this exquisite creature loved him, had given herself body and soul to him, was willing to spend her entire life at his side. It was a sobering thought and humbling, and he vowed he would be worthy of her and cherish her to his death. He caressed the long hair that cascaded down her back, and spread the reddish tresses around her like a cape, then gazed at her in awe, thinking she looked like a goddess in her fiery covering, standing proud and incredibly desirable. Spying one pert, rosy nipple peeking through the strands of hair that covered her chest, he bent, kissed it, then licked it, the hot wet lash making Felicia's breath catch and her legs tremble.

For each caress Hawk had given her, Felicia had reciprocated, and this was no different. She wrapped her arms around his broad shoulders and brushed her pebble-hard nipples against his chest, taking delight in his gasp of pleasure. She traced the powerful muscles on his chest, slowly descending from his bulging shoulder to one dark nipple, then stroked it until it hardened. Leaning forward, she licked the bud, just as he had done hers, and heard him moan. Spreading her fingers, the better to feel every ridged hollow and every corded sinew, she ran her hands down his sides, hips, and outer thighs. Hawk trembled, then drew her down to the pallet with him.

Just as he was leaning over her, Felicia caught his shoulders and rolled him to his back. Knowing he loved her made her bold. She wanted to show him her deep feelings with no reservations, no inhibitions. She whispered in a husky voice, "Let me show you how much I love you. Don't do anything. Just lie there. Let me pleasure you."

Taking the passive role in anything was not in Hawk's nature, and he had been trained since childhood to be aggressive. But his love for Felicia at that moment was so strong, that he would have given her anything she wanted, even submission. He nodded his head in silent agreement.

Felicia knew she had won a victory of sorts,

433

and smiled triumphantly. Then she came to her knees beside him, taunting him with featherlike strokes, caresses that left a trail of fire in their wake. Her fingers lightly explored the wide expanse of his chest, then smoothed across the hard planes of his abdomen, moving lower and lower to brush back and forth across his groin, teasingly close to the bold, magnificent muscle between his legs that ached for her touch. She bent her head and dropped tiny kisses over his neck and shoulders, then down his chest and abdomen, whispering between the kisses how beautiful she thought his body was. She stopped to pay homage to his navel, her tongue flicking and swirling, then, slipping lower, nipped at the tight skin there, delighting in seeing his muscles contract, then tremble. Her hand slipped between his legs, and she lightly raked her fingernails over the inside of his thighs, then she soothed the tiny stings by licking them away.

Hawk had discovered that playing the submissive role could be wildly exciting. When Felicia took him into her hands and stroked his rigid flesh, the blood ran hot and thick in his veins; passion raged in every part of him; his head pounded; his throat turned dry. Then feeling her hot mouth hovering over his erection, he sensed what she was about to do. He went very still, his heart racing furiously in anticipation. Weakly, he lifted his head, seeing her long reddish hair falling around his hips like a silken curtain. When she kissed the tip of him, he jerked, feeling as if a hot poker had been set to the sensitized skin. Then, as her devilish tongue danced over his throbbing length, each fleeting touch jarred burning nerve endings and made him feel as if he were dissolving in hot flames. When she took him in her mouth, his excitement reached the breaking point. "No! Stop!" he muttered. "Before I explode!"

Felicia raised her head and said, "Sssh, I'm doing this. Just relax and enjoy it."

She lowered her head to continue her ravishment and heard his tortured groan, felt his body go stiff. But Felicia didn't want to bring him to fulfillment with her mouth. Pleasuring him had excited her unbearably. She, too, was trembling with need and burning for release. She wanted him inside her when it happened, wanted to share in the climactic experience. She lifted her head and straddled him, then lowered herself over his splendid rigid length, shuddering as she took him in inch by inch. She paused in her descent and their eyes met, his like glowing coals and hers, molten gold. Their mutual awareness only intensified the exquisite sensation of their joining; both felt as if they were being consumed in a scorching heat.

When Felicia began to ride him, Hawk was tempted to take the aggressive role from her and throw her to her back. Then he remembered that this was her loving. His turn would come later.

They had all night, all the rest of their lives to make love. She rode him magnificently, and Hawk surrendered to sheer sensation as Felicia took them higher and higher on that dizzying ascent. She swiveled her hips, spiraling down on him in a fiery heat, the tight muscles of her sheath threatening to squeeze the life from him. His excitement became unbearable, his arousal so acute it was painful. His skin felt as if it would burst, and he heard a roaring in his ears. He broke into a cold perspiration, his muscles quivering uncontrollably. It was heaven; it was hell. He didn't think he could hold back another second. Then Felicia became suddenly still and arched her back, as a glazed look came into her eyes. Knowing she was teetering on the shattering brink, Hawk let out a exultant cry and allowed himself release, his scalding seed deep inside her lifting Felicia over that trembling peak to her own blinding climax.

Still straddling him, Felicia collapsed weakly over him, her head buried in the warm, salty crook of his neck. Hawk caressed her back and whispered love words and endearments, feeling incredibly weak. Then, when his strength finally returned, he took Felicia by surprise and, holding her hips firmly to his, flipped her to her back.

Looking down into her wide eyes, he said, "Thank you. That was beautiful. And now it's my turn to show my love."

His mouth came down on hers in a hot, plundering kiss that robbed her of her senses and sent her passion spiraling anew like a sky rocket. He plunged into her over and over with a wild urgency, making her quiver from head to toe, taking her breath away, filling her with unbelievable electrifying sensations, reaching for her very soul in his possession, then giving it back as he poured himself into her, showing her the sweet, savage splendor of his love.

When they drifted down from paradise, they felt reborn. Neither spoke, feeling that there were no words to express what they had just shared, both content to drift in that warm languidness. Feeling sated and blissfully happy, Felicia dozed off.

Hawk gently disengaged himself from her, rose, and lit a candle. Then he lay back down by her side and cradled her in his arms while she slept, his mind busy making plans for their future. It was much later when she roused, and asked groggily, "What time is it?"

"After midnight, I'd guess."

Felicia shot to a sitting position, saying, "Oh my God! What if Sarah and Daniel are waiting up for me?"

"I doubt that very seriously. They're bound to know we're lovers."

"But we've always been discreet. I've never stayed this long."

Hawk pulled her back down, saying, "Sweetheart, we're going to tell them in just a few hours

437

that we're going to be married. Now, do you really think it matters? Besides, I want to know what you think of my plans for our future, before we talk to them."

At the reminder of the future, an all too familiar dread filled Felicia. "I know you're not going after Tarleton, but are you planning on going back to war?"

"No, I think it's pretty much winding down, and I'm anxious to get us settled in our own cabin before winter comes. But there's something I need to find out from you, before we can do anything. Do you want me to take you back to your home, so we can explain to your parents what happened, and they can meet me before we marry?"

Felicia knew her parents must be worried, but she didn't want Hawk getting anywhere near where the fighting was going on, for fear he'd change his mind. Besides, she knew her parents weren't going to approve of her marrying a frontiersman. Best to let them get used to the idea, before they met him. "No, I can write them a long letter explaining everything. Then maybe we can visit later. I'm anxious to get settled, too. Have you a piece of land in mind?"

"Yes, I have. My father gave me some land in the Shenandoah Valley in western Virginia. Have you ever heard of it?"

"No, I haven't," Felicia admitted. "Shenandoah," she muttered, letting the musical word roll off her tongue. "That's a beautiful name. Is it Cherokee?"

"No. It's Indian, but not Cherokee. The valley was once claimed by the ancient ones, and they named it. It means daughter of the star. It's a beautiful place, a long valley of rolling hills and sparkling rivers, with high mountain ranges on both the eastern and western side."

Felicia smiled. Naturally, Hawk would stay near the mountains. They were in his blood. "It sounds lovely." She snuggled closer. "Tell me more."

"Well, it's not as heavily wooded as it is here. It was the ancients' hunting ground, and they burned most of the thick forest away to flush out the game. But there is still plenty of wood for buildings and fences. It's excellent pasture land, and that's what I was thinking of doing, raising some cattle, along with my gunsmithing. I'm simply not the farmer Daniel is. I don't mind putting in a small field of corn for winter fodder, but not raising it for a living."

And certainly not for making whiskey, Felicia thought.

Hawk was unaware of her wry observation. He continued, saying, "I think you'll like it. It's more thickly settled than out here, mostly Dutch and German, but lately more English and Scots-Irish have been moving in. There's even a real town in the upper valley, with shops, inns, a church or two. Lancaster, it's called."

Hawk felt good about his plans. The valley was claimed by no modern tribe of Indians, and therefore Indian attacks were unheard-of. He would be taking no Indian land, nor would he be bound to fight them, as he had vowed. It would be a safe place for Felicia and their family. It was also more civilized than this wilderness, although it, too, was considered the frontier. Hawk was proud of how well Felicia had adjusted to the rigors of frontier living, but he didn't want things to be too hard on her. He wanted to be able to give her a few luxuries and some social life. Frontier women lived short, often lonely lives, subjected to a harsh, dangerous environment with little or no comforts. And it was even harder on infants and small children. He certainly didn't want to go through the heartache Sarah and Daniel had, he thought, remembering the four small graves on a nearby hillside. He wanted his children to live long, happy lives. Yes, Hawk thought, the Shenandoah Valley was far enough removed to satisfy his need for spaciousness, yet civilized enough to give Felicia and their family some degree of safety and comfort.

Hawk had been so occupied with his thoughts, that it took a while for him to notice Felicia's long silence. "Is something wrong?" he asked.

When Hawk had said Scots-Irish, Felicia had remembered Sarah and Daniel, and realized that she would probably never see them again. The two farms wouldn't be close enough for them to visit. Neither could leave their animals untended for that long. A sadness had invaded her, robbing her of much of the joy she had been feeling. "I just remembered Sarah and Daniel. I hate to leave them."

"You've really become fond of them, haven't you?"

"Yes, particularly Sarah. My mother and I were never close. Most often, we were at odds with one another, and to be brutally frank, I couldn't admire her. She was so selfish and shallow. So Sarah has been more than just a friend and a teacher, she's been like a second mother to me."

"Yes, I know. I don't want to leave them either. That's why I came back. I missed them. And that's why I'm going to ask them to go with us."

Felicia sat up, and asked in surprise, "Leave their farm here and settle in the Shenandoah? Do you really believe they would?"

"We'll find out in a few hours."

Sarah and Daniel were sitting at the breakfast table, when Felicia and Hawk walked into the cabin. An awkward moment passed before Daniel broke the silence by remarking dryly, "Well, Hawk, I'm relieved to see ye're still alive. I had my doubts. The lass had murder in her eyes when she stepped into the barn."

Felicia was surprised. She had not realized that Daniel had a sense of humor.

441

Hawk chuckled, remembering how angry Felicia had been, then replied, "Indeed she did, and with good reason. But we've finally settled things between us." He drew her close to his side and looked down at her lovingly. "I've asked Felicia to marry me, and she's agreed."

It was obvious that the older couple were pleased with the news. Sarah let out a happy shriek, jumped up from the table, and hugged the two, while Daniel followed at a more sedate pace, grinning from ear to ear, clapping Hawk on the shoulder, then astonishing Felicia by hugging her.

The four sat at the table, while Hawk told them about his and Felicia's plans for the future. When he was finished, Daniel said, "Ye never told me yer father gave ye any land. When did that happen?"

"He told me about it when he took me back east. We even passed through there, so he could show it to me. Seems he was with the group that surveyed the valley years ago, and never forgot how beautiful it was. He said he couldn't leave me anything in his will, that naturally, his tobacco plantation would go to his other son, but he thought I might like the land, since it was on the frontier. I didn't think I'd ever have any use for it. That's why I never mentioned it. I guess it's a good thing I didn't throw away the deed."

"Aye, Daniel agreed. "I've heard that's prime farmland.

"How much land is it?" Sarah asked Hawk.

"Two thousand acres." Seeing the astonished looks on the Scots' faces, Hawk shrugged his shoulders and said, "I guess my father was thinking in terms of plantations and not farms."

Daniel frowned, feeling a little jealous that Hawk's father could be so generous with him, while he had so little to offer the man who had become a son to him. "It must have cost him a pretty penny."

Hawk had a good idea of what Daniel was thinking. "I don't think he paid all that much. The valley was still a deep wilderness then, pretty much cut off from the rest of civilization. It probably sold for just pennies an acre." Hawk paused, then said, "But I certainly don't need that much land. There's enough there for several farms. We'd like for you and Sarah to come with us."

Coming like it did out of the blue, Sarah and Daniel were too stunned to react for a moment. Then Daniel said, "Nay, Hawk. I won't accept any of yer land, if that's what ye're thinking."

"Please reconsider," Felicia said. "We don't want to leave you. You're more than friends. You're like family to both of us."

Daniel knew better than to suggest the young couple settle here, not when Hawk already owned land far superior to anything he could find in these mountains. That would be foolish. And if Hawk already had land, there would be no point in leaving this little farm to him. That was why Daniel had suppressed his natural Scots-Irish restlessness and stuck it out so long in one place, thinking to leave it to Hawk when he died. Daniel glanced at Sarah and knew by the expression on her face that she wanted to go with the younger couple, despite all of the years of hard labor they had put into this place. And he had a good idea why. Not only was she thinking of being close to the two she loved like a son and daughter, but of their children, babies she could cuddle and love, babies to take the place of those she had lost.

Daniel made his decision. "We'll go. But I won't accept any gift of land from ye. The valley is in Virginia. We'll claim cabin rights."

"What's cabin rights?" Felicia asked.

"It's a Virginian decree that says any man that puts up a cabin in the wilderness, and plants an acre of corn, can claim four hundred acres without paying for it," Hawk explained.

"And what if there isn't any unclaimed land close to Hawk's?" Sarah objected. "Then we might have to settle just as faraway as we already are."

Daniel scowled.

"What will you do with this farm?" Hawk asked him.

"Sell it. I've had several offers, but I've never paid them any mind."

Hawk knew Daniel's pride would never let him

accept an out-and-out gift of land, not even if he had been his natural son. To Daniel's way of thinking, the giving should be the other way around, and Daniel was not a man to break with tradition. "Suppose I sell you four hundred acres of my land, at what my father paid for it?" Hawk suggested. "That way you should have a little left over from what you get for yours to start your new farm, and I'd have a little cash to put into mine."

Daniel didn't know that Hawk had a little nest egg set aside and didn't really need the money. He made it sound as if Daniel's buying land from him would benefit them both. "Agreed, then. But Sarah and I will have to wait to move, until we sell this land."

"Ye're welcome to stay here until we do sell," Sarah offered, her eyes twinkling with delight at the plans. She'd be sure there was a porch on her new cabin, she thought.

"No, I think we'll go ahead," Hawk answered. "I'm anxious to get things started."

Sarah turned to Felicia, and asked, "Where will ye get married? If ye want to do it here, ye're welcome to use our cabin."

Felicia remembered what Sarah had told her about the wild frontier weddings, and wanted no part of them. "No, I'd like to get married by a minister. I just wouldn't feel married, if I wasn't." She turned to Hawk. "Didn't you say there was a church in Lancaster?"

"Yes, I know there's a Presbyterian for sure."

Felicia had belonged to the Church of England, but she wasn't going to quibble. "Is it alright with you, if we get married there?"

Hawk really didn't feel the need of any ceremony. In his opinion, they were already married, and had been since they had admitted to their love and made their vows to one another the night before. But he knew Felicia felt the need for something more, and if they were going to repeat their vows before a minister and witnesses, he was determined Felicia would have a real wedding gown, and not a nightgown. "Lancaster will be ideal," he answered, thinking of the shops there.

"When are you leaving, then?" Daniel asked.

Hawk thought that there was really no need to dally here any longer, and he was anxious to be alone with Felicia. They deserved some private time together. "As soon as we've eaten and packed up."

A few hours later, Felicia and Hawk were on the trail, riding double. Hawk pulled her closer, so that she was almost sitting on his lap, and lovingly kissed the skin below her ear. Felicia leaned her head back on his broad shoulder, relishing the feel of his steady heartbeat against her back, and thinking how very much she loved him. She had found her special man, the man of her dreams. Her magnificent savage was the rock she stood on, the air beneath her wings, her sun, her moon, her stars, her everything; and they were going to have a long, wonderful life together.

Her happiness was sublime.